# Praise for Kinsey W. Holley's
## *Yours, Mine and Howls*

"The romance is hot and heavy and the sarcastic conversations between Cade and Allison are filled with an underlying passion that will keep readers glued to the page. The many storylines offer excitement and adventure throughout and the magical world of the werewolves and fae creatures is extremely well written."

~ *Romantic Times*

"Kinsey Holley has created a very lovable cast of characters that will make you happy and leave you wanting more… *Yours, Mine and Howls* is a fierce love story and I'm Joyfully Recommending it!"

~ *Joyfully Reviewed*

"Ms. Holley writes this story with a lot of humor. There's plenty of snark and funny lines to go around that had me giggling. It lightens up the tension within the story… If you enjoy alpha wolves, mystery, a strong feisty heroine, and humor, then you may want to howl along with this book."

~ *The Long and the Short of It*

"I loved all the characters in the story and hope that some of them will return in books yet to be imagined. This is definitely a book I will recommend to my friends."

~ *The Romance Studio*

Look for these titles by
*Kinsey W. Holley*

*Now Available:*

*Werewolves in Love Series*
Kiss and Kin
Ready to Run

*Print Anthology*
Shifting Dreams

# Yours, Mine and Howls

*Kinsey W. Holley*

Samhain Publishing, Ltd.
11821 Mason Montgomery Road, 4B
Cincinnati, OH 45249
www.samhainpublishing.com

Yours, Mine and Howls
Copyright © 2012 by Kinsey W. Holley
Print ISBN: 978-1-60928-404-6
Digital ISBN: 978-1-60928-356-8

Editing by Mary Hamilton
Cover by Kanaxa

This book is a work of fiction. The names, characters, places, and incidents are products of the writer's imagination or have been used fictitiously and are not to be construed as real. Any resemblance to persons, living or dead, actual events, locale or organizations is entirely coincidental.

All Rights Are Reserved. No part of this book may be used or reproduced in any manner whatsoever without written permission, except in the case of brief quotations embodied in critical articles and reviews.

First Samhain Publishing, Ltd. electronic publication: February 2011
First Samhain Publishing, Ltd. print publication: February 2012

# Dedication

For Ashley, Belynda, Vickie, Wendy and the Other Wendy. This one is special, because it's The First.

And to Inez Kelley, who's very good with titles.

# Chapter One

*Outside Lake Charles, Louisiana*

"His daddy was an alpha! A *real* wolf! Not a drunkass loser like you!" Humans could've heard the woman screeching in the next parish. Werewolves probably heard her all the way to Houston.

"You're a lyin' whore! The brat's mine! Where is he? Dylan? *Dylan!*" The werewolf, smashed on moonshine, couldn't change easily. But a drunken wolf on two feet could still tear a human apart.

"Get outta my trailer, asshole!"

"It's *my* trailer and I'm not going anywhere, you fuckin' bitch!"

Next came the sound of breaking glass, followed by the bellow of a liquored-up beta, more breaking glass, the woman screaming, rinse, repeat...

Allison Kendall, exhausted after a day's work at the stable, turned up the television and longed for a remote to mute Guy and Gracie Fontenot. Her trailer and the Fontenots' stood a hundred feet apart, the last two left in the otherwise deserted Bayou Estates Mobile Home Park. The next nearest house lay a half mile away. It made living next door to the violent couple creepy, even though they were kin.

The window unit in the living room sputtered, useless against the suffocating August heat. Listening to the White Trash Werewolf Show was better than stewing in her own sweat, though, so she left the windows open. At least the unit in her bedroom still worked.

Carefully she opened the door to her room, where five-year-old Dylan Fontenot slept. The din of domestic war couldn't keep the tiny veteran awake. She dropped a kiss on his forehead and tiptoed out. When the phone rang, she dove to catch it before Dylan woke up.

"Hey. I just got home," said her cousin, Seth. "You up for something?"

"Can't. I've got Dylan. Gracie brought him over this afternoon."

"Shit. How bad?"

"Real bad." She slumped as she sighed, her emotional exhaustion equal to her physical fatigue. "Your bimbo sister just told her psycho husband he's not a daddy." The rest of Lake Charles had figured it out five years ago.

"I wish you'd stay out of that mess."

"Seth, we're family! I'm not leaving him in that hellhole when they go at it."

"But you can't keep him all the time, either. He doesn't belong to you. We're only—oh, fuck it," he muttered.

She didn't feel like arguing again either. "Guy's lost it this time. Should I call the cops?"

"Don't. Gracie won't press charges. She'll just get pissed off at you and take it out on Dylan. God, our family sucks."

So did living in the middle of a never-ending episode of *Cops*.

"I guess it's pizza again," said Seth. "Want me to re—"

Gracie Fontenot's shrill, skull-piercing scream drowned out the rest of his words. Her terrifying wail ended as abruptly as it began, like someone had snipped a cord.

Or snapped her neck.

The world held its breath. Then Guy Fontenot's moonshine-maddened roar shattered the night. The Fontenot trailer door opened and slammed.

Seth screamed, "Get the shotgun—I'm on my way!"

She dropped the phone and raced for the second bedroom at the back of the trailer.

*Aunt Jackie always kept it loaded, please God, please, let it still be loaded, it has to be loaded...*

Thank God. She pumped it once and started back for the living room, shaking with fear. The shotgun rattled in her hands. Bile rose in her throat as hysteria began to squeeze the air from her lungs.

"Ally?"

Dylan's sweetly sleepy voice stopped her cold, instantly quelling the panic. She paused outside her bedroom door.

*Mine or not, no one touches him.*

"Stay in bed, baby," she called softly. "Everything's all right."

She reached the living room and found it empty. No sound came from outside.

Maybe Guy had passed out.

Maybe he was stumbling to the biker bar a mile down the road.

*Maybe he'll get run over.*

The front door went flying as if sucked out by a whirlwind. Guy Fontenot lurched across the threshold, staggered, and steadied himself with one hand against the doorframe. His slack, sallow face gleamed with sweat. He squinted at her as he tried to focus. The acrid stench of moonshine and unwashed werewolf filled the tiny room. She stifled a gag while her mind raced.

Guy couldn't move that fast, this drunk—but he didn't have far to reach her. The shells were silver-loaded—but how much would it take to stop him? If she fired and missed, she wouldn't get another chance.

She'd never imagined she could die at eighteen.

"Where's m'boy?" He looked ready to pass out. *God, please.*

"Go home, Guy. You can see Dylan tomorrow." Her voice came out several octaves above normal, but still steady. A human's fear pheromones could push an enraged wolf over the edge. Moonshine made it worse. She swallowed, silently begging her heart to slow down and her hands to quit shaking. She kept the shotgun pointed at the floor.

"Gracie's dead. M-my wife. I killed m'wife."

Learning his wife had borne someone else's child could drive a stable werewolf to murder. No one would mistake Guy Fontenot for stable.

He sagged against the jamb, but she hesitated to raise the gun. She'd never killed anyone before. If she held him off until Seth showed up, she wouldn't have to.

"It'll be all right, Guy. You need sleep. Tomorrow you can figure out what to do."

"Want the boy."

"No, Guy, I'll take care of Dylan. You go on home now."

He stared at her for a moment. His eyes widened. He snapped his mouth shut as he stood a little straighter.

Guy was slow, not stupid.

"You wanna get ridda me so's you c-can call the cops." He sneered at her and she shuddered. "Think you can shoot me, girly? You wanna sh-shoot me?"

She watched in horror as his nails began to lengthen and the bones of his hand began to move beneath his skin, twisting, stretching, popping. *Oh, shit.* She'd been so focused on his body she'd ignored his eyes. The irises had begun turning yellow. He stank so of moonshine and sweat, she hadn't caught the rich, earthy scent that was another signal of impending change.

Guy stumbled toward her. She couldn't back up. She didn't want him near Dylan.

The howl of an enraged werewolf on four feet filled the air, and she nearly fainted with relief. *ThankyouJesus.*

Seth was here.

It happened so fast, and all at once. Through the open door behind Guy, she glimpsed a streak of brown fur as Seth reached the front yard. Guy didn't turn to see death running at his back, but rushed at her just as she raised the shotgun.

Her trembling hands betrayed her. The shot went wide.

Guy closed the distance. She swung the gun at his head. He knocked it from her hands. With a strength born of terror she kicked, sole first, straight into his balls. It didn't stop him. He clutched at his groin with one half-changed hand as the other swiped wildly. His claws raked her belly. She stumbled backwards.

It took a moment for the pain to penetrate. She looked down to see a blossoming red stain soaking her T-shirt. Touching it, her hand sank into a gaping wound.

She looked up at Guy's yellowing eyes and saw tears.

In dreamy slow motion, he grabbed her by the throat and flung her aside. Guy roared as Seth landed on his back. Ally went flying across the room, her skull striking the metal window ledge. A brilliant, bright white pain exploded behind her eyes, like a camera's flash going off at the end of her nose. She crumpled to the floor as someone whispered in her head.

Dylan's cries, Seth's howls and the disembodied voice were the only sounds in the trailer now. Guy was dead.

A second later, so was Ally.

She was never the same after that.

# Chapter Two

*13 years later, outside Fremont, Colorado*

Cade MacDougall struck a match against the porch railing and lit a cigarillo. He took a long, satisfying drag as he leaned against a column and surveyed his domain in the blinding sunshine of a postcard Colorado summer's day.

In the distance to his right, horses ran in the pasture while grooms cleaned the stables. To his left, saws, hammers and drills sang in the woodshop. From inside the house wafted the aroma of baked chicken and fresh bread. And ten yards in front of him, beside a swing set in the grassy center of the compound, a young wolf tormented the person Cade loved most in the world.

Aaron crouched while Rebecca grabbed a fistful of fur and swung a stubby leg over his back. She pulled herself up to sit astride, legs dangling three feet off the ground. Aaron turned in circles, around and around like a dog chasing his tail until Becca, dizzy and laughing, fell into the soft grass. When she stood, Aaron poked her in the butt with his nose, or nudged her in the stomach with his head, or lightly tapped her on the back with his tail. She plopped back down. Then she stood up. Aaron knocked her down again.

Soon, overcome with shrieking giggles, she lay for a while in the grass while Aaron yawned and scratched, waiting for her to catch her breath. Then they did it all over again for the sixth or tenth time while Cade looked on with quiet delight. He preferred Becca's giggle to any sound on earth, and he liked any wolf who made her giggle like that.

Mrs. Palmer would have no trouble getting Becca down for her nap. Cade would have a lot of trouble if she saw Becca and

Aaron. The latest nanny didn't approve of little girls roughhousing with werewolves.

"Baby Girl," he called. "Go inside and let Sindri wash you up for lunch."

"Da-deeee..."

"Inside, Rebecca. Now."

She pouted, but she seized a chunk of the good-natured Aaron's fur to pull herself up. Still a little dizzy, she toddled up the porch steps. He reached down to stroke her cheek and run his hand through her long hair, black and curly as his own. She hugged his knee and smiled up at him.

"I'm gonna try to be a cat again."

"Why don't you try being something else? I can't tell my wolf friends my baby girl's a cat."

"But I *am*, Daddy!"

He gave a rueful laugh. "If you say so, baby." It tickled him she pretended to be the only shape-shifting female on the planet. But a cat?

Becca went inside, Aaron right behind her.

Cade put out a boot to stop him. "No four-footed in the house, pup. It's a nanny thing."

Aaron bounded off the porch.

Mrs. Palmer had wolf issues, but she didn't drink or steal and she didn't have a thing for wolves. He'd fired all her predecessors. Premiere Professional Child Care didn't want to send another applicant, and he didn't want to hire one.

Sindri joined him on the porch. "The meal is ready. You should eat before it gets cold."

He nodded, lingering to finish his cigarillo. "Becca wants to be a cat."

"Buy her a kitten."

Cade did a double take. Sindri never said anything remotely in jest. "A kitten. On a ranch full of werewolves."

"The girl should have a pet."

"A cat's not a pet. A cat's an appetizer."

Sindri didn't respond. He clasped his hands over his stomach and gazed stoically at the landscape.

"Something on your mind, old man?" Cade smiled down at the top of the brownie's head.

"I make an offering to Eir this evening. I would have you

15

join me."

Cade sighed as he ground out the cigarillo and kicked it into the grass. Trying to keep the irritation out of his voice he replied, "Sindri. You know I don't do the old rites. The Church disapproves."

"You do many things your church disapproves of," Sindri huffed. "Your mother was a Christian, but she respected the Old Ones. She did not reject them or their ways. Eir loved your mother."

So had Cade.

"You do not do the old rites because they remind you of her."

Cade heard the love in Sindri's voice. It did nothing to lessen the ache he felt whenever he thought of his mother.

"Becca reminds me of her. Everything on this ranch reminds me of her. I don't do the old rituals because I don't give a..." No. He wouldn't be disrespectful. The Old Ones meant nothing to him, especially not Eir, but he wouldn't say that to Sindri. "What's the offering for?" he asked instead.

Sindri didn't protest the change of subject. "For finding your brother's son."

"Old man, the werewolf databank in D.C. found Carson's son. If Carson hadn't been in that hospital in New Orleans, we wouldn't know Dylan Fontenot existed. Maybe you should make an offering to the VA instead. You won't need to gather comfrey and copper. I'm pretty sure they take money."

He wanted the words back as soon as he said them. His childhood guardian didn't deserve his unthinking sarcasm. No one but Rebecca loved Cade as much as Sindri did.

Drawing himself up to his full three feet, two inches, Sindri turned to go back in the house.

"Sindri."

The wounded little brownie stopped.

He addressed the brownie's stiff back. "Eir can restore life, can't she? She can raise the dead?"

Sindri didn't turn to look at him. "Yes. She is the Healer. Death is not her equal."

"So. If Eir can raise the dead, and if my mother was beloved of her—" Eirny MacDougall had been named for her, in fact "—then why didn't Eir save her? Why didn't she pull Ma...my mother out of the sea?"

The brownie's voice softened. "Your mother made a choice, *barn*. Eir would not save her from herself."

Just inside the door, Sindri stopped again. Still without turning around, he added, "Your mother belonged to the sea."

Cade had hoped for a little more than that, thirty-three years after watching his mother throw herself into the North Atlantic.

# Chapter Three

Ally awoke in time to see *Fremont—40 miles* go whizzing past the window.

Seth drove. Their roommate of four years, Declan, slept behind him, his long frame sprawled across half the backseat, shaggy black hair in his face.

Dylan sulked in the other corner, behind her. She always rode shotgun unless she drove. The backseat didn't bother her, but Seth hated seeing her face in the rearview mirror. He said it gave him flashbacks.

"I still don't see why we had to leave like that. Just, like, boom, no warning," Dylan said.

Shouldn't an eighteen-year-old be past the petulant stage? *She* wasn't petulant at eighteen. She was dead at eighteen. *Kids today.*

"We didn't leave just like that," Seth snapped. "We've been planning this for three months."

"No, we've *talked* about it for three months. Then all of a sudden, we pack up and go. You didn't give me any warning, or ask if I wanted to go. I'm eighteen, in case you don't remember..."

Nothing set her teeth on edge like teenage sarcasm.

"Hey!" She sat up straight and turned to look first at Seth, then Dylan. Dec stirred in his corner. "Y'all have been arguing since we left home. Shut it, right now, or we're listening to Sarah McLachlan the rest of the way."

A terrified silence settled on the car.

Fremont straddled the Arkansas River two hundred miles south of Denver. Dec had lived in mountains before—it seemed Dec had lived everywhere before—but the other three hailed from a notably flat region where the only hills were freeway overpasses. They gawked with awe at the Rockies in the distant west.

"I gotta pee. Let's take a break," she announced as they drove into the city.

"Me too, and I need to stretch my legs." Seth had been driving all morning. This close to their destination, everyone was antsy.

Highway 50 became Main Street as it entered Fremont. The scenic little town of eight thousand boasted the best climate in Colorado. Tree-lined, partially cobblestoned Main Street ran through the downtown area and featured a mix of modern architecture and Old West-looking buildings. It was an altogether more picturesque place than the sprawling suburbs of Houston, Texas.

Seth turned into an unpicturesque gas station and fast food restaurant complex. "Don't take too long, people. I told Michael we'd be there by two."

"Whatever," muttered Dylan.

"I hate teenagers," Dec said with a crooked grin before heading off to the convenience store.

Dylan grabbed her from behind as she walked into the little restaurant, wrapping his arms around her waist and carrying her up to the order counter. He paused to jiggle her a little bit. He'd started picking her up when he was fourteen. He hated when she did it to him.

She laughed as she shrieked, "What? What do you want?"

"I'm rattling the piggy bank." He dropped his voice a couple of octaves. "Hungry. Feed me."

"Okay, but put me down! I have to pee and you're squeezing my stomach." She pulled out her wallet and peeled off a ten. Then she thought about Dylan's appetite and peeled off another ten. "Here. Get me a Diet Coke."

"You'll just have to stop and pee again."

"And shut up."

Dylan grinned and turned toward the counter. She put a hand on his arm.

"Hey."

He looked down. "What?"

"You know I love you, right? We both do."

"Jesus, Ally, why are you…?"

She reached up to butt his forehead with the heel of her hand. "Watch your language. I asked you a question. You know I love you?"

He rolled his eyes. "Yes, I know you love me."

"And you know I'll do what I think is best for you, even if it pisses you off?"

"What am I, six?"

"No, you just act like it. Fine." She pushed him away. "Go feed your face. Don't forget my Diet Coke."

She came out of the restroom to find Dylan didn't have his food yet, so she sat down at a table near the counter. This part of the restaurant was deserted but for two werewolves in the far corner.

She could hear their whispered conversation. As always, it made her acutely uncomfortable—it wasn't as if she tried to eavesdrop. She tapped her foot, whistled tunelessly and tried hard not to look in their direction.

The guy with the deep voice sounded young, frightened and angry. "I said I'd call if I had anything to report. I don't."

The other guy's voice was higher. He sounded confident, belligerent. "Aaron, you're not going to ignore me. We have an arrangement. That means you talk to me."

"But I don't want anyone to see us together!" Deep Voice Guy—Aaron—sounded a little frantic. "This could get me kicked out of the pack! That's why I want to talk on the phone."

As if on cue, her cell phone rang. Her stomach roiled when she saw the number. Unanswered, the call went to voicemail.

On the other side of the restaurant, the werewolves' heated discussion continued. No matter how much she tried not to listen, she still caught the words "I don't want to do this" and "you don't have a choice".

By the time Dylan returned with her Diet Coke, he had to go to the bathroom himself, so she decided to wait for him in the car.

She reached the door at the same time as the remaining wolf. Average in height, he had short brown hair and soft brown eyes. He held the door with a quiet, "Please, you first," and she realized this was Aaron.

Seth was alone in the car when she slid into the front seat.

"Seventy bucks. Seventy damn dollars to fill up the car."

She shrugged. "When the Fae give us that stuff they say everything can run on—"

"Yeah. When the Fae give us the formula for perpetual motion." Seth, a master mechanic, would be out of a job. "And when the Fae give us the secret to time travel, I'll tell my daddy not to go swimming when he's drunk off his ass."

She laughed and buckled her seat belt.

"I just got off the phone with Tomas." Seth's deep-set eyes were filled with worry.

"Yeah, he called me too, but I didn't answer." Tomas Alcevedo, a Fort Bend County sheriff's deputy, was a friend of theirs back home. "What did he want?"

"He said Lind's been talking about you around town. Says the guy looks like shit and he's telling people you beat the hell out of him. Tomas asked me flat out if one of us did it."

When werewolves and humans fought, the wolves were usually assumed guilty until proven innocent.

Her stomachache got worse. She did some deep breathing exercises and focused on slowing her blood pressure, not wanting Dylan or Dec to smell her anxiety.

"What did you tell him?"

Dec and Dylan piled into the car before Seth could answer.

No one said anything for the next couple of miles, but Dylan's twitchy restlessness was audible. He inhaled the burgers he'd just bought. Then he fidgeted, and he sighed, and he shifted position over and over. His long legs kept banging into the back of Ally's seat, but she grit her teeth and didn't say anything, lest the tension in the car be ratcheted up still further. Although she didn't turn around, in her mind's eye she pictured Dec slouched in the corner, grinning at the adolescent angstfest.

She babied Dylan. Seth argued with him and Dec laughed at him. Not one of them had any idea what to do with a remarkably strong alpha werewolf poised on the brink of adulthood. He still regarded Seth as a father figure, and so, for the moment, the beta still retained a measure of control. That couldn't last. Dec was a beta too, a cross between an uncle and a big brother. Two betas and a female, even one as strong as Ally, were not enough. Dylan needed a real pack, with a real Pack Alpha.

Hopefully, he needed Cade MacDougall.

And Ally needed to get out of Houston, but she kept telling herself that they would've made this trip anyway.

"Sweetie—" she began.

"Look, y'all, I—" Dylan said at the same time.

They both stopped.

"Go ahead, Dylan," Seth said quietly. "What is it?"

"I just—I know I can be a pain in the ass, okay? But that's not what I'm trying to do here, I swear."

As Dylan spoke, she and Seth communicated via sidelong glances.

"I know you didn't want to come up here, pup," Seth replied in a tone both gruff and tender. "But we wouldn't be doing this if we didn't think it was a good idea. Can't you just chill and see what happens?"

"Seth's right, baby."

"*Seth's right, baby,*" Dylan echoed in a sing-song, nyah-nyah, toddler voice.

When he grinned, she started laughing herself. "You're such a brat."

"I wish Dec had never told us about the databank," the teenager groused.

A national databank specialized in connecting werewolves who'd lost track of their relatives during the social upheavals of decades past. At Dec's suggestion, they'd submitted Dylan's DNA and learned the identity of his birth father. Carson MacDougall had died a few years ago, but Carson's brother, Cade, wanted to meet his nephew.

She reached into the backseat to pat Dylan's leg. He didn't push her hand away. Lately, she'd take any affection she could get from the moody teenager. "Dylan, I love you. We all do."

"I wouldn't say I *love* you," Dec muttered.

"Shut up, Dec," she laughed. "Our weird little family's been pretty happy, yeah?" Dylan started to speak; she didn't stop to let him. "But you need a pack to help you finish growing up. And we need to figure out what to do next. Seth and I are just thirty-one."

No one knew Dec's age. All werewolves between thirty and seventy looked thirty-five.

"No, listen," she said when Dylan tried to interrupt again.

"Most teenagers would love to find out they've got a rich relative. I mean, does this sound so awful? We're going to a ranch with horses. We'll be in the country, with mountains and rivers. Maybe you could look at this as an adventure or a vacation, not some kind of torture we dreamed up just to make you miserable. You know?"

She paused, but he didn't say anything. "Okay. You can talk now."

Dylan said nothing for a minute. Then, sounding less like the sullen stranger he'd been lately and more like the pup she'd loved all his life, he said, "It sort of sounds like...well, like you just want to get rid of me."

"Well," she echoed, "that's just dumb."

Everyone laughed, even Dylan.

"We don't have to drive a thousand miles to get rid of you, pup. We could just kick you out of the house," said Seth.

"That's what I voted for," Dec said.

"But I reminded him you were there first, and he didn't get a vote," she interjected.

"What if I hate this guy?" asked Dylan. "What if he doesn't like us?"

"Everybody likes me," Dec answered promptly. "You and Seth might have a problem. But if he takes a shine to Ally, maybe we'll all get a free ride."

"You'd really pimp me out?" she asked, feigning insult.

"Sure, if you're his type." Dec's Irish accent got stronger when he teased her. "He might just like 'em little and cute."

"What if he's not *my* type?"

"I don't see how a rich and handsome wolf with lots of horses wouldn't be your type. And don't tell me you don't need a man, darlin'. Or a wolf."

Dylan snorted in disgust. "You don't know what she needs, Dec."

Dylan hated any mention of her dating. Or having sex. Or being a girl.

Dec just grinned at him. "New days, pup. No more Lost Boys, no more Wendy. Allison Kendall, how long's it been since you spent time with a man you really fancied? The Dane doesn't count."

No, Jakob Lind didn't count. "I can't remember."

Dec sighed. "You see there? That's just sad, that is."

Maybe so, but it didn't matter. She no longer trusted her own judgment.

Dylan wouldn't be distracted. "But what if he's a dick? What if we all hate it there? We can just turn around and go home, right?"

*You can. I probably can't.*

"If MacDougall turns out to be a jerk, we'll deal," she said, trying to sound breezy and unconcerned, "but Nick Wargman said he was a nice guy."

Nick, the Houston Pack Alpha, had put them in touch with Cade MacDougall.

"That's not what he said." Seth brushed his dirty blond hair out of his face. He was overdue for a cut. "Nick called MacDougall a strong leader and an honorable wolf. That's not the same thing as a nice guy."

"Seth..." *Breezy! Keep it breezy!*

"Let's be realistic." Seth did breezy the way Dec did somber. "Pack Alphas don't become Pack Alphas by being nice guys. They're tough. They're dominant."

She rolled her eyes. "In other words, they're alphas."

"That's not what I mean. Pack Alphas..." Seth waved a hand in frustration. "You know what it takes to *be* one? To make a bunch of wolves do what you tell them? Nick, MacDougall, guys like them—they've killed. And a lot of the Rocky Mountain Pack are Lones and outcasts. They're even harder to control."

Dylan and Seth had never lived in a pack. Dec had obviously not liked living in a pack. Yet here they were, possibly joining a pack. Once again, she wished they'd had more time to think this through.

"I just think we shouldn't count on hugs and kisses. We don't know what MacDougall's expecting. Does he think Dylan is joining the pack? Me and Dec? How long's he going to let *you* stick around?"

They hadn't discussed any of this with the Rocky Mountain Alpha. MacDougall's offer came just when they—she—needed it. They were making this up as they went along. For the second time in their lives, Seth, Ally and Dylan were on the run.

This time, though, it was her fault.

The Valkyrie's words echoed in her mind: *Yours to raise, yours to protect.*

Dec broke the uncomfortable silence a short time later. "It's all pretty feckin' moot now, kiddos. We're here."

Cade locked himself in his office to get paperwork done before his guests arrived. Becca napped upstairs. He hadn't seen Sindri since lunch.

His office was soundproofed, but he smelled Michael before the latter knocked on the door.

"It's open," he called, grateful for a break from numbers and breeding charts.

His second-in-command stuck his head inside the office. "Got a minute?"

"Sure."

Michael sat down facing Cade's desk. "Seth Guidry called from Raton about nine, so they ought to be here soon."

"Good. The rooms ready?"

"Yeah, Sindri did it."

"Okay." He waited for Michael to say something else, but the big wolf just sat there. "It wouldn't take telepathy to know you're not here to give an ETA on my nephew. Out with it, wolf."

His lieutenant and best friend of twenty-five years tipped his chair back and laced his hands behind his head. "Maybe you should tell Aaron to call his father. If Aaron just talked to him, Rufus might realize you're not trying to lure wolves away from their birth packs."

Cade was scheduled to meet Rufus Stapkis and two other Pack Alphas in an effort to gain formal recognition for Rocky Mountain. Most packs hadn't acknowledged Cade's wolves as the legitimate successors to his father's pack. Cade thought fifteen years was long enough.

"What's the point? I'll see Rufus in Denver on Friday. He can wait." The idea of placating the half-mad Seattle Alpha repulsed him.

"I think Aaron should talk to him before that. Maybe put him in a better frame of mind for the meeting."

Cade would rather fight the old bastard than talk, and he knew Stapkis felt the same. But he couldn't ignore national pack politics, and he couldn't afford to alienate the St. Louis and Chicago Pack Alphas.

"Fine," he grunted in disgust.

He swiveled his chair to stare out the open window facing the front yard. The summer breeze ruffled the sheer curtains and fluttered the papers anchored on his desk.

"You think I should tell all my wolves to call their daddies? I could have them write letters home to Mommy. This is a pack, not a fucking summer camp."

Michael didn't crack a smile. "But we've got a woodshop. And the guys live in cabins, and we ride horses. Let's ask Sindri if we can make s'mores."

"You know, if you were Rufus' second, he'd rip your throat out."

"You know, you're a hell of a wolf."

Cade tried to scowl. "All right. Tell Aaron to call tonight. It won't make the crazy bastard like me, but it'll make me look magnanimous to the other Alphas. I like to look magnanimous. 'Cause I'm a hell of a wolf."

The two old friends laughed. Then they both winced and jumped out of their chairs as Mrs. Palmer emitted an ear-splitting shriek.

"What the fuck?" Cade shouted. Michael was already out the door. Cade vaulted over the desk after him.

# Chapter Four

A gated road interrupted the trees lining Highway 50. Beside it, a stone plinth bore a plaque with stylized Celtic letters reading *RMP Nordics*.

They'd arrived.

Her stomachache returned.

"You know much about Icelandic horses?" Seth asked. She'd run a small stable in Sugar Land for the last seven years.

"Just what I've read on the Internet. They're good-natured and can carry heavy loads."

"Is that why they're good for wolves?" Seth wasn't into horses. If it didn't have an engine, he didn't pay attention.

"That, and the fact they don't have a fight-or-flight response. Some people think wolves have been riding them since the Dark Ages."

No one knew much about how werewolves lived in the distant past, including werewolves. They weren't the most introspective of the non-human sentients. Recorded werewolf history started in the late forties, when they came out just before the other shifters, followed shortly by the dwarves and other Fae. Everyone knew they played a part in the Allied victory of WWII. Other than that, the werewolves didn't say much.

If female wolves existed, Ally suspected, some of them would've taken the time to write stuff down.

"Norwegian and Danish kings liked 'em," Dec said.

Surprised, she turned to look at him. "What?"

"Icelandic horses. The kings of Norway and Denmark liked them. They're related to Faroese horses. Ever heard of them?"

"No. Where are they from?"

He laughed. "From the Faroe Islands, of course."

"Those are in Scotland, right?"

"Not exactly. North of Scotland, halfway to Iceland. Beautiful, wild country. Bleedin' cold, of course. You don't swim in the North Atlantic."

"Since when do you know about Icelandic horses?"

"I'm Irish, you know. The Irish are mad for horses." He flashed his lopsided grin.

"Yes, I've heard," she murmured.

No matter how long she knew him, she didn't feel she knew him. He never missed his rent, and he made the best cosmos in southeast Texas, and somewhere along the way he'd become one of their closest friends. It had seemed natural to bring him along, especially considering that they'd never have found Dylan's uncle without him.

Now, though, she wondered—why had he wanted to come?

Barbed wire on wooden posts lined both sides of the gravel road. All they saw were dense clusters of trees and expanses of rock, grass and scrub brush. A pond sparkled in the distance. Shadows punctuated sunlight as they drove beneath trees whose branches met to form a canopy above the road.

"I didn't expect something this big," she mused.

"His father bought the first piece of property back in the fifties, and Cade's been adding to it over the years. Remember how the Rocky Mountain Pack imploded?"

"We can't remember something that happened before we were born, Dec. How do you know so much about this?"

He shrugged. "I thought it'd be useful to read up on the wolf, is all. Considering as how we're staying with him a while— or longer."

Dylan snorted at *or longer* and gazed out the window, refusing to get drawn into the subject.

Dec ignored the teen. "MacDougall's parents were murdered while the family vacationed in Scotland." His accent thickened as he spoke. "After the pack fell apart and the survivors left, no one bought the MacDougall land. Cade came back here fifteen years ago and started putting the place back together. He's also bought a lot of property in town."

Dec fell silent, watching the scenery roll past with a

faraway look in his bright green eyes.

More trees, more grass, more scrub brush.

More stomachache.

She was about to ask Dec another question when they rounded a bend in the gravel road. A spectacular vista opened up.

Mountains filled the horizon in the far distance, foothills in the near. Fields of green and gold, a couple of stables, neatly painted outbuildings, and several houses filled the foreground. The stables stood next to a section of fenced pasture about fifty yards away. Inside the fence stood the Icelandic horses Cade MacDougall bred, powerful little things with lavish manes and floppy foretops. She hoped MacDougall would let her ride.

To the right, a prefabricated metal warehouse squatted among large wooden structures. Behind this group of buildings stretched more uncleared land. A small yard held a wooden play system and a trampoline.

Directly in front of them stood a large house with cabins on either side and slightly behind it. The large two-story stone and timber structure looked like a cross between a Swiss chalet and something out of a western—cowboys and goatherds, maybe, or Heidi on horseback. The front door, arched with stone, soared into the second story, where windows sported balconies. The overall effect was both rugged and lovely.

Her stomachache got a little worse.

Cars and trucks and six or seven motorcycles sat in a graveled area. She grinned in spite of her nervous stomach. Rich or poor, urban or country, assimilated or feral, werewolves loved bikes.

Seth pulled into the gravel lot. Everyone in the car gasped and winced as a woman's piercing scream split the still, sunny air. Ally and Seth stared at each other. She knew they were both remembering Gracie's death cry.

The screamer, however, was quite alive. An older woman of ample proportions thundered down the front steps of the large house, heading for a late model Cadillac parked at the other end of the gravel lot. The old lady moved with impressive speed for one so large. Wolves came running from all directions to the center of the compound.

The old woman slammed the door of the Cadillac and peeled out backwards in a squeal of tires and a spray of gravel, fishtailing as she threw the car into drive and roared out of the lot.

The two wolves reached the porch just as Mrs. Palmer's car disappeared in a cloud of gravel. Cade looked at his second in shock.

"Goddamn. What is it with the nannies?"

Upstairs, Becca began to cry.

He turned back to look at the house, as if he'd find an answer there. "It's not Becca. Mrs. Palmer loves her. Why do I keep getting nymphos, drunks and crazy women?"

"Cade..."

"I talked to her at lunchtime. She was fine. I would've known if she was upset about something."

If wolves possessed Fae talents, Cade's would've been telepathy. While he couldn't read minds *per se*, he had an uncanny gift for reading emotions. Mrs. Palmer had been just fine two hours ago.

"Cade, they're here," Michael said. "Oh shit, she really is hot."

"Who?"

"The female. The foster mother."

"Huh? Oh." He'd been so dumbfounded at Mrs. Palmer's getaway he hadn't noticed the three wolves and a young woman with a centerfold body getting out of a Jeep Cherokee. The four new arrivals gazed in astonishment after the latest ex-nanny's car.

"No, can't be," he told Michael. "The female's in her thirties. Shawn! Go help them with their luggage. I'll be there in a minute." He slapped Michael on the back. "You do the introductions. I have to go see to Becca."

"No, that's her. I know that's her," Michael muttered as Cade headed back into the house.

They huddled together by the Cherokee, choking on the dust stirred up by the departing Cadillac. A redheaded werewolf with a friendly grin trotted up.

"Hey! Welcome to the ranch, we've been expecting y'all. 'Course, we weren't expecting that." He waved in the direction of the vanished Cadillac.

"Dude, what happened? Who was that?"

"*Dylan!*" Ally elbowed him. "That's none of our business."

The amiable werewolf laughed. "It's okay, I don't mind. Don't ask Cade about it, though. I think we just lost another nanny. Anyway, my name's Shawn."

Seth introduced himself and everyone else. When he got to Ally, Shawn looked her over with unabashed interest. "You're the girl who lives with three wolves. I didn't realize you'd had a pup yourself. Seth's your cousin, right? So Declan's your mate?"

She understood his assumption, but the bluntness caught her off-guard.

Dec put a hand on her shoulder. "She's not mine, and she hasn't had a pup. She looks this young naturally."

Shawn gaped. "How old are you?"

"I'm thirty-one."

"Holy crap! You look eighteen!"

"All right, Shawn, show some fucking tact."

The new voice belonged to a werewolf with beautiful yellow hair, more reminiscent of a lion's mane than a wolf's coat. The smile he gave them looked uncomfortable, as if he didn't wear it very often.

"This is Michael Wargman, Cade's lieutenant and the one who keeps the rest of us in line." Shawn made the introductions all over again. "Michael, can you believe she's never had a pup?"

"Ally, I apologize for Shawn. There's no filter between his brain and his mouth." Shawn ducked as Michael took a swipe at the back of his head.

She couldn't help laughing, disarmed by the redhead's humor and obvious lack of fear. "It's all right. I get that reaction a lot."

Wargman looked nothing like his younger brother Nick, the Houston Alpha. He was taller, bigger and broader. The hard, sharp angles of his face combined with his bulk to give him an intimidating air.

Shawn and Michael offered to help the guys unload the truck. Ally left them to it. She didn't lift heavy loads in front of others.

The wolves who'd come running earlier had dispersed. The little yard at the center of the compound was empty again, which suited her. She wanted to be alone for a few minutes.

Her stomach unclenched a tiny bit.

She couldn't be sure they'd done the right thing until they met MacDougall, but simply arriving had already eliminated some of her tension. With any luck, Dylan would soon settle in. Then she'd worry about her own future.

# Chapter Five

He couldn't imagine anything a four-year-old could do to make a woman of Mrs. Palmer's age and experience go nuts like that. Becca was rambunctious, a bit spoiled and liked to take her clothes off. Mrs. Palmer knew all that. He asked if there'd been any wolves in the house. Becca and Sindri said no.

If it were up to him, Sindri would be Becca's permanent caretaker, as the brownie had been his and Carson's. But Cade was a single wolf raising a daughter on a ranch full of wolves. While no one knew where Becca's mother was, her maternal grandmother in Savannah had always wanted to raise her. Courts never took sons away from their fathers or their fathers' packs, but single wolves often lost custody of their daughters. He had to find another nanny.

And he had to get back to his guests. After assuring Baby Girl she hadn't done anything wrong and he wasn't angry, he tucked her back into bed, hoping she'd resume her interrupted nap.

Shawn was showing the three wolves their rooms on the other side of the landing.

"We were gonna put you all in these four rooms, but since Mrs. Palmer... Oh, wait, here's Cade. Cade, this is Seth Guidry, Declan MacSorley, and, um...your nephew, Dylan Fontenot. He looks just like you, doesn't he? Well, I guess I mean he looks just like Carson, you know?"

Shawn stopped, stuffed his hands in his pockets and stepped back, not looking at Cade's face. Shawn had grown up in the pack with Cade and Carson. He knew how much finding his nephew meant to Cade.

Trying like hell to keep his voice steady, Cade shook the

teenager's hand. "Dylan. I'm very glad to meet you, son. I wish Carson had had the chance. I want you to think of this place as your home as long as you're here."

"I'm...thank you. I'm sorry I couldn't meet my— Your brother too. Sir. Thank you for inviting us." The pup's emotions were a noisy riot of confusion, reluctance and fear. Dismayed, Cade was searching for words to put him at ease when Dylan's face suddenly lit up. "Your house is awesome!"

Cade laughed. "It is, isn't it? Your grandfather built it, but I've added a lot to it."

He shook hands with Seth Guidry, who appeared outwardly calm but was nervous as hell on the inside, even a little afraid.

The third wolf, a tall, dark-haired beta, grinned at him with a familiarity that grated on Cade. There was something inexplicably smart-assed about his glee. Cade couldn't trust anyone who liked him so damned much at first sight. When the wolf shook Cade's hand, he held it a little too tightly for a little too long.

"'Tis a real pleasure to meet you, Mr. MacDougall," said the wolf in a light Irish brogue. "We've all been looking forward to it. Haven't we, lad?" The beta elbowed Dylan in the ribs. The teenager curled his lip and made an annoyed sound. The Irishwolf just laughed.

*Presumptuous asshole.* Cade pointedly returned his attention to his nephew.

"Where's Ms. Kendall, and who's the girl I saw down by the car? Is she your girlfriend?"

Behind him, Shawn snorted. Guidry and the Irishwolf looked uncomfortable. The teenager blushed almost purple.

"I don't— She's not— I mean..."

"I don't mind if you brought an extra guest, son," Cade hastily reassured him. "We've got plenty of room. She can stay with you if you want." The pup had excellent taste in females.

Shawn shouted with laughter. "That's not a teenager! That's Ally! She's thirty-fucking-one, and she's never had a pup!"

Cade gaped at his wolf in astonishment. "*That's* the foster mother?"

The Irishwolf—Cade couldn't remember his name—piped up. "Shawn here mentioned you may have a nanny shortage. Our Ally's wonderful with small monsters, and they love her."

"That's interesting," Cade snapped. "Shawn, finish showing the wolves around while I talk to Michael."

Michael hung up the phone in Cade's office when Cade walked in, slamming the door behind him.

"I really thought she would work," Michael said with a dejected air. "She wasn't a nympho, a thief or a drunk."

"Mrs. Legget wasn't a thief. She was a kleptomaniac. And now Mrs. Palmer's crazy." Cade collapsed into one of the guest chairs.

"You want your chair back?"

"No, I want my day back. I want to rewind and start over." Taking a cigarillo out of the wooden case on his desk, he lit it up and tipped his chair back.

"Shit. What now?" groaned Michael.

Cade smoking indoors indicated a bad day.

He took a long drag. "I'm wondering if I made a mistake."

"You don't make mistakes."

"Watch it, wolf. I'm serious. This could be a problem."

"We'll hire another nanny, Cade. Sindri can handle things 'til we do."

"That's not the problem. The female outside? You were right, that's Dylan's cousin, his foster mother."

Michael leered. "I know. Great tits and ass. She's as tasty as any of the nannies were."

A sexy young female on a ranch full of single wolves was an invitation for disaster. He'd had to fire two nannies before instructing the service to send someone older and unattractive. One had had a drinking problem, the next had sticky fingers, and now Mrs. Palmer had flipped out. Five nannies, and Becca was barely four.

"How 'bout we try—?"

"No more hot nannies, Michael."

The blond wolf sighed. "Yeah, you're right. So the foster mom's got a smoking bod. What's the problem?"

"I made your little brother a deal about the three of them— the uncle, the foster mother, the weird fucking roommate."

Michael frowned. "A deal?"

"I told Nick I'd look after the girl and the two other wolves.

Let them stay as long as they want. In return he recognizes my pack."

"You didn't tell me you'd given them an open invitation."

Cade shrugged as he took another drag. "Getting Houston's recognition is worth some inconvenience. Nick should've said something about the female, though."

Michael shook his shaggy blond head, looking incredulous. "Damn, Cade. A woman we've never met, who looks like that, hanging around as long as she wants? After all the shit with the nannies?"

Cade leveled a gaze at his second while he took another drag on the cigarillo. Just because he chastised himself for an error in judgment didn't mean his wolf could do it. His tone was mild but tinged with iron as he drawled, "Last I heard, Michael, I was the Alpha and this was my home. I just figured I could decide who gets to visit and for how long. No one told me I had to put it up for a vote. Who's on the committee?"

Their gazes locked for a minute. Michael looked away first, as was proper. And safe. He exhaled. "Point made, point taken."

Neither of them spoke for a minute.

"Where the hell is she, anyway?"

Michael glanced outside and shrugged. "She's wandering around the yard, looking lost and luscious."

"Close the window, it's getting hot outside."

The phone rang as he stood.

"Oh, look," grunted his second, still seated at Cade's desk. "It's Seattle calling."

Cade grinned. "I'd take it myself, but I have to play host again." He turned to go.

"Hey, wait." Michael paused with his hand on the phone. "Listen. If this all blows up in your face, do I get to say I told you so?"

"No. But if you're good, I'll let you clean up the mess."

# Chapter Six

So Cade MacDougall and Michal Wargman were assholes.

She didn't find it flattering that they found her sexy. Lots of guys found her sexy. It wasn't the compliment she'd imagined it would be when she was young. Whatever their opinion of her appearance, they didn't want her here.

Crossing her arms and hunching her shoulders, she told herself it didn't matter. She wasn't staying. Her numerous friends in Sugar Land would welcome her home. If she could go home, which she couldn't, because she'd beaten a guy half to death. She could explain *why* she'd done it. But *how* she'd managed to beat the crap out of a guy twice her size...that was a tough one.

*Butch up, Dead Girl. It's just a couple of jerks for a couple of weeks.*

Her back to the house, she listened as Cade MacDougall left his office, walked across a hardwood floor and opened the front door. She couldn't turn around until he was close enough for a normal human to hear him. It gave her time to tamp down the lonely fear and dismay she'd carried inside all the way from Texas.

By the time a mellow baritone said, "Miss Kendall?" she'd relaxed and pasted on her best coolly polite smile.

She turned. The most beautiful wolf she'd ever seen flashed a smile of his own—raffish, supremely self-assured—and Ally forgot to breathe.

For a split second, she feared she might reach up to run her fingers through his loose curls, jet-black like Dylan's. His closely trimmed beard matched his hair. His eyes were crystal green (like Dylan's), with lashes way too thick for a big tough werewolf (like Dylan's). His mouth was full and sensual. (She'd never thought about Dylan's mouth. She refused to start now.)

The wolf could really rock a pair of jeans. A tattoo on his well-developed right biceps peeked out from his polo sleeve. And the way his white collar framed the top of his chest, highlighting the hollow of his throat...

*You're pathetic,* she sneered to herself. If she hadn't recently sworn off men for the rest of her life, she wouldn't be hyperventilating like a virgin in a locker room.

"Miss Kendall?" he repeated, probably accustomed to rendering women mute. "I'm Cade MacDougall. Welcome to my home." He spoke in a slow, sexy drawl. Her hand retained his heat after he let go.

"Thank you. Please call me Ally." Hey, she was speaking normally. *You go, you tough little freak of nature, you.* As soon as she thought it, her mind went blank again.

He waited, apparently expecting her to say something else. After an agonizing second or two, he cleared his throat and said, "I apologize for the confusion earlier. I'd intended to greet you all myself."

"That's okay." She laughed self-consciously, in a weirdly high pitch. "Shawn said that was your nanny peeling out of here." MacDougall frowned. Belatedly, she remembered Shawn's warning. "Oh, I'm sorry, I wasn't supposed to... I mean, Shawn said not to ask... And I wasn't, I was just..."

*Crap.* She'd already pissed him off.

When she glanced up, he was smirking at her. The more she tried not to blush, the more she blushed. Just before her face spontaneously combusted, Dylan dashed out of the house.

A sincere smile replaced MacDougall's arrogant grin as he watched his nephew run toward them.

"Ally! You gotta see the house, it's awesome! Did you know I'm Scottish?"

She laughed. "Yeah, baby, I did. When I heard your father's last name was MacDougall, I kinda figured." She turned to Cade. "Dylan spent the first semester of his senior year on a study program in Scotland."

"You enjoy it, Dylan? My dad was very proud of our heritage."

"Yeah— I mean, yes, sir. I did."

"So where'd you go for your senior trip?" Cade asked as the three of them headed for the house.

"Oh God, please don't get him started," Ally groaned.

"I didn't get a chance to go," the teenager muttered. "We came up here instead."

"You mean they dragged you up here before you had one last fling with your bros?" MacDougall threw an arm around Dylan's shoulders. Something proprietary and offended flared within her. She mentally slapped herself. She'd brought him up here to meet his uncle, to find him a pack, to *let him go.*

"He's been to Florida a dozen times already," she said with forced lightheartedness. "And I know he's been drunk before, even though he thinks he's good at sneaking."

MacDougall grinned at her over his shoulder, and she had to remind herself to breathe again.

She scrambled to keep up with the two long-legged wolves. MacDougall, a hair taller than Dylan, swaggered with an easy grace the teenager was just beginning to exhibit.

Shawn appeared on the porch as they climbed the front steps. "I'll pack up Mrs. Palmer's stuff. Ally can have her room." He grinned at Ally. "It has a huge bathroom." He turned to Cade. "Chicks dig big bathrooms."

"That won't work." Cade turned to look down at her. They were standing so close she had to tip her head back to see his face. He smelled wonderful—musky and male, with an overlay of sweet tobacco.

Humans couldn't make eye contact with alphas, and she avoided doing things humans couldn't do, so she had to stare at his mouth. Her fingers itched as she imagined running one over his mustache and then down across his firm, wide bottom lip. His black beard, close-trimmed, looked soft to the touch. She'd never kissed a guy with a beard before. What would it feel like on her neck?

She looked eighteen. She wasn't accustomed to *feeling* eighteen.

"That room connects to Becca's with a door that doesn't lock. You won't get any peace. She likes to ramble."

"Becca's your daughter?"

His smile this time was tender, erasing all signs of his earlier annoyance. If she could've looked at his eyes, she knew she'd see the smile there. "She just turned four. I have no idea what happened with Mrs. Palmer today. This house has some kind of nanny-repelling force."

Trailing Cade, Shawn and Dylan into the house, Ally found herself in a large entryway filled with light pouring in from the window above the front door. To the left was a large office, to the right an open room with a dining table that could seat twenty people easily. The foyer led into a cavernous living room made even bigger by a cathedral ceiling.

An open staircase led up to the second story, a loft ringed by an elaborately carved banister. She saw at least six rooms up there.

The back wall of the living room featured a massive fireplace with inlaid stones. Mounted in the stones above the fireplace was a coat of arms. She'd seen things like it in faux British pubs, but this one looked much more impressive. She noticed that Dec was staring at it with a strange expression on his face.

"I've never seen a coat of arms in someone's house before," she said.

"It's not a coat of arms, darlin'. That's the crest badge of the Clan MacDougall," he murmured.

"Is it the same as a coat of arms?"

"No. A crest badge identifies a particular Scottish clan. Coats of arms belong to families or individuals."

"You're gonna tell me you can read it, aren't you?"

"It's Scottish Gaelic. It can mean either *Victory or Death*, or *Conquer or Die*." He grinned, winked, and wandered off to look at something else.

A door to the right of the fireplace led into another room behind the wall. The huge chimney she'd seen sticking out of the middle of the roof must be for a double fireplace. The walls and floors were constructed of light-colored wood, with no sheetrock or carpeting. The Scandinavian-style furniture and plush area rugs spoke of understated wealth.

Dylan was right. This was indeed awesome. She couldn't live here, she reflected wistfully, but she hoped he could.

A little girl called out, "Daddy?"

Cade sighed. "I knew she wouldn't go back to sleep after all that commotion."

"I'll go find Sindri," said Shawn.

"No, don't bother him. I'll get her." He called upstairs. "Hang on, Baby Girl. I'll be up there in just a minute."

She fancied she could feel his breath on her neck all the way up the stairs.

When they reached the second floor and halted outside a large room, she saw her luggage on the bed.

"As I was saying, Becca gets up at night and goes walkabout. She's wide awake when she does it. She'll normally head for the nanny's room and if no one's there, she comes downstairs to me. You probably won't want—"

"Kids don't bother Ally." Dec emerged from a bedroom across the landing. "Like I was telling you, she loves the little monsters as much as she does the horses."

Cade shot him an annoyed sneer. Pack Alphas didn't like to be interrupted. But he raised an eyebrow at her. "You like horses and kids?"

"I've nannied a little. I've run a stable for the past few years. I do teach kids to ride."

"Do you teach them how to swim?"

She gasped. "How'd you know I swim?"

"I smell the chlorine."

"Oh. I, um, I swam at the hotel this morning and I didn't wash my hair. I did take a shower, though." *Shut up, Ally.* She blushed.

Cade smiled.

Her breath stuck in her throat again.

"There's a swimming pool in the gym. It doesn't get used as much as it should. You're welcome to it anytime you want.

"That's perfect!" She hadn't meant to squeal, and she blushed again. "I wondered where I'd find a pool. Thank you!"

"You're welcome. I'll show it to you after dinner."

"I don't mind staying next door to your daughter. Don't go to the trouble of fixing another room. Besides, Shawn's right about chicks and big bathrooms."

Cade smiled. "Fine. We can always move you if Becca gets on your nerves. I'll let you get unpacked."

"Thank you."

Dec hung back for a second. In a falsetto voice he whispered, "*I did take a shower though!*"

"Shut up, fur face." She said it with affection.

After getting the last, most disturbing of his guests squared away and Becca engrossed in a movie about cats, he joined Michael outside on the porch.

"So? What do you think?" his second asked.

"I think she's fucking cute." *I bet she's cute fucking too.* He surprised himself. He didn't normally go for cute.

"Okay... I was talking about the situation in general." Michael eyed him skeptically.

"Oh. Well. I think the kid looks more like Carson than me—it kind of hurts to see him, to tell you the truth." He paused. "There's something weird about the Irishwolf."

"Like what?"

"You didn't feel it? He doesn't feel like any beta I've ever met."

"Seems like a nice guy."

"And Ally Kendall—if she told me she was a senior in high school, I'd believe her."

Michael laughed. "Since when do you find high school girls fucking cute?"

Good point. Cade wasn't into jailbait.

"What kind of vibe did you get off them?" Michael was aware of his uncanny gift for reading people. Cade's mother had always insisted he tell no one about his semi-telepathic abilities. She said it would make others uncomfortable. As an adult he didn't advertise it because it was so useful in business, poker and pack politics.

He sank into a rocker and ran a hand through his hair. "Guidry's a good guy—solid, honest. Something's got him scared, though. There's something he's not telling me, and I don't know if it's just him, or all of them. Dylan's feeling shy and scared, which is understandable. That MacSorley guy is just damned weird."

"And Ally?"

Cade smiled to himself, remembering how she'd blushed when she'd blurted out what Shawn had said. The surprising strength of her grip, the alluring softness of her hand. The way she'd kept fiddling with her hair and glancing up at him, the weird pauses and nervous laughter.

Normally he could tell if a woman wanted him, but he couldn't read what Ally Kendall was thinking or feeling. She blushed, she laughed, she seemed nervous, she seemed nice—it was all surface impressions. He couldn't get a handle on her.

"Hello?" Michael, perched on the porch railing with his arms crossed, was smirking at him. "Hot foster mama getting to you? You seem a little flustered there, Alpha."

Cade blew out a long breath and snorted. "Flustered my ass. I was just thinking, I can tell she loves the pup. Other than that, she just seems...I dunno. Wholesome. Yeah. She's wholesome."

Allison Kendall radiated wholesomeness. She smelled of lavender and sunshine and swimming pools, he thought with a smile. And Michael was right about the body. She was all curves and muscles. He'd enjoyed the view walking up the stairs.

He couldn't understand how thirty-one-year-old tits could look eighteen, even if her face did. And what a great face, with gray eyes and a little snub nose. When she smiled, she showed dimples deep enough to swim in. The fresh-faced innocence look didn't normally do it for him, but...

But hell. She was his nephew's foster mother. His dick would have to wait until he got to Denver.

He stood and stretched. "I'm gonna go check on Baby Girl, and then I'm going for a run. I haven't been four-footed in days. Make sure Aaron tells you how it went after he talks to Rufus."

"Got it. Later."


Did she have time to take a quick nap before dinner? She should go ask what time...

"Daddy? Daddy! Where are you?" The cross little voice came from next door.

Ally heard tiny feet slapping rapidly across the hardwood floor. A miniature replica of Cade MacDougall—longer hair, Winnie the Pooh panties, no beard—ran into the room. The child stopped when she saw Ally.

"Who are you?" Mini-Cade demanded.

"I'm Ally. Your daddy's down the hall. Want to go see him?"

The beautiful little girl looked a lot like Dylan too. Her

green eyes took up half her face. "I'm Becca."

"I know."

"I'm a cat."

"That's nice."

"Pick me up."

"Okay."

They regarded each other for a moment.

Becca said, "My tummy hurts," and vomited down the front of Ally's T-shirt.

# Chapter Seven

As he reached the top of the stairs, he heard Becca gulping and sniffling while Allison Kendall soothed her.

"Here, baby, let me help you. It's okay, you're fine..."

He hurried to the bathroom.

"Daddy!" Becca wailed.

"Hey, baby. You feel bad?"

She scrunched her face in thought. "No."

Ally looked at him in the mirror and shrugged with a grin. "Kids puke. I see some chocolate chips in there."

"Goddamn it. I told Sindri to check with me before he gave her any cookies."

"Goddamn it's a bad word, Daddy."

"Becca, where are your clothes?"

A champion pouter, she stuck her bottom lip out halfway down her chin. "Cats don't wear clothes," she whined. "I kept my panties on like you told me."

Ally laughed. "If you'll throw me a washcloth, I'll sponge her off. It's all over her face and chest." It was all over Ally as well, but she didn't appear concerned. He watched as she sat Becca on the counter and briskly wiped her down. When all the solid chunks were gone, Cade scooped her up.

"Come on, baby. Let's get you in the bath and let Ally get cleaned up. Thank you," he said to Ally as Becca wrapped her arms around him and buried her face in his neck. She still smelled like vomit. He gave her a squeeze. "How did she manage to get it all over you, anyway?"

"I was holding her. She ordered me to pick her up, and I just obeyed. I didn't even know they made alpha toddlers."

He laughed. "Sorry about that—Baby Girl's a little bossy sometimes. Sindri and the wolves indulge her." He hadn't made a move to leave yet, and he didn't want to.

"Who's Sindri?"

"He looks after the house for me and takes care of Rebecca when we're between nannies, like now."

She sponged off her T-shirt as they talked, remarkably unselfconscious. He couldn't look away. There was nothing coy or flirtatious about Ally Kendall, and it made him feel slightly ashamed for enjoying the unintentional wet T-shirt demo. She didn't appear to notice his fascination.

"You're pretty comfortable with kiddy slime. Lots of guys get grossed out at this sort of thing."

"I spent eleven years in the Army. Plus, I roll around in the dirt and eat small animals raw. Takes a lot to gross me out."

She grinned at him. He had the strangest, strongest urge to stick his finger in one of those dimples.

"I know what you mean. I live with three wolves, so I don't gross that easily either. Long as they don't shed on the furniture or bring their roadkill in the house, I don't care what they do when they're furry."

He laughed as he carried Becca back to her room.

He wanted to see those dimples again.

A short but heavy nap, followed by a hot shower, left her feeling calmer and more optimistic than she had in weeks. Then a subdued Seth stopped by her room on the way down to dinner.

He closed the door behind him and leaned against it, dark circles under his hazel eyes and a worried expression on his face.

"You okay?"

"I was just about to ask you the same thing."

"I'm worried about you," both said at the same time.

"Okay, you first," she said.

"The Lind thing. Stop blaming yourself."

"I blame myself because it's my fault."

"It's your fault the guy attacked you?"

"It's my fault I didn't tell y'all or Tomas when he wouldn't quit calling me. It's my fault I threw him across the stable."

"What were you supposed to do? Let him beat you up?"

"I was supposed to find some way out of the situation instead of losing control. And it's my fault I used Dylan to get out of Houston."

"No!" He folded his arms tightly in front of him, hunching up like he did when he was stressed. "No. You weren't using him. We had to bring him up here anyway. He had to meet his uncle. Why else have you been protecting him all this time? If his line's precious to Eir, he needs to be with them, yeah?"

"But we did it so suddenly, and now I'm not sure it was necessary." She began to pace, a nervous habit that irritated the stolid Seth. "I haven't had any signs or anything from Eir in thirteen years. How do I know I was supposed to bring him up here? We're in a strange place with strange wolves and I could lose both of you and I don't know what the hell I'm supposed to do next and I..."

He threw his arms around her and held her close. She rested her head on his shoulder as she took deep, long breaths to calm herself. Panic never helped.

"Keep it together, Dead Girl. You can't lose us. But MacDougall's smart. He'll see right through bullshit. And he's gonna want to know what we've been doing, how Dylan grew up."

"Okay. Yes. Yeah, he will." She gave Seth a brilliant smile full of confidence she knew *he* knew damned well she didn't really feel. "We'll handle questions just like we always do, okay? Nothing to worry about."

They'd been spinning the stories for so long they didn't even think about it. Nothing threw them anymore. This was just a momentary stress attack.

"Do you trust me?" Seth asked.

"What? That's a silly question."

"So answer it. You trust me?"

"Of course I do. With my life. And with my death." She laughed.

He didn't. "Okay. Let's get this over with."

Cade walked into the kitchen to find Sindri deep in

conversation with the Irishwolf. He struggled to remember the name—Donal, David...Declan. Declan MacSorley. Sindri didn't generally speak to strangers in the house. Even weirder was the language they were conversing in.

They looked up to see him watching them. Sindri frowned, but MacSorley gave him a relaxed smile. Cade didn't return it.

"You speak Icelandic, Mr. MacSorley."

"Just a wee bit." The Irishwolf appeared unfazed at Cade's brusque interruption.

"My mother and Sindri are the only people I've ever met who could speak it."

"There aren't many Icelanders roaming the globe, that's true. Aren't many Icelanders, period, come to think of it."

"Is there—?" He stopped short when he saw the Irishwolf flinch, although Cade hadn't moved a muscle. MacSorley's careless grin faltered as he gazed over Cade's shoulder with a strange expression.

Cade turned, saw nothing, then looked down. Becca stared up at him. She wore her pajamas, both top and bottom. The no-naked-outside-your-own-room admonitions were getting through.

"What do you want, baby?"

"I'm thirsty," she pouted.

"You can have a glass of water, but then straight back up to your room." He paused. "Mr. MacSorley, this is my daughter Rebecca. Becca, this is Mr. MacSorley."

Becca moved behind Cade's leg with a barely audible "hi". She didn't meet new people often.

MacSorley continued to stare at her. Cade found he couldn't read the Irishwolf as easily as he had earlier. He seemed disturbed. A lot of Lones were uncomfortable around children. But then he flashed a wide grin, flippant once more.

"Well, now," he cooed. "I've only known one little girl as pretty as you my whole life. And I'm a very old wolf, you know. How old would you be, darlin'?"

Becca ventured a peek at him. "Four," she whispered.

"I was four once, but I don't remember anything about it."

Becca cocked her head at that, perplexed. "I'm a cat."

Cade sighed, but MacSorley laughed delightedly. "Really? That's cracker, that is! Are you a cat all the time, or just sometimes?"

"Just sometimes." Her smile annoyed Cade. He didn't want the Irishwolf charming his daughter.

"Can you do it whenever you want?" MacSorley asked Becca.

She shook her head.

"Well, that's okay, it's a wonderful thing anyway. Just remember, though—" here MacSorley lowered his voice conspiratorially, crouching with his hands on his knees and looking at Becca gravely "—kitty cats have to be careful around wolves. I'm sure Daddy's wolves love you to pieces, but what if they don't recognize you when you're a cat, hmm?" And then he winked.

Becca's eyes got huge. Her mouth made a little O.

"All right, Becca, there's your water. Say good night to Mr. MacSorley."

Still staring at MacSorley in solemn amazement, she whispered good night and fled upstairs.

"Now," Cade said when she was gone, "what brings you to the kitchen, Mr. MacSorley?"

"Just Dec, please." MacSorley looked like he'd forgotten what they were talking about for a moment. "Let's see, I—oh! I just smelled something intoxicating and had to follow my nose. I found this wee fella here, and I was gobsmacked when he told me he cooked it all up himself. Between you and me, much as I love the Wendy—and I do love the Wendy—cooking is not her forte. We eat out quite a bit."

Cade studied the wolf for a minute. He couldn't get a bead on him, couldn't read him at all. "Who's the Wendy? Are you talking about Allison?"

MacSorley laughed. "Yes. It's our little joke—see, she's Wendy and we're the Lost Boys. She sews our pockets and—"

"My mother read me the story. Which one of you is Peter Pan?"

"That would be Dylan, if we let him, but we won't."

"My nephew is reluctant to grow up?"

"And what eighteen-year-old boy isn't, when he's had a nice, clean home and plenty of food and someone who loves him as much as Ally does? He's her pup, you know, just as surely as if she'd birthed him herself. Of course, she'd have been thirteen years old, and that's skeevy to think about, but—"

"Dinner will be served in five minutes. Sindri will call you when it's ready. I need to talk to him right now."

The Irishwolf seemed incapable of taking offense.

"I hope it's okay if I don't join you. I figure the first night should be for family, and for you to get acquainted with your nephew. He didn't want to come up here, y'see, and it's gonna take him some time to relax. I'm sure you'll understand that."

"I'll deal with my nephew without help from strangers, wolf. And I'm sure *you'll* understand *that*."

"Well, then." The weird wolf beamed at him. "I believe I'll go for a run in those fine-looking woods. Enjoy your dinner, Cade. That little girl is a wonder. Pleasure meeting you, Sindri," he continued with a nod in the brownie's direction. "It's a beautiful kitchen you have here. Good night, all."

And the son of a bitch strolled out whistling a jaunty little tune, leaving Cade somewhat gobsmacked himself.

"Sindri, what was that about?"

"Nothing, *barn*."

The Old Icelandic word meant child. Cade didn't mind the appellation at forty-four. The way Sindri saw it, Cade was "born yesterday, and the young one this morning".

Cade watched the brownie scurry about the kitchen from step stool to step stool, putting the finishing flourishes on the meal he'd prepared. One didn't ask a brownie how he accomplished his tasks. Sindri cleaned like a fairy, cooked like Martha Stewart and looked like a cross between Julia Child and ET.

"Was he bothering you, old man?"

Sindri didn't stop fussing with his meal or turn around. "He smelled my food and came to see. He asked who I was, and I was pleased to tell him."

"There's something strange about that wolf. He annoys me."

"Too much annoys you, *barn*. Go. Sit. Eat."


"...and he met my mother while he was in Scotland researching his ancestry."

Cade paused to take a drink of wine. Ally had told him about leaving Lake Charles when Dylan was five, following

Gracie Fontenot's death and Guy's disappearance. Before he could draw her out with more questions, Dylan had started talking about Scotland, so Cade told them about the Clan MacDougall.

Louis MacDougall had been proud of his Scottish ancestry and his descent from Somerled, the twelfth century Scottish leader whose son established the clan.

"Of course, genealogists say Somerled has something like half a million descendants today."

"He drove the Vikings out of Scotland, didn't he?" Dylan asked. "I read about him while I was there."

"That's right. Nowadays, they think Somerled actually had Viking ancestry himself."

"I wonder if Somerled was a werewolf," Ally mused with a little smile. She still seemed wholesome. She still flashed those fuckably cute dimples. He still couldn't tell what she was thinking or feeling. And that was a problem, because the story she'd fed him about leaving Lake Charles was as thin and holey as her tight blue jeans.

The three adults had finished eating. Dylan was on his second helping of standing rib roast. They drank an excellent Chilean red, the teenager trying hard to act like he drank wine around his elders all the time. Everyone was enjoying themselves, which put Cade in a tough spot.

He'd been racking his brain for a diplomatic way to tell Ally he didn't believe a word she'd said tonight. That probably wasn't the best way to elicit another dimple flash, and it would ruin what had been a pleasant evening so far.

"So, Ally. How long were y'all in Beaumont before you moved to Sugar Land?"

Ally tucked her hair behind her ear. "We just stayed in Beaumont for a few months. We got in touch with a friend of one of my other cousins, who hooked Seth up with a job in Houston, and we moved there. Then we moved out to Sugar Land, a suburb of Houston. I nannied for a while and then I wound up at the stables. Seth ran an auto shop."

"When did you meet MacSorley?"

"Right before Dylan's first change, so, what—four years ago? He was bartending at this neighborhood place where we hung out."

"Who looked after Dylan while you hung out at a bar?" *Oh*

*well. I'm a Pack Alpha, not a goddamned diplomat.*

Ally barely paused. "We just took him with us."

"Excuse me?"

Seth sighed and hunched his shoulders. Dylan snickered.

Ally looked Cade straight in the nose. "We parked him under the pool table. We were teenage trailer trash. You wouldn't expect us to have the sense to get a babysitter, would you?"

"I didn't mean..."

"Yes. You did."

He admired her aplomb and even briefly regretted his snide question. But he knew Seth was lying, and therefore she was too. He wanted to trust her, but he probably couldn't.

He wanted to see those dimples again, but he probably wouldn't.

She took a deep breath before she spoke again. "We didn't go out together much. I had friends I traded babysitting with. We didn't bring people home, and neither did Dec when he moved in. I didn't want him moving in at all, to begin with. I didn't want people thinking we were... Well, thinking we were what you obviously think we are."

"Then why'd you let him move in?"

She sighed and closed her eyes. "We needed help with the rent, and Dec always has plenty of money. Seth liked him the minute he met him. I don't know anyone who's ever met Dec who didn't like him right away." She opened her eyes. He almost expected her to look him in the eye, so defiant was her gaze. "He's part of our family now. Dec suggested Dylan go to Scotland. He paid for half of it. If it weren't for Dec, we'd never have found the DNA match."

"I don't like him."

"I don't care."

They studied each other in silence while Dylan fidgeted and Seth slumped.

"So," he began, then stopped. "Dylan. Go in the kitchen. Sindri would love to stuff you with some more food. I want to talk to Ally and Seth."

Seth had hardly spoken. Ally seemed to do the talking for the three of them.

The pup looked at the female uncertainly.

"Dylan." He hadn't raised his voice, but his nephew jumped. "Son, when I tell you to do something, you don't check with her first. She is not the Alpha. I'm the Alpha, and this is my home. I shouldn't have to keep reminding people of this," he said, half to himself. "Go on, now. And close the door behind you."

Once Dylan was gone, Seth reached over and took one of Ally's hands. Her gaze remained fixed on the table.

"Ally." Cade tipped his chair back, stretched out his legs and spoke slowly, staring at his wineglass while he fiddled with the stem. "I apologize for the bar crack. But I've got a problem here. You and Seth—even MacSorley—seem like decent folk. Dylan acts like a kid who's been raised right. Nick Wargman spoke highly of y'all, and I respect his judgment. So I want to like you. The problem is..." And now he looked at her. "The problem is, I don't believe the story you're telling me. I just can't. It's preposterous, and I can't believe people have bought it for thirteen years." He couldn't read her. But he could read Seth, and that would be enough.

"Gracie asks you to keep Dylan for the night. She fights with Guy. You and Dylan both sleep through it. In the morning, when you take Dylan home, the trailer's torn up and Gracie's dead." He paused. "Dylan didn't see any of it, right?"

"Right," she replied flatly. "I left him outside while I went in. I figured they'd be hung over and beat-up and nasty."

"Right. So—Gracie's dead, Guy's gone. Seth comes over, y'all take Dylan and run. Your cousin, Seth's sister, is dead, but you don't call the cops. You don't call anyone in your family. You don't call anyone in the Lake Charles Pack. Wait—one more thing. Seth, are you Lone?"

"He's—"

"I asked Seth, not you," Cade said smoothly, watching the beta. He could feel Ally glaring at him in silent wrath. She was lying to him—why did it bother him that she was angry with him as well?

Seth Guidry frowned for a minute, then shrugged. "Yeah, I guess so. My daddy died before I was born, and no one in my family or the rest of the pack took much interest. I didn't really mind."

Cade sighed in disgust. He'd heard stories about Lake Charles for years, but what kind of pack would let a fatherless wolf grow up alone? He turned back to Ally.

"You take Dylan and drive straight to Texas. You stay with your relatives a few weeks. You find jobs in Houston, your family waves you on your way and you live in Sugar Land for the next thirteen years. Have I got that, Ally?"

"Yes." She practically ground her teeth as she spoke, visibly struggling to keep her anger in check. The aplomb of minutes ago had disappeared.

"Why didn't you call the Lake Charles Pack?"

"Because everyone knew Dylan wasn't Guy's kid. No one knew who his father was, if he was even a wolf. And if you look up white trash werewolves in the dictionary, you'll see a picture of the Lake Charles Pack. I wouldn't leave one of their own kids with them."

"Why not call Social Services?"

She rolled her eyes. "When's the last time you dealt with Social Services, Cade? You even know anyone who has? Anyone who's been in foster care?"

He didn't answer.

"Of course you don't. You're rich. You wouldn't know anything about it, so let me explain. Number one, foster care is usually worse than home. Number two, Social Services doesn't like dealing with wolves. There aren't a lot of wolves who want to be foster parents, and—"

"I killed Guy," Seth said quietly.

"—humans are afraid to fost—" Ally stuttered to a halt, eyes widening as she realized what Seth had just said.

*Now* they were getting somewhere. Cade smiled with satisfaction, sitting forward with his arms on the table. His instincts always told him when someone was hiding something.

He loved being right.

Until he saw the expression on Ally's face. Her composure punctured at last, she looked bereft, like a scared little girl. He didn't care how skilled a liar she might be. He wanted to comfort her, protect her, and that bothered him.

"You said you trusted me," Seth said to Ally.

"But I don't trust *him*," she replied, barely above a whisper.

Cade snorted. "*You* don't trust *me*? I'm not the one who's been lying, sweetheart."

They ignored him.

"He's Dylan's blood," Seth implored, glancing nervously at Cade. "Do you really think he'll call the cops?"

Ally clutched her cousin's hand so tightly it turned blue, but he didn't attempt to pull away.

"I'm tired of lying about everything all the time, Al," Seth continued.

"What will you tell him?" She sounded terrified.

"Just what he needs to know, nothing else." Seth sounded determined.

"Excuse me," Cade drawled. "I'm right here. And I expect you to tell me everything."

They still ignored him.

"We talked about this," said Seth. "If we're going to stay here—if Dylan stays here, and Dec and I stay here—"

"Dylan is staying here. MacSorley is not staying here. I haven't decided about you, Seth." And he was starting to regret his deal with Nick Wargman about the female.

They still fucking ignored him.

"We wanted someone to help us guide Dylan. That's Cade. There's one big dog in the pack, Ally, and he's it. We accept that or we leave."

Cade slammed his hand down on the table. "All right, that's enough. No one's leaving until you tell me what I want to know. What happened to—?"

The female went on as if she and Seth were alone in the room. "Fine, Seth, he's the big dog. That doesn't mean he has to know everything..."

"Goddamn it!" Cade roared.

"Shut up!" Ally yelled.

Cade stood and kicked his chair back. He'd never harmed a woman in his life, but he'd just come damned close to jumping this one. "Who the hell do you think you are?"

"She thinks she's the alpha," Seth said quietly.

"Why does she think that?"

"Because she's the alpha."

"She's a female, for Christ's sake! You *obey* her?" Now that he'd started yelling, he found he couldn't lower his voice.

"No, he humors me!" She was still shouting, standing now. Only Seth remained in his chair.

"Do you ever let the wolf speak for himself?" Everyone on

the goddamned ranch could hear this.

"He can speak for himself all he wants. I need some air."

She stormed out the front door, slamming it behind her with a lot more force than someone so small should've been able to muster.

Cade stared after her, furious, offended and impressed.

And aroused.

He could tell he'd frightened her, but she hadn't backed down an inch. Few people ever yelled at him, and no one had told him to shut up since—well, ever. That would've been deadly for a male, either wolf or man. It still pissed him off coming from a female.

But not as much as he would've expected.

She'd seemed so cute and polite, but as soon as he confronted her... No, he shouldn't be smiling. He couldn't tolerate such brazen defiance, and he wouldn't tolerate being lied to.

Still. She was different. Different intrigued him. Recurring visions of her naked body probably had something to do with it too.

Seth was watching him apprehensively. Cade sat down, picked up his wineglass and put his feet on the table. "All right. Tell me how you killed Guy Fontenot."


Trembling as the door slammed behind her, she took great gulps of air, both to clear her head and to relieve the treacherous tightness in her throat.

No crying. Alpha chicks didn't cry.

But she didn't feel very alpha when she was around Cade MacDougall. He scared the hell out of her. A guy that dominant, that shrewd, that rich *and* that pretty...there had to be something deeply wrong with him. Had to be.

She stuffed her hands in her jeans pockets to keep from twisting her hair out. Her heart pounded, her pulse raced, her stomach churned. She stumbled over to the little yard and sat in a swing, putting her head between her legs.

*Maybe this is what an anxiety attack feels like.*

Oddly enough, considering her life, it would be her first.

It wasn't just Cade MacDougall's dominance throwing her

off her game. There was that stupid episode with Jakob Lind, the decision to turn Dylan over to a wolf she'd never met... She should've thought this through. Fleeing from their home in a blind rush had been a huge mistake.

For the first time since she woke up in the back of the Cherokee thirteen years ago, she didn't feel in control. She'd dropped the reins, and her life was galloping away without her.

Her body vibrated with pent-up energy. She itched to run—fast, far, for a long time. But she couldn't go running through unfamiliar terrain, after dark, with God knew how many wolves watching her.

She smelled Dylan before he poked his cold, wet nose at her, trying to lick her face. On two feet he had to be asleep before she could peck him on the forehead. On four feet he turned into a big, hairy, kissy monster.

"Stop! Don't lick my face. I know, I love you too. Come on, roll over." Some wolves wouldn't deign to be petted and scratched like dogs. Dylan was still too young and frisky to care.

Clouds obscured the half moon. A faint, fuzzy glow illuminated the yard and the fields and woods beyond. She petted Dylan, and she rocked, and she listened to the voices and noises coming from the cabins on either side of the main house. When she got tired of all that, she started obsessing over what Seth had just done.

Why hadn't he bothered to warn her? *Do you trust me?* didn't constitute a warning. They'd been here a few hours, and already a door had been slammed in her face. Acting on impulse, rather than planning and forethought, led to blunders like this.

She heard the front door open and knew it was him; she could already identify his scent. He ambled over to the swing set with a loose, sinuous gait.

Embarrassed at the way she'd lost her temper inside, she concentrated on scratching Dylan and ignored Cade looming above her.

"Dylan, I still need to talk to Ally. Go run."

Dylan ambled off.

"I think your cousin is an honorable wolf."

"He is that. Absolutely," she agreed quietly, staring at the ground.

"If an honorable wolf is willing to kill and lie for you, I suppose you aren't a bad person, no matter how much you annoy me."

*Condescending creep.*

Cade smoked.

Ally swung.

Time passed.

"Seth just told me one hell of a story." Now he spoke gently, no mockery in his voice.

She looked up. "You believe him?"

"I believe people who aren't lying to me."

"So you're telepathic."

He grinned around the cigarillo. "I'm a wolf of much power."

"Good for you." *Bullshit.* Wolves didn't possess Fae talents. Wolves and Fae couldn't even produce children together. She tucked her hair behind her ear and put her head back down.

"Are you going to cry?" Now he sounded worried.

She started to laugh, but stopped before it turned into a sob. "No. I don't cry in front of people." She quit swinging for a minute. "I might throw up, though."

"I'd prefer that to crying."

"That's weird."

"Can't help it. Female tears annoy me."

She looked up and laughed shakily. "Me too."

He stared at her in silence, and she looked back down at the ground. Unnerving though it was, she enjoyed being the center of his attention. She liked the way he scared her, and it scared her that she liked it.

"Why'd you do it?" His drawl had gotten more pronounced since they'd started arguing at dinner, and it sounded appallingly sexy on him.

Her heart stopped for a moment. What had Seth said? "I had to."

"No, Ally, you didn't. That's just the point. You didn't have to do any of it. You could have called the cops, you—"

"There wasn't time."

"You could've let Guy take Dylan."

She gaped at him in shock, blinking back the tears suddenly pooling in her eyes. "How could I do that? How could I *ever* do something like that?"

"I'm just trying to understand how an eighteen-year-old girl faces down a wolf drunk on moonshine. Not many young girls would risk their lives like that, not even for family."

The wave of relief nearly knocked her over. Seth had told MacDougall what he needed to know and nothing else, just as he had promised.

She debated for a moment over how honest to be.

"I lost my parents when I was eight. My aunt Jackie raised me, and I loved her—she was barely twenty-one when she took me in—but she died when I was sixteen and I stayed in our trailer by myself."

"You didn't have other family?"

"I did. I had Seth and his mom, and some others. I didn't want to live with them. They gave me money here and there, but otherwise they left me alone. I didn't really fit in. I read books and made good grades and didn't drink and screw around and I wanted to go to college." She shrugged. "I was lonely and sad, and Dylan made me feel necessary. Gracie loved him—she did, but she was weak. She would never have given him up, but she'd take all the help I gave her. And when Guy showed up that night, I thought, 'Hell no. I won't let you hurt him'."

"So you faced down a drunken, rampaging wolf alone."

"It wasn't like I was unarmed. I had a silver-loaded shotgun."

"You missed."

"This is true." She paused. "I'm a much better shot now."

He grunted in exasperation as he ground out the cigarillo. "You shouldn't joke about it."

"Well, I'm not used to talking about it. We haven't even told Dec the real story."

"What about Dylan?"

"What about him?"

"How much does he remember?"

*Oh God, no.* She tried to keep the panic out of her voice. "He says he doesn't remember any of it. We don't ask him about it and we don't talk to him about it. Look, I'll tell you whatever you want to know. I'll leave if you want me to, but don't ask him about that night." She stopped, wondering what else she could say to make him understand. "Please, Cade. Leave him alone."

Once more Eir's words echoed in her head. *Yours to raise,*

*yours to protect.*

She didn't want to look at him, didn't want him to see the way she fought so hard to keep from crying. So she stared at his boots.

An instant later, he was on one knee in front of her.

He brushed the hair from her face, his fingers lingering for a second on her cheek. As he put his hand under her chin and tilted it up, his voice flowed through her, low and soft. "I know bad memories, Ally. I know what it's like to remember things you wish you didn't, things that still scare you no matter how old you get. I would never make Dylan talk about this."

He dropped his hand to her throat, running his palm lightly up and down, his thumb tracing her veins. His touch didn't disconcert as it had earlier, when they shook hands. Now it warmed and enervated. Ally closed her eyes. A small sigh leaked out as all the fear and tension drained away, leaving her deflated. A wolf's thumb on the jugular should make one real damned alert, but she was relaxed, even drowsy. She didn't want to cry anymore. She just wanted him to keep stroking her like this. If she fell asleep, would he carry her inside? That would be nice.

"You really are extraordinary," he murmured.

Before she could rouse herself to speak, the plaintive howl of a frightened wolf split the night.

Her eyes flew open. "That's Dylan."

She tried to stand up, but he pushed her back down. "You stay here." He took off in the direction of Dylan's howls, coming from the woods behind the little cluster of buildings.

"Hell with that," she muttered, and took off.

# Chapter Eight

She plowed into him when he came to a sudden halt. They were about a half mile from the house, amid dense trees.

Cade paused for a second before running forward to grasp the legs of a figure dangling from a noose. She gasped.

It was Aaron—the wolf from the restaurant where they'd stopped that afternoon.

Cade lifted the body up so that the rope went slack.

"He's not dead," she said stupidly.

"No, he's not." Cade fumbled in his front pocket with one hand while holding up the wolf's legs. He pulled out his cell phone. "Call 911 and get back to the house. Go!"

She took the phone and sprinted for the house, Dylan on her heels. Wolves met her as she raced out of the trees. Some were on two feet, some on four. Michael took some wolves and went to help Cade.

Sitting in the living room with Shawn much later, she asked, "Who was that poor wolf?"

Shawn shook his head. "Name is Aaron Stapkis. A good guy, just nineteen. His father is the Seattle Alpha, real old school."

"Old school?"

"Unpredictable, ready to rip some fur the minute someone looks at him cross-eyed. Most Pack Alphas used to be like that, back before we came out. Now it's just the older ones. Stapkis lost his wife last year. It makes some wolves a little funny in the head. He's always hated Cade."

"Why?"

Shawn shifted and stretched, rubbed his neck and didn't say anything. She waited, careful not to press him.

"Well, see, when Cade came back here fifteen years ago, he contacted some of the younger wolves born in the pack with us, back when Louis and Eirny were alive."

"You were in the—? Wait, back when who was alive?"

"Louis and Eirny, Cade's parents. Louis was the Alpha."

"How do you spell his mother's name?"

Shawn looked puzzled. "E-i-r-n-y. She was from Iceland. It was some kind of Viking name, I think. Ally? What's the matter?"

"What? Oh, nothing. Sorry, you just reminded me of something." It couldn't be a coincidence—Eir had said that Dylan's line was precious to her. Ally resolved to learn more about Eirny MacDougall. "Never mind. You said you were in the pack?"

"I was born in it, like Cade."

"Where'd he come back from?"

"Savannah. He and Carson went to live with Louis' family after Louis and Eirny died."

She wanted to know more about that but couldn't think how to ask without looking even nosier than she probably already did. "So Cade came back and started calling the wolves he'd grown up with. Did they want to come back?"

"A few. But others started showing up—Lones, or wolves who were unhappy in their birth packs. They were all Cade's age or younger, and all of them were unmated."

He took another pull of beer. "See, a pack is really made of families. Until we have wolves with wives and kids, most packs won't recognize us. Anyway. Nobody cared about the Lones, but the Pack Alphas didn't like losing their youngest and strongest. They started talking about Cade luring their wolves away. He wasn't—he isn't, I mean—they just come because they want to."

"So did the Pack Alphas do anything to stop their wolves from leaving?"

"I don't know anyone who's been, like, punished or anything. Besides, Cade's loaned money to a lot of wolves for business. He's like a—what do you call it—a guy who loans money to new companies…"

"A venture capitalist?"

"That's it—he's a venture capitalist. Even older wolves in the Ten Packs—they have business with him, and he's helped them make money."

"Cade sounds pretty smart."

"Oh yeah. Not just head smart, but people smart too, you know? He just knows who you can trust and who's no good. He's always been that way." Shawn's voice faded as he walked into the kitchen to get another beer.

"So Stapkis' son left his father's pack to come out here?" she called.

"Huh? Oh yeah." He sat back down on the large leather couch. "We're getting bigger. We've got a couple of wolves in town who've gotten married. We're the first new pack in over a hundred years. But until Cade came back, Stapkis was the biggest Alpha in the West. Aaron joining us makes Rufus look weak. He doesn't want Rocky Mountain recognized. Cade's supposed to go to Denver Friday to meet with Stapkis and two other Alphas."

"So Stapkis' son is here with Cade's pack, and Cade's supposed to meet Stapkis this week, and now Cade has to tell him his son tried to hang himself."

They thought about that for a moment.

"Holy shit," was all she could think to say.

"Yeah." Shawn took another pull on the bottle. "Man, I hope Aaron makes it. I had no idea he was depressed or anything. Suicide's a huge deal with wolves. We don't kill ourselves much."

They heard the front door open. Cade came in talking to a wolf Ally didn't recognize.

"Michael's going to stay there 'til three," she heard him saying. It was just after midnight. "I want someone in the room with him at all times, so he doesn't wake up alone. Anyone can go see him, but you need to make a schedule of four hour rotations and get people signed up."

"Got it. I'll check back with you in the morning."

The door closed.

Cade looked surprised to see them when he walked into the living room. "Hey. I didn't expect anyone to still be up. Shawn, you hear what I was saying about making sure someone's in the room with Aaron?"

"Yeah. I want to go to the hospital tomorrow. How is he?"

MacDougall ran a hand through his curls, looking haggard and haunted. His formerly crisp white polo was wrinkled and dotted with coffee stains. "Aaron's in a coma. Dylan found him just in time, but they can't tell the amount of damage yet." He heaved a sigh. "Goddamn it. I had no idea the wolf was in trouble. I should've sensed something."

He headed for the room behind the fireplace. "Shawn, get some rest. You've got a long day tomorrow."

Ally made up her mind as he walked away. "Cade, can I speak with you?"

He turned to her. "I'm really beat. Can it wait 'til the morning?"

"I don't know. It's about Aaron Stapkis."

"What about him?"

She stopped, suddenly self-conscious, and wondered if she should just tell him everything, here in front of Shawn. He sensed her hesitation.

"Shawn. Go get some sleep."

Shawn didn't protest being ordered off to bed like a child. He gave Ally a wide smile and a good night.

On his way out, he stopped and hugged his Alpha tightly. Cade returned the hug, ruffling Shawn's bright red hair and planting a kiss on top of his head. Pack wolves were more demonstrative than Lones, but Ally doubted Cade MacDougall went around hugging and kissing all his wolves like that.

Watching Shawn leave, she asked, "Does everyone just do what you tell them?"

He gave her a tired smile. "Yes. That's why I'm the Pack Alpha. What did you want to tell me about Aaron?"

His stare was direct and unnerving. "I saw him at a restaurant this afternoon, talking to another wolf. It sounded like they were having an argument, and—"

He raised an eyebrow and held up a hand to stop her. "Wait. Not here. In my office."


He closed the curtained French doors and sat behind his desk, motioning her to one of the two leather chairs in front of it.

There were no Scandinavian-style pieces like those in the living room and the bedrooms she'd seen so far. This furniture was what she'd always thought of as *high cowboy*. Cade's huge kneehole desk faced the foyer. Made of a dark, rough-hewn wood, it had a lovely dark green leather top.

A bookcase armoire covered almost the entire back wall of the room. It looked like something behind the bar of a fancy saloon in an old Western. It even had a large mirror stretching the length of it. People facing Cade's desk were forced to either focus their attention on him or look at themselves in the mirror.

Taking her seat, she resolved to keep her focus on him for as long as she could handle it. It wouldn't be that difficult. She'd never liked looking at herself, and she welcomed an excuse to stare at him.

MacDougall leaned back in his chair and ran his hands through his hair again, tugging at his dark curls. She found it strangely comforting to recognize a fellow hair torturer.

"Okay. You saw Aaron at a restaurant this afternoon. Can you describe the man he was with? How'd you know they were arguing?"

If she recounted the conversation, he'd have more questions about her, questions she didn't want to answer. But a guy's life might be at stake here, and she remembered Seth's words earlier, about finding a new way to live. The small bit of honesty she'd tried so far tonight was like standing up straight for the first time in years, long after you'd grown used to the weight pressing on your shoulders.

She briefly explained the visit to the restaurant and what she'd overheard. "I got a good look at Aaron, but I didn't see the wolf he was talking to, except from the back."

He frowned. "How did you know they were wolves?"

"I...I can just tell."

"Of course you can." He did deadpan sarcasm quite well. "You can just tell werewolves by barely looking at them."

"Yeah, I guess it's from living with three of them." She tried to smile and couldn't quite make it. She tucked her hands under her legs to keep them out of her hair. Of course he could smell her nervousness.

"How close to them were you sitting? At the next booth over?"

"I don't know— I mean, no, not right next to them. No. I was some distance away."

"Some distance away. But you heard the conversation clearly, even though you weren't looking at them. You weren't looking at them, were you?"

"No. I didn't want them to think I was listening, so..."

"But you *were* listening."

"Yeah, but not on purpose. I mean—"

"So you inadvertently heard two wolves having a confidential conversation clear across a restaurant." He sat forward now, leaning on his desk and watching her closely. His expression was blandly polite, his posture tense. He smelled agitated. She reminded herself not to meet his eyes.

"Yes."

"Yes what?"

"Yes, I heard two wolves having a private conversation clear across a restaurant, and no, I wasn't looking at them, and no, they didn't realize I could hear them." She blew out a long breath, leaned back in her chair and closed her eyes.

"That's some damned good hearing you've got, Ally."

She didn't open her eyes. "Yeah. It's not that fun, actually. I hear a lot of stuff I'd rather not."

"Like maybe two wolves discussing your tits and ass?"

Her eyes flew open. She tried to keep her expression as neutral as his. He wanted her to say something, so she said nothing.

"Good night vision you've got too."

"Really?"

"Obviously." He flashed a beautiful, predatory smile, teeth bright white in his dark black beard. "Humans can't maneuver in the woods at night, not without some kind of light. Yet you followed Dylan's howls straight to Aaron. You got there almost as fast as I did. And you could tell from looking at Aaron, in the dark, that he wasn't dead."

She stood up and hugged her arms across her body, jiggling a leg nervously. "Look. You're stressed out. I feel like I've been awake for three days. We barely know each other and we've already had a screaming fight. I wanted to tell you because I thought it might be important, and I did, so I'm going to bed now. Good night."

She turned, walked to the door, and bumped into his forearm. He stood right behind her, one hand on the French doors to prevent her opening them.

"I can move faster than you. That's a relief."

Her face, scant millimeters from his arm, flushed hot. She couldn't tell if the heat came from her or him. She wanted to taste the warm skin of his smooth, muscled arm.

She didn't often yearn to press her tongue to unfamiliar flesh.

That heady scent of coffee, tobacco and Cade set her pulse racing and her skin tingling. His breath stirred her hair.

She had an absurd, and absurdly powerful, urge to relax and lean back against his chest. She'd thought he was looming over her earlier, in the yard outside, but that wasn't looming. *This* was looming. He made her feel small and weak, which she hadn't felt in thirteen years. He made her feel safe and warm, which she hadn't felt in twenty-three years.

"Ally." Even though they weren't touching, she could feel the vibration of his voice in his chest. It soothed her.

"Ally. Turn around." His voice was softer now, like earlier on the swing.

This was a power play. She wouldn't submit, even though she'd love it if he touched her again.

Which he did, kneading the back of her neck with strong, skillful fingers. She couldn't suppress a contented purr. His touch induced contradictory sensations. It was soporific—she wanted to curl up against him and go to sleep. It was electrifying—she wanted to curl up against him and...not go to sleep.

"What are you doing?" she asked irritably.

She could sense his smile. "I'm massaging your neck."

"That's wildly inappropriate, don't you think? We hardly know each other. Do my shoulders too, they're killing me."

He chuckled and obliged, working deeply into tense muscles.

"Do you typically give massages to women you barely know?"

"No. Do you typically let strange wolves rub your shoulders?"

She smiled. "No. It's been an odd night. I'm not really the

touchy-feely type."

"Me neither."

"You hugged and kissed Shawn." That sounded weird. "I mean, I thought it was sweet."

"Shawn is like my little brother. I take special care of him."

One hand moved to the base of her skull, where he began to massage her scalp gently. She loved it when someone played with her hair. In Cade MacDougall's hands, it became an erogenous zone.

She really should stop this. She really didn't want to.

When she turned around to face him, her nose hit him right at the sternum. Intoxicated by the scent of him, she stared at the strip of tan flesh framed by his unbuttoned polo. The outrageous desire to lick him returned.

She pressed her back against the door to look up at him. She couldn't raise her gaze much past his mouth and those full, sensuous lips in the beard that looked soft to the touch. He rested his hands lightly on her upper arms.

"Thank you," she murmured. "That was wonderful. I think I should leave now. Will you kick me out tomorrow?"

"No. I'm not going to kick you out 'til I've figured you out."

"I wasn't lying about what I heard at the restaurant."

"I believe you. I don't know why, but I do." He released her arms—reluctantly, it seemed, but maybe that was just what she wanted to believe—and she groped behind her for the doorknob. She tried not to stumble as she walked out backwards, Cade following, still looming.

As they walked out into the foyer, he said, "Tomorrow I'll show y'all around a bit and you can see the swimming pool."

"That would be great. Thank you."

"Good night, Ally."

"Good night, Cade."

She walked up the stairs without looking back. She could feel his eyes on her all the way to her room.

# Chapter Nine

He slept like hell, woke up surly and called the hospital. Aaron's condition remained unchanged.

The suicide attempt had blindsided him. His near-telepathic ability to read other people worsened the guilt. He hadn't been looking after his pack as he should. He'd let personal matters—nanny drama, the other Alphas, Dylan's discovery—absorb too much of his attention. Unfortunately, those were all important issues. He couldn't ignore any of them, and certainly not the Alphas.

The phone call to Rufus Stapkis had been even worse than expected. Stapkis accused Cade outright of trying to kill Aaron. Stapkis and Cade had never even met. The meeting planned for tomorrow was supposed to facilitate some kind of détente. No chance of that now.

Stapkis would want to visit Aaron at the hospital. Protocol demanded he pay a visit to Cade first. But Stapkis didn't recognize Rocky Mountain, and Cade couldn't allow Stapkis to enter his territory without permission.

He might end up fighting the old wolf after all.

Michael had called Chicago and St. Louis to cancel the meeting. They'd indicated they still wanted to meet with Cade, so he would go to Denver tomorrow as planned. He'd worry about Stapkis after that.

Today, he would spend time with his guests. And tonight, with his wolves.

He went in search of Ally first. He told himself he did it because she'd know where the others were, and not because he wanted to see her the most.

Ally and Becca were getting along famously in Becca's

room, Ally clapping and cheering while Becca danced to *The Wiggles* on TV. Baby Girl begged to go with them. It reminded him that his daughter didn't spend enough time with other children or with him. More guilt.

He filled Ally in on Aaron as they walked downstairs.

"I think Seth and Dec drove into town after lunch. They wanted to look around."

"I guess it's just you, me and Dylan," he replied. The prospect of spending time with her, without the other wolves, pleased him—which annoyed him. He'd honor his deal with the Houston Alpha, but he didn't want Ally staying any longer than necessary. He needed one less complication in his life.

Dylan was perched on the pasture fence chatting with the hands and observing the Nordic ponies. At Cade's gesture, he jumped down and joined them as they walked to the stables.

"Have you ever been to Iceland?" Dylan asked him.

"I've always wanted to, but I just haven't gotten around to it. Your grandmother never wanted to take us there. She lost her parents when she was young and said it made her sad to think of going back. But she was happy when my dad decided to raise Icelandics and Nordics. She rode them when she was young."

"Where in Scotland did your parents die?"

"Dylan!" Ally gasped.

Cade put a hand up. "No, it's okay."

They had stopped just outside A-Barn. He cleared his throat and closed his eyes for a moment, startled at how the question had kicked him in the gut. Dylan look frightened.

"I'm sorry, Cade, I shouldn't..."

"No, it's okay," he repeated. "Someday soon we'll sit down, just the two of us, and I'll tell you everything about our family. Anyway—" he cleared his throat and tried to smile at the pup "—they died on Scarista Beach, in the Outer Hebrides."

"You went there, didn't you?" Ally asked Dylan.

"Yeah!" the pup replied excitedly. "On the Isle of Harris. It was a really cool beach. I wanna go back."

Ally caught Cade's eye and mouthed, "I'm sorry." He shook his head and grinned in spite of the pain. Eighteen was a heedless, invulnerable age. You didn't think about dying at eighteen, and other peoples' deaths didn't seem completely real.

Allison Kendall had thought about dying at eighteen, though, hadn't she? Did Dylan ever think about that? Did he ever stop to think that at his age, Ally had risked her life to save him?

She jolted him from his musings when they entered A-Barn.

"This is gorgeous! How many stalls do you have?"

"Forty. Twenty in A and twenty in B-Barn. We normally don't have more than twenty horses at a time, though. Nordics and Icelandics here in A, and a few Irish Hunters in B-Barn."

"Those are your only breeds?"

"For now, yeah. I keep thinking about Cobs, though. I was in Ireland last year and almost bought some stock."

Her eyes lit up like sparklers as they walked down the runs between the stalls. He expected her to start jumping up and down, Becca-like, in her excitement. Christ, those dimples were going to kill him. Why did a brazen, lying little stealth-alpha female have to be so goddamned cute?

"You've never seen Icelandic horses?" Observing her glee made it hard to stay in a bad mood.

"No. They're beautiful! Who's the mare about to drop?"

"That's Snowmane. We're on standby. She'll drop in the next day or two."

Ally cocked her head to the side. "Snowmane. That's a horse in Tolkien, right?"

"Very good. Yes. Tolkien used a lot of Icelandic and Old Norse names. My mother liked naming horses from his books."

"Do you ride the Icelandics?" asked Dylan, eyeing the little animals doubtfully.

Cade laughed. "No. I feel silly as hell on a horse that short. Some wolves don't care, though. A lot of them like the ponies for their kids. I ride a Hunter. His name is Sleipnir."

Ally said, "That's not Tolkien, is it?"

"No. Sleipnir was Odin's eight-legged horse."

"You're into Norse mythology?"

"My mother was an acolyte of Eir, an Old One. The Norse thought she was a goddess. They made her one of the valkyrie."

"Really," she said quietly.

She had a strange look on her face—shock, maybe, or fear? A lot of people didn't even like to admit the existence of the Old

Ones. Some, like Apocalyptics, found human contact with them abhorrent.

Cade crossed his arms and regarded her steadily. "Does observance of the Old Ones disturb you? I don't pay much attention to it, but I should tell you that Sindri is devoted to Eir."

She shook herself and smiled apologetically. "No, no, that's not it at all. I've got Apocalyptic relatives and they offend me. No, I just... I used to know an old lady in service to Eir. I was just surprised. I didn't think she had many acolytes in the U.S."

"You're right. She's not widely known outside Scandinavia. Sindri's from Iceland, like my mom—he came to the States with her when she married my dad."

She gave a little laugh and shook her head again. "Well, anyway. I've read Tolkien two or three times. I always thought if I ever had a horse of my own, I'd name him Shadowfax."

She turned to stare at Snowmane again, looking downright dreamy.

Dylan grinned. "Horses make her happy."

"I can tell." He returned his nephew's smile, oddly relieved. "When I get back from Denver, we'll go for a ride. We don't have time today. I'm taking the Wrangler to show you around the property."

"Oh, that's right—you were supposed to meet with Aaron's father tomorrow, weren't you?"

"How'd you know that?"

She looked embarrassed. "I'm sorry. It's just... Shawn and I were talking about Aaron last night, and the pack, and he mentioned it."

"Shawn talks too much."

Ally tilted her head back. For a second, once again, he thought she was going to look him in the eye. "Cade, if I've annoyed you again, I'm sorry. I promise I'm not doing it on purpose. I'll head back to the house and you can show Dylan around without me."

"Wait a minute—"

"Hush, Dylan." She backhanded the teen lightly across the shoulder and then looked up at Cade again, still a little red-faced. "I mean it. I just talked to Shawn a little bit before you got back from the hospital. I don't want my mouth getting him in trouble."

Cade didn't want her mouth getting *him* in trouble, so he quit staring at it. "I'm in a crappy mood," he muttered. "It's making me snap more than usual."

And that was all he'd give her. He wasn't in the habit of apologizing to cheeky females, not even ones with bottomless dimples and smooth lips and perfect tits.

Dylan had watched the whole exchange in mortified silence. His nephew cleared his throat diffidently. "Look, I was gonna go for a run anyway. Y'all can go without me, I don't—"

"You can go for a run later, son."

"Yes, sir."

Ally's eyes widened at that. She looked like she was struggling to keep a straight face. Those fucking dimples were showing, though.

Soon they were out on the property, bouncing up and down the hills and cutting through acres of uncleared brush and trees. He'd taken the doors and top off the Wrangler.

He didn't attempt to cover all ten thousand acres but showed them his favorite parts of it. On the western side of the property, about five miles behind the main house and separated from it by dense trees, they got out of the Jeep and hiked down to an offshoot of the Arkansas River that cut through a shallow ravine.

This was one of Cade's favorite spots. The pine and cedar trees stretching out over the water on either side kept it cool even in the height of summer, providing the prettiest and most peaceful spot on the ranch. Ally and Dylan were excited with everything Cade showed them. It surprised him how happy their reaction made him.

He'd loved this land since he was old enough to recognize it. He remembered his life here until the age of eleven like some kind of dream world—he didn't remember ever being unhappy, or scared, or sad, or his parents arguing, or anything bad at all ever happening. He knew it wasn't so, of course. The MacDougalls had been a normal, albeit wealthy and very happy, family. They had had problems like anyone else. But because the events of his eleventh summer were so horrific, everything that went before tasted impossibly sweet in his memory.

When he'd returned fifteen years ago, to find Sindri and Shawn living in the main house while the cabins and outbuildings crumbled around them, he knew he'd never leave again.

Screams of laughter startled him. He'd just run the passenger side of the Wrangler through a big patch of muddy water, drenching Ally. Wet and dirty for the second day in a row, she laughed it off.

So did Dylan, perched in the backseat. "Dude, you totally soaked her! That was so awesome!"

"Don't ever call me dude. But you're right, that was pretty awesome."

"Did you do that on purpose?" Ally shrieked.

"No, I swear." He almost managed not to laugh as he said it.

The sun wouldn't set for a few hours, but the temperature had dropped. She shivered.

"Dylan. You said you wanted to run, didn't you?"

"Yeah."

"Strip off and give your shirt to Ally. You can get back to the house on four feet."

"Cool!"

He threw his clothes to Ally. Minutes later, furry, he bounded away.

Cade looked at Ally. "Damn. He changes almost as fast as I do."

"Dec and Seth couldn't believe how fast he does it in broad daylight. I don't think he's finished growing yet."

The stronger the wolf, the faster and less painful the change, and the less vulnerable he was to changing against his will. Alphas as powerful as Cade could change at any time and could resist the change under duress.

"Turn around," Ally said.

He turned his back and waited 'til she said "Okay." When he turned back, she was out of her wet T-shirt and into Dylan's much larger one. She rolled her shirt up—and bra? Yep, she'd taken her bra off—and threw them in the backseat.

He needed to get to Denver in a hurry.

"Now. Can we check out that swimming pool?"

"Fine with me, ma'am."

After a few minutes of driving in companionable silence, she said, "Can I ask you something personal without pissing you off?"

"What the hell do you care? Pissing me off doesn't bother you much."

"It does too! I swear I'm not doing it on purpose." Her ponytail was coming loose, strands of dark blond hair whipping across her face. Her cheeks were rosy from the wind and her eyes still shone with glee. She smelled of lavender and sweat, and he'd swear he could smell happiness on her as well. He wanted to put his face to the back of her neck and inhale her.

This had to stop.

"Oh, all right," he grumbled. "Ask."

"Okay." She paused a minute, choosing her words. "When you get mad at me for arguing with you, or the way I talk to you—is it because you're a Pack Alpha or because I'm a woman?"

"It's both," he said carefully. "I'm not used to women arguing with me, and I can't remember the last time someone told me to shut up." And he couldn't understand why it hadn't made him angrier—that kind of defiance would normally trip all his alpha wires.

"Well, I shouldn't have said shut up. That was ugly. So when you were surprised, thinking Seth obeyed me—that was because I'm a woman? And even betas shouldn't obey a woman?"

He knew where she was going with this. It came up with a lot of women, and it was one of the reasons Cade avoided serious dating. "It's unusual. It's just weird to see a woman dominate two wolves, even if they're both betas."

She made that contemptuous clicking sound with her tongue that only females could do. He could feel her rolling her eyes at him.

"I don't dominate them. I just tell them what to do. 'Cause...they're laid back, and I'm not, so it's easier that way."

"Whatever you say, Ally. It's still weird."

"Are all alphas sexist?"

Now he laughed out loud. "I knew you'd get to that. No. Wolves aren't sexist. We're just wolves. We don't submit to women. Not permanently, not... It's tough to explain."

"What about mates?"

"Oh, well, mates are different. That's a whole other psychological, physical relationship. When a wolf bonds to a mate...yeah, it's different. It's not really submission, but I guess it's similar. My parents were mated, and my mother could play my dad like a piano. And he knew it."

But *when* did he know it? Cade had never thought about that before. He frowned to himself as he downshifted to get up a small hill and back onto the paved road.

"So...Becca's mother isn't your mate?"

"No, she wasn't." He carefully emphasized the last word and waited for the question he knew would come next.

"Where is she? Is she still involved with Becca?"

"Mary Ann's not around. I paid her a lot of money to go away, and I expect her to stay there. It's best for Rebecca."

She didn't say anything after that.

They were back on the main road leading to the complex. It was easier to hear and talk now that that they weren't bucking across the bumpy terrain.

"Now I have something to ask *you*," he said.

"And you don't particularly care if it pisses me off."

"Not really." Somehow she made him smile when he should've been annoyed. When he actually was, in fact, annoyed. "You haven't spent much time around any wolves but yours, have you?"

"No, just casual acquaintances. Seth's the only one I was related to—well, him and Dylan. Since we left Lake Charles, we've avoided other packs." She turned toward him with newfound animation. "See, when we first got to Texas, we kept a low profile. I think Lake Charles suspected Seth killed Guy, and they let him get away with it because Gracie was his sister. They must've figured he had a right. But even though they didn't come after us, we decided it was best to stay out of Louisiana. So—"

"Hang on," he interrupted, holding up a hand and glancing at her as he drove. "About that. What happened with Guy's body? The cops? Your trailer?"

"Seth made an anonymous call and told the cops they'd find Gracie in her trailer and Guy in mine." Her accent had gotten a little twangier as she talked about the past. It was sexy as hell. She chattered on, oblivious to the way he was staring at her and probably risking a rollover. "Once the cops realized Guy had killed Gracie, they didn't care who killed Guy."

"Yeah, but, I mean, what about *you?*"

She shrugged. The wind had whipped more hair out of her ponytail. He fought the urge to reach out and tuck the silky strands behind her ear.

"I called a friend, told her to send me a few things I wanted and I'd deed the trailer and everything in it over to her. All it cost her was getting the place cleaned up, so she was happy. And then we—"

"No, wait, Allison, that's not what I meant. How did y'all explain *your* disappearance? Yours and Dylan's? Even if the cops didn't care who killed Guy, he's dead in your trailer, and you're nowhere around, and neither is the pup. What did they think when they saw all that blood?"

She cocked her head with a lopsided little grin, like he'd said something funny and she knew he didn't realize it. "Cade, we lived in an empty trailer park on a bayou fifteen miles outside of town—me, a drunk werewolf, his stripper wife and their little boy. The cops don't wonder about folks like us."

When he didn't say anything—what the hell could he say? He had no idea what it was like to grow up like that—she went on cheerfully.

"I'm still not sure what stories are out there, but the Houston wolves weren't anxious to have Seth around. I think Nick would've let him in anyway, after he got to know us, but Seth never wanted to join. I don't think Seth is a born Lone, it just worked out that way. Dec is definitely a born Lone."

"MacSorley is strange," Cade muttered.

She busied herself redoing her ponytail before saying, a little crossly, "I'll take your word for it. He's popular back home. There aren't many wolves in Sugar Land, just a few young betas who followed Dylan around. They didn't have fathers."

Wolves needed to be raised by wolves, if not necessarily in packs. Fatherless wolves had higher rates of alcoholism, domestic violence and imprisonment.

"That's one of the reasons I decided to bring him here." Finished messing with her hair, she turned her attention back to him, where it belonged. "Dylan needs to be around werewolves, and I didn't think Houston was the best choice."

"Of course it wasn't. You had to bring him here."

She cocked her head at him. "Well, no, I didn't *have* to. I wanted him to meet his only paternal relative."

He couldn't let that one go. "You had to bring him here. I'm his uncle."

She shrugged deliberately. "So is Seth."

"I wanted to meet him. You didn't have a choice."

"I always have a choice," she responded calmly.

He threw the Jeep into park. For a split second, he feared she'd bang her head into the windshield, but she had amazing reflexes. She simply stretched out a hand for the dashboard. He would've been ashamed to hurt her, but goddamn. She took turns pissing him off and turning him on.

"Do you enjoy baiting me, little girl? Is that why you keep doing it?"

"No. But let's get something straight." She took a deep breath and bit her lip. He could smell her anger and her fear, but she didn't cower. Her words were clipped and precise. "Dylan's not just my cousin, he's my kid. I saved him, I raised him, he's mine. If he wants to join your pack, fine. If he wants to leave, fine. But I didn't have to bring him. I don't have to do anything."

"You'll sure as hell have to leave when I tell you to," he ground out.

He heard her breath catch in her throat. Blinking against tears, her jaw clenched, she put a foot up on the dashboard and rested her head on her knee. Ally Kendall talked a tough game, but he wasn't buying it anymore.

Or maybe she just wasn't as tough when the subject was her pup or her future. Somehow he knew, without asking, that she had no place else to go.

And just like that—just like last night—he regretted his words. Without thinking, he reached out to her, but she turned her head away. The skin on the back of her neck was warm and soft beneath his calloused hand. He stroked her neck with his thumb as they sat in silence for a few long minutes, he trying to think of something to say, she trying not to cry.

"Ally. Look at me."

"Don't," she said shakily, sitting back and staring straight ahead with dry eyes. She pushed his hand away. "Don't say something nice. Because I'll like it, and then you'll turn around and be an asshole again."

"I'm not trying to be an asshole."

It discomfited him, how much he needed to gaze at her. Her face, in profile, looked so young and fragile. He'd managed to memorize its lines and curves in the space of just one day. The golden blond eyelashes resting against the smooth, soft cheeks. The spot where he knew a dimple could appear, but not for him, not anymore.

He shouldn't be sitting here trying to patch things up. They were in sight of the complex. Wolves were strolling about, looking at the Jeep stopped in the middle of the road.

Cade stretched his arm out again, letting his hand just brush her shoulder, but she still wouldn't look at him. "I'm a Pack Alpha, Allison. You keep challenging me, and I don't know why you do it."

Or why he kept letting her do it. A suspicion had taken root in the back of his mind, but he didn't want to look too closely at it.

"I'm not challenging you. I just don't like being told what to do."

Her voice was steadier, but still so forlorn as to break his heart. He couldn't stand being the one who made her sound like that. She seemed so scrappy and determined, but so small and alone. Even with three wolves—or perhaps *because* she was with three wolves—she was so alone.

"I hate the way you make me feel," she muttered in the same hurt tone.

Recoiling at her words, he threw the Jeep into first and drove much too fast back to the house.

They didn't speak again. Cade jumped out of the Jeep and stomped into the house, leaving Ally staring after him. Just as well—tears still pricked at her eyelashes. She couldn't bear to cry in front of him.

In a minute, Michael came out of the house. He scowled as he approached her.

"Cade wants me to show you around." He turned and began to walk toward the cabins.

"I'd rather just..."

"Cade told me to show you around, so I'm gonna show you around." Now that she was on the outs with his Alpha, Michael didn't bother trying to be polite. "The sooner we get started, the sooner it'll be over."

"Well gosh, Michael, when you put it that way."

They checked out the cabins—three large bunkhouses for wolves, two empty cabins for guests. They didn't visit the woodshop. She suspected Michael could tell she didn't give a rip.

Why did she keep fighting with Cade?

The gym was right behind the main house and constructed of the same beautiful wood and stone. Michael said it was as old as the house. Louis MacDougall and his wolves had built it some fifty years ago.

Why was he harsh with her one minute, tender the next? As soon as he'd seen that he'd hurt her, he'd tried to soothe her. Was claw/caress/claw a Pack Alpha thing?

When they walked into the building, her own reflection assaulted her from three of the main room's four walls. This was why she hated commercial gyms—all the damned mirrors.

One minute he was about to kick her out, the next he was stroking her neck with that warm, hypnotic touch.

The gym was indifferently furnished with an old plaid couch, a Formica-covered table and some chairs.

He was the most confusing male she'd ever met—charming, brusque and overpowering.

His mother had served the Old One who had restored Ally's life.

She barely glanced at the showers and sauna. What really impressed her was the pool room, which held a full-sized saltwater pool. She'd never swum in one before.

He was going to take all the family she had and kick her back out into the world by herself.

And she couldn't wait to see him again. She both dreaded it and longed for it.

She wanted to put on her swimsuit and jump into the pool, but she didn't feel comfortable doing that. It would feel weird, having just had another fight with Cade, to help herself to his facilities, even though he'd offered them. Besides, going back and forth across a pool wasn't enough to quell this dammed up, kinetic misery. She needed to be outside. She needed to run.

At first she sprinted, overjoyed to move freely and naturally with no one to see her, no one to note her speed and agility. She left the compound behind in seconds.

As she ran through a small copse and back into the open, she heard the howling. It was one of her favorite sounds. She could discern the nature of different howls, and tonight Rocky Mountain sounded alternately forlorn and exuberant. They mourned Aaron, even if he wasn't dead, and they rejoiced in their wolfish nature.

She wished she had a pack to belong to, someone else with whom to rejoice in her nature. Uniqueness sucked.

So did maudlin self-pity.

She ran for two hours, heading back to the house when it got dark. Later, emerging from her shower, she found Becca perched on her bed, wearing only Hello Kitty panties.

"You should be in bed, baby. Want me to tuck you back in?"

"I heard the wolves," the child said sleepily. "Can we go look?"

She debated for a second, then decided there'd be no harm in a quick peek.

"Hang on. I'll get dressed."

She sat down at the top the porch. Becca promptly claimed her lap.

The house sat at the apex of the horseshoe formed by all the buildings clustered around the yard. From the porch she could see all the way down the main road, across the open fields and beyond the stables. Nothing moved. All she heard were wolf howls in the distance.

Becca put her head on Ally's shoulder, eyelids heavy. Ally pressed a kiss to her temple. They sat in silence for a while before a few wolves walked out of the trees behind the woodshop and headed in their direction, taking no notice of the two females.

Becca pointed in the direction of the stables and said with a groggy grin, "Look. There's my daddy."

An enormous black wolf loped gracefully across the fields. As he approached the yard, he slowed to a walk. Ally caught her breath.

Full moon was a few nights away. On this cloudless, starry night the yard received enough glow to give everything a faint silver sheen. No outdoor lights spoiled the effect. She could see without the moon glow, but the way it glinted off the wolves and shone on the whispery fields and trees, the howls of the unseen wolves and the breeze across her skin, and the bundle of warm, sleepy child in her arms—all of it together brought tears to her eyes. If she could paint herself into a home of her choosing, it would be here. This wasn't self-pity, just an acknowledgement of what she didn't have and wished she did.

The black wolf stopped in front of the porch and stood watching them with unblinking eyes. She rested her cheek on Becca's head.

Becca said, even more sleepily now, "Hi, Daddy." The wolf put his cold, wet nose to her cheek. Becca laughed. Then he looked up at Ally, and it was weird and scary to have that face so close to hers, those yellow eyes holding hers.

Ally whispered, "I'll put her to bed now."

He watched her as she walked away, just like he had last night.


She hit the pool early the next morning. Losing herself in the rhythm of the laps, she swam hard, back and forth, back and forth, all movement, no thought.

She didn't know how long she'd been in the water when she ran out of strokes. She had just enough energy left to swim to the ladder and hoist herself out. She took a couple of steps and looked up.

Cade stood a few feet away, watching her.

Yet again, she stopped breathing. She tried to look away, to look anywhere else, but he commanded her attention without word or movement. His gaze, intense and unreadable, caressed her skin, and she shivered.

His dark blue button-down shirt accentuated tanned skin and taut muscles. He leaned with his back against the wall, arms crossed, one foot braced behind him. Faded jeans hugged his lean hips and long legs. The worn denim looked soft to the touch. An image popped into her mind unbidden—her running her thumb along the inner seam of his raised leg, the friction of her fingers on the denim heating her hand as it went higher up his thigh.

Blushing, she forced her eyes back to the fierce, beautiful face. Her hand itched to brush the curls out of the startling green eyes that held her pinned in place. How could he stalk her without moving a muscle?

A wolf that pretty shouldn't look so dangerous. A wolf that big shouldn't be so graceful. If only she...

"I hate this place."

"I'm sorry?"

"This room. The pool. My mother swam every day, sometimes more than once a day. It irritated my father—he'd say he didn't know he'd married a mermaid." He paused, temporarily releasing her as he looked about the room. "I don't know why I keep it running. The smell of the saltwater reminds me of her." He smiled slightly. "I don't think I want to associate my mother's scent with you."

"Cade, I..." She faltered, too nervous, tongue-tied and aroused to continue.

He pushed off from the wall and crossed the distance between them in two long strides, picking up her towel on the way.

Her brain yelled at her to run, her body insisted on staying put, so she did what every small animal did when confronted with an inescapable predator.

She closed her eyes.

"Allison."

She loved the feel of his voice. Deep and slow, it flowed through her like warm brandy.

"Ally. Look at me."

She opened her eyes, careful not to meet his gaze. Instead she stared at his strong, sensual mouth and imagined his beard against her skin.

Cade pulled the swim towel tight around her shoulders and drew her in. Before she could react, his mouth came down on hers.

She gave a helpless little moan. His tongue was hot, and she shivered again when he let go of the towel to bury his fingers in her hair and kissed her harder. She stood on her tiptoes and leaned into him, her arms going around his waist, her hands running over the smooth, hard muscles of his back.

Slowly he released her mouth, pausing to bite her bottom lip ever so softly. He lifted his head from hers, but he didn't let go of her face. She glanced at his eyes, just for a second. The heat and the hunger in his gaze melted her bones. Her breath caught in her throat as his finger softly traced the outline of her mouth.

Cade inhaled sharply when she parted her lips and tentatively, shyly, licked his finger. His skin was rough beneath her tongue. His thumb traced a line of soft fire down her cheek as his finger explored her mouth. A hot, exquisite ache inflamed her core, weakening her legs.

With eyes half closed, Cade watched her mouth as she swirled her tongue around his finger. She sighed as he withdrew it.

"Tell me you lied," he rasped.

"What?"

"Yesterday. When you said you hated the way I make you feel. Say you lied."

She'd meant she hated the way he made her feel weak. But his fingers were tracing her jaw and wandering across her lips and stroking her throat, and she didn't want him to stop. So she replied in a shamefully shaky voice, "I don't hate the way this feels."

He cocked an eyebrow and brought his dark head down closer to hers until their mouths were almost, but not quite, touching.

"I'll be back in two days. You'll be here."

Though she barely knew him, she'd never been so weak or willing for any man. Stupid with desire, she would let him take her right here on the concrete floor if he wanted.

And yet she managed to be annoyed with the way he gave her an order and expected her to obey it.

"You can't tell me to—"

"Goddamn it," he growled, crushing her to him and kissing her again—harder this time, rougher, but it didn't hurt her and it didn't scare her. She kissed him just as hard and hungrily, her fingernails digging into his back.

When they stopped to breathe, he held her face still and forced her to look up at him.

"Allison, I'm having a bad week. You will be here when I get back. Shut the fuck up and say yes."

Every inch of her was pressed against him now. She wondered, a little deliriously, if steam might rise from their bodies, hers so wet and his so hot. She swallowed hard and whispered, "Yes."

His expression was still hungry, but now there was tenderness there as well, and an uncertainty she didn't understand. He muttered another curse and held her head tight against his chest, running his fingers through her wet hair. His heart hammered against her ear. She tightened her arms about him.

"I'm soaking wet and I have a hard-on. Think any of my wolves will notice?"

"Oh," she gasped, staring at him in dismay. "What are you going to do?"

He ran his thumb down the bridge of her nose and over her lips. "I'm the Alpha—I don't have to do anything."

"But they're going to smell me on you!"

He gave her a slow, cocksure grin. "Yeah. Even better, they're going to smell *me* on *you*."

She must have looked mortified, because his grin widened.

"You're adorable." His thumb lazily teased her mouth again. "I swear to God, you annoy the hell out of me, and it just turns me on more."

He tilted her chin up and kissed her softly on the cheek, and then he walked away. She wrapped the towel around herself, feeling cold and lonely and exposed.

At the door he paused and smiled at her. "Keep an eye on Becca for me. Everybody here spoils her rotten, and I think she's taken a liking to you."

"All right," she whispered.

And he was gone.


He ran into Michael just outside the gym.

The two wolves stopped in their tracks and regarded one

another in silence. Michael wasn't entitled to explanations. Cade didn't want to talk. But after twenty-five years, he couldn't keep much from his closest confidant.

His front was still soaking wet. Every wolf within miles could smell her on him. That wasn't the problem, and now they both knew it.

"Oh, boss," Michael muttered in dismayed sympathy.

He grunted. "Yeah, I know. Not what I need right now."

"I'm sorry. I mean—should I be sorry? Are you sorry? Do you...?" Michael drifted off helplessly.

This would be so much easier if they were both furry. They wouldn't have to talk.

Michael tried again. "Look, maybe it's not even...it's been three days. That can't be enough time..."

"It happens. Hell, it happened to my father." He scuffed a boot toe on the ground and looked up at his second. "Yeah, it happened."

Michael opened his mouth, closed it, shook his head. He opened his mouth again, closed it again because really, what was there to say?

Cade shrugged. "I can't do anything about it right now. I'll see you on Sunday. You call me if there's a problem."

They fell into step as they walked to his car.

"I'm not calling you, boss—whatever comes up, I'll deal. You concentrate on the meeting. Try not to think about the female."

Like that would work.

Once at the car, the two of them grasped forearms for a long moment.

"Ally's going to keep an eye on Becca for me. I want you to keep an eye on Ally. Make her feel at home. Make her feel safe."

"Of course, Alpha. Don't worry about anything here. I'll see you Sunday."


He should've spent the two-hour drive thinking about the most important meeting of his life. Of course, he couldn't think of anything but Ally Kendall.

The image of her body slicing through the water arose in his mind. The way she melted when he touched her, the tiny catches in her breath when he stroked her face, her tongue on his skin...

He couldn't see himself calling any women in Denver now. The one who'd caused the craving was the only one who could fill it.

She was strange. She was sweet and stubborn and defiant. She liked his daughter. She smelled like sunshine.

She smelled like home.

That was what his father had always said about the first time he'd met Cade's mother, on a cold, empty beach in the Outer Hebrides. He'd spent a few hours in her company when he realized she smelled like home. He had thought he knew what home smelled like, he said, but he didn't.

Not until the mate bond claimed him.

# Chapter Ten

"Shit! I don't... SINDRI! SHAWN! That bitch! That, that...that sneaky—"

The office door stood wide open. Michael froze when she and Becca walked in the house. He sat at Cade's desk, holding the phone in his hand, anger clouding his handsome face.

Michael stared at her. She stared at Michael. Michael looked at Becca.

Becca began to wail.

"We're going upstairs now," Ally muttered, scooping her up and taking the steps two at a time. Becca cried all the way.

"Shh, it's okay. Come on, let's chill up here."

They'd spent the day together, reading books and hanging out at the stables with Dylan and Seth. It had done her spirit a world of good. Looking after Becca wasn't the best way to keep her mind off Cade, but she didn't think she could do that anyway.

"Why's Uncle Michael yelling?" Becca had stopped crying once they'd reached her room. Now she just sniffled loudly.

"I don't know, sweetie, but I promise he's not mad at you or me."

The little girl curled up into a ball on her bed, eyes shut tightly and face screwed up as if holding her breath.

Vaguely alarmed, Ally put a hand to her cheek. "Becca? Baby, what's the matter? Do you feel bad?"

"No," she whispered, "I'm scared. I wanna be a cat for a while."

"Oh, baby. You don't have to be a cat. I promise. Uncle Michael isn't really that mad."

"He's mad at Sindri! I heard him yelling at Sindri!"

Ally sensed another wail coming on. "No, he wasn't— Shh, sweetie, calm down." She stretched out on the bed and put an arm around the girl, resting her cheek against the lustrous black hair. "He was calling for Sindri, he wasn't yelling at him. How about you do some *Wiggles* and I'll go see what's wrong with Uncle Michael, okay? I'll come back up here and we'll play some more."

*The Wiggles* could take Becca's mind off anything.

It was none of her business what had the normally laconic werewolf so pissed off. But her curiosity—not nosiness, curiosity—forced her to investigate.

She found Michael in the kitchen with Sindri, no longer yelling. Now he paced, apparently arguing with himself. The brownie looked concerned but said nothing.

"...I told him when he left yesterday I'd handle everything here. I didn't pay any attention to—damn. This meeting's the most important thing that's happened to this pack since Cade put it together—if he has to turn around and come home... The Alphas expected him to show up even after Seattle's own son tried to kill himself, and—"

"Will Aaron's father be there?" Sindri interrupted quietly.

"What? No. He and Cade had it out on the phone. Rufus called Cade a murderer. But St. Louis and Chicago still want to see him. He can't just call them and say 'hey, sorry—I'm a single father, I have to go home and meet my daughter's grandmother'. I mean, Jesus, these guys are old school to begin with, they can't—"

"Mary Ann's mother's coming here?" She blurted it without thinking. Michael frowned, surprised to see her.

"Ally, I have a crisis here. What do you want?"

"I-I just..." She stammered to a halt, embarrassed. She wanted to know what was going on, even though it didn't concern her. "Is there anything I can do to help?" she finished weakly.

Michael waved her off. "No. I have to call Cade," he said to Sindri, pointedly ignoring her.

"That is not necessary. The *barn's* grandmother is no

threat. It is good for the girl to see her."

"Sindri, how do we know that?" Michael addressed the brownie with a gentleness and respect he hadn't shown Ally. "You remember how furious she was when Cade wouldn't let her have Becca last Christmas? If she shows up here, and Cade's gone and there's no nanny—there's just you, me, Shawn, the wolves—what's that going to look like?"

"Michael?" Ally interrupted.

"The wolves leave. You and Shawn remain. You tell her I look after the small *barn*."

"Sindri, you're great, and Becca loves you, but I don't think—"

"Michael?" Ally said again.

He spun on her. "Ally, I'm trying figure something out here."

"That's what I'm trying to tell you! I have an idea."

"And what would that be?"

"What about me?"

"You?"

"Yeah, me. I could, you know, pretend to be the nanny? Until Cade gets back?" It had sounded better in her head.

Instead of replying with something along the lines of, "God you're pathetic—are you really that desperate to impress him?" Michael folded his arms and made a *hmm, that's interesting* face.

"That's not a bad idea," he said to Sindri, who nodded.

"Cade asked me to keep an eye on Becca while he was gone," she pointed out. And yes, she was that pathetically desperate to impress Cade.

"Oh. Yeah, I forgot about that..." Suddenly, oddly, Michael's whole demeanor changed. He became almost friendly. "You know, that could work. I'm sorry I blew you off. I should show you some respect."

"You should?" She blinked in surprise. "Why?"

"Oh, well...because, you're a guest, and— And you raised Cade's nephew, and because... I'm a grouchy bastard sometimes, I guess." He and Sindri exchanged a look and Sindri smiled.

Whatever the reason for the abrupt mood swing, she'd take it. "All right, Michael. Thank you. So, what do we do? When's she going to be here?"

Michael looked at his watch. "About thirty minutes."

"*What?*"

"Exactly." He grimaced. "I don't know what she's up to, but Sarah Jane's a proper Southern lady—she'd never do something this rude by accident. If we're going to do this, you need to... Well, you don't need to do anything, just be ready to meet her. I'll go tell everybody to get the hell out."

"What about my guys? Is it okay for them to be staying in the house? Are you worried what she's going to think of wolves in the house with Becca?"

He thought for a minute. "No. I think it's okay for them to be here, since you're here. I don't want the whole pack around until Cade gets back, but it's not like Sarah Jane has never met wolves. She's known Cade since he was a teenager. She knows a lot of the Savannah pack."

"Really?"

"Yeah, I'll tell you about Savannah sometime, it's interesting. An unusual pack—they've been there forever. A lot of the wolf families go back to before the Civil War."

"What's she like? I mean, so I'll be prepared."

The strapping werewolf shrugged. "You know rich Southern ladies. Cotton candy you can break your teeth on."

They both laughed.

"But she's not crazy like Mary Ann. We don't know she's trying to take the kid. Maybe she just wants to see Becca, and she's not giving Cade a chance to say no, even if it pisses him off."

"She's not afraid to piss off a Pack Alpha?" That just sounded unwise on so many levels.

"Like I said, she's tough. And besides—he's a single wolf with a bunch of other single wolves. He's gotta be careful. Cade's too smart to go loco on Sarah Jane—CPS would yank Becca out of here in a second. Okay." He rolled his shoulders, stretching his neck like he was trying to get the kinks out. "You get Becca ready, I'll throw the guys out, and if this works, we meet back here for a beer or twelve after everyone goes to bed."

She grinned, pleased and surprised to find herself bonding with the dour wolf. "You're on. And when I get some beer in you, maybe I'll get you to tell me about Mary Ann."

He laughed again. "No, ma'am. No way. You can't get me drunk enough to tell you about my Alpha's women."

"Where are you from, Miss Kendall?" Mrs. Ferguson spoke in the soft yet forceful voice common to many Southern belles, her Georgia accent stronger than Cade's. Ally, a swamp rat who'd spent her life trying to suppress her Louisiana/Texas twang, had always envied gentler Southern accents.

"Lake Charles, originally, but I've lived in Houston for thirteen years. And please, call me Ally."

"Thank you. Call me Sarah Jane. Do your parents still live in Lake Charles, Ally?"

"No, ma'am. They passed away when I was eight. I lived with an aunt after that."

"Oh, how awful."

They were in the living room—Michael, Ally, Sarah Jane and a sleepy Becca, who'd stuck to her grandmother's side since before dinner. Mrs. Ferguson had last seen Becca when she was two. Becca started off shy but quickly warmed up. When Ally introduced herself as the nanny, Becca squealed in delighted surprise.

Ally sat at the other end of the couch from Becca and Sarah Jane, while Michael sat with one leg thrown carelessly over the arm of the leather recliner. Wolves were loungers, not perchers, and Michael didn't seem inclined to be any less informal for the older woman's benefit.

Becca lay with her head in Sarah Jane's lap, slowly drifting to sleep while the adults talked around her. Ally remembered doing the same thing as a child when her parents were alive, and the warm, snug, safe feeling it had given her. No reason to hustle Becca off to bed right away. Besides, Michael had made it clear he didn't want to be alone with "that woman", which Ally found funny.

Sarah Jane Ferguson was formidable in a thoroughly refined, gently implacable way. Ally had assumed she'd be in her fifties or sixties, and she probably was, but she could have easily passed for forty-five. She wore her ash blond hair shoulder length, and she dressed in fitted capris and jeweled flip-flops that Ally figured cost fifty bucks. Everything about her was chic, tasteful and understated. Ally hoped she would age that gracefully.

Actually, Ally just hoped she would age.

"Michael tells me Carson's son has been living with you?"

"That's right. His mother was my cousin. When she and her husband died, I took him in."

"You would've been just a teenager yourself, wouldn't you? That's a remarkable thing for a young girl to do." Sarah Jane stroked Becca's hair as she spoke, glancing down at her frequently.

"I'd been on my own since I was sixteen. And when we moved to Houston, I had family there to help me out."

"I see. Michael says there are two other wolves with you?"

"Yes. Seth is Dylan's uncle, and Dec is our roommate."

The front door opened. They heard Dec and Dylan's voices. The two wolves halted when they saw the group assembled in the living room.

Michael stood to introduce them. "Guys, this is Sarah Jane Ferguson, Becca's grandmother. Sarah Jane, this is Declan MacSorley and Dylan Fontenot."

"Oh my God. He looks exactly like Carson, doesn't he?" For the first time that night, the older woman's elegant poise slipped. She rose to greet Dylan with an outstretched hand and he shook it shyly, taken aback at her interest.

"You look so much like your father it's scary, honey," she murmured. "Which means you look just like Cade and Rebecca—doesn't he?" she asked, turning to Michael and Ally. "All those green eyes and black hair—they all look just like Eirny." She laughed. "You can't see Louis MacDougall at all. Or me."

"You knew my father?" Dylan asked quietly.

"I knew him when he was a teenager." She smiled. "I can tell you some stories about Cade as well."

Ally wanted to hear those.

Sarah Jane turned to Dec. "Forgive me, I didn't catch your name?"

"Declan, ma'am. Declan MacSorley. It's a pleasure to meet you." Dec pressed her fingers gently, giving her the most sincere smile Ally had ever seen on him, without a trace of his customary flippancy. "Your granddaughter's the loveliest little girl I think I've ever seen, Mrs. Ferguson. You must be very proud."

"Thank you, Declan. And please, just Sarah Jane. Rebecca's pretty precious, isn't she? I know I was horribly rude for barging in like this, but I just had to see that little girl." She smiled brightly—and completely unapologetically—before she bent to kiss a sleeping Becca. "Well. I'll leave you young folks to stay up and talk. Ancients like me need all the sleep we can get."

Ally noted with interest that Dec's eyes followed Sarah Jane until she'd left the room. She turned to Michael.

"Wouldn't she be more comfortable in the house with Becca?"

Michael shrugged and flopped back down in the recliner. "She's lucky I'm letting her stay here at all. I don't want her watching everything we say and do. Her cabin's very comfortable."

Dec sat on the raised hearth, elbows propped on his knees. Dark brows knit in worry, he wore a rare frown. "Michael, are you sure you don't want to call Cade? He's bound to think Sarah Jane ambushed him, and he'll want to know why you didn't tell him. I'm thinking you're taking a big gamble here, lad."

"Dec!" she exclaimed, appalled.

But Michael merely stared at Dec thoughtfully as he dangled a leg over the arm of the recliner and rocked. "No," he said after a minute. "No, I don't think I will. You're right, it's a gamble. Cade might rip my fur, but I'm thinking about the pack here. This meeting is huge. Thanks to Ally, Sarah Jane shouldn't find much to object to around here, and if Cade's pissed off, that's her problem."

"All right. You know your Alpha better than I do," Dec said somewhat sadly as he stood. "Well, the lovely Mrs. Ferguson is right. Ancients do need their rest, and I'm off to get some. Good night, all."

He winked at her. She shook her head in disbelief as he climbed the stairs. Was there anyone he couldn't dazzle with his charm? Well, Cade, certainly. And her and Dylan. That was about it.

"Didn't that piss you off?" she asked Michael.

"What?" he asked, getting up to leave.

"Dec! Didn't it piss you off when he questioned you like

that?"

Michael laughed and shrugged. "Nah. Not Dec. He's cool. Good night, Ally. And thanks again." He had lovely blue eyes. When he tried, he could be downright pleasant. "I appreciate it. And so will Cade."

# Chapter Eleven

"My granddaughter needs a haircut. I don't see how she can hold her little head up under the weight of it."

They were washing Becca off after a finger painting session. Paint covered Ally head to toe. Her hair was frizzing out. Sarah Jane looked ready for a date.

Becca had spent the morning soaking up the attention like a tiny, lonely sponge. "Don't cut my hair!" she wailed.

"Don't whine. I agree," she said to Sarah Jane, "but maybe we should wait 'til Cade gets back?"

Sarah Jane gave her dubious look. "You're the nanny, aren't you? That's well within a nanny's discretion."

"Yeah, well, I mean—yes, but—it's just, I haven't been here that long and we hadn't really talked about how much I'm allowed to..."

"Oh, please." Sarah Jane waved a dismissive hand. "Males aren't concerned with little girls' hairstyles. I'm not suggesting we cut it all off. But just because she's being raised by wolves doesn't mean she should look like it."

"I guess you're right. And if Cade gets upset, I'll just blame it on you."

"There you go." Sarah Jane smiled in triumph, wiping up the leftover paint. "Cade MacDougall doesn't scare me. I'm going to my cabin to freshen up and I'll meet you downstairs, okay?"

"All right."

She'd wanted to look around town anyway, and she longed for something to take her mind off Cade MacDougall.

Two days later, the scene at the pool seemed less real. She knew she hadn't imagined it, but she had a hard time believing he was seriously interested in her. Surely he had lovers. Women probably dissolved into little puddles of helpless goo whenever he looked at them. Lord knew *she* did. She cringed a little when she recalled how squishy she got as soon as he touched her, how quickly she agreed to whatever he said.

Once she had Becca clean and dressed, Ally realized nothing short of a shower would get all the paint off herself. And once she was naked in the shower, her mind went back to Cade.

Her whole body flushed at the memory of his touch and his hungry, possessive gaze. She'd always been a little sexually reserved. Not repressed, just...slow to warm up. In Cade MacDougall's hands, she burned, instantly. Whether they were talking, or arguing, or doing whatever it was they'd done at the pool, her typical inhibitions disappeared in his presence.

Houston seemed thousands, not hundreds, of miles away. This ranch, these wolves, Cade and Becca—she'd known nothing of them a week ago. Now the thought of leaving them behind scared her nearly as much as the thought of losing her own wolves.

She followed the aroma of fresh baking into the kitchen, where she wasn't surprised to find Dylan scarfing muffins as fast as Sindri could happily serve them. At ten o'clock in the morning. After he'd consumed a huge breakfast two hours earlier.

"I wish I'd known about y'all a long time ago," she told Sindri as she sat down at the table. "He started eating twenty-four/seven when he turned twelve."

Dylan rolled his eyes.

Sindri smiled in his mysteriously placid way. "It is good to feed a young wolf again."

"But there's other young wolves here, Sindri," Dylan said. "You feed them, don't you?"

"Yes. But they are not of my *hefoar kona's* line."

"His *what's* line?" she asked Dylan, rhetorically.

To her amazement, he seemed to know. "His important lady's," he said, starting on another muffin.

"How do you—?"

"Where's my Nana? When're we going?"

They turned to see Becca in the doorway. She wore the jeans, T-shirt and tennis shoes Ally had put on her, and the feather boa and sunglasses she had put on herself. She looked like a backup singer for David Bowie circa 1975.

"We're leaving as soon as your Nana gets here. Did she tell you to call her Nana?"

"Yes. It means Gramma."

"I know."

"Where are y'all going?" Dylan asked.

"We're taking the munchkin to town for a haircut."

"Can I come?" He'd stopped eating for the moment.

"Sure. I haven't had any time with you since we got here. I've missed you. Stop rolling your eyes. Come on, sweet girl," she said to Becca. "I hear Nana. Let's go see if she's ready."

Sarah Jane looked just as fresh as she had thirty minutes earlier. So Ally was disappointed when she said, "On second thought, hon, I'm just exhausted. I don't think I'm up for a trip into town. Why don't you go on without me?"

"Are you sure? We can do it some other time..." Ally would never have thought to get Becca's hair cut if the older woman hadn't suggested it.

"No, no, y'all go on. Are you going with them, Dylan? That's lovely, y'all can have a nice day together. Shall we take Rebecca to Mass tomorrow?"

"Um, sure. Look, we don't have to go today..."

"I wanna go! I wanna go, Ally, please?" Becca clutched Ally's hand in both of her hot little ones, pulling on Ally's arm while staring up at her and doing the *pl-eee-eee-eee-ase* little kid bounce.

She squealed in delight when Dylan swung her up into the air. "Yeah, let's do it. It'll be fun to get off the ranch. I might even talk to you. You can ask me questions and stuff."

"I can't pass that up, can I?"

"Good! Just take the Lexus. I had the rental place strap in a child seat." Sarah Jane pressed keys into Ally's hand. "Rebecca," she said, kissing the child's cheek, "are you really going to wear those glasses and that feather thing?" At Becca's emphatic nod, she sighed. "Well, be good and have fun."

Dec was coming in as they were going out. Ally asked if

he'd like to join them. He looked past her, to Sarah Jane standing in the living room.

"I don't think so. I'm feelin' a mite knackered. I'm thinking I'll take a nap after I see if the wee fella's cooking anything tasty." Sindri had appeared behind Sarah Jane. Dec went inside the house and closed the door behind him.

"Dec has a crush on Sarah Jane," Ally said in wonder.

"You think so? Cool."

"You don't think it's weird?"

"Nah. Who knows how old he is? He needs a female. So does Seth. Maybe with me out of the way, they can settle down." He dangled a shrieking Becca over his shoulder as they walked to the car.

Michael hollered to them from the front porch of the woodshop.

"Hey, Stinky Butt. Where you off to?"

"I'm getting a haircut!" she crowed.

"You think Cade would mind?" Ally asked him.

Michael shrugged as he jogged over to meet them. "Not if you think she needs it. You got any plans tonight, when you get back?"

"I have a date. He's picking me up at seven."

He laughed. "Very funny." She liked Laughing Michael. She hoped to see more of him. "We're playing poker tonight. Seth says you play, and we've never had a female at a game. What do you think?" He slouched against the Lexus, hands in his jeans pockets.

"Who's we? It's just you and Shawn—my wolves don't play."

"The guys will be up here after dark. I'm hoping Sarah Jane turns in early like she did last night. So, you in?"

She smiled innocently. "Yeah, that sounds fun. It's just friendly, right? No hundred dollar pots? I'm not a big gambler."

Michael smirked. "It's twenty to buy in, chips go for a quarter, fifty, and a buck."

"Great! I can handle that."

"Yeah, I figured you could. Seth says sometimes you pay the rent with poker."

"Aw, shit. When is he gonna learn?"

"Boss, I'm telling you, everything's fine here." Michael sounded cheerful, which made Cade suspicious.

He'd called home before sitting back down with St. Louis and Chicago. The Brown Palace Hotel was the finest in Denver, but Cade had never slept alone there. He wondered if he could take Ally any time soon. She probably hadn't spent a lot of time in luxury hotels.

He wanted to spoil her. He wanted to impress her. He wanted to know her, because finding yourself mated to a virtual stranger was disconcerting as hell.

"Cade? Are you going to fill me in, or do I have to wait 'til you get home?"

*Goddamn it.* His mind had wandered again. How long had Michael been talking?

"It's going great, in fact. St. Louis and Chicago are ready to recognize us. I think your little brother's recognition has a lot to do with it."

"About damned time. That's great news." Michael laughed. "So yeah, you were right to make the deal with Nick."

"Oh, now you don't mind having Ally around?"

"Not at all. She's been a lot of help with Becca and everyone likes her. Honestly, boss, if you're stuck with a mate, you could do a lot worse."

"Michael, what the hell's going on?"

"It's under control. Fuck, Cade, how long have I had your back? You've trusted me under fire, you trusted me to build a pack, but you can't trust me when you're in Denver for two days?"

He relaxed when he heard the irritation in Michael's voice. "All right, all right. Don't get your panties in a bunch. Look, the main reason I called is I have news about Rufus. If it weren't for Aaron I wouldn't care, but we've got to be alert. No one's seen him since the other morning when I talked to him—he just dropped out of sight. The pack's trying to keep it quiet, but they're worried. He hasn't been right since his wife died. With Aaron in a coma, who knows what he might do."

Michael was silent for a minute. "Fuck. You think Rufus might be headed down here?"

"That's what I expected," mused Cade. "Now I'm wondering. He's probably senile, he hates me, his pup's almost dead...who knows? Spread the word so we hear about it if anyone sees him." All the wolves in Colorado, never more than fifty at a time, communicated with the Rocky Mountain Pack, even those who didn't belong to it. Cade and Michael had spent years establishing their network, and even Lones respected them.

"I'll put some guys on perimeter watch."

"Good. Shit. I can see him challenging me, maybe. I just don't know if he's crazy enough to ambush me. He's a Pack Alpha, for Chrissakes." It was unimaginable for a wolf of Rufus Stapkis' stature to engage in such behavior.

Personal honor was paramount in wolf culture; personal confrontation was part of that. A fight could be a formal challenge or an old-fashioned brawl, but a surprise attack was the depth of dishonor. It rendered the offending wolf liable to prosecution. Courts didn't meddle much in the affairs of wolves. The Sentients Equal Rights Act of 1965 included the right of wolves to engage in combat without the threat of human law. Though many humans disliked it, courts consistently upheld the principle. Ironically, once wolves came out officially in human society, and even more after SERA passed, wolf on wolf violence had decreased dramatically.

"Then again," Cade mused, "I don't like what Ally told me about Aaron and that other wolf in the restaurant. What if Seattle tried to pressure Aaron? The pup's barely out of his teens—he'd be vulnerable to something like that."

"I'm putting some of the guys out on the edges at night for a while—just 'til we get a better feel for what's going on. And a second wolf in Aaron's room," Michael said firmly.

"Good." Cade exhaled. "Shit. I know I'm invincible—" they both laughed "—but I'm tired." He rubbed his face and lay back on the hotel bed. "Between Aaron and Rufus and this meeting and now Ally..." Hell. Michael was his second, not his shrink.

"You've got a lot on your mind. That's why I'm here. I've got it covered on this end."

"Yeah, I know you do, wolf. I know you do." He paused, trying to figure out a way to say it without sounding like he was femming out. He couldn't. "How's Ally?"

Michael didn't laugh, but Cade heard his smile. "She's great. She and Dylan have gone into town to get Baby Girl a haircut. Oh, and the nanny service called again."

He laughed. "Whatever it is, you handle it, I don't care." He thought for a minute. "So. Ally likes Becca, doesn't she?"

"Yep. And Becca likes Ally. I've been thinking—if our Alpha's got a mate, a lot of wolves will stop with all the 'you're not a pack, you're fraternity or a gang' bullshit. And we could use a grown female around here."

"Michael," Cade said sharply. "I'm glad you like my mate, but you're way too goddamned cheerful. What's going on down there? You know I don't like surprises."

"Yeah, I know, boss." Michael's laughter rang a little hollow this time.

"You're not in the way."

"Huh?" Dylan sounded like he'd been drifting off to sleep.

"What you said earlier. You're not why the guys don't have women."

She shot him a glance to see his reaction. He appeared to be studying her rather...adultly.

"I'm the reason you don't have a man, though."

"No. *I'm* the reason I don't have a man. Lots of single moms manage to have a social life."

"You mean a sex life."

"Dylan!" Surely he was teasing her? But when she stole another look, she didn't see him laughing.

"Since when are you comfortable thinking about me with a sex life?" Her voice came out in a higher octave than normal.

"I'm not comfortable with it, exactly, but you're the one who said you needed to figure out what to do with the rest of your life. And you were right—I'm a big wolf now. I need to let you go."

"No, I need to let *you* go." They both laughed nervously. "And, baby, I'm not ever really gonna let you go. You're stuck with me."

"I know," he said quietly. "You're my mom. But I can't put you in a nursing home yet. You need a boyfriend."

Flustered, Ally glanced in the rearview mirror to check on Becca, bent over double in her car seat. How could small children sleep like that? With any luck she'd be refreshed, not cranky, when they got to town.

"What happened with Lind?"

"What?" That one came out of nowhere.

"Lind. Why'd you stop seeing him? Is he the reason we left home so quick?" He didn't sound upset or angry, merely curious.

She closed her eyes for a second to collect herself, then quickly opened them when she remembered, oh yeah, she was driving.

"If I said yes, would you be mad at me?"

"No," he said after a moment. "I didn't want to come up here, but now I'm glad we did. I'd feel better if you'd had a reason besides me to leave."

"Okay." She hesitated. "Then the truth is yeah, he's one of the reasons. We already wanted to bring you up here, but Jakob kind of, um... He sort of went psycho on me, and..." There were certain subjects Dylan and Ally didn't discuss directly, and she'd always thought it was by mutual, unspoken agreement.

"Did you get a little redneck on his Danish ass?"

She laughed shortly, relieved. "Yeah, I guess you could say that. Stupid, but I just couldn't stop myself at the time. So we thought maybe I should clear out for a while. I wanted to take off somewhere on my own, but Seth insisted we come up here. I honestly don't know why Dec decided to come with us."

"I think he needs us more than we realize."

"You're being awfully mature today," she teased. "It makes me feel old."

He grinned. "Deal with it. I'm growing up."

Dylan shattered the companionable vibe a few minutes later when he said, "He wants you, you know."

"What the hell are you talking about?" she asked in a strangled sort of voice, but of course she knew. At the oblique reference to Cade, her hands had started to shake a little on the steering wheel.

"Sorry. I'll shut up about it."

"No, I'm sorry, you don't need to..." *Deep breath. Start over.* "I'm the one who's always bugging you to talk to me. I'm just not sure I can talk about *this*."

"Okay."

Another mile flew past. They'd be in town soon.

"How do you know he does?" she asked him quietly. It unnerved her to talk to Dylan as an equal.

"Everyone knows, Al. He's the Alpha—everyone can tell when he wants a female."

"Oh my God," she whispered to herself. She recalled Cade's grin—and her own mortification—when he'd said all the wolves would smell him on her.

"It's okay. Don't be embarrassed, it's not...it's not dirty, you know? It's not like he's a human guy who just wants to get you into bed, it's—"

"How'd you get all clued in to werewolf stuff?" she snapped, reddening. But she wasn't angry. God help her, she was turned on, and scared, and, yes, a bit thrilled, and she couldn't deal with any of those emotions in front of Dylan.

He shrugged. "I've listened to the guys at the ranch. I've been... I can't really explain it. It's not all words, you know? Some of it's like, mental, or just instinct. That's why I like being there. It feels natural." He cocked his head at her, a disconcertingly shrewd expression on his handsome face, and then hit her with another one. "Ally, how come you never think a guy wants you?"

Balls were flying out of left field faster than she could hit them. "I don't know," she muttered, and he didn't press.

She sighed. "Because...look. You don't remember back before it all happened, do you? I know you remember that night, but you don't remember much about me before that, right?"

She couldn't believe they were having a Major Conversation like this in the car, with a sleeping child in the backseat and her trying to keep her eyes on the road while navigating the emotional landmines of the past and talking to her little boy about stuff she never wanted to talk to him about.

"I remember my parents," he said slowly. "I remember always being scared except when you were around, but no—it's weird, but I don't remember much about you."

"Okay. Well, see, I didn't date much. Like, at all. So, after it happened..." She'd always planned to explain *It* to Dylan when he grew up, which meant...now? No, not right now. "I mean, when I came back, I still looked like me, but completely different. It felt like walking around in someone else's body."

She found it hard to explain to someone who'd been born beautiful how difficult it was to go from chubby and cute-ish to hard and hot. "Guys liked the body, but it didn't feel like mine.

Sometimes it still doesn't, if that makes sense."

"It does."

"It's still weird," she continued, feeling reflective now. She propped an elbow on the window and leaned her head on one hand while she steered with the other one. "I still forget about the strength sometimes. I'm used to the eyesight and the hearing, and I've learned to ignore the smell."

"Yeah. For wolves, it's automatic to tune out certain sounds and smells when we're on two feet, you know? Otherwise we'd have sensory overload all the time."

Fremont came into view, and she welcomed the distraction. Soon they were on Main Street.

She loved small towns whose Main Streets were actually the main streets. She started looking for a parking place and hoped her assumption that she'd locate a salon nearby proved correct. Fremont was so small, she hadn't bothered looking online for a map.

"But I'd never thought about how *you* handled it. I mean, holding back my strength is automatic for me. It isn't for you?"

"Not always," she replied absently. Downtown Fremont was busy on Saturday afternoon.

"Wolves just keep their strength in check by instinct. Same thing with speed, when we're on two feet." He turned to her as much as the seat belt would allow as she cruised slowly, still looking for a parking spot. "See, we passed for thousands of years, right? 'Cause when we're on two feet, it's just instinct not to move too fast or show too much strength. That must be evolution, like the way a female stops aging if she has a wolf, so she keeps pace with her mate."

Ah. She spotted a parking spot up ahead, in front of a manicured grassy area with a small fountain and some benches. People were sitting around the fountain or throwing Frisbees with dogs.

"I never understood why evolution didn't do that for women who birth daughters with wolves," she muttered. "Evolution seems sexist sometimes."

"Oh yeah, it can be. It's totally unfair to females." He cocked his head at her. "Hey, I just thought of something. That would make sex kind of weird, wouldn't it?"

"What would?" she asked uncomfortably.

"The strength thing, when you're having sex."

She gaped at him, appalled. He wasn't joking.

"If you're really getting into it," he continued blithely, "and you forget to concentrate on holding back, you could lose control and hurt a guy, couldn't you? See, when I'm with a girl, it's just natural for me not to use all my strength, I don't have to think about it—"

"Sweetie." She stomped on the brake halfway into the parking spot. The car behind her honked in annoyance. She unbuckled her seat belt and turned to face him. "I'm glad you want to talk to me, and maybe—*maybe*—I could talk to you about Cade. But I cannot talk to you about your sex life, or mine. I just. Can. Not."

He raised an eyebrow—damn, he looked just like Cade doing that—and smiled at her affectionately. "Okay. I don't want to embarrass you. It's just kind of cool to talk like this, you know? You're talking to me like I'm grown."

"Don't I normally?"

"Not really. But it's okay, I don't mind. Usually."

"Yeah, you do." She sighed. "Okay. I'll work on it."

"Thank you." He leaned over and kissed her on the cheek—while not furry, sick, sleepy, hungry or prompted.

They pulled a limp Becca from her car seat. She wrapped her legs around Ally's waist. Dylan went to put money in the parking meter.

Something tripped her instincts as she stood there rubbing Becca's back and coaxing her awake. She gently pivoted from side to side, rocking Becca as she scanned the streets and sidewalks.

There. Tall, weird guy at two o'clock, staring straight at them from the doorway of a building five blocks ahead, down the nearest cross street. She had a clear view of him across the little park. Long white hair, almost silver. A relatively young face with a thin scar running diagonally almost the length of it, right temple to left cheek. He wore sunglasses, so she couldn't see his eyes. Despite the summer heat, he wore slacks and a long-sleeved shirt open at the collar. She kept swaying back and forth, letting her eyes roam. He wouldn't know she could see him from so far away, but she didn't want to be obvious. When Dylan rejoined them, he stood with his back to the guy, obstructing her view.

"Hey." She stood Becca on her feet between them. "There's

a strange guy directly behind you, down this side street about five blocks. He's watching us."

"Weird. Give me the keys." He walked around to the back of the car and opened the trunk, as if looking for something. He did a fine job of scanning the area surreptitiously.

"Yep, he's definitely scoping us. I get the feeling I've seen him before."

"You're kidding. Where?"

"I dunno. I mean, he's interesting looking—I wouldn't think I'd forget someone like that. But I can't place him. He looks spooky. Maybe you and Becca shouldn't run around by yourselves."

"No, I can handle it. Let's split up and see if he follows one of us."

They planned to meet for lunch. Dylan went to explore the town a bit, Ally and Becca to look for a salon.

If attention were a tornado, Rebecca MacDougall would've been a mobile home. Ally found it slow going down the cobblestone streets, with passersby stopping to say hello to Becca as she strutted in her sunglasses and boa. They asked her name and age and exclaimed over her adorableness. A number of people recognized her as Cade's daughter because the resemblance was so striking and he was so well known, but they all acted like they hadn't seen much of her.

For her part, Becca basked in the attention, bouncing along holding Ally's hand and jabbering nonstop. Ally tried her best to keep up. They talked about Daddy, nannies and Sindri's pancakes, how Becca sometimes turned into a cat but not on purpose, werewolves, *Wiggles*, why bees stung you but butterflies didn't, horses, her imaginary friends, people passing them on the street, her Nana, and more.

For a minute, Ally forgot she wasn't really the nanny. Maybe she'd tell Cade she was enrolling Becca in a preschool program. Right before he kicked her out for getting his daughter's hair cut.

Downtown Fremont was charming—lots of funky shops, antique dealers and regular retail stores. A number of buildings had historical markers which Ally would've loved to stop and read if she didn't have Becca dragging her along. She kept looking around, but she saw no sign of the weird white-haired guy. She no longer had the feeling of being followed.

They found Cute Kids' Kutz two streets over from where they parked. After a wait of twenty minutes, an empty chair beckoned. Ally told the stylist—Heather—to tame the curls all over and take two inches off the bottom.

Heather was nineteen. Heather had lived in Fremont all her life. Heather wanted to move to Denver or some other big city because Fremont was absolutely dead. Heather talked more than Becca.

"She's just beautiful. Sweetie, you are too cute! And you're being so good. I bet your mommy's very proud of you, isn't she?" Heather beamed at Ally.

"Ally's my nanny," Becca said softly. Ally couldn't tell if it was the mention of a mommy or the haircut that turned her little face so suddenly grave.

"Oh, well—that's great too!" She looked at Ally appraisingly. "Wow. You're young to be a nanny. Where do y'all live?"

"Outside of town," Ally replied. "I've just been there a week—"

"Oh my God!" Heather squealed, and Becca jumped a foot. Ally's sensitive ears nearly bled. Humans weren't supposed to make noises like that. The young woman noted Ally's grimace and lowered her voice, looking sheepish.

"Sorry. It's just that I figured out where I'd seen Rebecca! She's Cade MacDougall's daughter, isn't she?"

"You know him?"

"God no, I wish." Heather snorted. "But my girlfriend Celine, see, she was Rebecca's nanny for a while! Isn't that wild? Hey, sweetie," she said, putting her head next to Becca's and looking at her in the mirror, "do you remember Celine?"

Becca concentrated. "No."

"You were too little. Just as well," she said to Ally. "Celine has a thing for fur, you know? Someone said she even went after—" She stopped, looking at Becca, then back at Ally. "You know. And he fired her. I can't really blame her for trying. He is so hot, isn't he?"

"Who's hot?" asked Becca.

"No one you know, baby," Ally said as she and Heather laughed. She got a silly warm glow from knowing Cade had fired a nanny who came on to him.

Every woman in the shop suddenly turned toward the door, so Ally did too. Sure enough, it was Dylan. As he made his way toward them, she caught a breeze from all the female heads whipping back around to watch him walk past.

Heather looked at her in amazement. "Is he with you?"

"Yes," Ally smiled. "How'd you find us?" she asked Dylan.

"I asked someone on the street where you'd go to get a kid's haircut." He wasn't looking at her. He was smiling at a mesmerized Heather.

"Dylan, pay attention." She slapped his arm lightly. "Did you see the guy?"

"What? Oh yeah, I did. He followed me after I split off from y'all. He..." He stopped and looked at Heather, hanging on his every word. "Excuse us a sec," he said smoothly. When had he learned to speak *smoothly* to women? He and Ally stepped aside for some privacy.

"He was really good at it," Dylan continued. "If you hadn't seen him, I don't think I would've known he was following me. I walked around for a while, waiting for him to approach me, but he never did. Finally I got bored and just asked him what he wanted."

"You *what?*" She didn't mean to squeal.

He raised an eyebrow and grinned. "I asked him what he wanted. Why not? I didn't see a gun or anything."

"But— Oh, forget it. What did he do?"

"Well, I shocked the hell out of him. He looked around like he was gonna try to dodge me or something, but he didn't. So I walked up and said, 'Dude, why are you following me?'"

"And what did he say?"

"He seemed kinda scared—like, he didn't know what to say, or he was embarrassed, I don't know. He had a weird accent—kind of like Swedish or German, you know? He asked me who my mother was."

At her appalled squeak, he held up a hand. "Let me finish. He looked surprised. He said 'no, that can't be, you look just like her' and I said 'well, sorry, my mom was Gracie Fontenot', and he asked what I was doing here, and I said that was none of his business, because I'm not totally stupid, okay?"

He paused and then said, more quietly, "Then he asked me

who Becca was."

Ally's head snapped up. "Who Becca...why would he want to know that?"

"I don't know, but that's when I got pissed off and I said, 'Dude, stay the fuck away from us, it's none of your business who we are and I don't want to see you again'."

She swallowed. "Okay. Good. That's more like it. Don't say fuck. So? What'd he do?"

"He looked straight at me and said, 'You didn't see me'."

"*What*?" She laughed uneasily.

"Yeah. He said 'you didn't see me', and I said, 'Uh, dude, I'm standing here looking at you'. 'Cause now I'm thinking he's tripping on something, right? And he gets this weird—like, even weirder—look, and he said, 'but you are war gulf'."

"*War gulf*? What does that even mean?"

"Who knows? He said, 'but you are war gulf,' and then he said, 'you didn't see me', one more time and I was like 'yeah, still seeing you, dude', and then he disappeared. He ran away as fast as a wolf, and that's when I decided he was some messed up high Fae who was out of his head on something."

She sagged with relief. "Oh, thank God. You're right—that must be it. He thought he recognized you, then tried to pull some mind whammy on you, but he was too stoned to do it." She smiled in embarrassment and bumped her head gently against his chest. "Sorry, but that really freaked me out for a minute."

There were few pureblooded high Fae—the ones known in earlier times as elves or fairies—in the U.S., and most of them were in a sorry state. High Fae didn't handle certain aspects of modernity well. Many of them preferred to live on special homelands in Canada, Iceland and parts of Scandinavia. They were impervious to human diseases but unfortunately susceptible to human vices, particularly drugs. Drugs that suppressed the human nervous system gave the Fae a treacherously sweet high. It also suppressed their talents and wrecked them mentally and emotionally. The drugs wouldn't kill them—full-blooded high Fae lived hundreds of years and were tough to kill—but long exposure could leave them in a state worse, in some ways, than death. It sounded like their weird guy was more to be pitied than feared.

Dylan declared Fremont boring and himself hungry. Ally

went to pay. She realized Dylan wasn't behind them and when she looked back, she saw him chatting up Heather. She almost—*almost*—went back to drag him out, but she remembered what he'd said about her treating him like a grownup. So she and Becca waited outside. Ten minutes later he joined them, looking pleased with himself.

They had a nice lunch with no further signs of Pitiful Fae Guy and headed back to the ranch.

# Chapter Twelve

The sight of so many werewolves in the woodshop that evening had surprised her, because the gravel parking lot remained virtually empty. Michael had grinned and explained the wolves had sneaked back onto the ranch on four feet. A few of them also came up every night for guard duty.

Now, two hours into the game, Ally sat behind the fattest pile of chips.

"Michael, my wolf—she's good. She's really good," laughed one now—Roman, if she remembered correctly.

"Oh yeah, our Wendy is dangerous," Dec drawled, sitting on an empty workbench and dangling a beer between his outstretched legs. "It's that whole sweet and innocent thing."

All the tools and work tables had been pushed up against the walls with the lumber. The large, custom-made poker table sat in the middle of the room. Wolves who weren't playing drank beer and watched the game.

She'd been a little hesitant to play poker in a room full of alphas, but aside from the testosterone dripping down the walls, there'd been no trouble.

"I knew it was an act," Michael said over his shoulder. "Nobody could be that sweet and innocent."

Dec took a long drag on his beer. "Actually, the sweet and innocent is genuine. But it distracts poor saps such as yourselves from her fearsome poker skills."

Everybody except Michael laughed.

Dec's nonchalance in the presence of so many alphas was odd, and the alphas' easy acceptance of him even more so.

Dec was odd, in fact. She'd never really noticed it 'til she'd been able to compare him to lots of other werewolves.

"Are we playing cards here or what?" Michael groused.

"Bet's to me, right?"

"Yeah. Ally, if you can't beat three of a kind, you don't need—"

"I know how to play the game," she said without looking up from her cards. "That's why my stack's so much bigger than yours."

More than one wolf snickered. Michael looked around with a fearsome scowl and the room settled down.

"'S not *that* much bigger than mine," he said under his breath.

"It's about to be," she cooed, and threw in two dollars. Everyone else stayed in. When the bet got around to Michael, he raised. Ally called him and tossed in two more dollars. Everyone else folded.

"Okay, Wargman," she said, propping her elbows on the table and leaning forward. "Show 'em."

He grinned at her as he laid down his hand. "Here you go, Kendall," he growled triumphantly to a chorus of wolfish "whoos".

She stood up and leaned forward on the table a little more, peering at his full house as he watched her smugly. She looked up at him in wide-eyed gravity, and a couple of wolves began to chuckle.

"Michael," said one, "that doesn't look like a female about to lose some money, bro."

Michael's smile froze, his eyes narrowing at her expression.

"You know what, Michael? Most of the time a full house would do it, but tonight I got—" now she began to lay her cards down one at a time "— a seven, and a nine, and another nine, and another nine *and*...one more nine." She beamed as widely as he had just a moment ago. Wolf-whistles and applause erupted.

Michael couldn't speak for a minute. "I don't believe it," he whispered.

"Neither do I!" she laughed once she'd finished high-fiving everyone in the room. "I had three of 'em to start with. I mean, when am I gonna get dealt something like that again? And why doesn't it ever happen in a casino?"

"Did anybody bother to shuffle the fucking cards?" Michael

addressed the air with feigned heartbreak. "Hey, where you going?" he asked as she scooped up her chips.

"I'm going inside. It's late and I'm tired and I don't want to take *all* your money, because that would just be mean." Michael started to smile but managed to turn it into a grimace. "Besides, I want to check on Becca." Another wolf had already slid in to claim her seat at the table.

"Ally, you don't have to check on Stinky Butt." Michael shuffled a fresh deck and looked up at her with that sardonic smile. "You're not really the nanny. Cade would never let you work for him."

"Why not?" she huffed, wounded.

"Well, I mean—because, you know, he'll hire someone to do that, and you..."

"I do know how to take care of children, Michael." She hadn't realized the idea was rolling around in her head until he shot it down.

"Oh yeah, I know, I know. I just meant, you're a guest, and Cade wouldn't expect..."

"Whatever. I'm going inside," she muttered.

Michael stood up. "Ally, wait, you don't understand..."

Stung, she stuffed her winnings in her jeans pocket and hurried out of the woodshop, nearly running into Seth as she rounded the corner at the front of the house. He grabbed her elbow as she brushed past.

"Hey, what's up? Where you going?"

"Nothing. Inside." She pulled away and hurried on.

"Wait, what—? Ally! Stop! What's the matter?"

She didn't want to explain it to him. If he knew how messed up she'd allowed herself to get over Cade MacDougall, how much she wanted to stay here and was afraid to leave, he'd worry. She wouldn't allow that. Seth was enjoying himself here, she could tell, and he deserved the chance to relax and let himself be part of a pack for the first time in his life.

And besides, what the hell did Michael know? Cade might think hiring her was a great idea.

Just because they bickered didn't mean she couldn't work for him, she thought as she stamped into the house. They wouldn't fight all the time if she just shut up and let him be the boss. And she could. She could be polite, do as she was told.

She could live here, take care of Becca, stay with Dylan and Seth.

And Cade.

Could she work for him, feeling the way she did? She paused halfway up the stairs to ponder that. Why not? He'd soon be distracted by some other woman—maybe he already was. Besides, constant proximity offered the surest cure for infatuation. And Becca already adored her.

*Okay, Ally, there you go—a practical, efficient solution to the pitiful-Dead-Girl-has-no-place-to-go problem.*

She could make it work. She had to.

She walked into Becca's room to find an empty bed. A Hello Kitty nightgown lay on top of the sheets, but there was no sign of the little girl who'd been wearing it.

For a split second she suffered one of those heart-stopping panic seizures, like when she'd lost Dylan at an Astros game for all of ten minutes.

*Wait a second—she's just rambling.*

A quick check revealed no Becca in Ally's room, so she headed downstairs. Sarah Jane and Sindri were talking in the kitchen. She didn't pay attention as she hurried to Cade's room.

His bedroom. Where his bed was. Where he slept and showered and dressed. And made love to hundreds of women... No, that was stupid. He wouldn't bring hundreds of women up here. Maybe just dozens. He probably got most of his nookie in town, away from Becca.

Cade's four-poster bed stood at least two feet off the floor. The kid couldn't climb up there by herself. A quick glance in the spacious bathroom revealed a garden tub that set her heart to racing. No sign of Becca, though.

Maybe she'd joined her grandmother and Sindri.

Once out of Cade's room, she was about to turn left into the kitchen when she paused. Sarah Jane and Sindri were whispering. Ally had no trouble picking up every word and, only somewhat ashamed, she couldn't resist.

"How can I tell him now, after all these years? He would never forgive me. Why have I waited? Why did I not talk to him when he returned?" Sindri sounded as if he were weeping.

"Calm down, honey, please," Sarah Jane urged. "Don't do this to yourself. I promise you, everything will be all right. We'll talk to him soon, and in the meantime, the three of us can keep an eye on her. That's the main reason I'm here, to look after her. You've got to quit fretting, baby. Shh..." They fell silent.

Very quietly, Ally padded back the way she had come, stopping when she got to the door of Cade's room.

Sindri and Sarah Jane were friends? And who were *the three of us*? Should she mention it to Cade? She'd have a hard time explaining the circumstances, especially since it didn't concern her and eavesdropping wasn't an attractive habit.

But she'd pay close attention to them in the future. That wasn't nosiness, it was just...interest.

She walked back through the den and into the kitchen, calling out to make sure they heard her coming.

"Sarah Jane? Sindri? Have you seen...oh. There she is."

Sindri sat at the big kitchen table with his head in his hands. He didn't look up when she walked in. Sarah Jane, cradling a nearly naked, soundly sleeping Becca in her lap, smiled warmly. "Ally, honey, were you looking for our girl? It seems she likes to wander at night. I found her clear on the other side of the house."

"Yeah, Cade had told me she does that sometimes." She dropped into a chair across the table from Sarah Jane. "I was pla—" she almost blurted out that she'd been playing poker with the wolves "—planning to take a walk when I decided to check on her. I got scared when she wasn't in her room, but I figured she had to be somewhere in the house."

"Sindri gave her some milk and she fell asleep before she finished it."

"Would you like some? Or hot tea? I will make you something to eat..." Sindri stood up and pushed his chair back, his wizened face drawn but dry-eyed.

"No, Sindri, that's okay, really. I'm ready to turn in myself. Sarah Jane, I'll take her on back to her room. Unless you'd rather do it?"

Sarah Jane laughed. "Oh, honey, these old legs can't make it up those stairs with thirty pounds of sleeping girl. I'll let you do it."

"Okay." Ally stood up and gathered Becca in her arms. "Well, good night."

"Good night," they both replied.

She listened as she climbed the staircase to Becca's room, but she heard nothing more from the kitchen.

# Chapter Thirteen

"Has Cade called yet?"

"Yeah. He'll be home around eight."

Ally knew Michael didn't want to talk, but anticipation was killing her. "Did he say how the meeting went?"

"It went fine." The tension in Michael's voice was contagious.

She couldn't leave it at that. "Did you tell him about Sarah Jane? How'd he react? Was he okay with you not telling him sooner?"

"Yes. Bad. Fuck no."

He stalked off in the direction of Cade's office.

Ally was nervous about Cade's arrival as well, but for a different reason.

She and Sarah Jane had taken Becca to Mass that morning and then to lunch. It thrilled the child just leaving the ranch two days in a row. Becca had to start spending time with other children. She needed a real nanny, someone young and active. Someone who took a personal interest in her development. Someone, despite what Michael might think, like Ally.

Asking for the job would cost her nothing except maybe her dignity. When it came to Cade MacDougall, her dignity wasn't all that safe anyway.

Only Michael, Ally, Dec and Sarah Jane were in the house for dinner that night. A heavy blanket of tension smothered their halfhearted attempts at conversation. Becca took her dinner in the kitchen with Sindri. Seth and Dylan were now eating and sleeping in the bunkhouses with the rest of the pack.

It felt weird, not seeing them every night and each morning, but they both seemed happy. Seth was more relaxed than he'd ever been, and Dylan had shown no signs of teenage angst in over seventy-two hours. She didn't feel she had any right to whine, no matter how much she missed them.

Everyone scattered immediately after dinner. Michael shut himself up in Cade's office, Dec disappeared, and Sarah Jane said something about needing to go to town.

Ally thought equine company would be preferable to anyone else's under the circumstances, so she pulled on her boots under her sundress and headed for the stables.

But not even the horses could relax her tonight. She didn't know what disturbed her more, the prospect of asking Cade for a job he wouldn't give her, or simply seeing him again. It made her neck tingle and her pulse pound and her stomach flip to think about being in the same room with him.

*And you think you can work for him? Stupid Dead Girl.*

Walking back to the house, lost in thought and worry, something in the twilight shadows caught her eye. If there'd been a lot of wolves around as usual, she might have missed the two figures standing close together between the house and Sarah Jane's cabin. As she got closer, she observed Dec and Sarah Jane deep in conversation. She was surprised, since it had been less than two hours since Sarah Jane left for town.

She took care to approach unobtrusively, walking softly toward the north side of the house to remain out of their line of sight. For one of the few times in her second life, she liked being able to hear like a wolf. She didn't even know why she wanted to eavesdrop. It just seemed weird to see them talking like that. First Sarah Jane and Sindri, now Sarah Jane and Dec? She'd figured Dec had the hots for the older woman, but if so, they'd already hit turbulence.

Sarah Jane stood stiffly, glaring up at the Irishwolf with her arms folded tightly beneath her breasts. Dec paced restlessly, gesturing as he peppered Sarah Jane with questions in cold anger.

"Are you *trying* to provoke him, girl? Do you *want* an alpha wolf at your throat?" Dec's accent was heavier than she'd ever heard it before. It almost didn't sound Irish—it was thicker, more guttural. "Or," he grabbed Sarah Jane's upper arms as if he were about to shake her, "are you thinkin' you can provoke him and take the *barn* away? Because I'll not let you do it, darlin', you better know that right now, I'll..."

"Leave off, Declan MacSorley!" Sarah Jane exclaimed, putting both hands on his chest and shoving him away. Her accent, too, had changed, but the difference was subtler. The soft Southern smoothness was gone, the words harder around the edges. Her voice had taken on a strange but pleasant lilt. "I don't want to take her away from her father. I just want some time with her and I can't ignore what I'm sensing! Something's wrong, something bad is coming..."

"Aye, and we'll handle it. Cade can take care of himself and his daughter, and we can... Ally, what are you doin' here?" They both turned to look straight at her.

Fascinated by the fight, she'd crept closer without realizing it. And Dec could smell her, of course. She didn't attempt to act casual or make up some lame excuse.

"I was coming back from the stable and I heard y'all arguing."

Dec folded his arms, waiting for her to go on. Somewhat defensively, she continued, "Sarah Jane, how'd you get to town and back so fast? I didn't even hear the Lexus come back."

Sarah blinked in surprise. "What? Oh. Oh, well, I got halfway there, realized what time it was, and decided I'd rather wait and go tomorrow, when I don't have to worry about driving home late at night. Besides, I'd rather spend a little more time with Rebecca before her father gets home."

At the mention of Cade, Dec shook his head and muttered something about Sarah Jane being an idiot.

"I've already put her down for the night," Ally replied. "I'm sorry, I—"

Sarah Jane appeared to brighten a little. "It's all right, dear. She wasn't asleep yet. So I took her out to my cabin and we had a little slumber party, just the two of us." She beamed with grandmotherly contentment, and maybe a calculating glint in her eye.

"What? You just hauled her out of bed? I mean, that's—" She stopped, flustered. Granted, Sarah Jane was Becca's grandmother, but still, it seemed...weird. Presumptuous.

"Daft, is what it is," grunted Dec. "And maybe suicidal."

At Ally's shocked gasp, Sarah Jane rolled her eyes and patted Ally's arm. "Don't pay any attention to him, Allison. He's a fine one to be calling other people daft."

Ally, still stuck on Dec's "suicidal" crack, recalled Michael's tension earlier in the evening, and his report of Cade's reaction. "Dec, do you think Cade will be upset when he finds Sarah Jane here?"

"I think he'll be 'upset'—" his tone put audible quotes around the word "—to know that Mrs. Ferguson showed up unannounced. I think he'll be livid to find Becca in Sarah Jane's cabin tonight on top of it."

"And *I* think that if the young whelp's going to be furious with me just for showing up, Rebecca doesn't need to hear it."

"That young whelp is a Pack Alpha! You do not ambush a Pack Alpha on his own feckin' turf, woman, especially not when he thinks you're after his child!"

"But if Sarah Jane just explains how she wanted to see Becca..."

"And if she just explains it before Cade's so enraged that he shifts, maybe all's well. But it's not the kind of thing I'm comfortable assuming. And since when do you spy on me, Ally girl?"

"Leave the child alone, Declan," Sarah Jane said from behind him. Her normal accent had returned. Ally wondered if she'd imagined her losing it.

He held up a hand. "I'm asking Allison a question."

Sarah Jane thumped him on the back, hard. He stumbled forward a bit.

"And *I'm* telling *you* to leave the girl alone, you arrogant gobshite. I've no reason to be afraid of Cade MacDougall, and you know it." She smiled at Ally again, and this time Ally was certain about the gleam of calculation in Sarah Jane's eyes. "As long as Ally's here, Cade will be fine."

"What?" Ally squeaked. "What on earth are you—?"

"Good night, dear," Sarah Jane said calmly. She looked up at Dec, rolled her eyes, and walked back to her cabin muttering something about "daft" and "hundred years".

"Dec," Ally said slowly as the older woman walked away, "is Sarah Jane crazy?"

"Eh," he said heavily. "It's hard to tell with females like

that, love. Very hard to tell."

Before she could ask what the hell that meant, he ambled over to the house and flopped down in a rocking chair on the porch. "Would you care to join me for a while until the fireworks start?"

Ally got a little chill down her spine. This grave and troubled wolf was a stranger to her.

When she had settled on the top step of the porch, she asked, "You think I should go get Becca and put her in her own room?" She didn't care if it made Sarah Jane angry as long as it kept Cade from freaking out.

Dec didn't answer right away, running his hands through his dark hair and scratching at his unkempt beard. "Shite. I don't know— No, she's probably right. If he goes mad, the child shouldn't be in the house."

"Why'd you call her a barn?"

"What?" he said, looking startled. "Why'd I call who a *barn*?"

"Becca. I thought the word was *bairn*."

He smiled. "Oh. It is, it is. That's what I called her. You must've misheard me." He gazed at her appraisingly, one eyebrow cocked. "Y'know, Ally girl, I've always found your nosiness rather charming, but it could land you in trouble one day."

Her face burned as she stammered, "I'm not nosy, I'm— I'm curious."

"All right, then. Your curiosity could land you in trouble one day. Cats and all that, y'know."

"Never mind that, Dec," she said impatiently. "Look, Cade already knows Sarah Jane is here, so it won't be a complete ambush. Don't you think he can control his temper when he gets home?"

"Under normal circumstances. With all the stress he's under right now, the way she just showed up—it was stupid."

"I like Sarah Jane."

"I like her too, Ally. Always have. Shite," he repeated. "Ah, well. Maybe we'll get lucky and he'll attack Michael first."

"*What?*"

Dec abruptly ceased rocking and stared out across the front yard. He spoke slowly and softly. "Maybe Cade's spent the drive thinking about what Michael told him, and by the time he gets here he'll be angry but calm. Or he could've spent the two hours thinking about how Sarah Jane showed up without warning, and Michael didn't call him, and he's already got Aaron and his father to worry about, and he just had the most important meeting of his life, and he's exhausted, and he'll get madder and madder with each passing mile, and when he gets home he goes straight for Michael's throat. It's occurred to Michael. That's why he's so tense."

"That's too awful to think about." She felt a stomachache coming on. "But...he did leave Michael in charge. Everything's under control, and Cade didn't have to leave Denver, and the meeting went well. So..."

"You're right. And just like with Sarah Jane—if Michael explains all that before Cade rips his throat out, all's grand. The two have been best friends for twenty-five years. That counts for a lot. But if Michael can't explain, or Cade won't listen... It could be bloody. And this pack couldn't handle something like that right now."

"Why?"

Dec appeared to consider his next words carefully. "A pack feeds off its leaders' emotions. Joy, anger, fear—everything flows out of the Alpha to his second, to the other alphas and then to the betas. Rocky Mountain's thrived, even without recognition, because Cade and Michael and the lesser alphas are strong leaders. But if Cade feels his family is threatened, and he loses faith in Michael, and the two of them go fang to fang—Christ. Louis' murder destroyed the old pack, and it happened four thousand miles away. The psychological backdraft drove half of them crazy and turned the other half against each other. If Cade and his second fall out at a time like this, it could be just as bad."

Ally's spine was frozen now. "Dec, maybe the wolves told you how long Cade and Michael have been friends—"

"Michael told me," he said smoothly. "He likes me. He tells me everything."

"Maybe. But I don't think Michael told you all about Louis MacDougall and the old pack. And I don't believe you read it all on the Web. On the drive up here, you kept calling Cade by his first name and talking about stuff like you remembered it."

He rocked slowly, eyes closed.

She could barely whisper her next question. "How well did you know Eirny and Louis MacDougall?"

He opened his eyes. "I never met Louis. I never met Carson or Cade, but I followed their lives. I knew Eirny well. Very well."

She'd expected him to laugh her off. Having it confirmed so bluntly shocked her.

"Is that why you like Cade? Because he reminds you of Eirny?"

He shook his head sadly. "Cade looks like her, but he's his father inside out. No. Carson took after Eirny. That's why he's dead." He was staring out across the fields again. "Cade got past his parents' murder, but Carson never did. He was okay as long as he was in the army. Once he lost that structure, he fell apart. Eventually the drugs and the drink did him in."

"Were Carson and Eirny weak?" She couldn't imagine that of a Valkyrie's acolyte.

"Eirny wasn't weak, she was...heedless. Undisciplined. She gave herself over to whatever she felt, or wanted, and never stopped to think about consequences. I think Carson was the same way. More feeling than thinking. Cade's not like that."

"How'd you know Eirny?" She sat riveted there on the step, not daring to move for fear of dispelling the mood. But apparently it was already over.

"I don't think I want to talk about it right now, darlin'. And I don't want you telling Cade anything about it either. I'm trusting you not to."

"Why?"

His gaze returned to her face, and his emerald eyes bored into hers. "Why? Because I've been your friend for years, and I've been a good one. Because I've never asked you to keep a secret, and because I've kept your secrets without being asked."

"What secrets, Dec?" she whispered.

"Ally, darlin'. You've never explained your youthfulness. Or why you never get sick, never bruise or hurt yourself. You hear things you shouldn't hear, see things you shouldn't be able to see. Don't get me wrong, you're careful. Usually. If I didn't live with you, I'd never notice. If I didn't live with you, I'd never have seen you lift the entertainment center with one hand. Now, I've heard of mothers who manage to lift cars off their children, but no one gets that kind of adrenaline rush from vacuuming the den. I've never asked you about it, have I?"

She was getting chilled again. "I guess we've both been a little dishonest."

"We're not dishonest. We're circumspect." He flashed his normal grin, but it didn't reassure her.

"Wait a minute, Dec." She spoke slowly as her mind raced ahead of her words. "Now I'm thinking—the stuff you've done for us, it didn't come out of nowhere, did it? Like when you thought Dylan should go to Scotland. The MacDougalls are Scottish. And you're the one who suggested we send Dylan's DNA to the databank. You already knew who his father was, didn't you? How, Dec? How'd you connect Dylan and Carson? There's still a lot you're not telling me, isn't there?"

"And there's a lot *you* haven't told *me*. I've never asked about the Dane, or why we left Texas in such a hurry."

Wait. She was supposed to be grilling *him*.

"You didn't like me at first, you remember that?"

She nodded, though the *non sequitur* confused her.

"You were reluctant to let me move in. Seth, who never does anything without thinking about it a few months, liked me right away. Which is what I'm accustomed to, tell the truth. You ever wonder why it took you longer?"

She shook her head.

"Well, I have. You are not what you appear to be, my Wendy, but I still trust you. You trust me?"

She was thinking about that when they heard a car coming up the main road far too fast. Scant seconds passed from when it turned off the highway to when it came flying around the last bend, screeching to a halt in a tornado of gravel. The driver threw himself out of the car.

It was Cade, of course. He hadn't spent the two hour drive absorbing and adjusting to Michael's information.

Rage twisted his beautiful face as he ran toward the house. Dec stepped down from the porch into Cade's path, presumably in order to— What? Commit suicide by Alpha? What the hell was Dec thinking?

Cade didn't stop to find out. He vaulted the steps onto the porch, sending Dec flying with a dismissive flick of the wrist. Dec went over the porch railing and caromed off the swing set into the grass in front of Becca's little trampoline.

Cade slammed the door behind him with such force it

should've splintered on its hinges. But this house was made to hold, and withstand, werewolves.

She was glad she'd left Becca in her grandmother's cabin. As she listened to Cade bellowing at Michael, she realized he was too enraged to think about his daughter sleeping upstairs. It would be safest to stay outside, preferably farther away. But in the rashest move she'd made since facing down Guy Fontenot, Ally followed Cade into the house.

What the hell was *she* thinking?

## Chapter Fourteen

She stopped at the entrance to the living room. The wolves weren't there, but she heard them.

"Where the fuck is she? What do you mean letting her in *my* house with *my* daughter? What has she seen?"

"She's staying in the cabin. Cade, I told you on the phone, everything's fine, Ally's looking after Becca, Sarah Jane likes her, the wolves have stayed scarce..." Michael was speaking almost too fast to be understood.

"Why didn't you call me, goddamn it?"

"I talked it over with Sindri. He thought—"

"Sindri's not my second! I didn't leave him in charge!"

"Cade, I decided Ally had it covered, Becca was fine and Sarah Jane..."

"You think you know what's best for my girl?"

Cade's voice sounded guttural. Ally realized with a shock that he'd started to change. He either couldn't stop it or didn't want to. An Alpha as powerful as Cade, changing in a rage... *Oh God, Dec was right.*

Stay, or run like hell? It didn't matter—just like that day at the pool, her legs wouldn't move.

They emerged from the west wing of the house, Cade moving in long, angry strides with Michael behind him.

The change slowed Cade down. He couldn't run like he had a minute ago. She caught a glimpse of his face when he made a sharp turn to go upstairs.

The unfamiliar expression on Dec's face had given her chills. Cade's expression froze the blood in her veins.

Michael stopped at the bottom step as Cade went up the

staircase.

He was headed for Becca's room.

She moved her lips, but no sound came out. Just as she tried again, Cade roared, "*Michael, where's Becca?*"

"With Sarah Jane," she croaked.

Michael stared at her, aghast. Cade leaned over the railing, noticing her presence for the first time. The physical change had not begun in earnest, but the musky odor of a changing wolf hung heavy in the air. His eyes were rimmed with yellow, his breathing rapid and shallow as he stood utterly still with a white-knuckle grip on the railing.

"What did you say, Allison?" Cade's quiet tone felt far more menacing than his roaring.

Her voice came out in a terrified squeak. "I said she— She's in Sarah Jane's cabin. They get along so well, and she likes..." For the second time that evening, she remembered the night she died. Once more she was throwing herself in front of a maddened wolf, but this time she wasn't the only one who could stop him—that was Michael's damned job. So why was she here?

Michael said, "I'll go get Bec—"

"No," Cade cut him off. "I'll go." He cleared the loft railing in one fluid leap, dropping straight down to land on his feet in front of them.

He was panting, though not from exertion. His black T-shirt, wet with sweat, clung to his torso. His face had assumed a saturnine cast, wet curls plastered to his forehead. His eyes weren't yet fully yellow, but the pupils had narrowed and elongated as the change set in.

Before she even knew she was doing it, Ally jumped in front of him, put her hands on his chest and began pushing him back. A voice in the back of her head kept screaming, *Are you insane? Run this time! Run!* She barely heard it over the sound of Michael's voice and her own, babbling simultaneously.

"Cade, you can't go out there like this! You'll change before you get there and you'll rip someone to pieces. Becca will see you..." Her voice climbed ever higher, into the Really Scared register.

"Ally, get out of here. I'll handle this. I won't let him leave, but you can't be here..." Michael said, without making any move to pull her away from Cade.

"If you kill Sarah Jane—God, Cade, the cops! They'll take Becca, they'll pump you with silver..." She grunted with effort as Cade leaned harder against her hands, clearly perplexed that she'd stopped his forward motion.

He stared at her, bemused, pushing against her as she pushed against him. She held him in place a whole five seconds. You couldn't judge a werewolf's strength by his physical size. Cade was six-three and looked to weigh about two-twenty, all of it lean muscle. Even with her strength, trying to push him back felt like pushing against a boulder rolling downhill. He had far more force and weight behind him than the eye could see.

His strength terrified and excited her. By now it came as no surprise to find she reveled in the contact with him, even as she feared imminent dismemberment. He moved slowly forward, pushing her back an inch at a time, like in a cartoon. Maybe if she let go, he'd fall over.

She glanced back to see Michael still rooted to the spot in front of the stairs, watching Cade with some concern but no apparent intention of intervening.

"What the hell *are* you?" Cade asked hoarsely.

"Scared," she replied, turning back to look him in the face.

He jerked to a stop and she banged into him, her head thunking against his chest. His big hands grasped her at the waist. He picked her up as if she weighed nothing at all, holding her there, her head level with his and her feet dangling.

She clutched at his shoulders to steady herself and couldn't help squeezing a little, testing the hard muscles. The urge to press her tongue to his skin returned, so strong her mouth watered. She could almost taste him as she breathed deep, inhaling his sweet, wild scent. She closed her eyes and put her head back, Cade-drugged, her self-control a whisper away from shattering. Her whole body trembled and she couldn't stop it.

"You're scared of me, Ally?" He still spoke in that low, deadly tone, but his voice was a shade clearer than moments ago.

"Oh hell yeah," she muttered.

Cade didn't take his eyes off her. "Michael. Get out."

She heard the door slam and tried to yell *"Stop! Take me with you!"* but couldn't get the words out.

Cade pulled her closer. She gasped at the hot breath on her neck. Maybe she could break his hold if she tried, but arousal now competed with fear. She hesitated to move, so strong was the urge to wrap her arms around his shoulders, her legs around his waist.

"I could never hurt you. No more than I could Becca." She shivered at his voice in her ear. If she turned her head, she'd meet his mouth. His voice was definitely clearer now.

She couldn't hold still like this much longer, but he showed no sign of releasing her. He held her, rubbing his face against her shoulder, then her neck, then back to her shoulder.

"Cade, what are you...?" She gasped again as his lips brushed her shoulder. "Cade, are you *sniffing* me?"

He growled as he nuzzled her neck. "I like your smell. I hated taking a shower in Denver because I wanted to smell you. I wanted the other wolves to smell you on me."

Those words, in that voice, through those lips against her skin, left her breathless and shaking as a wave of hot, liquid desire washed through her.

A little moan escaped her. She slid her fingers through his hair as she'd ached to do, pressing his head deeper into her neck. Giving up, giving in, she wrapped her legs around his waist as she laid her cheek against his head. She didn't resist when he shifted his grip to her bottom. His hot hands warmed her through the thin cotton sundress and soaking wet panties.

"Thank you, Ally."

"For what?" Her voice trembled as badly as the rest of her.

"For stopping me. For saving me."

"Do you—" damn, even her voice trembled "—do you want me to go get Michael now?"

He laughed against her neck. "I don't need Michael," he rasped. "I need your throat."

She tensed. "What?"

"Your throat, Allison. Give it to me."

The ultimate expression of submission—offering your throat to a wolf. She shouldn't want to lose herself in him like this. She shouldn't want to submit. "Cade, I can't..."

He pulled her tighter against his body, his erection straining against his jeans, pressing against her core.

"Now, Ally," he groaned against her neck, and her body

responded before her mind could object.

She threw her head back, her hands still tangled in his silky hair. Then his mouth was at her neck, hot and wet and open, his tongue licking fire along her veins as he trailed greedy kisses to the hollow of her throat. He nipped at her collarbone and licked the sting away. His teeth and tongue glided gently across her jaw, and she shuddered at the rough caress of his beard against her skin. Her whole body ached for that caress, for every inch to burn beneath his kisses.

"Cade, kiss me," she implored.

He did, and any last resistance crumbled to ashes when she abandoned herself to the fire he'd started. His tongue demanded, she surrendered, and her arms tightened around his neck as he kissed her stupid. She couldn't think and didn't want to, didn't want anything but his mouth and his hands and his body on hers.

She whimpered in frustration when Cade broke the kiss, but he ran his tongue lightly across her bottom lip, gently sucking it. She sighed and put her hands on his face so he couldn't take his mouth away again. Scattering kisses across his cheek to his ear, she smiled in primal triumph when he shuddered, groaning her name.

She'd never been drunk on a man's touch. She'd never been with a man stronger than her, a man with whom she could shed all restraint.

Maybe she'd needed a wolf all along.

She moaned and wriggled at the sudden motion of his hips between her legs. Her sanity feebly attempted to assert itself as she realized they were headed for his bedroom.

This was a mistake. She had to stay out of his bed. Didn't she?

Reluctantly lifting her head, she cupped his face in her hands. His eyes were liquid green once more.

"Cade," she murmured, stroking his jaw and watching raptly as he turned his head to plant open-mouthed kisses in her palms. Then his lips returned to the hollow of her throat and she almost went under for good.

"Cade," she pleaded again. "Wait. We have to stop."

"Why?" he murmured against her throat. "What's the matter, baby?"

It wasn't just the *baby* that stopped her heart. It was the tenderness with which he said it. This wolf, so powerful and dominant, so hard with wanting her, so carelessly capable of taking her against her will, had told the truth. He wouldn't hurt her. Her body and her mind urged submission, but there was no threat of harm.

"I... I don't..." She forced him to look at her as she tried to speak coherently. "I don't do this. I don't... I've never gone to bed with a guy I barely know..." She trailed off, embarrassed.

That slow, rakish, arrogant smile, the one that weakened her knees and moistened her panties, reappeared as he said in a low growl, "It's okay. You'll never do it again."

She had no idea what to say to that, wasn't even sure what he meant. "Cade..."

"Allison," he said against her mouth, "take your hair down." Holding her effortlessly with one arm, he slipped his other hand inside her panties, his thumb skimming the smooth cleft of her butt while his palm squeezed her cheek. She moaned and bucked against him.

They were in his room. He kicked the door closed.

Sanity gave a shrug and called it a night.

She burned hot from the inside out, like someone had left a light on in her chest. She tugged the clip loose, letting her hair tumble into his face as she stared at him, dazed with wanting.

"You can drop it now," he murmured with a smile.

The clip fell from her hand.

"That's good. Now kick off your boots."

They clattered to the floor behind him.

Cade sat down on the four-poster bed, Ally in his lap. His hips shifted beneath hers as he kicked off his own boots.

Her hands slid up his arms, fingers slipping inside the sleeves of his T-shirt. He laughed softly when she batted his arms away so she could lift the shirt over his head. She pushed on his shoulders to make him lie down so she could explore his chest and his stomach, but he laughed again and didn't budge.

"No, sweetheart. Alphas on top."

He slipped one hand under her sundress and ran it all the way up her thigh 'til his thumb came to rest against the wet crotch of her panties, pressing against her clit.

"Cade..." she moaned.

He watched her face as he rubbed his thumb in a slow

circle. When she began to thrust against him and rake his shoulders with her nails, he smiled. "There we go. You smell so sweet. I knew you'd smell this sweet. Lose the dress, Ally."

She couldn't do it fast enough, yanking it over her head and tossing it aside. She gasped as cool air rushed over bare skin. He cupped a breast in his free hand, rubbing his thumb across the nipple before taking it between his teeth and tugging softly while his other hand tortured her through her panties.

She'd always been too shy to make noise during sex. Tonight she heard sounds she'd never heard before, and she realized they were coming from her.

Cade stood up and laid her on the bed, removing her panties in one smooth stroke before stepping back to regard her in silence. Fighting the lifelong urge to cover up, to hide from attention, she forced herself to lie still under his gaze.

He shucked off his jeans. When he was naked she stared at him in wonder, inhibitions forgotten.

She'd become used to that face. It filled her mind nearly all the time now. But she'd relied on her imagination for the rest of him, and it wasn't equal to the task. He was even more beautiful than she'd expected. She took in the broad shoulders and chest tapering down to hard, sharp obliques and long, powerful legs. Dark black hair on his chest narrowed to a fine, furry line running over the rippling muscles of his stomach, past his hips and down to his cock. Her mouth went dry at the sight of his erection.

She shivered at the thought of him, all of him, inside her. She'd never wanted anything so bad. She'd never thought she could *have* anything she wanted so bad.

And with that, just for a second, she was back in her right mind. Just for a second, she could think clearly. *What the hell am I doing here? He can't really want me. He won't want me when it's over, and I'll be sorry I ever...*

"Stop it, Ally. Stop thinking."

How did he know?

Instantly, he was on top of her, pushing her back to the bed and taking her mouth. Nothing could stop her mind like his feverish body, the weight of it pressing against every inch of her skin. All the times they'd touched before had been too brief, too light, leaving her aching. Now she could finally touch him as she'd longed to do.

But when she put her hands on his shoulders, he grabbed her wrists and pinned them to the pillow while his tongue invaded. She tried to pull free. He held her fast. She whimpered with frustration, amazed at how it turned her on to be subdued like this. She quit struggling and kissed him back with an ardor as new to her as the cries of passion and the taste for submission.

Cade broke off with a groan and rested his forehead against hers. Closing his eyes, he took a few long, deep breaths. He didn't release her hands.

"I want to touch you," she whispered.

"Later," he laughed shakily. "I'm barely hanging on here." He lowered his head to her breast, bathing her nipple with his tongue and then blowing on it. It got so tight and hard she whimpered, and when he took the nipple back into his mouth and sucked, the sensation echoed between her legs. His chest hair tickled her stomach as she wriggled beneath him.

"Cade... I can't stand it, I need..."

His breathing was as ragged as hers. "I'll give you what you need, sweetheart. I promise I will."

He released her hands, and when she reached for him he slid down her body, pressing her to the bed. His mouth never left her skin as he worked his way down. When he got to her stomach, the kisses and nibbles were little jolts of electricity, her hips jerking in response to every tiny shock. She loved the feel of his beard against her tender skin.

Then he stopped. He simply froze, his mouth hovering above her lower belly. His fingertips slowly skimmed her skin. And she froze as well, suddenly remembering something she'd never had to think about before, because she'd never slept with a werewolf.

They could see in the dark, of course. Even if he hadn't touched the ridges and the bumps, he could still see them—the reason she never wore two-piece swimsuits or cropped shirts, why she always made love with the lights out and showered alone. Why she let her lovers think she was repressed rather than let them see her naked in the light.

The only spot on her body that didn't heal itself.

Her stomach. Her scars.

She stiffened, fighting panic. Cade sensed her movement before she made it. He grabbed her wrists and pinned them above her head. He lay atop her, his hair spilling across her breasts. She strained against his hands, trying in vain to buck him off.

"Stop it," he whispered.

She tried again.

"Stop, baby—*stop*," he repeated, more forcefully this time. He pulled himself up and kissed her hard, then more gently, her lips and eyes and neck, all the while murmuring sweet words she couldn't understand but could feel, words to calm and soothe her the way she calmed and soothed panicked horses.

Soon enough, his lips and his voice and his hot, hard body were all she could focus on. The panic ebbed. Passion rushed back in. She quit struggling, parting her lips to his tongue. He cautiously released her wrists, holding himself up on his elbows and kissing her with open eyes. She didn't move for a moment, and they stared at one another. Slowly she brought her hands up to his face and kissed him as hard as he'd kissed her, twisting her fingers in his hair and crushing his mouth against hers. She bit his lip and sucked it gently before she plundered his hot mouth with her tongue, reveling in the taste of him.

He groaned, and his hands—strong, safe, saving hands—swept back down her body. Once more his kisses followed his hands, and she gasped and squirmed at the wet heat of his tongue licking her scars.

He chuckled softly as she thrust against his head, silently urging him lower. His hands were gentle but unyielding when he pulled her legs apart and held them still. She screamed and arched off the bed as his tongue dipped into her crease and then up over her clit. His silky hair grazed the inside of her thighs and she tried to press them together, but she couldn't. She wanted to buck her hips, but she couldn't. His hands held her so firmly she could barely move. It was the most delicious agony she'd ever experienced, and she desperately hoped no one in the house heard her screaming.

His tongue dipped in and out, licking and swirling, his hands still firmly clamping her hips to the bed as he pulled her lips apart. He very lightly stroked her clit with his tongue. She screamed again.

"Cade! Cade, I can't..." Her fingernails dug into his hands atop her thighs, and she pushed against him, straining to move as the tip of his tongue went 'round and 'round.

"Cade! I need..."

He knew what she needed. He sucked gently at first, then harder. When he took one hand off her thigh, she bucked wildly against his mouth.

Slowly he drove one hot finger into her, then another. He took his fingers out almost all the way and plunged them back in, deeper this time. Then he did it again, in and out, his tongue and his fingers pushing her ever further into madness.

"Cade," she moaned, loving the sound of his name in her mouth, "I'm coming, I'm coming so hard, I can't..."

His fingers didn't slow and his tongue didn't stop as the waves got bigger and her screams got louder. The last wave crested, taking her under, and she sobbed in ecstasy as the orgasm racked her body. She was still trembling when Cade began to kiss his way back up. She'd never liked tasting herself on a man before, but she didn't hesitate when his mouth claimed hers again.

He lifted himself up on his hands and watched her face as she parted her legs to him. His bright green eyes glittered in the dark. She sucked in her breath at his expression—hungry, possessive, wild. She cried out as he entered her, at the length and the size of him.

He startled her by shifting back on his knees and grasping her hips, pulling her butt off the bed. He began to move with hard, smooth strokes, not taking his eyes from her face. She gasped out loud, astonished at the sensations he was creating in her. She'd never known simple intercourse could feel like this.

"Harder," she gasped.

He didn't break his rhythm as he grunted, "I can't, I don't want to hurt you."

Panting between the words as he drove into her, she whispered, "I'm stronger than you think. Please."

"No, I won't, you don't know..."

"Cade," she said sharply, in a voice she didn't recognize as hers, "as hard as you can, *now*, and don't stop 'til you come."

A look of amazement flitted across his face, and then he groaned. He closed his eyes, threw his head back and began to thrust harder. She grabbed the headboard and watched him, enrapt at the wild beauty of his expression and the raw power of his body. He'd been so deliberate while driving her into a frenzy. Now he was loosed, uncontrolled and uncontrollable. *She* had done this to him. He had lost himself in *her*. Nothing had ever set her ablaze like that did.

"Ally. God, Allison, what've you..." Through half-closed eyes she watched him approach his climax. He slipped his thumb into her mouth. She bit, and she licked, and she whimpered when he withdrew it, but then he put his thumb to her clit and stroked once. She tumbled over the edge in one long, shattering release.

He took a last, deep thrust and held himself inside her, shuddering as he came, and then they collapsed, insensible. Neither could breathe, so neither spoke.

A shaft of moonlight, the sole illumination in the otherwise pitch black room, sliced across the middle of the bed, bathing Cade's dark head and sleek torso in pale silver light. Her fingers trailed across the tattoo on his right biceps—crossed rifles over a laurel wreath—before drifting back into the disheveled curls she couldn't stop touching.

It scared her, how much she relished laying there safe and drowsy beneath his warmth, listening to him breathe, stroking his hair as the aftershocks subsided. He kissed her palm as she ran it over his cheek. Life had assumed an air of unreality ever since she arrived at the ranch, but nothing seemed as unreal as this moment, lying in the moonlight beneath this beautiful werewolf with his head on her stomach and his hand caressing her thigh.

She wasn't sure he'd want her to stay all night. She wasn't sure they'd do this again, and she wasn't sure they should've done it at all.

She was pretty sure she couldn't ask for the nanny job now.

"How often do you throw yourself in front of enraged wolves?" His voice had regained its normal mellow drawl. He sounded tired and content.

"Just twice so far." Her hand paused in his hair. "This time was a lot better."

She felt him smile against her skin. "Smartass." He laid his palm against her scars. "What did he do to you, baby?"

*He killed me.* "After I shot and missed, he started changing. Seth showed up, and I thought he'd get Guy before... But then

Guy charged me. I kicked him, but I couldn't stop him, and... His claws were so sharp, I didn't realize he'd cut me at first."

He was quiet for a minute. "Those were deep cuts."

"Yes."

"Ally..." he said softly, "Ally, y'all couldn't just jump in the truck and run. You were bleeding, you must've passed out, how..."

"Yeah, I was out of it. Seth threw me in the truck and got me to a doctor, a werewolf. While he fixed me up, Seth went back and got Dylan. The doctor doped me up, told Seth to keep my bandages clean, and we were gone. We stayed at a motel in Beaumont 'til I could walk again."

Afraid to embellish any more, she stopped. She'd spent thirteen years lying to everyone about everything that had happened. Lying had never bothered her. With Cade, she felt ashamed.

She opened her eyes. He still watched her—trying to determine if he believed her, she imagined, or if he needed to question her further.

"Are you high Fae?" he asked.

She gave a small shout of laughter. "*What?*"

"You heard me," he said evenly.

She grinned at him. "You like to catch people off-guard, don't you? It's one of the power games you play."

He cocked an eyebrow but didn't return the grin. "Power is never a game. And answer the question, Allison." The mild tone didn't disguise his steely seriousness.

She quit laughing. "I'm not Fae."

"Are you sure?"

"Positive. If I have any Fae, it isn't much. Why?" Why would he care if she were Fae?

His eyes narrowed and he looked away, his hand still idly stroking her stomach. "Mary Ann always swore she was high Fae. Said she had a lot of Fae blood, and it came from Sarah Jane."

How intriguing. "Sarah Jane's got Fae blood? Huh. I'd think a rich Southern lady wouldn't want anyone to know about that."

"Oh, she wouldn't. It'll still keep you out of the best clubs. But I always believed it. Mary Ann's gorgeous and crazy as hell." The high Fae looked human and tended to be beautiful, creative and nuts. It was no accident that most actors and artists were largely Fae. "That's why I figured she couldn't get pregnant." He laughed softly and started tracing patterns on her stomach again.

"Were you upset when she did?" She'd been curious about Becca's mother, and she'd use anything to get him off the subject of her own weirdness.

"At first, yeah. I thought she'd pretended so I wouldn't worry about birth control. But she went hysterical, swore up and down she was really Fae. She never quit claiming it, even though it'd be impossible if she was having my kid."

"There's no way Becca isn't your daughter."

He laughed. "I couldn't be sure of it at the time. I figured she had other lovers, but she swore I was the father. And then a DNA test proved it."

"How'd you get involved with her in the first place?"

He looked a little embarrassed. "We'd had a fling when I was in my thirties. I ran into her again about the time I found out Carson was dead." He cleared his throat and looked away. "I hadn't seen him in years. By the time the investigator I'd hired traced him to New Orleans, he'd been dead a couple of months. I didn't take it well. I wanted a little self-destruction, and Mary Ann's good at that."

"You don't seem like the self-destructive type."

"I'm not. I had to work at it. Anyway. I went to Savannah to tell the family, and we got started again. It was all drama, all the time. Then she turned up pregnant, and the day she hit five months, she got an amnio. She wanted to know if it was a boy or a girl."

"Oh shit," she murmured. "You think she got pregnant hoping she'd have a wolf?"

"Maybe. Or once she found out, she just hoped it'd be a boy. She flipped out when they told her it was a girl. She wanted an abortion." He frowned at the memory.

The idea of no Becca in the world made her want to weep.

"What did you do?" she whispered.

His bitter, brittle smile almost frightened her. "I may have threatened to kill her. Or something. I don't remember. I'm pro-choice, as long as it's not my kid we're talking about, and I couldn't be sure it wasn't my kid. I promised her a lot of money if she'd take care of herself and have the baby. Three weeks after Becca was born, Mary Ann dumped her on Sarah Jane and ran off to New York. I decided I didn't want to share. I gave her a lot more money and she signed away her rights."

"Wow. That's kind of...you basically bought her baby."

He cocked an eyebrow. "Rebecca was my baby too, and Mary Ann didn't have to take the money. I knew she would. Sarah Jane's always blamed me for it, but she knows better."

"Did you ever think about marrying her?"

"No. She wanted to get married. I said no way."

"Why? I mean, I get that you didn't love her, but maybe for the baby..."

"No," he said flatly, looking straight at her. "I swore a long time ago I'd only marry my mate. If I didn't find a mate, I'd never marry, and if I did find a mate...I'd never let her get away."

She hoped he couldn't tell he'd just punched her in the heart. Still stroking his hair, she gazed out the window as she fought back tears.

*I can't stay here.*

She didn't know how long he went on talking, unaware that he'd opened a vein. Eventually, though, she realized he'd asked her something and was waiting for a reply. "I'm sorry, Cade," she said as normally as she could. "I drifted there for a second. What'd you say?"

"How many wolves have you slept with?"

*What the hell?* "Counting you? One."

"Really. You ever date a wolf?"

"No." He seemed to expect her to say more. "I already have three at home. Four wolves would feel like a pack, you know?"

"But you've had boyfriends."

"A couple. Nothing that lasted." What difference did any of this make?

"Why?"

"Why what?"

"Why nothing that lasted?"

"Because I lived with two adult wolves and I was raising a third. When guys find out I'm a den mother, they scram. I'm not normal." She didn't care that she sounded irritable and bitter. It was how she felt.

She waited for him to say something. He just lay there, propped up on one arm with the other slung carelessly across her belly, staring at her. For one ludicrous moment she imagined him looking straight into her head and seeing all the weirdness and all the pain. She felt truly naked.

"I need to get up."

"Why?" he asked, his voice quiet and gentle.

"I have to go to the bathroom." *And then get dressed and sneak upstairs without anyone seeing me.* She couldn't hear a thing outside the room, so she had no idea who was in the house.

"All right."

He rolled off to let her up.

She took a long time in the spacious bathroom—sitting, peeing, thinking, delaying. Maybe if she stayed in here long enough he'd fall sleep? Get bored and go find something else to do?

But when she came out of the bathroom, he was sitting up in bed, holding her dress. Like he knew she was going to run.

"Come back to bed, Ally." His gentle tone just made it worse.

"Cade, I need to go."

"No, you don't. Look. I never question the women I sleep with— I'm never that interested. I'm interested in you. You don't want to talk about men, I won't ask. Come back. I need to hear about Becca, anyway." He paused. "Please."

A nice touch, that *please*. It still didn't feel like a request, but he'd made the effort. She didn't want to leave, of course, not really. Nothing sounded better right now than climbing back into bed with him, curling into his warmth and strength. She so rarely shared a bed with someone else.

"Okay. I'll get back in bed. But I want you to hold me."

God have mercy, she was possessed. Naked or not, she had to bolt. Now.

He grinned so tenderly her heart broke all over again.

"You're not being a smartass right now, are you?"

She shook her head, certain he could see her blushing in the dark.

"I never know what the hell you'll say next."

"Neither do I," she whispered.

His grin widened.

"Holding you is all I want to do right now, Ally. Get over here."

So she climbed into bed and he pulled her hard against him.

"Wolves are made to cuddle. But—wait. Wait." He rested his chin on her shoulder. "Women always want to talk about feelings when they cuddle. I don't do feelings. Are you about to do feelings?"

Her face still burned, but she closed her eyes and snuggled back against him. "I can hurt you. I may not look like it, but I can mess you up."

He settled back down behind her, smiling into her neck. "I think you already did, ma'am. Now tell me about Sarah Jane and Becca."

She recounted the past two days—the fun she'd had with Becca, her own impressions of Sarah Jane.

"You got her hair cut?"

"Well, she looked like a little troll doll."

He laughed again, his beard rubbing against her bare skin, his arm tight around her. This was nice. This was unbearably nice.

"Thank you," he said quietly. "For stepping up, for helping Michael. For helping me."

"I didn't mind. I enjoyed it. I took a bunch of Michael's money at a poker game."

He chuckled. "I need to hear about that."

So she told him.

She hadn't decided how, or whether, to tell him about Sarah Jane and Sindri, or Sarah Jane and Dec. It might sound like stirring up trouble. Or sucking up for a job. After she'd just slept with him.

This was getting complicated.

She was getting sleepy.

"Cade."

"Hmm."

"You don't think Sarah Jane would pack up in the middle of the night and leave with Becca, do you?"

"Won't happen. Michael's got wolves watching her right now."

She shivered when he gently nipped at her shoulder and ran his tongue up the back of her neck. "When did you tell him to do that?"

"Didn't need to. He'll know. That's why he's my second."

"I thought you were furious at him for not calling you."

"I was." Cade went still for a moment. "I went a little *loco* there. I shouldn't have lost it, but Michael handled it the right way."

"Have you told him that?"

"Don't need to. He knows. That's why he's my second." His tongue moved to her ear.

"Do Pack Alphas apologize?"

He barked a laugh. "Not to their seconds, no."

"But what—"

"Shh. Not now—we can talk more tomorrow."

He pulled the sheet up to her breasts and tucked it beneath her. She felt him relax against her back, his arm under her head, his other hand making lazy circles on her hip.

As she drifted off to sleep, he murmured, "Tomorrow we talk, baby. Tomorrow we talk about you."

# Chapter Fifteen

Ally awoke with a start. Her internal clock, unfailingly accurate since her second birth, told her the sun would rise soon. Cade had flipped over onto his back, one arm on the pillow above his head, the other flung across his stomach. She slipped out of bed.

As she lingered to gaze at him, she knew she'd be replaying last night in her mind for years to come, but she couldn't face more questions. Emotionally spent, psychologically raw, she needed an escape plan.

She pulled on her panties and sundress, then cautiously opened the door and peeked out into the living room. She neither heard nor smelled anyone. Racing up to her room, she remembered at the last moment not to let the door slam behind her.

Her cell phone was beeping to indicate a voicemail message. Tomas had called last night. She needed a shower, food and coffee before she could tackle that.

Once she'd taken a long, hot shower it was just past sunrise. She'd thought she might be up before anyone else in the house, but Sindri smiled gently when she walked into the kitchen.

"Good morning. You are well?" he asked.

"Good morning. Yes, thank you."

He poured her a cup of coffee and resumed fussing about the kitchen. She watched him as she sipped her coffee. They'd never talked much, but he seemed to like her.

"How is Cade?" he asked her.

"I'm sorry?"

"Cade came home last night. You were with him. He is

well?"

*Great.* Who else knew?

"Um, Cade's all right. He was— He was upset, at first, about Sarah Jane, but once he calmed down he was better. He's still asleep."

"Good." Sindri nodded firmly. "It is good that Sarah Jane is here. We need her. And Cade needs you. This is well."

*No, this is weird.*

Dec and Sarah Jane appeared. Sindri placed two more coffee cups and a plate of fresh biscuits on the table.

"Good morning, darlin'." Dec kissed Ally on the head. "Did you sleep well?"

The traitorous burning in her cheeks made her put her head down.

"I know you know," she muttered into her coffee cup.

Dec sat down. She heard him pour two cups of coffee. Sarah Jane reached over and put a hand on Ally's arm. "Honey, are you okay?"

Oh God. What did Sarah Jane think of daddy-screwing nannies? How many others would know about this?

"What did you hear?" she asked quietly, head still bent over her cup.

"Nothing," Dec replied. She could feel six eyes on her. "Ally," he said, as gently as she'd ever heard him, "whatever happened last night is no one's business but yours and the Alpha's. Trust me, darlin', it's not like you think it is. There's nothing for you to be ashamed of."

She slumped a little. "I guess everyone has to be polite to the Alpha's female guests."

No one replied. She peeked up to see Dec looking at Sindri, and Sindri looking confused.

"Cade does not have female guests," Sindri said.

"What? You mean— Women don't spend the night here?"

"No. Never. You are different. You are special." He smiled in his usual mysteriously serene manner.

Dec said, "Ally, you need to know—"

"I forgot something in my room." Her stomach churned. "I'm sorry, I just don't feel like talking to anyone right now."

Then, coward that she was, she fled.

Cade drifted in twilight sleep, vaguely aware of a small animal burrowing in the ground beside him amid a rustle of leaves, snorts and giggles.

Not the ground—his bed. Not leaves—sheets. And giggles?

Eyes closed, he patted the sheet beside him. He felt a small, warm, wiggly lump—round on the top, skinny in the middle, then round, then skinny. Shorter than Ally, and Ally never giggled like this. He smiled despite being angry—very angry—at his mysterious mate for running away before he woke up.

He gave the top lump a squeeze.

"Ow! Daddy, that's my head!" The indignation in Becca's voice made him laugh.

He rolled over with a big Daddy growl. She responded with an elated shriek. He dragged her over on top of him, making munching noises as he played "eat the Becca" before hauling her across him and planting her on the floor beside the bed. She began to bounce.

"I sure missed you, Baby Girl. Have you had breakfast?"

"No. Nana and me just got up. Sindri's cooking breakfast."

"Nana?"

"My Gramma. She likes me a lot."

"I see. Where is she now?"

"In the kitchen with Sindri and Uncle Dec."

*Uncle Dec? Oh hell, no.* "Do you know where Ally is?"

"I think she's in the kitchen too. Ally's my nanny now. We went to town and got my hair cut. Everyone told me I was pretty."

"You are pretty. Go get some breakfast. I'll be there as soon as I shower and dress."

But once Becca was gone, instead of getting up to shower, he lay in bed thinking about his strange, absent mate.

Making love to Ally last night wasn't the smartest thing he'd ever done. Claiming your mate without telling her she was, in fact, your mate might strike some people—for instance, your mate—as arrogant. Cade had once heard an old alpha, a mated wolf, compare the difference between the mate bond prior to claiming and after claiming as the difference between cement and fusion. In other words, when the mate bond claimed you,

you were fucked. Once you'd claimed your mate, you were even more fucked.

The mate bond didn't tie the woman to the wolf as it did the wolf to the woman, and the woman could always choose to walk away.

But Ally wouldn't do that, he thought as he smiled to himself. She wanted him as much as he wanted her. Last night had been very consensual, even if he hadn't been totally up front about everything.

And why would she want to leave, anyway? He was a rich Pack Alpha, he could offer her a life she'd never been able to have, and she could stay with Dylan and Seth. Sure, she was bossy as hell, and it would take her a while to get used to not being in charge. But she wanted him.

Smiling to himself, he got up to shower and then go look for his mate.

His first stop was the kitchen.

"Good morning, Alpha."

Cade ignored the Irishwolf. "Becca, are you done with breakfast?"

"Yes."

"Good. Go play in your room. And Mr. MacSorley is not your uncle. You'll call him Mr. MacSorley."

"Can Nana come with—?"

"Nana's going to talk with me. Go."

Becca paused to kiss Sarah Jane, who hugged her tightly. "Promise you'll remember what we talked about, all right?"

Becca nodded and scampered out. MacSorley rose to follow her.

"MacSorley. Wait. Do you know where Ally is?"

The Irishwolf paused in the doorway. "No, I don't. She left in a hurry a while ago."

Cade frowned. "Why?"

MacSorley leaned in the doorway and regarded him levelly. "She was embarrassed. I tried to explain she needn't be, but Ally's rather...shy in matters like this. Good Catholic girl, y'know. And I think everything that's happened recently has frazzled her a bit." He paused. "I'm not sure how to say this, but—"

"Then don't. It'll just piss me off, anyway."

"Aye," MacSorley murmured, eyes fixed on the floor. Somehow he managed to be vaguely insolent even while submitting. Cade recalled something from last night, something he'd forgotten as soon as he saw Ally.

"Why'd you get in front of me last night?"

The other wolf shrugged, still looking at the ground. "I'm not sure. Instinct, I guess."

"Since when the hell does a beta's instinct put him in front of an alpha on the rampage?"

"I think I was trying to protect Ally. Or maybe Sarah Jane. I'm not sure, to tell you the truth." He sounded sincere this time.

"You are the strangest wolf I've ever seen in my life, and I don't like you."

Sarah Jane gasped.

"Yeah. Yeah, I can believe that. It's understandable."

Cade heard sadness in MacSorley's words. He hadn't expected to wound the Irishwolf. It irritated him. "Well. If you see Ally, tell her I want to talk to her."

MacSorley left.

"Cade, maybe I should talk to Allison, I could—"

He spun around to face Sarah Jane. "What the hell are you doing here?"

Her hands trembled as they gripped the back of a chair. The scent of her fear filled the kitchen, but she didn't flee. She stared hard at a spot somewhere above his head as she stuck out her jaw and said tightly, "I was in the area and I wanted to see my grandbaby. I didn't call until I got here because I thought you'd say no."

"I can't imagine why I'd do that, Sarah Jane. Can you?"

She closed her eyes. "I've said things in the past, Cade. Thoughtless things. I made stupid, reckless threats because I was angry and scared and unhappy about Mary Ann." She opened her eyes and tried to look him in the face. "I don't want to take Rebecca away from you. That's not why I'm here. I swear."

She seemed sincere, but he couldn't sense whether she told the truth or not. What had become of his mystical powers of discernment in the last week? Had his new mate shorted out his mojo? He stared at Sarah Jane for a minute, then shook his head to clear it. He was a civilized wolf. He didn't threaten old women.

"Sit," he ordered.

She sat while he got himself coffee, pouring more into her cup as well. They drank in silence across the table from each other.

The silence got uncomfortable.

"How's Mary Ann?"

"No idea. I haven't heard from her in two years. I assume she's still in California."

"I see."

"It's my fault."

He raised an eyebrow. "Why? Did y'all have a fight?" Sarah Jane normally gave Mary Ann anything she asked for.

"No, I mean the whole thing. All of it." She made a vague sweeping gesture with her hand. "Mary Ann is my fault. I spoiled her. I excused her for everything she ever did because her daddy died and I never wanted her to suffer anything again. That's no way to raise a human being."

"You're right," he agreed, "it's not. But at some point she became responsible for herself. You can't take the blame for everything."

"It's one thing to say that. It's harder to believe it." She sighed and took a long sip of coffee before continuing. "Well, I decided I want my granddaughter to know who I am, and I calculated that if I just showed up and begged you to let me see her, your innate nobility of spirit would assert itself and you'd take pity on me."

He nearly choked on his coffee trying not to laugh. "Fuck." He knew she hated the word. "Sarah Jane, I could've killed you last night."

"I didn't think you would. You're too much like your father."

"Don't try to flatter me."

"I'm not. Declan worried how'd you'd react, but I thought if you came home enraged, it would be best if Rebecca weren't here."

He'd never admit she'd made the right decision. "Declan, is

it? You two look pretty comfortable with each other."

"He's charming. I can't imagine what would make you dislike him so."

"I'm not getting into it right now."

"All right. Let's talk about Rebecca and Allison."

"You first."

"Well, Rebecca is perfect. But she needs to be around children and women."

"I know that. And Allison?"

"And Allison is no more the nanny than I am." Before he could respond, she held up both hands and said gently, "I'm not criticizing. I know Michael was worried about what I would think, so he got rid of the wolves and Allison volunteered to play Mary Poppins."

"We've had some nanny trouble lately."

"I've heard. Cade, if I thought you weren't taking care of Rebecca, or she was the least bit unsafe, a pack of werewolves couldn't stop me taking her. But I'm not going to interfere when I see how happy and loved she is. And she certainly seems to like Allison." Leaning across the table, she smiled at him the way an older woman smiled at a male who'd been leashed and brought to heel. "When are you going to tell her you claimed her?"

He stared at her. "Who told you she's my mate?" Maybe he needed to rip some fur off Michael after all.

"No one had to tell me, Cade. I can see it, just like I saw it when your father brought Eirny home from Scotland. You're bonded, pup."

"If you can tell that from seeing me for ten minutes, maybe Mary Ann was right about the Fae blood. Don't tell the ladies in the Junior League. And don't call me pup."

She laughed and leaned back. "I've been around a lot longer than you. You have no idea what I pick up on." Suddenly, she looked pensive. "Cade, is everything all right?"

He frowned. "In what sense?"

"I'm not even sure. I'm not talking about Allison, or the trouble you're having with the other packs."

"And what do you know about that?"

She waved the question off. "I just mean, has anything unusual, or unusually bad, happened?"

"One of my wolves attempted suicide this week. That's very bad."

"No, that's not what I mean. I mean something closer to you, something about you or Becca? Maybe Dylan..." She played with the rings on her hands as she talked, her brows knit in worry. A strange anxiety had crept into her tone.

"No. The packs, the nannies and Aaron. That's it. Why?"

"It's nothing. I think I'm just turning into a superstitious old woman. Forget I brought it up." She beamed at him. "Oh, and that Dylan. What a beautiful boy! He looks just like you and Carson at that age. Allison must be a remarkable girl to have raised a kid like that."

He didn't attempt to hide his smile this time, secretly glad for the opportunity to talk about Ally. "Yeah, yeah I think she is. She's definitely remarkable. I'm just not sure how. There's a lot about her I haven't figured out yet. In fact," he said, draining his cup, "that's what I'm about to do now. I need to have a chat with Ally."

"I think I'll take Rebecca into to town with me, if that's okay with you?"

"You'd better bring her back."

"That's not funny."

"I'm not joking."

"Do you honestly think I would kidnap my own—bah." She broke off with an exasperated wave of her hand. "Never mind. I'm not about to start a fight at this point."

"Wise decision."

On her way out, she paused at his chair and placed a hand on his shoulder. "Thanks for letting me stay."

He looked up at her with a half smile. "I didn't say you could stay. I'm just not kicking you out right now."

She startled him by laying a hand against his cheek as she looked at him almost fondly. "All right, then. I'll be here to help as long as you let me."

"I don't need your help, Sarah Jane."

"I hope you're right, Cade. I really do."


He smelled Ally's lavender scent as soon as he walked out of the kitchen. It came from her room. On the way up the stairs, he called out to Michael to get the wolves back. They were his pack and this was their home.

He knocked on Ally's door. "It's me. Can I come in?"

A pause.

"Just a minute."

He heard some scraping and bumping, and she opened the door.

His heart started tripping to a happy staccato when he saw her there in bare feet, faded jeans and a soft yellow tank top. She looked drawn and tired, with heavy eyelids and dark circles under her eyes. He should pick her up and carry her back downstairs to bed. He stepped forward, intending to kiss her, but she backed up to open the door wider, so he walked in past her.

She stood with one hand on the doorknob, the other stuffed in her pocket, not looking directly at him. MacSorley was right. She was uncomfortable about last night. That touched him, arousing his protective instinct.

He had to tell her he'd claimed her.

"Hi," she said.

"Hi yourself. Why'd you disappear?"

"I woke up early, and I couldn't go back to sleep, so I thought I'd just get up." She tucked her hair behind her ear as she glanced from the bed, to the carpet, to him, and back to the bed.

"Why don't you come downstairs with me, and..." Something in the closet caught his eye. Or, rather, something didn't catch his eye, because he saw nothing there. He knew she'd hung some clothes up, but now the closet was empty. He turned back to Ally, who wouldn't meet his gaze.

He walked into the bathroom. The counter was bare. When he walked back into the room, he spied the corner of a suitcase sticking out from under the bed. He reached down to pull it out.

It was full.

He dropped the case and stared at her. "What do you think you're doing?"

She flinched and crossed her arms tightly, looking down as she whispered, "I think I need to— To just..."

"To just what? What, Ally? What do you think you need to do?"

He advanced on her. She retreated until her back hit the bedroom wall, hugging herself with her eyes downcast and her hair obscuring her face. He didn't care if he frightened her. He wanted to yell at her, to shake her 'til her teeth rattled, to lock her in that goddamned closet 'til he could figure out what to do with her.

"I think I need to leave."

He heard it, but he couldn't quite believe it.

"Why?" he snarled.

No response.

"Why?" he roared, and she shrank back, covering her face with her hands. A part of him was ashamed of frightening her like this. But a bigger part, the bonded wolf with a mate he couldn't trust part, didn't care.

She'd made him feel like a fool.

He placed his hands against the wall, trapping her between his arms. Leaning in until their bodies almost touched, he stared at the top of her head and willed her to look up at him.

"How did you plan on leaving, Allison?"

"The Cherokee," she whispered, close to tears.

"It's yours?"

"No, Seth's."

And here came the tears. She'd get no comfort from him, not this time.

"Okay." He stalked out of the room. Leaning over the railing, he called for Seth and waited in the hallway while Ally stayed in her room, quietly sobbing.

She was a better actress than Mary Ann, he'd give her that. She'd tried to slink away without a word to him and when he caught her, she manufactured tears. A wolf's mate could manipulate him six ways from Sunday and he might never know it, so strong was the bond. Ally had a gift for manipulation. He'd be a fool if he gave her the chance to use it again.

Seth came jogging up the stairs, slowing when he saw the expression on Cade's face.

Her eyes widened when she saw Seth. "Why did you—?"

Cade cut her off, holding out his hand to Seth. "Give me your car keys."

The beta, ashen-faced, looked from Cade to Ally. "What?"

"Your keys. Give them to me."

For a minute he thought Seth would ask him for a reason, but Guidry was smarter than that. He handed the keys over silently, casting a worried sideways glance at Ally, who stared at Cade with mounting sullen anger.

"You can't make him do that," she said through gritted teeth.

Cade smiled grimly. "I just did, sweetheart. My wolf does what I—"

"*Your* wolf?" She looked stricken.

"My wolf," he replied with satisfaction. "He's in my pack now, and he'll do what I tell him."

His resolve almost faltered at the agony that crossed her face, an expression bleaker and sadder than the one she'd worn the night Seth confessed to killing Guy.

But as soon as he saw it, the look disappeared, replaced by one of glowering fury. She balled her fists at her sides as her chest heaved in short, shallow bursts. This petite female smelled deadly furious. If she were a wolf, he'd be in defensive posture by now, expecting an imminent attack.

"Cade, for God's sake, what's going on?"

Another spasm of pain crossed Ally's face at Seth's plaintive question, but then the anger returned.

"Why don't you ask Allison?"

Seth turned to her. "Ally?"

She kept her gaze on Cade as she said with exaggerated calm, "I think it's time I left, sweetie. I was going to borrow the Cherokee to get to town, but it looks like Cade objects."

She smiled at him then, a cold, hostile grin, the kind he saw more frequently on males than females, a smile that challenged and defied without a trace of tears or hurt or weakness. A fuck you smile, from one alpha to another.

"Where are you going?" Seth whispered.

"Home first. Then I'll figure something out."

Seth was shocked. "What about Lind?"

"Tomas called. No one's seen Jakob in a week."

"But he might—"

"Oh fuck no, we're not doing this again. Seth," he barked, and the beta's attention snapped back to him, "who's Tomas and who's Lind?"

He could see that Seth wanted desperately to look over at Ally, but his Alpha's command was too strong. He submitted, lowering his head. "Tomas is a friend of ours, a cop. Jakob Lind's a guy who— A guy Ally went out with for a while. He turned out to be a head case—"

"Went out with?" Cade asked sharply as he stared at Ally. "How long?"

She shrugged as Seth replied, "Not long. Couple of months."

"Were they lovers?"

Ally rolled her eyes.

"No," Seth said.

"How do you know?"

"I always know who she sleeps with." The wolf sounded more miserable by the minute.

"What's he got to do with Ally going back to Houston?"

"Well, see, she, um..."

"She what?" Cade barked.

"I beat the crap out of him."

She wasn't hunched up and shaking any longer. She stood with her hands on her hips, watching Cade and Seth's exchange with something like amusement. He'd never seen a female so cocky while so pissed off.

"Why'd you beat him up?" he asked, intrigued.

"I broke up with Jakob because he seemed too interested in Dylan. His ego couldn't handle it. He showed up at the stables one night and tried to attack me."

Rage clouded his vision at the thought of someone harming his mate. "What happened?" he ground out.

"I threw him across the stable. Then I hurt him."

"You *what?*"

She shrugged again. "He shouldn't have tried to jump me when I was on my period. I beat him up a little too much, and it would've been hard to explain since the scumbag is twice my size, so I dumped him in the parking lot of a nasty wolf dive. Then I thought maybe I should get out of town for a while in case he talked about it."

"So you came up here."

"I wanted to go somewhere by myself, but—"

"I didn't want her to," said Seth, still in submission to

Cade. "We'd talked about bringing Dylan up here, and it seemed like a good time to do it."

"Pretty goddamned convenient for Ally, wasn't it?" Cade said quietly. "Good thing you had the pup for an excuse to leave town."

Ally flinched as if he'd slapped her. Then her eyes narrowed. Her lips curled in a sneer, drawing out the words with contempt. "Fuck you. Seth, I'll leave the keys at the bus—"

"You're not going anywhere."

"Excuse me?"

"I'm keeping the keys to the Cherokee, and you're sure as hell not taking any of our vehicles."

"You can't keep me here!"

"I'm the Alpha, sweetheart. I can do anything I want."

"What, you're going to post a wolf outside my door?"

"Oh, you don't have to stay in the house. It's thirty miles to town. I think it'd take you a while to walk it."

She cocked her head. "An hour if I jogged, thirty minutes at a flat run. Of course, that's without the luggage. If I had to carry suitcases..."

He grunted in disgust. "On second thought, smartass, you can stay in the fucking house."

"Hell I will."

"We'll talk later."

"No. We won't."

"Seth, go. Remember, Allison—" he couldn't help grinning at her fury "—inside the house. If you try to leave you'll only embarrass yourself."

He almost imagined he heard a low growl. As he reached the bottom of the stairs, she slammed the door so hard the floor vibrated. A picture fell off the wall.

*Where'd she get that kind of strength?*

Michael had heard it all.

"Cade. You can't hold her here. That's false imprisonment. What if she calls the cops?"

He sighed. "I'm not gonna keep her locked up for long, Michael. Just...for a while."

"Well...I think it's a bad idea. But we've got another problem."

"Great. I need another problem."

"I just got off the phone with Trey. He was at the hospital with Roman and Shawn. Rufus Stapkis showed up."

"What happened?" Cade barked.

"Shawn was alone in the room. Rufus attacked him—"

"*What?*"

"Shawn's fine. The guys heard him yell. Hospital security showed up, ten kinds of hell broke loose. Stapkis got away and no one knows where he is now."

"Fucking hell."

They sat down in his office.

"What do we do?" Michael asked.

"Was he alone?"

"Yeah, I think so. No sign of any strange wolves."

"Hmm. You said the Seattle pack acts spooked, right?"

"Yeah. There's been talk about him being *loco*, and we know they don't know where he is."

"So. There's no reason to assume we've got a pack war brewing. This could be one crazy old Alpha acting alone."

"Probably."

"Good. Call Seattle. If anyone hears from Rufus, he needs to know if I see him, he's mine."

Cade wouldn't have to challenge at this point. His unprovoked attack on one of Cade's wolves left Stapkis without any rights, especially since he'd entered Rocky Mountain's territory without notice or permission.

"I want every wolf in the state on the lookout for him. He knows we'll be after him now. He's not entitled to protocol, so he's got no reason to behave with honor."

"You going up to Colorado Springs?"

"Shit. I should." His mate or his enemy? Take care of the problem at home, or the problem roaming around somewhere in the vicinity of the whole fucking state?

"How's Aaron?" He should've asked before now.

"No change. They're not calling it a vegetative state yet, but he's still out."

Cade ran his hands through his hair and tugged hard. If wolves could go bald, this week would do it. "All right. Stapkis might show up, so I'm staying here. I want you to go to Colorado Springs. Talk to the guys, ask around, start putting out the word."

"Leaving now."

"Good."

Cade had heard his wolves outside. Everyone had returned from exile. He stretched in his chair and closed his eyes.

He didn't often find himself without a clue how to handle a situation. He could handle Rufus Stapkis. He could handle Sarah Jane and his daughter's need for companionship. Apparently, though, he couldn't handle his mate.

He couldn't even tell her she *was* his mate. He'd thought after last night she'd be all soft and gooey, radiant with, if not love, at least affection for him. Instead, he hesitated to turn his back on her.

Worst of all, underneath his anger still lay the primal urge to cherish and protect her. He couldn't forget the pain in her eyes when Seth submitted to him, or the head-swimming rage he'd felt when he heard about Jakob Lind. Maybe he should try to talk to her...

*Hell no.* Let her stew.

So here she sat, under house arrest and the paw of an arrogant, control freak alpha asshole who was happy to screw her, needed to dominate her, and had no long-term interest in her.

She regretted slamming the door. Losing her temper had put her on the path to Colorado in the first place. For thirteen years she'd maintained control of her strange nature. That control had slipped when Lind attacked her. Since she'd arrived here—since she'd met Cade—it was disintegrating bit by bit, and she didn't know how to stop it.

She lay flat on her back, trembling, clenching and unclenching her fists. Counting to five hundred, she took long, deep breaths and waited for the ache in her chest to subside, the knot in her throat to ease. She was as livid as she'd ever been, but just beneath the fury lay stark terror and more heartbreak. Everything she'd feared would happen had happened.

She'd lost Seth.

She didn't blame her cousin for submitting to a powerful Alpha. Seth needed a pack. If he hadn't felt he had to stay with her and Dylan, he'd probably have settled down with a woman by now.

No, she didn't blame Seth for submitting. She blamed Cade for making him. He'd done it on purpose—to hurt her, to teach her a lesson, just to prove he could.

"Remember, Allison," she said out loud in a perfect imitation of Dylan's *nyah-nyah* tone, "inside the house."

Asshole alphas.

Seth belonged to Cade now, and Dylan probably did too, and it hurt. It hurt so bad she could barely breathe.

But if Cade walked in the room in the next five minutes and tried to kiss her, she'd let him.

She hated herself for not hating him.

She sat up. Maybe she couldn't think clearly enough to figure out her next move right now, but that didn't mean she would just sit here like a good little prisoner. She didn't need a door to escape.

After donning shorts and running shoes, she opened the bedroom window, which faced the back of the house. There was no one out there right now. It looked about thirty feet to the ground, forty at the most—nothing to a wolf or a woman with wolfish abilities.

At the very least she'd burn off some rage. Best case scenario, Cade would come looking for her and have a heart attack when he saw her gone. Grinning as she imagined his reaction, she jumped.

"You cannot treat your mate like this. It is shameful."

Cade turned away from the computer in exasperation. "Sindri, I'm not going to discuss it. Allison and I are having issues, and you don't know everything about—"

"I know more about her than you think. I know she is a good female, and she is supposed to be here." The brownie's wizened face tightened with anger.

"Well, *she* doesn't know she's supposed to be here, because she was getting ready to leave without telling anyone."

Sindri frowned and pursed his lips.

"Yeah. She tried to make a run for it. And she hasn't been telling the truth, and—"

"None of that matters. She does not deserve this treatment.

Your parents would be ashamed of you. I am."

Cade stood up. "Wait a goddamned minute, old man. You don't tell me how to treat—"

"I am going to see the girl. She may be afraid." Sindri spun on his heel and hurried out.

Cade was too surprised to react right away, but he caught up to Sindri before he got to the stairs.

"Hold up." He put a hand to Sindri's shoulder. The brownie angrily knocked it away. Cade couldn't remember him ever doing something like that.

"You do not tell me what to do, *barn*." He stretched his arm to stab at Cade's chest with one long, skinny finger. "I am not your wolf. I am not your servant. I do not obey you. I care for you, as I cared for your mother and your brother. I failed them. I will not fail you."

Cade watched, open-mouthed, as Sindri shuffled up the stairs and knocked on Ally's door. When she didn't answer, he let himself into the room. A moment later he came back out and peered down at Cade through the slats of the railing. Cade didn't think he'd ever seen Sindri smirk before.

"She is gone. Your mate escaped out the window."

# Chapter Sixteen

He knew she hadn't left the room. The window was open, but he didn't see her crumpled body lying on the ground below. At this point, nothing she did surprised him.

It still scared the hell out of him.

Now that he'd claimed her, finding her would be easy. But how? On horseback? On two feet? Four? If he caught up to her in wolf form, what then? Would he change back and start yelling at her, buck-ass naked? After their recent scene, being chased by him on four feet might frighten her.

Or it might just piss her off.

He'd go on horseback. She had a head start, but a horse could catch up to her in no time.

Sindri acted oddly unconcerned, even a little amused, insisting Ally would be safe. Cade worried the four-hundred-year-old brownie might be going senile.

On his way to the stables, he ran straight into Dylan. "Ally jumped out the window. Any idea how she might be able to do something like that?"

"Um, well," Dylan stammered, "I can't— I mean, I can, but it's kinda..."

"Never mind. Once I find her, we're all going to sit down, and the three of you will answer every fucking question I ask."

Dylan muttered, "Yes, sir." Cade ignored him. He got Sleipnir saddled in record time and went after his mate.

She'd been running with defiant abandon for a while when she noted she was picking up a strange scent. She normally didn't pay much attention to scents. Here on the ranch were so many different smells, from plants, wolves and other animals, she didn't bother trying to keep track. Scent became background noise, like traffic in Houston.

Now she realized the new scent was one she'd smelled recently. She closed her eyes and began sifting through all the scents crowding her mind, plucking and sorting, separating them like tangled threads.

When she thought she had it, she tripped and fell, one knee banging into a large, jagged rock. Panting, she knelt in the scrub grass on her hands and one good knee, watching blood seep from the other one. She'd smelled that scent for a very brief time, but it had stuck in her memory, she guessed, because it was so closely associated with Aaron's subsequent suicide attempt.

The scent came from High Voice Guy, the wolf who'd argued with Aaron at the restaurant.

He didn't want to hear more lies. He didn't want another fight. No enemy's fangs could rip him up like her brash, bitter anger did. He knew she had feelings for him, but for some reason, she wouldn't trust him enough to tell him what was going on.

Or else she really was a manipulative, cold-blooded female and she'd played him the way his mother had played his father. But his mother had loved his father, so Louis MacDougall's life had been a happy one, whereas Cade's life would be hell for the next five or six decades.

Maybe he'd get lucky and she'd die young.

Ha ha.

He'd already ridden ten miles. His mate ran faster than any human should. He'd noted her speed the night they found Aaron. That speed, combined with her hearing and her eyesight, and the strength she'd exhibited when she slammed the door, led to one conclusion:

His mate was a wolf.

Ha ha.

None of this was remotely fucking funny.

Another scent crossed Ally's track—a wolf scent, but one

he'd never smelled before. He jerked sharply on the reins. A stranger had entered his territory. Stapkis? Whoever it was, his mate and the strange wolf were now in the same vicinity. He didn't like that.

He rarely visited this remote, heavily forested part of his holdings. Highway 50 lay five miles south. Aside from cutting juniper-pine for the woodshop, they left the area alone.

Both scents were stronger now, and they came from the northeast, where the trees were densest. He needed wolf form to track faster, smell better, and, if necessary, fight harder. But he needed human form to think and plan. If the wolf lurked in the woods, he'd had plenty of time to see Cade already, and Cade would be vulnerable while changing, so he saw no point in getting furry right away.

Ally appeared from behind a large boulder about a quarter mile away, running toward him from the east, parallel to the trees. Heart soaring, he grinned in spite of his anger, because she seemed so eager to get to him.

"Cade!" she shouted. "Someone's here! It's the guy—"

A rifle boomed. A bullet whizzed past his ear, missing him by a hair. Ally screamed.

Sleipnir reared. Cade, distracted, lost his seat for the first time in years and tumbled to the ground. Sleipnir pounded off in panic. Ally froze, looking from Cade to the trees. She broke for the trees as he got to his feet.

"Ally! Get away from there!"

Why was she running *toward* gunfire? Another shot rang out. This one hit him in the left shoulder.

It was a silver bullet.

Silver tore through muscle and he grabbed his shoulder, twisting in agony. One silver bullet couldn't disable him, but the more he moved, the faster the poison would spread. If he took another hit, he'd have a hard time defending his impossible mate.

A third shot boomed. This time, no bullet came near him. Ally screamed again.

Rage drowned out the pain that should've slowed him down. A wolf who would attack by ambush—with a gun, no less—wouldn't hesitate to kill a female. Terrified she'd been shot, Cade raced for the woods as the unknown wolf roared. The trees blocked his view, but he heard the fight and could make no sense of it. Ally couldn't fight a wolf. What was he doing to her?

He found them just inside the outer ring of trees. The strange wolf clutched the barrel of a lever-action rifle in his hands, swinging the stock at Ally. She was on her feet, weaving and dodging the gunstock with wolf-like speed and agility, coming in under it to land roundhouse kicks on the wolf's lower body. All this Cade noted as he charged the wolf, bringing him crashing to the ground in a flying tackle. The gun went sailing out of the stranger's hands.

Cade regained his feet first, aiming a powerful kick at the stranger's ribs while the latter still lay on the ground. The bastard managed to grab Cade's leg and pull him back down, where they continued to punch and roll. Cade outweighed his enemy and soon had the wolf pinned on his back beneath him.

"Ally, get out of here!"

He pummeled the wolf's face while the guy struggled to get free. Ally, damn her, didn't answer or obey, dancing around on the edges of the fight like she was waiting to jump in.

The wolf still had one arm free, which he used to reach into his pants pocket and pull out a silver knife. Thanks to the silver already in his system, Cade's reflexes were shot to hell, and the knife missed his jugular by an inch.

Ally screamed.

Why was she still here? Why hadn't she run?

He was still pinned on his back beneath Cade but with that one arm free, the wolf slashed madly back and forth with the silver knife. Cade was weak and dizzy, his reflexes deteriorating more rapidly now. Any second the knife would find a vein or a chunk of muscle and that would be that. Cade made one last desperate grab for the flailing blade. The motion knocked him off balance and he started sliding off the wolf's body. The guy drove his knee into the back of Cade's head. Cade jumped off and rolled to his feet, shaking his head to clear it.

The other wolf looked exhausted, but not particularly angry, as if this were nothing personal. He stood, and they circled each other warily, each feinting here and there but not closing.

Cade stared at him, trying to figure out why a stranger was trying to kill him. Then, suddenly, he knew.

It was the clearest glimpse he'd ever had into another

person's mind—not simply an emotional impression, but true telepathy. In his own mind, he could see what the other wolf was thinking. It lasted only seconds, but the force of it left him dizzy. He stumbled, recovering before the other wolf could rush him.

"Whatever Stapkis promised you, is it worth your honor?"

The wolf froze, blinking in confusion.

"I asked you a question. What does an Alpha have to pay a wolf to throw away his honor?"

The stranger hadn't been angry before, but he was now. Confused and frightened, he started to move again, feinting and dodging and slashing out with the knife.

"It's the guy I heard in the restaurant with Aaron," Ally called.

"I know, baby. What did you threaten Aaron with? What did you say that made my wolf try to kill himself?"

The stranger froze in shock for a second, looking from Cade to Ally. Cade closed, grabbing the wolf's knife hand with both of his, intending to flip the guy over his shoulder. The wolf stomped on Cade's instep, which was a bullshit pussy tactic. It worked too, thanks to the silver bullet still oozing its poison a little at a time. The shock of the pain caused Cade to lose his grip. The wolf spun in one fluid motion, burying the knife high in Cade's left ribcage and slicing down.

The knife went in like hard, cold fire. Every nerve in his chest, and then his whole body, screamed in agony. He stumbled back, forcing himself to stay on his feet and keep moving, until he found himself with his back to a tree. He pressed a hand to the blood flowing from his side. It didn't staunch the bleeding.

He couldn't see into the wolf's mind anymore. A window had opened for a few seconds, but now it had slammed shut again. Didn't really matter, since he wouldn't be alive much longer.

As he stood there, unable to run or fight, forced to wait and watch his enemy coming at him, he thought of another silver knife, another wolf. For a minute his attacker morphed into the tall, gaunt Fae with long silver hair who'd murdered his father on that beach in Scotland while his mother knelt screaming in the sand.

Ally let out a savage howl and launched herself across the

clearing in one long, graceful, impossible leap, landing on the wolf's back. If Cade hadn't known she was about to die—he'd defend her to his last breath, but he didn't have many left—he would've smiled. She looked like one of the Valkyrie in Mama's stories, all beautiful vengeance and divine wrath.

They slammed into Cade, who roared with pain. Ally reared back, teeth bared. Cade watched in awe and anguish as she grabbed the wolf's head from behind and broke his neck, nimbly alighting before his body crashed to the ground.

What a gorgeous hallucination. He even heard the neck snap.

She would've been a good mother for Becca. At least there was Sarah Jane...

Ally was leaning over him, her honey blond hair in his face, her precious lavender scent enveloping him, crying his name as he passed out.

This time, she was the one who killed a wolf seconds too late to save a loved one.

*No.* Cade wouldn't die. He was a wolf, stronger and fiercer and much harder to kill than her weak, human self had been. She had to get him back to the ranch.

She was afraid to move him and more afraid to leave him. She could get back to the house in minutes, but they'd need to get a car, and that would take time, but if he were in shock and she tried to carry him... And while she dithered like a useless idiot, he was turning gray and his breathing was shallow... His cell phone. He always carried his cell phone.

Her hands trembled as she searched for Michael's number on speed dial.

"What's up, Boss, I—"

"Michael! Cade's been shot, and—and—he's been stabbed, and I'm going to carry him, but I need—"

"Ally! *Ally!* Calm down! I'm in Colorado Springs. I'm calling Roman. Stay put!" He hung up without another word.

She pressed down harder on the stab wound, wishing she had something long enough to tie around his chest to keep pressure on it. If she could get her T-shirt off with one hand, and hold it in the wound, then...

The phone rang.

"They're almost there," Michael said. "Who did it? Where is he?"

"Some wolf. He's dead," she hiccupped. "I saw him with Aaron a few days ago but— They're here."

The blessed Range Rover roared toward her, Dec and Shawn leaping out before Trey came to a stop. They lifted Cade gently and put him in the back—still breathing, weakly, but God, he was so pale. She climbed in and wrapped an arm around him as they took off over the rough terrain.

"Hang on, baby," she whispered into his hair. "Please, hang on. I don't care if you act like an asshole. Just don't die."

Dec leaned over from the backseat, keeping a finger on Cade's neck. He looked as sick with fright as she felt.

"He's so cold, Dec. Why is he so cold?"

"His pulse is weak but it's there," Dec said tightly. "It looks like we got to him in time. I need to get that bullet out. The wee fella is gathering his herbs and poultices—"

"*Herbs*? We've got to get him to the hospital!"

"No, love, there's no time." Dec's voice and expression were both grim. "He'll never make it. The silver's already workin' in him. I've got to get the bullet out and cleanse the wounds, and Sindri has the poultices and the comfrey mead to neutralize the silver."

"Dec, what the hell are you talking about?"

"Listen to me, girl!" She saw real fear in his face. "I know what I'm talkin' about. I know what to do. I did not come all this way to watch the wolf die. You will do as I tell you and we'll— shite." His phone rang. Ally heard Sarah Jane's voice.

"What happened? I know something happened, Declan, who is it—?"

"It's Cade. He's been shot and stabbed. Where are you?"

"In town, with Rebecca."

"Stay there 'til I call you. She doesn't need to be around this." He hung up.

Wolves immediately thronged the Rover. They carried Cade to his bedroom, where Sindri was assembling an array of surgical tools so calmly and methodically one might've thought the place doubled as a surgery all the time. She smelled a strange odor, sweet and woodsy, not unpleasant but very

167

strong.

Dec ordered all the wolves out. Even the alphas obeyed. Ally hung back at the door, expecting Dec to kick her out. "I don't want to leave him."

Once again, Dec surprised her.

"I don't want you to go. Just stay out of our way for a bit, there's a good girl."

She collapsed onto a vintage-looking sofa covered in rich green suede and standing on brass-tipped walnut legs. More stylish than comfortable, suitable for sitting but not for lounging, it wasn't the kind of couch a male would buy. Somehow, Ally knew Eirny had picked it out. This had probably been Eirny and Louis' bedroom. She wanted to cry again.

Dec and Sindri got Cade undressed. Sindri cleansed the wounds while Dec reached for a scalpel and retractors lying on the bedside table next to a small steel bowl. She was glad he had his back to her. She could've watched the procedure in an ER, but it looked barbaric when performed in a bedroom. She closed her eyes and breathed deeply through her mouth.

"You all right over there, Ally girl?" Dec asked absently.

"I think so," she said between gulps of air. She couldn't bring herself to ask him if he thought Cade would be all right, couldn't even consider the possibility that he might die. It terrified her almost as much as the prospect of leaving and never seeing him again.

She heard the ping of metal hitting metal as Dec dropped the bullet in the bowl.

"All right, *barn*," he said to Sindri, "get your comfrey and mint and then I'll close him up."

Ally watched with interest as Sindri, kneeling on the bed across from Dec, applied compresses to Cade's shoulder and side. The cloying order she'd smelled earlier now permeated the room.

"What's that stuff, Dec?"

"Comfrey and marshmallow, red sorrel and bits of other stuff the wee fella would never tell me about. It'll draw the poison from Cade's system. We'll need to get comfrey tea inside him to raise his temperature."

A werewolf's normal temperature was one hundred five. Silver poisoning lowered it dangerously.

"Is knowing how to do this a brownie thing?"

"No, it's an Old One thing, a Viking thing. Cade's mother was an acolyte of Eir, an Old One. The Vikings called her a valkyrie, a handmaiden to Freya."

"I know Eir."

"Is that so?" He turned to gaze at her thoughtfully, his arms crossed. "Interesting choice of words. Well. Eir is a healer. She passes her art to womenfolk. Eirny never had the patience for healing, but the wee fella has a gift. I don't think Eir minds a male doing it if he's not human. Or wolf." He rubbed his chin, still smiling at her in his shrewd, amused way. "I'd like to hear more about how you know Eir."

Sindri interrupted. "You may finish, then we will change the sheets."

Dec turned back to stitch up the wounds. Sindri gathered his materials and came to stand in front of her.

"Michael has returned. You need food. Come."

Not hungry in the least, she followed.

Michael grilled her for an hour, making her repeat the morning's events several times, as if telling the story over and over would cause her to suddenly know something she hadn't known the first ten times.

They were sitting at the table in Sindri's domain once again, the little brownie resolutely attempting to shovel food down their throats.

She told Michael about seeing Aaron in the restaurant the day they got to Fremont, and about the argument.

"And you're sure the guy who shot Cade was the guy in the restaurant with Aaron?"

"I'm positive. Same voice, same sce— Same voice." She remembered something Cade had said. "Cade seemed to know who the guy was. At least, he seemed to think Stapkis had sent him."

"It makes sense. I've got Seth taking pictures of the body. We'll email them to Seattle and see if he's one of theirs." He took another swig of coffee, watching her intently. "How are you doing?"

"Aside from killing a guy and watching Cade nearly die, I

guess I'm doing okay." She pushed her plate away and leaned on the table, her head in her hands.

"You've never killed anybody before," Michael said gently.

No, but if she hadn't done it, Cade would be dead instead of High Voice Guy. What really bothered her was she couldn't explain how she broke a werewolf's neck. The scrutiny she'd dodged for thirteen years loomed. She shook her head without looking up and said dully, "What am I going to tell the cops?"

Michael snorted. She raised her head to look at him, confused.

"The cops won't find out about this. Once we've identified him, we'll dispose of the body. And that's that."

She couldn't believe what she heard. "What if someone comes looking for him? Won't someone talk? What about his family?"

Michael shrugged, clearly unconcerned. He leaned back in his chair and laced his fingers behind his golden head. "The wolf dishonored his family and his pack, if he had one. No one will expect his body back. He's not entitled to burial under our custom. His family won't speak of him, not even to each other. And none of our wolves will say anything. You saved our Alpha's life. They'll do anything for you now."

"Oh." She hadn't considered the ramifications of her actions. She'd been doing a lot of that lately. Every time she meant to stop doing it, something else happened to make her do it again.

"Meanwhile," Michael continued, "there's one other thing I'd like to know."

"Okay."

"How the hell did you manage to break the wolf's neck?"

Just when she thought she'd dodged it again.

Her eyes met Sindri's. He shook his head so slightly she didn't know if she imagined it.

"I don't know," she said calmly. "By the time Cade couldn't fight anymore, the other guy was pretty beat-up himself. It must've been that and adrenaline that let me do it. I jumped on him and the next thing I knew, he was dead."

Michael looked at her with an unreadable expression. "You were that freaked out?"

"Well, yeah! Cade was about to get killed!"

He was staring at her shrewdly. "So you risked your life to save him. You do that kind of thing often?"

"No. Why?"

"I'm just trying to figure out how you feel about my Alpha."

"That's none of your business, Michael."

"Yes, it is, Ally." His tone wasn't unkind. "Packs aren't like human families; we don't have human attitudes about privacy. Everything that affects Cade affects us—he belongs to us. I'm just looking out for him."

"Fine. Once I've had a shower, and we know how Cade is doing, you can drill me about my intentions."

He grinned. "Cade's right. You're a smartass."

"Whatever." She stood. "I'm going to take a shower."

He'd hurt worse, but only in combat. He couldn't move and he couldn't speak and he couldn't tell if he was awake or not. He floated just below the surface of consciousness. Voices sounded muffled, distant.

At some point, he sensed Sindri in the room. It comforted him. The brownie put a strong, gnarled hand to his neck and lifted his head. Something warm and tangy slid down his throat, and he gulped reflexively. He tried to open his eyes but couldn't manage it.

If he was alive, did that mean Ally was too?

Later—minutes? Hours?—he opened his eyes. The moonlight coming in through the window fell across Mama's sofa. Sindri lay fast asleep with his head in Declan MacSorley's lap.

*What the hell?*

MacSorley sat with his head back against the wall, eyes closed as he stroked the dozing Sindri's hair.

He opened his eyes and returned Cade's stare. "You're dreaming, *barn*," he said with a sad, exhausted smile. "Sleep. Your mate will be here soon."

*Bullshit.* This was no dream. He struggled to speak.

No use. The pain and Sindri's medicine took him under, and he fell into a deep sleep.

Dec napped on the sofa. She stood beside the bed, watching Cade sleep. Brushing the hair from his eyes, she smiled with relief to feel his warmth. Sindri must've given him that tea stuff.

"How's my girl?" Dec asked groggily from behind her.

She shrugged without turning around. "This is ludicrous," she whispered.

She didn't have to look at Dec to know he'd cocked an eyebrow. Just like Dylan, and just like Cade.

"What's ludicrous, love?"

"Feeling this way about a guy I've known for a week."

"Oh, I'm sure it feels strange." He yawned. "And I'll grant it's unusual, but I don't know I'd call it ludicrous. Seems rather intense to me."

"It's just that I— I mean, I don't, I've never..." Why did she find it so difficult to discuss her own feelings? Why couldn't she talk about things normal women talked about?

"You've never fallen for a man, or a wolf, like this before, and you haven't had many lovers, and you're not used to being around someone so much stronger than you, and you're scared."

She put a hand to her mouth and closed her eyes, willing herself not to cry. "Shit," she whispered. "Am I that obvious?"

"I've known you four years, love. There's not much I don't see."

"Oh, right. I forgot. You've noticed my weirdness." That didn't bother her anymore. She sat on the edge of the bed, next to Cade's hip. His deep, regular breathing didn't falter as she stroked his beard with the back of her hand.

"There's very little I haven't seen in my life, Allison Kendall. But I can safely say I've never seen anything like you."

She turned her head to look at him. "How old are you, Dec?"

His mouth quirked in a half smile, half grimace. "Older than I look, younger than I feel."

"Are you Cade's father?" She'd seen such love in his eyes when he talked about Eirny MacDougall...

Dec laughed quietly. "No, I'm not."

"It's just that I never noticed, 'til we got here, that you look a lot like Dylan, and Cade too. Same hair, same eyes, same—"

"I'm his uncle."

She'd already suspected a family relationship, but it still surprised her. They regarded each other in silence for a moment.

"So you're Louis' brother?"

"No. Eirny's."

"Okay, then—wait. Eirny was from Iceland. You're Irish."

"It's a long story," he said curtly.

"Hmm." She bit her lip, considering. "Okay. I guess we don't need to get into it right now. I didn't know Eirny was a wolf's daughter."

"Neither does Cade." Dec walked over to the bed to gently lift one of Cade's eyelids, then let it fall. "I don't want him to find out this way," he murmured, "but I think he's safely out of it."

"Are you going to tell him?"

"I want to. We got off to a bad start. I've been waiting for an opportunity, but other things keep popping up. Like you, for instance." He smiled down at her.

"Me? What, you mean my little roll in the sack?"

He cocked an eyebrow clear up into his hairline. "Little roll in the sack? Girl, I know you've not had many lovers, but you're not stupid."

Suddenly restless and self-conscious, she stood up to pace.

He blocked her path.

Rather than go around him, she crossed her arms, thrust out a hip and stared at the floor. "Dec," she said in as petulant a voice as Dylan ever mustered, "I'm really tired of people talking about my sex life and asking how I feel about Cade."

She felt his gaze boring into the top of her head. "I know how you feel about Cade. Do you know how *Cade* feels about *you*?"

She winced. "I'm not sure he feels anything. I know he wants me, or he did, but he doesn't— He's not interested in anything long-term. I mean, he flat out said it, so—"

"Really?"

"Yes, really."

"What exactly did he say?"

"He just— He—" She stopped at the familiar tightening in her throat, the trembling mouth, the eternal damn stomachache.

"Do we have to talk about this, Dec? I'm tired, and my heart hurts, and there's more important stuff going on than what Cade and I did, or what he feels, and..."

Dec wrapped his arms around her in a loose bear hug. He laughed as she banged her head against his chest.

"Ally girl, it's all...related, if you will. I know it's none of my business. I'm askin' because I care about you, and I think my nephew might be an idiot. What exactly did he say to make you think you were just a momentary tumble?"

"Oh, nothing important," she mumbled into his sternum. "Just that he'd never marry unless he found his mate, and if he found her he'd never—"

Her vocal chords locked up and skidded to a halt while her mind raced on ahead. A choking noise escaped her. It sounded a bit like "eep". She pushed Dec away to find him staring at her with a patient, almost pitying expression. She stared back, slack-jawed.

She turned to look at Cade, sleeping so quietly, weak and wounded. She remembered how forceful and strong he'd been in that bed last night, how he'd stared at her face as he carefully explained that if he found his mate, he wouldn't let her go.

She remembered his fury when he saw her packed suitcase this morning.

*I never question the women I sleep with...I'm interested in you.*

She'd said, *I can mess you up.*

He'd said, *I think you already did.*

"You think I'm his *mate?*" she squeaked.

Where did Sindri keep the paper bags? That's what you needed for hyperventilation, right? Rapid, shallow breaths into a paper bag. Deep breaths just made it worse. A pediatrician told her that, years ago.

Alphas were arrogant. They did what they wanted and didn't stop to ask for permission or forgiveness. But if she was his mate, then that meant he'd claimed her. He'd slept with her, thereby allowing the mate bond to bind him to her completely, before he'd even confirmed that she'd accept him. That was beyond arrogant. If she rejected him, he'd spend the rest of his life emotionally and physiologically tethered to a woman he couldn't have.

"Oh, I *know* you're his mate, darlin'. Every wolf on this ranch knows it. I was just trying to help *you* figure it out. Cade should've mentioned it. I thought if you knew, you might not be so anxious to leave."

She turned slowly to look up at him again. "The whole ranch knows about that too?"

"Probably. Seth told me right after it happened. It tore him up pretty good."

"I know." God, not more tears. "It wasn't his fault. It was mine." She rubbed her temples. "This is very, very weird, Dec."

"It's not the weirdest thing that's ever happened to you, though, is it?" He looked at her shrewdly, appraisingly, again. It made her feel transparent.

"No, it's not, but—oh. Oh hell. Does Dylan know?" She hugged herself tightly and sat down on the bed again, leaning back against Cade. He hadn't stirred. His body warmed her through her flannel lounge pants. The size and the solidity of him soothed her.

She tried to ignore the tiny seed of joy taking root deep inside. But it was sending out tentative little shoots, and she could feel them poking up through her defenses—her caution, her prudence, her restraint and reserve. As she contemplated the prospect of life as Cade's mate, the only thing comparable to her budding joy was her blooming panic. Because she found the prospect very freaking damned scary.

"I don't know, but I'm sure he can handle it."

"Who? Oh. Dylan. Right. He understands a lot more than I give him credit for." She shifted, planting her arm on the other side of Cade's body. With her free hand, she brushed the hair out of his eyes once more.

"Well, the whole falling-in-love-in-a-week thing makes more sense now." She kept her voice low, even though Cade showed no sign of waking.

Dec sat down on the couch again, elbows on his knees. "You think so?"

"Well, yeah. Isn't there some kind of reciprocal response when a werewolf bonds to a woman? When the physiological switch in his brain gets flipped, it triggers something in her. At least, that's what I've read. I never knew a bonded wolf."

"That's what it looks like in many cases," he said slowly.

"Wolves don't find mates that often, so it's hard to say. I've been around a hell of a long time, and I haven't met that many who did. And there have been women who rejected wolves."

"Yeah, and werewolves who went psycho from it."

"I know a psycho wolf when I see one, and Cade's not."

"Dec," she whispered as her fingers traced the line of Cade's jaw, "I don't know what to do."

"At least you have a choice. Cade doesn't, but you do," he mused. "What the hell was he thinking? If you'd rejected him before you slept with him, it would've been hard enough. But if you reject him after he's claimed you, it's...it's unimaginable. That's the kind of recklessness I'd expect of his mother, not him."

She grinned tenderly at the unconscious werewolf. At *her* unconscious werewolf. "He's not reckless—he's arrogant. It probably never occurred to him that I'd reject him. That's why he got so incensed when I tried to leave. There's no control freak like an alpha."

"Can you live with that? You wouldn't be the boss in this house, love."

"Maybe I'm tired of being the boss. I might like someone else driving for a change."

Dec snickered. "You might find that's more difficult than it sounds. It's just one of the things you're going to have to think long and hard about, Ally girl."

He dropped a kiss on her forehead and gazed for another moment at his sleeping nephew. "I'm going to eat and then crash for a few hours. Get some sleep yourself, please."

Alone now with Cade, she sat and stroked and stared for a long time. Then she shucked off her lounge pants and crawled into bed. She pressed herself against his side with one arm around him, listening to him breathe. It took a long time to fall asleep.

## Chapter Seventeen

He knew it was the silver knife wound summoning The Dream after so many years of peace. As a teenager, when it tortured him all the time, he'd learned to control The Dream—alter it, rewind it, make himself wake. Sometimes he even changed the ending, and Mama and Papa lived as long as he slept. He couldn't do that now. He had to let it run while he watched it like a movie.

Papa put them to bed. Carson fell asleep, but Cade couldn't. He lay there and listened to the fighting, the crying and the pleading. Mama and Papa argued in hushed tones. Mama cried, as she'd cried for weeks, ever since their arrival in Scotland. It scared him as nothing had ever scared him in his short life. His parents never fought. Since they'd arrived in Scotland, they argued every day.

They'd come here because Mama wanted to show them where she and Papa had met, but now she sulked and cried and spent every moment alone on the beach. Nothing Papa said could make her come inside. She sat and stared at the ocean for hours, ignoring the three of them. At first, Carson and Cade tried to cheer her up. They begged to go to the cold, lonely beach with her, but she smiled sadly and told them she needed to go alone. They stopped asking.

The front door of the little cottage opened, then closed. Cade heard no more voices. Footsteps approached. Cade closed his eyes, feigning sleep, as Papa peered into the room. Satisfied that both boys slept, he closed the door. A few minutes later, the front door opened and closed again.

Mama had left the house, and Papa had gone after her.

Cade briefly thought about waking Carson, but his older

brother would stop him. Fifteen and swollen with pride after completing his first change, Carson thought he was such a grownup. He ordered Cade around as if he had a right to, and he pretended to understand their parents' new troubles. He told Cade to leave Mama alone, that Cade was just making it worse.

That wasn't true. It couldn't be true.

He slid out of bed and pulled on his clothes, including his jacket. He hated the cold Scottish summer. He wanted a real beach, like in California or Florida or Texas, where kids and dogs ran in the surf and teenage girls jiggled in bikinis. The only other people at this beach were a honeymooning couple and old folks who never left their cottages.

Scarista Beach was a five-minute walk from their cottage. To avoid overtaking Papa he hung back, creeping along the winding path. Papa said the ocean interfered with his sense of smell. Cade hoped the surf's roar interfered with Papa's hearing as well. As he approached the beach, he dropped to all fours, creeping through the grassy hillocks of sand. Nothing out here would interfere with Papa's night vision.

Cade didn't have a wolf's hearing yet, and he didn't need it. The people on the beach weren't trying to be quiet. He heard Mama talking to a strange man. It sounded vaguely, but not quite, like Icelandic.

The strange man sounded angry. Mama sounded angry and scared.

Cade crept behind a sandy hump to the left and peeked over the top just in time to see Papa run onto the beach.

Mama and the strange man stood at the water's edge.

In The Dream, Cade never saw the strange man's face. He knew he'd seen it that night. But in The Dream, the man's face was a blank spot, a hole in the movie screen.

The stranger stood too close to Mama. He shook her as they shouted at one another. Mama's long black hair and the stranger's long black cloak snapped in the wind, billowing around them, binding the two of them together.

*"Eirny!"* The wind carried Papa's howl up and down the beach, a howl infused by a blend of heartbreak and rage the eleven-year-old Cade couldn't understand and the adult Cade could never forget.

Mama and the strange man turned, Mama's face a mask of grief and terror.

The stranger yelled something to Papa in the unknown tongue. He held Mama back for a second, but she broke free with a shout and flung herself across the beach.

"Louis! Leave, please! Go!"

The stranger shouted something, though whether at Mama or Papa, Cade couldn't tell. Mama, crying and pleading, threw her arms around Papa, who pushed her roughly aside.

Cade cried out as she tumbled to the sand. The adults didn't hear him. He wanted to run to Mama, but terror held him paralyzed.

Papa snarled and charged the stranger standing at the water's edge. As Papa closed the distance, the man's hand moved to his belt. Mama screamed. Cade barely had time to register the glint of silver.

Papa leapt. The man's arm flashed out to meet him, plunging the knife into Papa's stomach and thrusting it deeper as he shoved Papa away. Papa's yowl of pain and rage joined Mama's terrified keening. He fell to the sand on his back, the enormous knife embedded to the hilt in his belly.

The strange man stood there, unmoving. Even though, in the Dream, Cade couldn't see his face, he sensed him smiling. The stranger didn't move until Mama ran back to the water's edge to throw herself on Papa's motionless body, wailing in the same foreign tongue. When he bent down to grasp her arm, she erupted with an animal snarl and ripped the knife from Papa's body.

Whirling around, she slashed madly, blindly. The stranger roared and flung an arm across his face. Mama slashed again, but he tore the knife from her hand and threw it far out into the ocean. Clutching at his face, he turned and ran off down the beach, disappearing from sight as quickly as a werewolf.

The sight of the knife sailing through the air and dropping into the water broke Cade's paralysis. With a guttural cry of "*Papa!*" he ran to his father's body and fell to his knees.

When Mama raised her face to him, he didn't recognize her.

The blood gushed from Papa's belly, clotting the sand. Mama's hands were wet with it as she raised them to her face, her eyes wide and wild. She let out a keening wail. Cade stared at her, transfixed. Who was this woman?

She rose to her feet, wild grief written on her blood-smeared face, and reached out her hand to him. Trembling and sobbing, he extended his, but before they touched, she gave a harsh shout and turned her back on him. She ran straight into the pounding surf. She didn't stop, and she never looked back.

He screamed as she vanished beneath the waves. He kept screaming when the old couple from the cottage next door came stumbling down to see what had happened. He screamed for Mama as the policemen raced down to the beach, and he screamed for her as they peeled him off Papa's body.

He was still screaming when he woke up, but this time, for the first time, he wasn't alone.

His eyes snapped open. His body, locked in the nightmare, refused to move. He heard his heart pounding in his chest, his blood pulsing in his ears—and Ally stirring next to him.

"Cade? Cade! Wake up, baby. Look at me. Here. That's good."

She held his face while she kissed his forehead and his eyes. Then her mouth covered his, pouring sweet relief into him like cool wine.

He tried to take her in his arms, but the left side of his body erupted in fiery pain. She seemed to sense it, pressing a hand to his chest, urging him not to move. Her tongue stroked inside his mouth, easing the panic, calming the terror. His body shuddered as the nightmare surrendered its hold.

His mate had saved him.

"You broke his neck," he whispered hoarsely, wonderingly.

"Like a fucking toothpick," she murmured with a shy smile.

He chuckled, light-headed. "You're cute when you say fuck."

She kissed him again. "Go back to sleep. I'm here."

His head fell back against the pillow. He let sleep take him, untroubled this time by dreams or pain.


He awoke to someone knocking on the door and fading sunlight peeking through the drawn curtains. The clock said five p.m. Ally was gone.

"Cade?" Michael called.

"Come on in," he croaked, clearing his throat. "You seen Ally?"

"She's swimming. Uh-uh, no way, bro," Michael laughed,

pushing him back against the bed when he tried to stand. "Ally said you're not getting up."

"What the hell is wrong with—" he lost the intended effect when he had to stop, panting, and wait several minutes 'til he had enough breath to finish "—you?"

"Ally said if I let you out of bed she'd kill me."

"Ally's not your Alpha, wolf." Some of his strength had returned, but not enough to intimidate his second, who knew it.

"Yeah, well, my Alpha can't do much to me right now, but his mate kind of scares me. There's something strange about that chick, Cade."

"I know. I don't care. Help me up."

"Cade, I just told—"

"I need you to get me into the bathroom, Michael."

"Oh. Okay, sorry."

"I need a shower," he wheezed as he put his hands on Michael's shoulders and pulled himself to standing.

"Cade, I'm not sure that's a good idea."

"Before she comes back."

"Ally doesn't care—"

"*I* care. I want a shower before my mate comes back."

"Ah. Gotcha. You do stink. But I'm getting in there with you, just in case."

"Whatever."

They hobbled to the bathroom, Cade's arm around Michael's shoulder, Michael's arm around Cade's waist.

"She killed the wolf," Cade panted.

"I know." Michael grunted under the weight of Cade's body. "It bothers me."

"She can see in the dark."

"That bothers me too."

"When she slammed the door, the house shook."

"Bothering me."

"She runs almost as fast as I do."

"Bothering the fuck out of me."

"She called me baby."

"Oh, well then, we've got nothing to worry about, do we? Hope she's not the jealous type. Wouldn't want her breaking my neck if she catches us in the shower together."

"Shut the fuck up and help me get undressed."

Michael waited by the shower door, but Cade didn't need him. The wooziness was gone. He leaned against the wall of the capacious stall as hot water pummeled him, massaging and reinvigorating his battered body while the soap scrubbed away the lingering scent of silver, grass, blood and dirt.

It left him exhausted and exhilarated.

Michael handed him a pair of clean sweats.

"Hold up," he said as the big wolf wrapped an arm around his waist to hustle him back to bed. "I need to shave."

His beard, which he kept trimmed close to his jawline, had reached island castaway/mad backwoodsman status. Would Ally care how clean he was if she couldn't find his mouth?

He stood at the mirror with the warm washcloth on his face as he inspected the damage to his body. The scars would all disappear in the next couple of days. He knew he'd have invisible scars for longer than that. The return of The Dream meant the attack had messed with his head. He didn't want to think about it right now.

"The gunshot wound looks clean and pink," he said to the mirror.

Michael, lying on his back on the bathroom rug with the *Sports Illustrated* swimsuit issue, grunted his agreement.

"Sindri does good work."

"Sindri didn't stitch you up," Michael said distractedly. "MacSorley did. Looks like he knew what he was doing too. ET assisted with his herby stuff."

Cade paused mid-lather. "What the hell are you talking about?"

Michael tore himself away from the bikinis. "When we brought you in. Dec removed the bullet and stitched up the cuts."

"And you let him?"

"Why not? Sindri was okay with it. Look at your chest. That's some nice sewing."

Cade stared at the mirror. "You like the bastard, don't you?"

"Yeah." Michael shrugged. "I can't figure out what he's done to make you hate him."

"I don't hate him," Cade whispered in frustration. He closed his eyes, listening to the rhythmic drip of water in the basin, and tried to figure out what he was feeling. "There's just something about the wolf that sc—" he caught himself before he said *scares* "—rubs me the wrong way."

Michael smirked. "Maybe you're jealous. He's lived with Ally for four years, and he looks an awful lot like you. Maybe the mate bond doesn't like it."

Their eyes met in the mirror. A foreboding crept over him, a deep unease that hadn't plagued him since he was a lonely, sullen teenager. Was it The Dream? Or was it MacSorley?

"He doesn't look like me," Cade said softly, staring at himself again. "He looks like my mother. *That's* why he gives me the creeps."

"Okay, that would be disturbing."

"I had The Dream." He didn't look at Michael as he said it. "Earlier, when Ally was with me."

"I figured," said his best friend, returning his attention to supermodels. "I heard you screaming. I thought I'd give Ally a shot at it before I came in. She took care of it, didn't she?"

"Yeah." He started shaving, his mind wandering as his hands worked without any direction from his brain. "Michael," he said as he swished his razor in the water, "why don't you ever dream about your father?"

"Because I know I didn't kill him, and I don't care who did."

He knew Michael meant it. Cade was the Alpha, but in some ways, his second was harder. Or maybe just more damaged.

"Are we gonna talk about feelings now?" Michael yawned.

"Shut up."

"Thank you."

They shaved and ogled in comfortable silence.

"Hey," he said suddenly. Michael looked up. "You hear anything from Seattle? Anyone see Rufus around?"

"Oh yeah. I've got info on the wolf who's trying to kill you. I just somehow forgot to mention it 'til you reminded me. Because I'm stupid like that." He muttered "sheesh" under his breath and returned to the girls.

Cade's cheeks reappeared. His beard and moustache lost their depth. He patted his newly mown face dry.

"Hang on." Michael scrambled to his feet. "I'm coming."

"I don't need help," he snapped, "I can walk by—"

That's when his legs decided not to hold him up anymore. He didn't fall over. He just sort of wilted in place. Michael caught him before he hit the floor.

"Not a fucking word."

"Who, me?"

He threw his arm around Michael's wide shoulders and they started the journey back to the bed.

Ally knocked on the door. He knew it was her before she called out, "Cade? May I come in? Oh my God, what happened?"

She rushed to his side, but stopped when she realized she couldn't grab his left arm. She stood there bouncing on her heels, fluttering her hands, obviously dying to interfere as Michael unhurriedly walked him to the bed.

"Sweetheart," he huffed, hoping she couldn't see the effort it cost him to talk, "you're supposed to wait 'til someone says *come in*. That's the whole point of *may* I come in?"

"Asshole," she muttered, and Michael sniggered.

He sat down on the bed and gave Michael a *back off—no weakness in front of the mate* look which his second immediately recognized.

Ally frowned down at him. He noted the way her eyes avoided his face. Michael threw a friendly arm around her shoulders and gave her a squeeze.

"He's had a bath and shaved his fur." He gave her a little shove. "Go on. Climb in, I don't mind."

"Michael!" she squealed, blushing.

"You're making m— Her uncomfortable," Cade growled. She looked damned tasty when she blushed, though. She wore soft blue flannel pants and a thin, sky blue T-shirt—too thin, actually, for him to be comfortable with other wolves seeing her.

Michael lowered his eyes, grinning insolently. "Like I said, it's still a couple of days before you can rip me up. I'll get my jollies while I can."

"It's okay," Ally murmured. "I'll get used to it. I think."

She walked around the bed and got in on the other side. He was still growling at Michael, who was still grinning at him, when she snuggled up against his back. She ran a hand up into his hair. He shuddered and sank back between her legs, resting his arms on her bent knees, acutely conscious of her pelvis cradling him.

Michael tried to smirk, but it turned into a genuine smile. "I guess I can leave him now. Be gentle with my wolf."

"I'm gonna fucking kill you," Cade said conversationally.

"Gotta catch me first. Later." He turned to go.

"Wait a sec. I need to know something." She kissed the back of his neck softly and then lifted her head to Michael. "How long have y'all been together?"

Michael burst out laughing. Even though it hurt like hell, Cade joined him.

"What's it been—" Cade started to say.

"'Bout twenty years," Michael said simultaneously.

"No, twenty-five," they both finished.

She laughed with them. "How'd you meet?"

He let Michael answer. "Army—we were Rangers."

"Whoa," she interrupted. "I'm impressed."

Michael shrugged with false modesty. Cade put his head back against Ally's shoulder, the better to feel her hair against his cheek.

"It's easy for wolves. Anyway, we met at sniper training. I was his spotter."

"He had me at 'take the fucking shot, dumbass'," Michael said dreamily.

Ally dissolved into giggles, her face against his neck. Desire shot through him, hard and fierce. His eyes met Michael's—*get out of here, now.*

She stopped laughing and looked up. "Did he leave?"

"Yep." He breathed deep, inhaling her freshly showered, lavender-and-Ally scent. Her nipples rubbed his bare back through the thin T-shirt. He could sit there all night while she messed with his hair.

"Okay," she said in a small voice after a long moment, "what now?"

He smiled, eyes still closed. "It'll be another day or so before I'm strong enough to do what I want to do to you. You keep breathing in my ear like that, I might hurt myself."

She rested her chin on his shoulder. "You feel yourself healing that fast?"

"Hmm. Tomorrow makes three days, and Sindri's poured a

lot of comfrey in me."

"Dec did a good job cleaning the wounds out too."

He let that pass, pressing her hand to his mouth and running his tongue across her palm. She rewarded him with a shiver. "We could talk about how you killed the wolf."

"We could talk about your nightmare."

"Yeah. No. Explain the strength. And the speed and the hearing and—"

"Rock paper scissors?"

It really fucking hurt to laugh. "God, you're cute. Okay. One, two, three—"

He threw scissors, she threw paper.

One look at her face wiped the smile off his.

"What are you so scared of, baby?"

She started scooting to the other side of the bed in a backwards spider crawl and gasped when he grabbed her foot to drag her back, scissoring her legs to either side of him. He pulled one leg across his lap, clamping his hand to her thigh to hold her still.

He grinned through the pain. "Are you going to make me fight you to keep you here on the bed? Because I will, even if it rips me open."

Leaning back on her arms, she looked him right in the eye and held it, her expression both fearful and defiant.

"Who told you you were my mate, Allison?" he asked quietly.

"I figured it out myself."

"No you didn't."

She tugged her leg. He wouldn't let go.

"Fine," she said tightly. "Dec told me." Not giving him a chance to erupt, she continued, "But I could already look you in the eye. I didn't do it because it would freak you out."

"I'd imagine it would, since I hadn't claimed you yet, and the only alpha you could look in the eye would be the one mated to you."

"I can look any alpha in the eye."

"I see. So you can do eye contact like you do speed, and strength—"

"And hearing and scent. Yes. I have all the characteristics of an alpha. I just don't change, and I'm not as dominant." She paused. "And silver doesn't hurt me."

"If all that were true, it would make you pretty fucking unique."

"It is. I am."

She never broke eye contact. Her voice, devoid of emotion, and her matter-of-fact demeanor disturbed him. Still, he could see her trembling. She smelled scared to death.

Suddenly, sickeningly, he wondered—what if his beautiful, brave, shy, defiant, funny mate was delusional?

"I'm not crazy, Cade." Her tone was softer now, a little sad. "Seth will confirm everything I say. I think Dylan can back it up too. I'm just not sure how much he remembers."

"How much he remembers about what?"

"About the night I died."

"The night you—shit." His throat went dry. He had to swallow before he could speak again. "You're not making this up, are you?" he whispered. "You really think you died."

She sighed and looked away. Then she blew out a breath and fell back on the bed. When she spoke again, she addressed the ceiling in a tired voice.

"I don't think it, Cade. I know it. I remember it, Seth remembers it, and I think Dylan remembers it. Guy Fontenot killed me. Not when he clawed me, but when he knocked me across the living room and I slammed my head on the window ledge. My heart stopped beating. I died."

"For how long?" He'd read of humans revived after several minutes without a heartbeat.

"Five hours."

"Five hours," he repeated.

"Five hours."

"Five hours."

"Yes, Cade. I said five hours."

"You were dead for five hours."

"No breathing, no heartbeat. I got stiff and cold and everything."

"Jesus," he breathed.

"No, Eir."

His own heart stopped then. A dull roaring sound filled his ears.

She propped herself back up on her arms. "You okay?"

He stared at her, not really seeing her. "I don't like Eir."

"Why not? Didn't your mother—?"

"Yes. And Eir didn't stop her from killing herself. Or bring her back."

"Oh." She sat all the way up to reach out a hand to him. Something made her stop.

He stared past her, remembering. "I grew up hearing about Eir," he said half to himself. "I knew she was supposed to be able to raise the dead. At least, the Vikings thought so. Sindri said she didn't save my mother because Mama made a choice."

"I'm so sorry," she whispered.

His eyes returned to her. "Old Ones aren't around anymore, though. Not in our world, our plane of existence, whatever. They haven't messed around with people in a thousand years."

"I didn't think they could, either."

"So why'd she save you?" he asked, more harshly than he intended. But as soon as he thought about it, he knew the reason. "Dylan."

"Yeah." She looked down for a minute, her fingers idly plucking at the bedspread. "She said I died in battle, and the Valkyrie gathered fallen warriors, so... Anyway, she said I had a choice. I could be with God and my parents, or I could come back to raise Dylan and protect him. She said she'd give me what I needed to do that. She said she didn't want to see another of his line die, that his line was precious to her."

Since he'd claimed her she couldn't lie to him, but if she were delusional he wouldn't be able to tell. He didn't think she was, though. He believed that what she told him had really happened, because it was the only thing to explain her inexplicable abilities. It contradicted everything he knew about the way Old Ones operated, however.

"She didn't save Mama, or Carson, so she saved you?"

Ally nodded, her eyes welling up with tears. Her chin trembled again. "Cade, could you come over here? Please?"

"I don't need to be held, Ally," he snapped.

"I do," she whispered.

Something in him broke. The icy anger washing through him was for Eir, maybe even for Mama, but not for Ally.

The lies, evasions and panicked retreats made sense now. It didn't mean she wasn't moody, or that he knew her any better than he had five minutes ago. But if he could wrap his head around what she'd experienced—what she *was*—he might be able to woo her, induce her to stay put.

Maybe it was like breaking horses.

"Why are you smiling at me?" she sniffled.

Skittish—that was it, what he hadn't put his finger on before. She was skittish like a fine, spirited animal that wanted to stand still but didn't know how.

He shook his head. You couldn't tell a woman she reminded you of a horse. She wouldn't understand.

"You're kind of amazing." He shifted to the end of the bed and put his good arm around her.

"I'm not." She sniffled again. "I'm a freak of nature."

"Yeah, and you're amazing," he said into her hair. "Weird and beautiful."

He lay back and pulled her down with him

She hiccupped and shuddered, then laid her cheek against his heart and tucked a leg between his knees. He stroked her hair and back. When her breathing had slowed and she'd relaxed a bit, he said in his most soothing manner, "Tell me the rest."

He tried to ignore his blood singing in his veins as she pressed against him, her thigh resting against his hard cock, or how the lavender scent made him want to bury his head in her neck and go to sleep. He focused on her softly shaking voice instead.

She'd found herself in her childhood bedroom, in the home she'd shared with her parents before they died. That was her "happy place", the place she associated with safety and comfort. A woman was there. Ally couldn't describe her, couldn't name the color of her hair or eyes or the expression she wore. There was only an impression, a memory of a feeling, that the woman was beautiful, kind but distant, good but not friendly.

"It wasn't a warm, snuggly, I'm-with-Jesus feeling. It was more a *this very powerful being has taken an interest in me and that might be good or it might be bad* feeling. I asked her if she was an angel, and she seemed to find that funny, but I don't think she laughed or anything. She said no, and I asked her if she knew God, and she said yes, but no better than I did.

"And we talked about my parents, about Seth, and Dylan, and my death, and what I'd done, and why. The choice, to stay dead or go back. I asked if I went back, would I still go to Heaven when I eventually died again and she said yes, she couldn't do anything God didn't allow her to do, and my soul was my own.

"None of this is really a memory, you know." She tilted her head to look up at him. "It's not even like a dream. It's like someone stuck someone else's memories in my mind. I can see it all, and I know it happened to me, but I don't feel a personal connection to it. Does that make sense?"

"A little," he mused. "Sometimes that's how I feel when I remember things that happened to me four-footed. It's kind of fuzzy, removed."

"Yeah. Removed is a good word for it." She lowered her head and snuggled back into him. "I don't think she even told me her name. I just knew it when I came back, like it was part of a program she'd downloaded in my head. I knew her name but I had to look her up to find out who she was. Once we were in Texas, I met an old lady who was one of her acolytes. I have to think Eir arranged that."

"What happened to Seth while you were busy being dead with Eir?"

She stretched and wiggled a little in his arm, flexing against him. If he hadn't been listening to his mate describe her own death, this would've been one of the most enjoyable experiences of his life. Ally drawing circles on his chest beat any three-way or model, or three-way with models, he'd ever had.

"Seth freaked out. I was dead. He'd killed a Lake Charles wolf, and that pack is full of nasty trash. He couldn't call the cops, and he didn't want to call anyone in his family, because then the pack would find out."

"Where was Dylan?"

"In my room, screaming for me. Seth told him everything was okay and to just wait there for him. Dylan wanted to know where I was, and Seth yelled at him, and after that Dylan wouldn't say anything. Then Seth wrapped my body in a comforter and put it in the back of the Cherokee."

"What the—?"

"He didn't want someone else taking my body. He's not sure what he thought he'd do with it. He had some idea about taking me back to my father's family in Texas."

"Okay. And then?"

"He went to Guy and Gracie's place and took all the cash he could find, and he went to his house and got all the money he'd saved."

"I'm impressed he held it together like that. That kind of trauma would make most betas change."

"Seth's a strong beta. And he's got guts to spare." She stopped talking. He listened to her taking deep, quivering breaths.

"So, now he's driving around with a little boy and a dead girl..." he prompted.

"Yeah, a dead girl in the back seat and a catatonic little boy up front. He knew he should probably drop Dylan off with someone in Lake Charles, but he hates our family as much as I do. So he kept Dylan and took off for Beaumont, where my cousin TJ and some others lived." She paused. "He did pretty good, considering."

She took a deep breath. "And right after he crossed the Sabine River, just outside of Orange, I sat up."

He jerked. Her head bumped up and down on his chest.

"You *what*?"

"I just woke up. I was talking to Eir, I made my decision, I opened my eyes and I started to suffocate—I had a hunk of goose down in my mouth. They didn't hear me thrashing around back there, I guess, because they were kind of surprised when I sat up."

"You just sat up?" He almost laughed at the image it conjured. This shouldn't be funny, not even in a gallows humor sort of way.

"Yeah. I don't think I remembered, just at that moment, that I'd been dead. I sat up, saw them and said, 'Why is Dylan in the front seat?'"

"First thing back from the dead, you start bitching?"

He heard a small smile in her voice. "Well, you can't put a five-year-old in the front seat. Then Dylan turned around and said "Ally!" all happy like, and Seth turned around and saw me, and he screamed like a girl and drove the Cherokee into a ditch."

When she didn't say anything else right away, he nudged her impatiently. "And?"

"And...there was some screaming and crying, but we had to

get the car out of the ditch before the cops saw us, so we did. We stopped to buy me some clean clothes and then we showed up at TJ's parents' house a little after midnight. I couldn't explain why the boys had luggage and I didn't, or why Dylan was with us. When I opened the door of the backseat, I pulled it off, and that's when I first realized that something deeply weird had happened to me, and...life went on. We dealt."

"Who else knows about all this?"

She sighed and shifted. He tightened his arm around her lest she be tempted to get up. She relaxed.

"Just Mrs. Olsen, the Eir acolyte I mentioned. I met her at church right after we got to Sugar Land. Other than her, and Seth and Dylan, only you know."

"Dec doesn't know?"

She took a sharp breath, but her voice sounded normal when she answered. "He knows I'm weird. He doesn't bug me about it."

She stopped, and this time he didn't prompt her to go on right away.

They lay together in the quiet darkness. The more he played with her satin honey hair, or ran his thumb up and down the back of her neck, the more she relaxed and nestled against him. Her hand trailed idly up and down his stomach while her warm breath tickled his chest hairs.

He thought about her first night at the ranch and the fight at dinner, when he'd been so certain she and Seth were lying to him and she'd been so scared when Seth admitted to killing Guy Fontenot.

He thought about an eighteen-year-old girl who gave her life for a little boy, then chose to postpone Heaven so she could take care of him, and of the guts and brains and selflessness it took for two teenagers to do what they had done.

He thought of how she'd lived thirteen years with superhuman abilities she was forced to hide, raising someone else's kid.

Unique, hell. She was awe-inspiring. A badass Army Ranger Pack Alpha might feel inadequate for just a moment.

The moment passed, of course. The awe remained.

He could give her what she'd never had—security, privacy, rest. She wouldn't have to hide her nature among humans. He could protect her, cherish her. Most wolves said the mate bond felt just like love. He suspected he would've felt this way even without the bond.

There was still one thing he needed to know.

"Ally."

"Hmm?" She sounded sleepy.

He rolled her over onto her back, propping himself up on his good arm. She gazed up at him through half-closed eyes.

"Wait a minute." She opened her eyes all the way. "Be careful, Cade. Watch your shoulder. Lay back—"

"Shh." He stopped her mouth with his own, shuddering when, after a moment, she dragged her nails gently down his back. Their tongues met, soft and lazy. He drank until he was dizzy. She sighed contentedly as he broke the kiss. She wanted him, that was obvious.

Which made the question even more important.

"Ally," he said against her mouth.

"Hmm?" she purred.

"Why'd you try to leave, baby?" He raised his head slightly to look at her eyes, and she closed them again, no longer eager to challenge him.

"Ally, look at me," he ordered. "I thought the night we had was good, I thought—"

"It was wonderful. The best I've ever had."

"Then why—?"

She spoke in a rush. He realized she was embarrassed and wanted to get it over with. "Cade, you looked straight at me and said you'd never marry unless you met your mate. I thought you were trying to tell me that, you know, I didn't have a chance with you or anything." Her eyes flew open. She blushed crimson. He loved her blush. It made him feel tender and horny at the same time. "To hear something like that right after what we did, and—it was just, it just..."

"It hurt your feelings?"

She squeezed her eyes shut and drew a shaky breath. He bent his head to kiss her eyelids. Her lashes were wet.

"I'm sorry, baby." He stroked his thumb across her cheekbone and down to her mouth. "I make you cry a lot, don't I? I shouldn't make you cry so much."

She smiled shyly, still not meeting his gaze, and pressed her hands into the small of his back, cradling him between her legs.

"You can make it up to me when you've got your strength back," she whispered.

"Yes, ma'am," he growled. "You're going to need all your strength yourself."

He cupped her breast for a moment, flicking his thumb across her nipple, and smiled with satisfaction when she gasped.

Reluctantly he rolled over onto his back once more and closed his eyes. She snuggled up tight, breasts pillowing his arm, and drew her leg up over his hip. They lay there, relaxed and tired and content to listen to each other breathe.

"Cade?"

"Hmm?" Why did females always wait 'til you were almost asleep to start a conversation?

"When are you going to tell me about the dream?"

Pause. "Later."

She smiled against his skin. "Fine. I'll bug you about it later."

Something jabbed her in the back once, then twice. She jerked sleepily to get away from it. *Jab.* This time in the ribs, hard. What the hell?

She woke with an "umph", sweaty and disoriented on the edge of the emperor-sized bed. Someone had left the curtains of the upper window wide open and moonlight streamed in. She loved the way it washed over the bed.

As she lay with eyes closed, pretending she could feel the moon's pull as wolves did, listening to Cade's deep, regular breathing, a second sound intruded—lighter breathing, more rapid, a little nasal. She had to roll over carefully, lest she tumble off the side of the bed. As she turned, a small fist shot out across her shoulder, just missing her mouth. Becca frequently fought unseen forces in her sleep, yet never cried out as if in a nightmare. She just swung and kicked and punched and wiggled, waking up happy and refreshed.

Ally captured the fist and lowered Becca's arm to her side. Gently but firmly, she pushed the little girl back to the middle of the bed, sliding over next to her. Becca flexed and mumbled, but she didn't wake. Cade slept on, his back to them, oblivious to the midnight tussle inches away.

A sleeping child was nature's sweetest furnace.

Ally pushed the hair out of Becca's hot little face and gazed at her a while. A warm, sleeping child and a warm, sleeping werewolf in a big, warm bed in a big, safe house. Her werewolf? Her child? Her bed and home? The prospect filled her with fearful hope and uncertain joy. So enormous a change, so abrupt a fork in the road, would take getting used to. She was scared this new life wouldn't really be hers, scared she couldn't cope if it was.

She wrapped an arm around Becca and pulled her close, giggling when the curly hair tickled her nose. Cade snorted, rolled onto his back and began to snore softly. Even his snoring seemed sexy—more evidence, if she needed any, that she was completely gone. She stared at his broad chest rising and falling, at his beautiful face mirrored so closely in his daughter's. Inhaling the sweet scent of baby soap and shampoo, she fell back to sleep.

# Chapter Eighteen

She'd been wearing the same T-shirt and lounge pants for she didn't know how long. Cade had been shot four—or was it five now?—days ago, and she'd left the house only to ride, swim, or play with Becca.

She got out of bed, stretched, and walked into an empty living room. All the action was in the heart of the house—the kitchen—where Sindri, Sarah Jane, Dec, Becca and Seth were talking and laughing. Becca shrieked in Dec's lap as he tickled her mercilessly.

"Good morning, honey. You get enough sleep?" Sarah Jane put a mug on the table in front of her and poured some coffee.

She yawned. "Too much, I think. What day is it, anyway?"

Sarah Jane smiled. "It's Friday."

"Holy crap."

Sindri fixed her a plate of freshly scrambled eggs and toast. Did he cook breakfast all day?

"Where's Cade?"

Seth answered. "He's at the stables. He wanted to get back to work."

"And y'all just let him go? Is he in any shape to be running around?" She looked first to Dec, then to Sindri, for confirmation.

Dec gave a lazy smile and shrugged. "The Alpha's a very strong wolf, love, and he's healed nicely. The poison's gone. Besides, you're the only one who could make him go back to bed."

Everyone laughed. She blushed.

"So you've checked him out?" That made her feel better.

"Oh hell no. Sorry," he muttered, looking over at Becca, now crawling all over Seth. "Um, no. The Alpha's no fonder of me than he was before he got shot. The wee fella gave him a once-over."

"He is healing well. His father was strong like that." Sindri looked at Sarah Jane, who laughed.

"Oh, Louis. Good Lord. I remember when he was a teenager, before the wolves came out. Some fool bet Louis he couldn't jump off the top of his family's house—four stories tall—and hit a blanket on the ground below." She shook her head and smiled at the memory. "He hit that blanket dead center. Broke his leg in three places. His father wanted to shoot him right there, just for being so damned stupid. Luckily there weren't any humans around to see it. Back then a break like that would cripple a human. Even for a wolf, it was an awful injury, and his father made the doctor set it without giving Louis anything for the pain first. He was up and around in two weeks, acting stupid again in three."

"You knew him well?" Ally asked.

"Well enough. Our families had been in Savannah for a long time."

Seth looked up from dangling Becca over his shoulder. "You have wolves in your family, Mrs. Ferguson?"

Dec and Sindri exchanged a glance, but Sarah Jane just nodded. "My uncle was a werewolf. Werewolves were in Georgia before the war. A lot of them fought in it, as a matter of fact."

"Yeah, sometimes I wonder how long it would've taken us to come out if it hadn't been for the war."

Sarah Jane laughed. "I was talking about the War Between the States, Seth. A lot of werewolves defended Atlanta. Didn't do much good, of course, but still. People remembered."

Ally hadn't thought she was hungry, but she'd cleaned her plate. Politely refusing Sindri's offer of seconds, she rose.

"I think I'll go find Cade, make sure he's not overdoing it. Unless you want some time to yourself?" she asked Sarah Jane. "In that case, I'll take over Becca."

"Oh no you don't. I get more Becca time today. Let's go, baby." Becca trotted out with her grandmother.

Ally put her dishes in the sink, thanked Sindri, and turned to go.

"Hang on," said Seth, still nursing a cup of coffee at the

table. "I wanted to talk to you for a sec."

"Okay."

Dec cleared his throat. "Ally girl, a word?"

"What is it, Dec?"

"I—" He paused, looking at Seth. "Let's step outside. Seth, would you excuse us for a minute?"

Seth laughed. "Seriously?"

Dec didn't crack a smile. "Yes. I'm sorry. I need to speak to Ally privately. It'll just take a second."

Her cousin looked incredulous, then shrugged. "Sure, wolf. Whatever." He shook his head and took another gulp of coffee.

They walked out to the front porch.

Dec sighed. "Now I've hurt his feelings," he said in a low voice. "I didn't want to do that. And I don't want to put you in an uncomfortable position, love." His brow was furrowed and he sounded apologetic. "I know you and the Alpha have had some problems, and I want you to be happy while you get used to all this, but—"

"But you don't want me telling Cade you're his mother's brother."

He had the grace to look sheepish. "I know I have to tell him, and I plan to, but I've waited almost three weeks, and he doesn't like me, and I just—"

"I think that's weird, you know? Everybody else here likes you. Even Michael likes you, and he's a lot grumpier than Cade."

"What can I say? Every once in a while the MacSorley charm bounces off its intended target."

"Sindri likes you."

"Aye, the wee fella and I get on."

"You've known him a long time, haven't you?"

"Sindri served my family long before Eirny married Louis."

"How long?" He didn't answer. "Of course, you're not going to tell me. Look, Dec, if Cade finds out I knew about this and didn't say anything, he'll be furious with me." Dec looked crestfallen. "On the other hand, I'm bound to piss him off about something else anyway, and I'm not sure how much difference it would make." He began to smile. "I mean, when I thought he was gonna kick me out every time I looked at him cross-eyed, maybe I wouldn't have agreed, but sure. What the hell. You need to be the one to tell him. But," she stopped him as he smiled and started through the door, "don't wait much longer, you hear? It'll just make it worse."

"Of course. Sarah Jane says the same thing."

"Okay. Then I'll keep quiet."

"Thank you," he said, giving her a brief, tight hug. "Thank you. I swear I'll tell him soon."

"You'd better."

Dec ambled off while she returned to the kitchen and Seth.

"Okay, what did you want to talk about?"

He hunched his shoulders and stared at the table.

"Seth? What's wrong?"

He looked up at her with a worried expression. "Are we okay?"

They hadn't talked since Cade got shot, but she immediately understood what was bothering him. "Sweetie, we're always okay."

"I just mean, the way I—"

"I know what you mean. And you didn't do anything. That whole *my wolf* bullshit? That was Cade's fault, not yours."

"It's weird."

"What's weird?"

"All...this, you know?" He held up both hands and looked around. "You're his *mate*, and he's my Alpha, and it's like we're different people all of a sudden."

"*No.*" She said it so fiercely it came out almost like a snarl. He started in surprise. She reached across the table to grab his hand, giving herself of a huge rush of déjà vu as she recalled sitting in this exact position at the big dining table their first night on the ranch, a lifetime ago. "No. We are *not* different people, not to each other, understand? You deserve to be happy, and you deserve to be part of a pack, and you don't need to be worrying about me."

"I want you to be happy too, though," he replied softly. "You are, aren't you?"

She nodded. If it were anyone but Seth sitting across the table, she might not have found it so easy to admit. "Yeah. Yeah, I really think I am. Everything's happening so fast, and I haven't had a chance stop and process it, but yeah. I've never been so happy." Saying it out loud somehow made it more real.

Seth was nodding, less worried now though still somber. "Good. Me too. But still. It'll never be the same again. It'll never be just you, me and Dylan. We can't up and run if we want to."

"No, but I don't think we're gonna want to."

As last he smiled. "No. Probably not."


It felt so good walking outside into bright sunshine and a cool breeze, she had to restrain herself from skipping.

The weather was perfect. So was her hair—she didn't miss the Houston humidity. Dylan and Seth were happy, and here she was, embarking on a relationship with a gorgeous, intelligent, sweet—deep down, at least—powerful werewolf who owned a ranch full of horses and was now biochemically programmed to adore her, and he had a precious little girl who adored her as well, and all the werewolves smiled and waved and acted like she was the shiniest thing they'd ever seen. She suspected that if she walked into the woods, birds and bunnies and assorted forest creatures would surround her and take food from her hands, and she would sing to them, and they would help her get dressed or clean the living room or something.

A sudden thought made her pause. Should it bother her that the mate bond was a lot of the reason for Cade's attraction to her? She couldn't bear to think it might be the only reason. There was no way to know how he'd feel about her without it. Did that make it less real, less meaningful?

Was it wrong to be happy a guy wanted to be with you, and no one but you, forever, because his body told him he had to?

No, damn it. She wasn't going to think like that, wasn't going to take the happiest time of her life and ruin it with fear and self-doubt. She deserved to be happy. All this happiness had been on backorder for years. She was going to sign for it, accept delivery, and get the fuck on with it.

She breathed deep when she walked into B-Barn, savoring the multiple layers of scents. Some women liked to smell flowers, some food. She enjoyed the smell of horses, hay and tack. The open doors at the other end of the breezeway framed the riding ring and, behind it, acres of green grass and dense trees beneath the kind of blue sky and blazing sun that made you want to adjust the brightness controls on the world.

One groom was mucking out a stall, another one cooling

down a Hunter in its stall. They turned as she walked down the breezeway.

"Good morning."

They stared.

"Hi. I'm Ally. I don't think we've met?"

One suddenly found something to stare at on the ground. The other clutched his shovel and blinked at her.

"Do y'all know where—?"

"Hi, pretty girl."

She smelled his wild, tangy scent before she turned to see him strolling up the other end of the breezeway, carrying a fully rigged saddle and followed by a groom leading a lovely piebald Hunter. The front of Cade's gray T-shirt was damp. Perspiration shone on his face and in the hollow of his throat. Twelve hours earlier he'd been unable to move his left side. Now he was riding and lugging tack.

The sight of him sauntering toward her with loose-limbed grace in his threadbare jeans left her dizzy with desire as the voice in her head whispered, *That's yours. You can have that.* Cade's lazy, sultry smile seemed to say he'd heard the voice himself.

How long before she could look at that smile without going hot on the outside and gooey on the inside? It took her a moment to remember she was annoyed with him.

"What the hell do you think you're doing?"

He stopped a couple of feet away from her and raised an eyebrow. "Coming to look for—"

"Have you eaten anything? How long did you ride?"

"I'm gonna go somewhere else..." mumbled the groom with the Hunter, leading the horse off to a distant stall. She ignored them.

"I had breakfast with Becca, and—"

"Why didn't you let the groom take the saddle? Do you want to rip something open?"

He shoved the saddle at her without a word. She took it without thinking. One of the grooms whispered, "*Dude!*"

She cursed silently as she realized she'd forgotten to react to a forty-pound load dropping into her hands. She held the saddle as if it weighed no more than a pillow. Cade just smiled wider.

Then he stripped off his shirt.

"See? No stitches. All healed."

The knife wound had shrunk to a thin, pale ribbon running down his left ribcage. The bullet hole was barely visible to Ally's wolf-keen eyes.

Reluctantly she tore her gaze away from the lean, sculptured torso and back up to his beautiful face. He didn't bother hiding the smirk.

"Would one of you please take this thing?" A groom shot forward to take the saddle from her hands.

"Fine. You're healing on the outside. That doesn't mean you're ready to run around—"

"I haven't run."

"Or carry loads of weight—"

"One saddle."

"Or go riding yet! Damn it, Cade, you still need rest!" She balled her fists on her hips as she glared up at him, furious at his silent laughter.

"Sweetheart," he drawled, "if you want to go back to bed, all you have to do is ask."

She closed her eyes and waited for the hot waves of embarrassment to recede.

"Are you going to stamp your foot?" His low, teasing growl was fuel for the fire licking at her insides. "Because that would be so goddamned cute, I swear I'd throw you in a stall and do you right there with the horses watching." He cocked an eyebrow. "Or maybe the hayloft. Yeah. You'd look hot in a hayloft."

She couldn't understand how he managed to arouse and mortify her all at once. "I'll show you how I stamp my feet all over you, asshole."

"Uh-oh." His voice was suddenly soft and low. "All right, pups. Out. Now. You're embarrassing my mate."

Eyes still closed, she heard tools dropping, feet pounding. Then there was silence. They were alone. She opened her eyes to see him regarding her solemnly.

"I was teasing, sweetheart. Don't be mad."

She nodded and crossed her arms across her chest, feeling bitchy and humorless now. It was easier to stare at his muscular pecs than up at his face. "I'm not mad, I just— I was worried about you."

"I'm a very tough wolf."

"I know. For a while there, I didn't think you'd make it."

"Bothered you, did it?" If she looked up, she'd see that cocky half grin. She could always hear it in his voice.

"Scared the hell out of me." She scuffed at the dirt with her tennis shoe. He was bare inches away. Why didn't he touch her?

"I thought you were dead too, you know," he continued quietly. "I thought I was hallucinating when I saw you break Courtlandt's neck. I was sure he'd killed you."

That made her look up. He wasn't smiling now.

She crossed her arms tighter. "Courtlandt? So Seattle ID'd him?"

"Yeah, from the photos Michael sent them. They don't know where Stapkis is."

"But they realize Stapkis was behind the attack?"

"Oh, definitely. They're already choosing a replacement. Rufus has been formally denounced and expelled from the Pack."

"What does that mean?"

"Means whoever finds him, kills him."

"But aren't you worried he'll come after you himself?"

He shrugged, tucking a stray hair behind her ear. His knuckles grazed her cheek before he dropped his hand. "Not worried. Hoping. I need to be the one who kills him."

She gaped at him, and he smiled grimly.

"What did you think I'd do? Stapkis sent someone to *ambush* me with a goddamned *gun*. His wolf nearly killed my mate."

He put his shirt back on and hooked his arm around her neck, pulling her to him. With her cheek against his damp shirt, she breathed deep, finally relaxing, and wrapped her arms around his waist. They held each other in silence until he put a hand under her chin and tilted her face up.

"So. The day's wasting and I have to go to Colorado Springs tonight."

"To see Aaron?"

"Yes. I haven't checked on him since I got back. Now, what—?"

"Can I go with you?"

"Of course. You sure?"

"Yeah. I've been thinking about him. I just saw him that once, when he held the door for me, and then— Seeing him in the woods, I just..." She couldn't explain.

"You're a wonder." He smoothed her hair back from her face, gathering it in his hands behind her head. His eyes ate her up, his expression both hot and tender. The butterflies in her stomach fluttered up to her throat.

In a soft, slow voice he murmured, "I was going to ask you, before you sank your teeth in my ass, if you wanted to go for a ride."

She whooped with glee and jumped up to kiss his cheek. "Yes! Let's go!"

"Well, now, wait a minute. If you think I need more rest, maybe we should—"

"You're fine. You're tough, you're healed, let's go." She grabbed one of his hands in both of hers and began tugging him down a row of stalls.

"You want an Icelandic or a—?"

"I've ridden the ponies, now I want to ride a Hunter."

"Really?" He stopped dead and yanked her to him. "Okay. Then we're going this way."

She shrieked when he bent down and scooped her up in a fireman's carry, wriggling and yelping as he nibbled on her hip. Cade halted abruptly and set her on her feet outside a large stall at the end of the row.

A dark brown head with a white strip appeared over the stall door. The horse nickered to Cade.

"Ally, this is Sleipnir. Sleipnir, my mate, Allison."

"Oh, Cade. He's wonderful."

The swaggering Pack Alpha disappeared for a moment. She gulped at the proud, almost shy, little boy smile he gave her, and she swore to herself she'd make him tell her about his nightmare soon.

He opened the stall door and led Sleipnir out, stroking and whispering while the horse rubbed his head against Cade's shoulder. Someone had already groomed him for a ride.

The handsome bay gelding was a deep brown from ears to buttocks, with a black mane, tail and legs. He had the powerful hindquarters that gave the breed its jumping ability, as well as the beautiful head and arched, muscular neck of the typical Irish Hunter. Enduring her inspection with good-natured calm, he lowered his head to her shoulder.

"Wow, he's tall. Seventeen hands?"

"Seventeen-two." Five feet eight inches at the withers, a few inches taller than normal for the breed and four inches taller than Ally herself.

She rubbed her cheek against his muzzle. "He's bombproof, isn't he?"

Cade laughed ruefully, rubbing the Hunter's nose as he nuzzled Cade's chest. "I thought he was, but the gunshot spooked him. He hasn't thrown me in years. You're getting old, boy," he murmured affectionately against Sleipnir's neck.

"Well, someone was shooting at him. Just 'cause he's named after a war god's steed doesn't mean he is one." She paused. "I wonder if Odin rode a gelding."

"I don't know about gods, but werewolves and stallions sure as hell don't mix. We breed 'em, but we can't ride 'em."

Something made her look up at Cade, standing on the other side of Sleipnir's head. He watched her intently, his dark brows furrowed, a half smile on his face and naked hunger in his eyes. The air got thick and heavy. Her stomach clenched. She licked her lips and waited for him to say something. He just stood there with a hip cocked out and an arm slung over Sleipnir's neck, eyeing her as if she were lunch but making no move.

"So," he said abruptly, "let's tack him up and get out of here."

"Um, okay." She frowned, confused and disappointed. She'd expected a kiss. "Who will I ride?"

"You're riding Sleipnir." He spoke over his shoulder as he moved to get the tack.

"You let other people ride your horse?"

He grinned as he threw the blanket and saddle across the Hunter's back.

"No. I let my mate ride my horse. Y'all need to get acquainted." He tightened and double-checked the saddle, then slipped the bit into Sleipnir's mouth. "Come on, give me your little foot. You're short, you know that?"

She punched his biceps, feeling perversely proud of the flinch he couldn't quite hide, then put her foot in his laced hands and bounded onto the big horse's back with glee.

"Who will you—? What are you doing?" she exclaimed as he grasped the saddle horn and swung up behind her.

"Push up, baby." He thrust his pelvis against her backside and chuckled when she scooted forward with an irritable "humph!"

She found it hard to concentrate—or breathe—with his arms around her, her head against his chest, his breath in her ear...his cock pressing into the cleft of her butt through her thin sweatpants.

"I've never ridden double with another adult," she fretted.

"Me neither. But it already feels like fun." He Elvis'd her again, pushing against her until her lady bits almost rubbed the saddle horn. She bit her lip, repressing both a giggle and a moan.

"Will he be okay with both of us? What about the weight?"

Cade's breath tickled her neck when he laughed. "He'll be fine. We're not running." Sleipnir gigged along easily. "You don't weigh anything anyway. Just mind your balance." He shifted behind her and thrust forward a little.

"Cade! You're gonna make me lose my seat!"

"Thought you knew how to ride."

"Asshole," she muttered.

He kissed her cheek again. "Oh, hush. Ask for a canter."

"That's too fast with both of us, he'll get—"

"Jesus, Allison. You argue with everything I say!"

"No, I don't! And watch your language!"

He put his hands over hers on the reins and shifted his weight deep into the saddle. She instinctively loosened her grip on the reins and deepened her seat as well. Soon they were cantering across the gently sloping fields beside the riding ring, headed west away from the compound.

In just a few seconds she and Cade were riding the canter in perfect tandem. She forgot her pique and lost herself in the joy of the ride.

His scent enveloped her as she relaxed into his broad chest and listened to his heart pounding against her back. She stared at the big, calloused hands gripping the saddle horn, hands she knew could stroke her tenderly or hold her down while he drove her wild. For now she was content to ride with the wind in her face and Cade at her back.

"Is the weather always perfect in Colorado?"

"Around here, in summertime, usually. Have you ever been in snow?"

"Just vacation snow. I saw it, I threw snowballs, I went home. I've never lived in it."

"You'll love it. We'll go up to the mountains for Christmas, just the four of us."

A few minutes passed before she said in a carefully neutral tone, "Must be nice."

"What?"

"Knowing that everyone's going to do what you want them to do."

"It's good to be the Alpha." He sighed. "The burdens are great, the responsibilities heavy, but the rewards are—"

"Shut up."

"Yes, ma'am."

Soon she recognized where they were.

"We're headed for the ravine!"

"Yeah," he replied, his voice suddenly husky and hoarse. "That okay with you?"

"Yes!"

"Good. Take him to a walk."

"Why?"

He snorted against her neck, and she giggled. "'Cause it's my horse, female. Now slow him down."

"Fine," she grumbled. "I don't see why we have to...oh."

Cade gathered her hair in one hand and pushed it aside. She giggled at the soft scratch of his beard, then moaned when he kissed the nape of her neck, tongue dipping into the hollow at the base of her skull. He slipped his other hand beneath her T-shirt. The heat of it penetrated all the way to her core, fanning embers smoldering since he'd smiled at her in the barn. The reins shook in her hands.

"Cade...I can't—oh!" She jerked a little as he nipped at her shoulder.

"Can't what, Ally?" he murmured.

His mouth traveled to her other shoulder and she arched

against him.

"Cade!" She squeaked a little. "We're out in the open!" She halfheartedly tried to turn her body away, but she didn't have much room to maneuver and she couldn't let go of the reins, and besides—even as her mind quailed at the exposure, her body flexed restlessly against his, begging for more.

He covered her hands with his and jerked back on the reins, holding them 'til Sleipnir had resumed a slow, steady walk. "There's no one around, I promise."

"No one can see us?"

"Nope. And we're about to be in the trees."

She opened her eyes. They'd almost reached the stand of trees fringing this side of the ravine.

"You planned this?"

He nodded and smiled against her skin. "Sleipnir knows where he's going. You don't have to guide him much."

"I can't guide him at all if you keep doing that to me."

Clever, calloused fingers were gently teasing and pulling her nipples. She shivered at the sensation of his hot, rough skin against her tender breasts

Soon they were in the cool shade of pine and juniper and cedar. Sleipnir ambled through the trees, stopping to nibble at the carpet of grass beneath the ceiling of branches. She smelled the river, heard it moving lazily through the ravine that dropped away to their left.

In a small clearing lay a blanket. On the blanket lay a pillow and some linens and another blanket, this one folded. A bottle of champagne sat nestled in ice in a beat-up metal bucket.

Her squeal of excitement turned to a gasp as Cade's hand swept down into her sweatpants. He cupped her mound, his finger dipping into her folds, pressing into her but not moving. She felt the first rush of wetness as her thighs tensed around his hand. Her sex began to throb.

"Show me, sweetheart," he breathed into her ear. "Show me you want it."

She bucked restlessly against him in the saddle. He knew she wanted it. His fingers stroked faster now, and she was dripping wet, juices flowing in a hot torrent of need.

She put her hand over his, outside her sweatpants,

grinding against his palm. "Right there, right...oh God, yes, that's good, Cade..." She gasped as he began rubbing circles around her clit.

"Do you like it like that?"

"I love it—a little faster, a little..." Rocking forward, she brazenly ground his hand beneath hers to show him the stroke she needed. When she sat at just the right angle, and his strokes matched the pulsing rhythm of her body, she gave a helpless, ragged cry and began to ride his hand with wanton abandonment.

"Is that better, baby?"

"It's perfect," she moaned.

"Good," he whispered. "Now take off your shirt."

"I can't...I can't hold the reins..."

Chuckling, he dropped her hair and took the reins, his other hand never missing a stroke.

She wouldn't have cared if anyone was watching as she peeled off her shirt and bra. He did that to her—he pushed her past herself, past her own restraint and reluctance.

She'd never been naked outdoors. The wind whispering across her skin and the filtered sunlight warming it, and the chance, however remote, that someone might see them, triggered the beginning of her climax. She was almost disappointed to start coming so soon. Grasping the saddle horn in both hands, she rocked forward further and faster.

Sleipnir had stopped and now stood patiently waiting. Cade dropped the reins to twist her head up to him. He kissed her hard, speaking into her open mouth. "Hurry up and come. I need to get inside you."

His words pushed her over the edge. She felt her sex throb and contract around his fingers. The orgasm burst over her without further buildup or warning. She cried out and held his hand in place while she thrashed against it as his tongue plunged into her mouth. When her release had wrung her out, she slumped against him, too blissed to think about his need or how hard and hot he was behind her.

He slipped from Sleipnir's back.

"I don't think I can stand," she said, woozy from the afterglow.

"I don't intend to let you." He laughed as she slid off the

saddle into his arms, and he laid her on the blanket. She lazily shed her sweats and panties while she watched him rip off his own clothes, graceful even in his frantic haste.

As he tossed his jeans aside, she rose to her knees and took his cock in her hand, laughing at his startled intake of breath.

He groaned her name. "Baby, I can't—"

"Shh. Yes you can." Taking the thick base of his penis in one hand, she ran her tongue up and down the length of it as her other hand wandered over the smooth, hard expanse of his stomach. Then her hand went around to cup his ass, stroking his hot skin. His hips jerked, his hands tightening in her hair. She felt his legs tremble.

Shielded by the trees surrounding them, excited by the wind blowing over her naked body, emboldened by Cade's whispered pleas, she lost all inhibition. A delicious shiver ran through her as he cried out her name again.

"Don't you dare come until you're inside me." She kept her eyes locked on his as she took him into her mouth. She sucked slowly, drawing him out like a lollipop, then took him back in, her mouth working in time with her hand, all the while watching his expression.

His eyes narrowed to slits, wonder and need illuminating his face. He took rapid, shallow breaths, the strain of holding back his release plain to see. Once again, she exulted in the power she held over him, the knowledge of how much he wanted her, what her mouth and her hands and her body could do to him.

He stroked her cheek with one hand while he pumped into her mouth. His expression began to harden, growing wilder and fiercer as his thrusts got harder and faster.

With a harsh cry, Cade withdrew from her mouth, pulling her head back. She gave a small cry of pain and surprise, but he didn't seem to hear. He was panting, his face twisted in ecstasy. He stepped behind her and shoved her forward, forcing her to her hands and knees.

She screamed as he dipped two fingers deep inside her. "Hurry up!"

He didn't answer. He withdrew his fingers, grasped her hips and yanked her back, impaling himself in her.

He held her ass in an iron grip while he drove into her

once, twice, three times. With every thrust she begged for more. On the fourth, he growled and exploded inside her. He shuddered as his hips rammed against her in the frenzy of his release. With a final growl, he collapsed on top of her.

She lay beneath him, stunned and almost sated, his lush hair spilling across her back. His breath was ragged and hot against her neck. Stars danced behind her eyes. Sex had never left her hyperventilating before. She started to laugh.

"Ally?" He brushed the hair away from her face, nuzzling her neck. "Baby? You all right?"

Her laugh turned into a small whimper. "I'm fine, but—ow. You're crushing me, sweetie. Let's switch."

He rolled onto his back, taking her with him. Happy and tired, she played her fingers across his stomach while he stroked her hair. She loved his stomach, loved its warmth and taut muscles and the fine, dark treasure trail that tickled her palms.

"I'm sorry." He sounded gruff and shy at the same time.

Her hand paused in its travels. "What for?"

"For being so rough. I got carried away. I promise, baby, I won't do it again. I know you haven't—"

She scooted her body 'til they were face-to-face. "Like hell. You *will* do that again. We're gonna do a lot more of that, werewolf. I loved that."

"But..." He grimaced in confusion. "You didn't come, did you?"

She laughed so loud it startled Sleipnir, who whinnied. "I didn't have time." She stopped laughing when she saw his mortification and kissed him tenderly. "You're a big, tough werewolf. You lasted a really long time. I just shouldn't have given you such a good hummer."

That elicited a sly grin. "You're right. It's your fault for blowing me so well."

Of course she blushed. Looking away, fingers nervously plucking at his chest hairs, she couldn't resist asking, "So...you really liked it?"

He put a hand to her chin, turning her head back to him.

"I think I said something like 'fuck, baby, don't stop,' yeah?"

She grinned. "Yeah. And you said you loved my mouth."

"Did I? Then I guess I liked it okay."

He rolled her over onto her back and nipped at her bottom lip, laughing and pulling his mouth out of reach when she tried to kiss him, nibbling at her neck and her breasts. Not until she tugged at his hair did he relent and return to her mouth. Their tongues dipping and sparring, she clung to his shoulders and sighed into his mouth as his warmth permeated her.

He broke the kiss to stare at her, their noses almost touching, his crystal green eyes boring into hers as he tangled his fingers in her hair.

"Admit it," he growled.

Her hands paused in their exploration of his biceps. "Admit what?"

"You're happy. I make you happy."

He was so shamelessly proud of himself—sure of himself, pleased with himself—and she wished, not for the first time, that Eir had given her the self-assurance of an alpha along with all the physical attributes and instincts.

"Yeah," she conceded softly, "I admit it. You make me happy." As his triumphant grin spread, she added, "And Becca makes me happy, and the horses, and the swimming pool—"

"And the pack?"

"And the pack."

His grin didn't falter. "But you can't have Becca and the rest of it without me. So I make you happy."

It was true. And it scared the hell out of her.

Cade nipped at her nose and rolled off.

"Hey! Where are you—?"

"Just lay there and look happy." He tossed her a small towel, then retrieved the champagne and glasses.

She stretched and sighed, watching the tree branches swaying above her, soaking in the sun's warmth, until he held out a glass and she sat up to take it.

"Oh, that's good. That's really good. I haven't had champagne in a while." She sipped, forcing herself to relax under his gaze, as if sitting naked and sipping champagne post-coitus came naturally.

She envied him his unconscious ease as he knelt on his haunches, drinking and watching her. He didn't need to make conversation or pose his body.

If he knew how badly he still rattled her, how she feared she'd never get used to this—to him—would he think her nuts? Would it even matter, given the mate bond? In spite of all the pep talks she'd been giving herself, she still couldn't get past the idea that he only wanted her because he had to.

"Stop thinking."

"Crap. How do you *do* that?"

"Put your glass down."

Some of the champagne spilled over on the towel in her lap as she started at the abrupt command. She carefully placed the glass on the blanket beside her.

"Toss the towel."

She liked the towel in her lap. It made her feel secure.

"Ally. Toss the towel and lie back down."

"Oh, the hell with it," she muttered and did as he told her. Everyone did as he told them. Eventually it was bound to get on her nerves, accustomed as she was to directing all the traffic in her life, but sometimes it wasn't so bad.

She lay back.

"Close your eyes."

She closed her eyes. Then she squealed and bucked as cold, cold champagne trickled onto her breasts and across her stomach, running off either side over her ribs. Goose bumps erupted all over her torso. Opening one eye, she saw him set aside his now empty glass. Before she could sit back up he was on top of her, pinning her hands to her sides.

She gasped again, not at the cold this time but at the tip of his tongue plunging into her belly button. Giggles turned to groans when he travelled up to her nipples, sucking each until it was taut and swollen and almost painfully sensitized. She arched her back, her shoulders pressing into the blanket.

His tongue heated the champagne against her skin. She twitched and twisted and giggled as he worked his way down.

His mouth travelled back to her navel, and then lower, and then lower still. She yelped when he put his hands under her butt and squeezed. Her legs fell open to admit his clever tongue, and she stretched to pick up the half-full glass by her hip. She caught him peeking at her. Feeling shameless, brave and spoiled, she held his gaze as she knocked back the rest of the champagne in one gulp and then collapsed against the blanket.

He didn't stop working that outrageous magic with his mouth, but he chuckled against her mound, and it tickled.

The ride home was sticky.

# Chapter Nineteen

Aaron remained in a coma. They wouldn't give up hope yet, but the doctors talked of transferring him to a long-term facility.

There was no word of, or from, Rufus Stapkis. They started to think he'd died. Seattle picked a new Alpha and was the second major Pack, after Houston, to recognize Rocky Mountain. Chicago and St. Louis followed immediately afterwards.

Cade bought a garage; Seth ran it. Dylan spent every spare moment in town. Ally suspected he had a girlfriend, but she didn't pry. She wanted him to go to college, but Cade expected him to do a stint in the military first.

Cade let Sarah Jane stick around. She moved into Ally's old room. He even ignored Dec, who spent all his time with Sarah Jane and Sindri and never managed to find the right time to talk to Cade.

They grew closer. He told her about the dream, about his parents' deaths and his family's life before the tragedy. She told him about her life. They told each other things about themselves they'd never shared with anyone.

They went back to the ravine more than once, but didn't make it to the hayloft.

She sat on the front porch at night and watched the wolves run, listened to them howl and contemplated with amazement the fact that this was now her home, the place she never thought she'd be allowed to choose.

She was happier and more relaxed than she'd been at any time in her life, and though Dec's secret hovered like a large black rain cloud on the edge of her suddenly sunny world, she managed to ignore it.

Cade didn't pressure her for a commitment. They never said "I love you", but as the weeks slipped by, she became convinced he felt the same way she did. She didn't even obsess over the love vs. biochemistry question.

She started to believe in happily ever after. Never did she stop to think all hell might break loose at once, threatening everything and everyone she loved.

Stupid Dead Girl.

He wanted to take her out on a real date, to his favorite restaurant in the heart of the historical district. He gave her a credit card and told her if she spent less than two hundred on a dress, the whole thing was off. She came home five hundred dollars later with a fitted, low-cut emerald green number and the hottest pair of black fuck me pumps he'd seen in years.

He was behind the bar, mixing drinks for himself and Michael, when she emerged from the bedroom. He let out a long, sincere whistle. Dressed up, she looked at least twenty-five. His eyes devoured the dress clinging to her every curve. Cut just low enough to be sexy and still decent, it accentuated her perfect tits.

Michael was staring at Ally with a disturbingly appreciative eye. Cade recalled his best friend's words the first time they'd seen her.

"You clean up pretty good," Michael said.

"Shut up," she purred, flashing those dimples and smiling at Cade with a look that said she knew what she was doing to him, and she liked it.

"Yeah, shut up, wolf."

"Where's Becca?" Ally asked.

Michael knocked his drink back. "Somewhere with Sarah Jane and Dec."

Cade put his hands on her hips and slid them around to her backside. "Those are some serious shoes." He loved what a pair of very high heels did to a woman's ass.

She gave a little wiggle and whispered, "I hope I can walk in them."

"You're doing fine. Walking's not what I've got in mind anyway."

Michael cleared his throat. Cade ignored him, kissing Ally lightly on the neck. "Take your hair down." She'd pinned it up loosely, wisps of it hanging in her face. It was pretty, but he wanted to see the lovely mass of honey gold spilling over her shoulders.

"What?"

"Your hair. Wear it down."

"Why?"

He laughed. "Because I asked you to."

She smiled back and nipped his chin. "You didn't ask. You ordered."

"Leaving now."

Neither of them turned to watch Michael go.

His thumb stroked her throat as he kissed her, knowing it made her go limp. "Come on, baby," he whispered. "I love to play with your hair."

She bit his lip. "It'll give you something to look forward to."

"Do you have to argue with everything I say?"

"Do you have to always tell me what to do?" She started for the front door, trusting him to watch her walk away. He didn't watch—he grabbed. He got her from behind and nuzzled the back of her neck, loving the way she shivered and laughed at the tickle of his beard.

"I'm too lenient with you."

"I'm too nice to you."

His cell phone rang.

"Let it go to voicemail. Come on." She spun from his arm, grabbed his free hand and pulled.

He looked at the number and frowned. "Fremont Police Department."

She sighed. "I guess you should take it."

"Hello?"

"Cade? It's me."

"Oh my God, Dylan?" She reached for the phone. He shook his head and pushed her away.

Dylan groaned. "Oh shit, is Ally right there?"

"Yes, son, she's here. Are you okay?"

"Yeah, I'm fine, I'm just in a little trouble."

"Let me talk to him."

"No. I'll handle it."

She put a hand to her mouth and glared at him.

"Cade, you there?"

"Yes. What happened, Dylan?"

"I'm in jail."

"Oh, God."

"Ally, hush. What happened, son?"

"Um, has Ally ever told you about a guy named Jakob Lind?"

Ally's face went white. Her fingernails dug into his forearm. He wrapped his arm around her neck and hugged her to him.

"I know who he is. What happened?"

"Well, I was at Cue's with Heather. We were just hanging out, playing pool. I looked up and there he was, staring at me."

"And?"

"Well, I didn't know what to think. I mean, we'd never had a problem. He seemed to like me, talked about taking me fishing or something stupid like that. I figured he wanted to get in good with Ally, you know? Then when she dumped him—"

"Dylan, son, they're not going to let you talk for long."

"Oh yeah. Sorry."

He winced with regret, because now he could hear the fear and worry in the pup's voice.

"He comes up to me and doesn't even say hi, just says 'where is she?' He was wasted. I said 'Ally's not here', and he looks at Heather and says 'tell your girlfriend to get lost, we need to talk', I say 'fuck off', he says if I don't talk to him, 'that weird fucking bitch will be sorry'."

Ally was trembling in his arms.

"I didn't want a big scene in the bar, since I'm technically not supposed to be drinking—" he wouldn't be nineteen for another two weeks, but the bartenders at Cue's were lenient with Cade's wolves "—and I said 'fine, let's go outside'. So we did." He took a deep breath. "And we get out there and he just goes nuts, screaming at me about how he knows there's something weird about Ally, and she almost killed him and he won't let her get away with it and it took him six months to find me and then we disappear…"

"Wait. Six months to find you?"

"Yeah, I know. We haven't been here that long. So I said I didn't know what he was talking about and I swear to God,

Cade, I didn't lose my temper, I just wanted him to shut up and go away." The kid sounded worried, but calm.

"Dylan, did anyone see this?"

"No. We were alone in the parking lot. I told him I knew he'd messed with Ally and he was lucky one of us didn't go after him, and he said she ruined his fucking life and cost him a lot of money, and he tried to hit me with a slapjack."

"*What?* Are you okay?" Ally shouted.

"Baby, hush. Obviously he's okay."

"I'm fine—I mean, he was drunk, I had plenty of time to block, but I knocked him out when I hit him. When he came to, he started screaming that I attacked him first—even though he was drunk off his ass and holding the slapjack. And the cop who was working security arrested both of us."

"So Lind's in jail too?"

"Yeah, in the squad car he was screaming that I attacked him and that my mom's some kind of ninja bitch, and the cop who took us in told him to shut the fuck up, then he puked and passed out and I had to ride the rest of the way next to him." Cade heard pride in those last words, and he hid a smile for Ally's sake. Lind was trouble, no doubt, but Dylan had acquitted himself well. Nothing like getting in a fight, getting busted and handling it better than your opponent to make a young alpha feel all grown up.

"Hang tight, pup. We're on our way."

"Okay. Thanks, Cade."

He followed Ally into the bedroom.

"Baby, you don't need to—"

"Don't tell me not to come."

She changed into jeans and a white cotton blouse with lace trim. With the loose tendrils of hair falling in her face, she looked soft and feminine and very touchable.

If Dylan had been sitting in jail because of a fight with anyone but the asshole who'd attacked his mate, Cade would've insisted they make time for a quickie. Every alpha wolf did at least one night in jail before he reached twenty-one. It was almost expected, like the military stint they did in order to learn self-control.

"I'm sure Shepherd will let me—"

"Who's Shepherd?"

"Dent Sheperd's the police chief. He's a good guy. He'll let me post bail and bring Dylan home tonight, but it could take a couple of hours."

"Fine. Let's go."

He caught her arm as she brushed past him. She tried to pull away, but he put both arms around her and hugged her close.

"He's fine, and he's going to be fine," he said into her ear. He felt her beginning to relax. "Trust me to take care of my wolves, sweetheart."

Immediately she stiffened. Before he could ask why, she pushed him away so hard he stumbled back and nearly fell onto the bed.

"What the—?"

"Don't give me that *my wolf* shit!" she snarled through tears which hadn't been in her eyes ten seconds ago. "You already took Seth away from me. You can't have Dylan."

"Baby, I didn't mean to—"

She put her hands over her face and took a few deep breaths. Another ten seconds later, she was in complete control again, no trace of tears. "I want to leave. Now."

After a quick word to Michael, they were on their way.

# Chapter Twenty

The first minutes in the car passed in brittle silence. She stared straight ahead with a shuttered expression. He could feel her misery, though. He'd learned to read all her moods, no matter how quickly they changed. Tonight she was wretched and angry, and it was his fault. While he wouldn't apologize, he had to try to explain.

He kept his voice low and calm. "Ally, that day in your room, I was out of my head. You tried to leave and I didn't know why. I thought you were playing me." She stared out her window as he talked. "I took Seth to piss you off and to keep you from leaving. If I'd known what was going on in your mind—"

Her head whipped around. "So it was *my* fault you did it?"

Irritated at the drama, he took a deep breath. "No. But if I had it to do over again, I wouldn't handle it that way."

"But you're not sorry."

He took his eyes off the road for a minute to look at her. "What do you want me to say, Ally? They've joined my pack. That makes them my wolves. And you're my mate, so why does it bother you?"

She went back to staring out the window until they got to town.

Zelma Holmes, a grandmotherly clerk who'd worked for the department since Cade was a pup, was on duty behind the intake desk at the quiet police station. Even on a Friday night, Fremont didn't get rowdy. She smiled at him as if he'd shown up for a social call.

"Hi, Cade! How are you tonight? Is this lovely young lady the mate I've heard so much about?"

Ally blushed, smiling and responding with her customary good manners. "Yes ma'am, I'm Allison Kendall. It's nice to meet you."

"Honey, you don't look old enough to vote!"

Ally started to answer, but he cut her off.

"Mrs. Holmes, I'd like to pay Dylan's bail and get him home. We're both worried about him."

She smiled gaily, showing a mouthful of badly fitting, smoke-stained dentures. "Oh, you don't owe anything. We told the boy he was free to go, just like that foreign idiot they dragged in here with him. Once the man showed up and explained how it was all a mistake, Hank told them they could go. The foreign fella hightailed it outta here, but your nephew said he'd rather wait for you. He seemed worried."

"I'm sorry? What man? Who explained what, and why did Cash let them go?"

Hank Cash, a middle-aged sergeant fated never to advance any further, was a vocal bigot who didn't like wolves. Cade had hoped he wouldn't be on duty tonight, or else bailing Dylan out might take longer than he'd led Ally to believe. Which was another reason he hadn't wanted her to come.

"Why don't you come with me? I'll take you back to see the boy."

There was no one else in the intake room. Still, it was odd that Zelma would leave the front desk like that. And she wasn't normally so cheery or chatty.

He started to tell Ally to wait, but she was on his heels as they walked through the security door to the holding tank. He wouldn't argue in front of strangers.

Hank Cash leaned against the open door of Dylan's cell. The only other prisoners tonight were a couple of disheveled frat types who whistled at Ally when she walked past. A look and a growl from Cade sent them running back to their benches. It earned him a grin from Ally.

"I'm telling you, kid, you've got plenty of time to get back to Cue's and that pretty girlfriend of yours. This whole thing was a— Oh, there you are, MacDougall." Cash straightened at their approach. For the first time in their acquaintance, he nearly smiled at Cade. He did smile at Ally, nodding his head and saying, "Ma'am." Cade didn't feel like introducing them.

"Cash, what's going on here?"

Dylan leapt to his feet. "Ally, you'll never believe who showed up!"

The sergeant interrupted. "MacDougall, I was just explaining to your nephew that since his altercation with the foreign guy was clearly not his fault, and I shouldn't even have arrested him to begin with, he's welcome to leave. He wanted to wait for you."

"Son? What happened?"

Dylan looked fit to burst, waiting for a chance to speak. "It was that weird dude we saw that day, Ally! He showed up here!"

"*What*?" She goggled, looking a little pale again.

"Ally, what the hell is he talking about?"

She ignored him. He fucking hated when she did that.

"What did he do?" she asked.

The words poured out of Dylan in an excited rush. "He came down here with this guy!" He pointed his thumb at Cash. "They were talking, and the weird guy was telling the cop that he knew me and Lind, and that Lind was a, a jerk or something, and he—I mean the weird guy—was sure it was Lind's fault, and the whole thing was just a misunderstanding, and they should just let us go. He seemed pissed off at Lind, told him he'd caused enough trouble and he didn't want to see him—Lind—again, and Lind got mad and started to say something but the old guy just said 'you won't argue with me, you'll leave town now' and so Lind shut up, just like that, and then...then it got really weird."

"Dylan," Ally said anxiously, "Just tell me what happened."

"He looked at me, and he said, 'Tell Eirny I'm sorry, I meant no harm. I want to see her'."

Ally gasped and looked at Cade.

The world tilted for a second. He grabbed a bar of the cell to stay upright. To hear his mother's name here, in such a bizarre context...

He knew he needed to ask Ally a question, but a painful buzzing noise in his head made it hard to think.

"Cade? Baby? You okay?"

Dylan and Cash were looking at him, Dylan worriedly and Cash in confusion.

223

He focused on Ally. "What's he talking about? What weird guy? And why would he know my mother?"

Dylan started to answer, but Ally stopped him. "Let's get out of here. Right now—we don't need to talk about it here."

The part of Cade's mind still working properly was grateful, and annoyed, at the way she quietly took over as soon as she saw he was in trouble.

"Dylan, come on, sweetie. Sergeant Cash—" the cop blinked and smiled at her "—we're going to talk to Chief Shepherd about this in the morning."

On their way out, Cade asked, "Ally, what the hell is going on here?"

She shook her head. "Wait 'til we're in the car."

He made no move to turn the car on once they were buckled up. His mind had rebooted itself and was functioning again. He turned to look at Ally, who sat lost in thought.

"High Fae?"

She looked up, surprised. "Has to be."

She had Dylan tell him about a strange man who'd watched them and followed Dylan the day she got Becca's hair cut. Something cold and slimy crawled across his skin as he listened to a description of the stranger. When Dylan recounted the man's questions about their mothers, Cade exploded.

"Why the fuck would you not tell me about this?" he shouted loud enough to be heard at the ranch. Behind him, Dylan whimpered.

Ally had been twisted around, talking to Dylan in the backseat. Now she turned to face him, but she didn't, as he expected, lose her own temper. She peered at him for a minute and then said quietly, "I'm sorry. We decided he was some doped out Fae, and then when you got home the next day, everything happened and I just forgot about it."

"What, you think a doped out Fae is *normal*? You think we get them around here all the time?"

She shrugged, face drawn with worry. "I didn't think about that. I've met a few in Houston, and I've never heard of them hurting anyone. They're too stoned to be violent, and with their talents dulled, they're not dangerous. We assumed he mistook

Dylan and Becca for someone else, and we forgot about it."

"But obviously he recognized them because he knows who my mother is!"

"So then why'd he ask who Dylan's mother was, or Becca's?"

"Yeah," Dylan piped up. "When I told him my mom was Gracie, he didn't believe me, and that's when he started with the war gulf crap."

"So did you talk to him when he showed up here tonight?"

"Not really. Lind was yelling, and he told Lind to get lost—oh! I see what you mean about Fae," the teenager mused. Cade snorted in exasperation. "He told Lind to leave, and Lind left. He told Cash and that old lady it was all a big mistake and they should let us go, so they did. But if he can mind whammy people, why didn't it work on me? That day in town, he looked at me and said 'you didn't see me', but I still knew I saw him."

"I have no idea how we figure that out. I'm more concerned with how he knows my mom." Mama had no family, and the pack members her age were long gone. Only Shawn and Sindri had known her. A Fae, a guy Cade didn't know, showing up here and mentioning her made no sense. He was missing something here, something important.

"Y'all still haven't told me what the guy looked like."

"Tall," Ally began. "Long white hair, almost silver, tied back in a ponytail."

"Eyes?"

"Eyes? Oh, right. No, I couldn't see them." She ran a finger across her face, from her eyebrow to her opposite cheek. "He had a scar across his face, though." She jumped. "Cade? What's wrong?"

He'd just shouted—a hoarse, sharp cry—and now he couldn't answer her because he was shivering and shaking like he'd swallowed dry ice.

"Cade? Baby, answer me! Right now!"

He put his forehead on the steering wheel. It rattled beneath his shaking hands. Ally's cool, soft hands stroked his face and neck.

"Baby? Please, can you tell me what's wrong?"

"It's him," he whispered, swallowing hard and concentrating on not throwing up. He wouldn't shame himself by falling apart in front of his wolf and his mate.

Ally slid across the seat to put her arm around him, but he pushed her away. To accept her comfort was to admit he needed it. Instead, he stilled the shakes, banished the sick and cleared his head, taking emotional refuge in dominance.

In the backseat Dylan whimpered, terrified by the stress his Alpha was shedding.

"It's who, Cade?" Ally asked quietly.

"The guy from my dream. The guy who killed my father."

After a few minutes' silence, Ally offered to drive, but he refused that as well.

"I thought you couldn't see the guy in your dream, couldn't remember what he looked like."

"Couldn't before. Can now. The scar. Mama cut his face with the knife that killed my dad." Now, for the first time in thirty-three years, he saw the guy clearly in his mind's eye, saw the lean, eerily handsome face and the long silver ponytail whipping in the wind.

Dylan whined again. Cade wanted to say something to calm the pup, but he couldn't summon the thought to form the words. He rolled his window down. The cool night air cleansed his lungs and dried the sweat on his face and neck.

"The guy who killed your mother shows up here," Ally said softly. "And he knows Lind. And he wants to know about Dylan's mother and Becca's mother, and he wants to tell *your* mother he's sorry. For what? For killing your dad? Thirty-three years ago? Doesn't he know she's dead? Dylan, honey, didn't you say the guy looked familiar?"

"Yeah."

Cade could barely hear him. Ally was the only one who didn't stink of fear and misery. Cade was grateful, once again, for her levelheaded nature, but he wished she'd shut the fuck up so he could concentrate on not changing while driving.

"Dylan?" he rasped. "You okay back there, son?"

"I think so."

"If it's the same guy, what does he want?" asked Ally.

"Don't care what *he* wants. *I* want to find him and kill him."

"Forget about finding him for a minute, baby. Think about

this. He saw us in town almost three months ago, but he didn't try to hurt us. He seemed almost frightened of Dylan when Dylan cornered him, didn't he?" She looked back at the teenager.

"Yeah. I thought he was gonna run away from me."

"So they talk, he does that pathetic 'you don't see me' bit, and he disappears. And tonight, when he sees Dylan, he gets him out of jail and says to tell Eirny he's sorry. That doesn't sound like a threat. I agree you need to find the guy, but I don't get the feeling he's out to hurt you or Dylan. Or Becca."

He didn't answer. What she said made sense intellectually, but his intellect wasn't working right now. The urge to run back to town, find the bastard and rip his guts out vied with the urge to run into the woods, find a deep hole and crawl in for a few months. Or just lock himself in his room and get well and truly shitfaced. Only the first option, of course, was available to an Alpha.

"Well?"

"Well what, Ally?" he yelled. He could feel her flinch all the way on the other end of the seat. "You want me to speculate on the bastard's motives? How the hell do I know what he wants? He killed my parents. You want me to give him the benefit of the doubt now? If you'd told me about the guy earlier, *when it fucking happened,* maybe I'd know by now what he wants!"

Cade locked his jaw and stared straight ahead, waiting for her to burst into tears. But no—that's what she would've done before, like the day he'd shown them around the ranch. Now she was his mate, and it had changed her as much as it had him.

His mate didn't cry. His mate busted his balls. He steeled himself for a tongue-lashing.

It never showed up.

In a soft voice, a voice full of love and concern he didn't deserve, she said, "Does emotional turmoil cause all alphas to act like assholes? Is it some kind of defense mechanism?"

It caught him so completely off-guard that he choked on a laugh. The tension in the car didn't evaporate, but she'd burned off a good fifty percent of it all at once.

"I don't know about all alphas, but yeah, I'd guess most." He rolled his shoulders and pressed them back against his seat as he stretched, forcing his body to loosen up a little bit.

Glancing up at the rearview mirror, he caught Dylan's eye and nodded shortly. His nephew closed his eyes and put his head back.

Ally unbuckled her seat belt, slid over and buckled the middle belt. She tucked her arm behind his and laid her head on his shoulder. "If you try to push me away again," she murmured, "I'll bite you."

"I might wreck the truck."

"So don't push me away."

So he didn't. And when she took his right hand and placed it in her lap, covering it with both of hers, he didn't take it back. Her touch eased the heartache, her scent calmed the rage. If she insisted he accept a comfort only she could provide, a comfort his body had been screaming for, then he would.

Sindri must've started cooking as soon as he learned of Dylan's arrest. The kid followed his nose straight to the kitchen.

Ally made an exasperated sound.

"Could anything kill his appetite?"

Cade laughed and drew her close. Glad to be home, she snuggled into his arms.

"Hey," he murmured into her hair. "You okay?"

"I am. Are you?"

Just then, her stomach growled loud enough to be heard outside. Cade's chest rumbled with laughter against her ear, and he squeezed her tighter.

"I will be, but I think I need to feed my girl. Come on, let's go see what Sindri's making."

Hand in hand, they walked into the kitchen, where Sindri toddled from stove to table as Dec laughed at Dylan.

"All right, pup. Can you stop eating long enough to tell us what you did to merit your first arrest? Please say a pretty girl was involved."

Ally sat down next to Dec. Cade fetched beers from the fridge and sat down across the table from her. Dylan paused in his inhalation of meatloaf long enough to grin. "I was with a pretty girl, yeah, but she wasn't really involved."

"Well, what was it, then?"

Sindri put two more plates on the table. Ally got up to fix

her own, but he shooed her back to the table. Her stomach growled again. No one noticed.

"Thank you, Sindri, this looks great. You're not gonna believe this, Dec," she said when she saw that Dylan was hoovering the meatloaf again. "Jakob showed up at Cue's."

"*Lind?* What's that gobshite doing in town? How'd he find us?"

"I'd like to know that myself," Cade said. "I think I'll take Michael and go back into town to look for him."

"Tonight?" She'd assumed all the drama was over for the evening. "I mean, you're exhausted, you've had a big shock. You should get some rest."

He reached across the table to squeeze her hand, a hint of irritation lurking behind his smile. Pack Alphas probably didn't like their females clucking over them in front of others. "Baby, I told you I'm fine. We need to know what Lind's doing in town and if we wait 'til tomorrow, he could be gone."

"Yeah," Dylan piped up. "Remember, the Fae guy told him to get out of town."

Dec paused with the beer bottle halfway to his mouth. "Fae guy? What Fae guy?"

Dylan started to answer with a mouth full of meatloaf. Ally backhanded him on the shoulder. "Not with your mouth full!"

Apparently over his earlier shock and anxiety, Cade answered for his nephew. "Well," he drawled, "a strange Fae followed Ally and Dylan and Becca around town a few weeks ago, but nobody bothered to tell me about it. And then tonight, the same guy showed up at the police station and told the cops to let Dylan and Lind go, and they did. But that's not the worst part."

Dec, no longer smiling, had put the beer down and now sat perfectly still. Sindri too, stopped in mid-motion, his back to them, holding a plate over the sink.

"So what's the worst part?" asked Dec with unnerving seriousness.

"The worst part is, his description fits the guy who killed my mother."

The plate Sindri was holding crashed into the sink.

Cade jumped up. "Old man! Are you okay?"

The brownie turned to stare at Dec with a horrified

expression. He said something that sounded like a question. Dec, not turning to look at him, replied in the same language.

"Why not, Dec?" Dylan asked, food forgotten.

Ally gaped at him. When had he learned to speak a new language?

Instead of answering, Dec asked, "Did he speak to you, pup? Did he tell you anything?"

Dylan nodded, wide-eyed. "Yeah. He said to tell Eirny he was sorry, and he wanted to see her."

An ashen-faced Dec said something in the foreign language again. Then, in English, "The mad bastard doesn't know she's dead. How the hell did he get loose?"

"Forget that," Cade growled. "What the hell do you know about my mother, MacSorley?"

"Oh shit," Ally whispered to herself. Like they hadn't had enough stress and surprise for one evening...

Cade's hands gripped the back of the chair he'd been sitting in. His knuckles were white, the veins and tendons of his forearm standing out ropey and rigid. He leaned over the table and stared Dec in the face.

"I asked you a question, MacSorley. Answer it or you're going out a window."

Dec didn't flinch, or whimper, or run like hell. He did none of the things a beta would've been expected to do with an enraged Pack Alpha inches from his face.

With an authority she'd never heard from him before, he replied, "I'm your uncle, pup. Eirny was my sister."

"Dude," Dylan breathed. "You're my great-uncle? How *old* are you?"

No one laughed. The only sound in the kitchen was Cade's harsh, rapid breaths. He didn't move a muscle, but his body vibrated with tension as he faced the Irishwolf across the table. Cade stared at Dec with loathing. Ally stared at Cade, watching for any sign he might start changing.

He hadn't mastered his earlier shock and anxiety after all. And this could push him over the edge.

His jaw was clenched so tightly his mouth barely moved, but there was no mistaking his next words. "Leave. Now."

Dec stood. Behind him, Sindri said, "No, *barn*. He must stay. There is so much you do not know."

Cade's expression went from surprise, to confusion, and finally to heartbreak. Seconds later, his face a stony mask, all he said to Sindri was, "Sounds as if there's much you haven't told me."

She heard the pain behind his words and she longed to throw her arms around him, comfort him with her touch as she'd done in the car.

Touching him didn't seem like a good idea at the moment.

"Cade," she implored, "he was going to tell you. He was waiting for the—"

His eyes cut to her. "You *knew?* Goddamn it, Allison, will I ever be able to trust you?"

She swallowed against the sudden ache in her throat.

Dec laid a hand on her shoulder. "Leave off, *barn.* It's my fault, I asked her not to say anything. I put her in a terrible spot."

Touching *her* wasn't a good idea at the moment, either.

Cade threw himself across the table with a roar. Dec shoved her out of the way as he was borne backwards, flying across the kitchen and slamming into the counter. Sindri moved just in time to avoid being crushed. Ally scooped the little brownie up and dove for the other side of the room.

To her amazement, Sindri lunged out of her grasp and was halfway across the huge kitchen before she dragged him back. Someone's elbow—she thought it was Cade's—clipped her in the jaw as she slid across the floor.

"Let me go!" Sindri screamed. "He will kill him! Let me go!"

Arms wrapped tightly around the frantic brownie, she huddled against the pantry door while Cade and Dec grappled and punched and rolled on the floor. The kitchen seemed much smaller with werewolves tearing it up. Chairs went flying. Fists and feet and heads punched holes in cabinets. The sound was terrifying, the smell worse.

Werewolf brawls belonged out-of-doors.

"Dylan!" she screamed. "Go get Michael!"

The teenager, whimpering and shivering beneath the table, stumbled to his feet and ran out, even as she heard someone crashing through the front door. From outside came the sound of panicked howling, the pack picking up on their Alpha's fury.

Cade was snarling like a wild animal. The two of them were

moving so fast she could barely tell them apart. She didn't know what was most incredible about the spectacle—the fact that Dec was holding his own, or that he kept trying to *talk* to Cade as they fought.

"Cade—Christ—listen to me! Stop it, *barn!* Calm down and give me—shite! I don't want to hurt you—*leave off, you fecking maniac! I need to talk to you!*"

She heard wolves in the living room all talking at once, but no one howling inside, thank God. Becca might actually sleep through this.

Michael, Roman, and another alpha raced in, paused a split second to gawk, then threw themselves on Cade. Eventually the three of them peeled him off his uncle, who lay panting on the floor.

Cade had sustained some cuts and bruises. They'd heal in hours, but she was impressed—and by now, strangely unsurprised—at the damage Dec had inflicted.

Sindri was still pushing and kicking to be free, so she let him go. Weeping, he ran straight to Dec and threw himself on the Irishwolf. Cade watched, still snarling, trying to break Michael and Roman's grip. They held him fast.

"Goddamn it, let me go!"

"No way, boss." Michael, blasé as ever, stood behind his Alpha with one hand on Cade's arm and one arm around Cade's neck. "You don't want to kill your mate's friend, and I'm not gonna let you." Roman held onto Cade's other arm as Cade twisted and fought.

Dec pushed himself up to his feet with a grunt, then leaned over with his hands on his knees, fighting to get his breath back. Now she saw that his right eye was beginning to swell. Blood seeped from a cut on his temple.

"Someone gonna tell me what this was about?" Michael asked.

Sindri was weeping, babbling beside Dec.

Ally stood up. "It's a long story, but—"

"It's my fault," said Dec as he reached down to hug Sindri to his side. "I've bollixed everything to bits. I never meant—"

"Get out."

They both fell silent at the guttural command.

Cade had quit struggling. His chest heaved as he panted.

Though his pupils were round and surrounded by white, his eyes held a distinctly Jack Nicholson "here's Johnny" cast as he stared at his uncle.

"Cade, this is too important," Dec protested. "There's too much I have—"

"You leave now," Cade snarled. "You're not welcome in my home or in my pack."

"You can't do that! Cade, for God's sake, hear what he has to say!" The group turned as one to look at Sarah Jane, who'd slipped in unnoticed amid the turmoil.

"Is Becca awake?" Ally asked quietly.

"Of course she is. I'll check on her in a minute." She stopped to take a look at Dec and drop a quick kiss on Sindri's head. Then she faced Cade with her hands on her hips. "Cade. You need to talk to us, all three of us. Declan, Sindri, me... There are things you need to know. Please, honey, calm down and—"

They all knew she was wasting her breath.

Ally still had a lot to learn about this wolf she'd probably spend her life with. One thing she already knew was that he hated lies. She and Dec had basically lied to him. He'd have to forgive her, eventually, but he wouldn't forgive Dec.

"You're welcome to go with him, Sarah Jane. In fact, I think you should."

Ally gasped. "Cade! You can't—"

He closed his eyes and grimaced, taking deep breaths. "Let go. I'm fine." Michael and Roman stepped back.

Cade squeezed his eyes shut and took another deep breath. He ran both hands through his hair, his face contorted as if in pain. When he opened his eyes and spoke, his tone was conversational.

"Ally, see to Rebecca. Sarah Jane, Dec, get off my ranch and don't come back. And Sarah Jane, you even think about challenging me for custody, I'll bankrupt you. Michael, get the pickup, we're going into town to look for Lind and the Fae."

"Okay..." said Michael, cocking his head. "Who's Lind and who's the Fae and why are we looking for them?"

"Now would be a good time to shut the fuck up and act like an obedient second."

"You'll explain later. Got it." Michael left, Roman behind

him.

Dec, Sarah Jane and Sindri remained huddled together.

"That wasn't a suggestion," Cade growled. "Move."

Sindri said something she couldn't hear and reached out a hand to Cade. Cade knocked it aside and stomped out, ignoring her as he passed.

The four of them looked at each other sadly.

"All right, old girl," sighed Dec. "We'll take your car. Get your things. I'll meet you outside."

Sindri threw his arms around Dec's waist, still crying. Ally found it profoundly disturbing to see the placid, inscrutable little brownie so distraught. Dec murmured something in that language again.

Sindri looked up at Dec, said something else, then disappeared down the hatch in the floor that led to his underground den beneath the kitchen.

"I don't—you can't—shit! Where will y'all go?" Ally threw her arms around Sarah Jane. "Becca will be hysterical. I can't believe this is happening. When Cade gets back, I'll talk to him. I'll make him sit down and listen, and then we—"

"He's too upset at us, and at you." Sarah Jane gave her a squeeze and pushed her away. "Look, honey. We're not going to stick you in the middle of this anymore. Dec will find a way to make Cade listen to him. I think Sindri can see to that."

"And Sarah Jane will be taking a little trip," Dec interjected.

"I will?" She looked up at him. "Where?"

"Keflavík."

The older woman's reaction was as startling as Sindri's had been. "Oh my God, Declan! He's here? He's *here?* I knew something was happening! I knew something was coming but I didn't see this, I never thought he—" Clutching at Dec's arm, she laid her head against his chest. Ally feared she'd faint.

Dec, though, seemed more annoyed than concerned. He patted her shoulder briskly before pushing her away to look at her. "Come on, woman, don't get weepy on me. We've too much to do."

"Just a goddamned minute!" Ally squealed. "What's going *on?* How can she just go like that, and where the hell is Kefwhatever?"

"Keflavík," Dec said calmly. "It's on the high Fae homeland

in Iceland. It's where Adnar's been imprisoned since he killed Louis. Sarah Jane will find out what happened. I'll stay and look for the bastard."

"Adnar—that's the Fae guy's name?"

"Yes. He's my first priority. Then Sindri and I will find a way to sit down with my nephew and make him listen."

"But he's gone into town himself! What if he sees you?"

Dec shrugged. "I can handle him. I'm not a normal werewolf, and Cade can't kick me out of Fremont." He put a hand to her back and gave her a little shove toward the living room, where he turned and went up the stairs.

"I need to get up there right away," said the older woman. "Those oblivious idiots probably don't even know he's gotten loose, and they're the only ones who can recapture him."

The night she died had been less confusing than this. Ally threw her hands up in frustration. "*Who*, Sarah Jane? What oblivious idiots? *What the hell is going on?*"

"We'll be in touch in a few days," said Dec as he came back downstairs. "And I'll explain everything, all of it, I swear, to you and to Cade. But we have to get going. I want to know why Adnar's here and how he's connected to Jakob Lind. I'm thinking maybe he's the reason Lind showed up back in Houston to begin with."

He and Sarah Jane walked out to the front porch with Ally at their heels, determined to get every scrap of information she could before they left.

"You think he sent Jakob to find us? Maybe dating me was a way to get to—who? Dylan?"

"Maybe. Maybe he knew Dylan was Eirny's grandson. I don't know. I intend to find out. Come on," he said to Sarah Jane.

"But, Dec, wait! You haven't told me anything! Who *is* Adnar anyway, and why'd he kill Louis MacDougall? Damn it, Dec! Why are you being so mysterious?"

"I'm sorry, Ally, truly I am." He wrapped one arm around her in a fierce bear hug. "Shite. This isn't the way I planned it. I fucked it all up, just like I fucked it up thirty-three years ago. I wasn't there for Eirny and her family then, but I'm here for Cade now, even though he doesn't want me." He put his hand to her chin and turned her face up. "It's very, very complicated, Ally girl, and I can't tell you about it before I tell Cade. Which I will, and soon. Trust me, love."

He kissed her forehead and released her. "Meanwhile, and this is very important, keep an eye on Becca at all times. Don't let her out of your sight."

"You think this Fae—Adnar—you think he'd harm Becca?"

"I'm not sure," Sarah Jane said. "He wasn't quite sane thirty-three years ago. There's no telling what state of mind he's in now. But Becca— Becca needs watching anyhow."

"Well, of course she does! She's four. Sarah Jane, how the hell do *you* know about all this? Can you at least tell me that?"

Apparently not. They hugged her one more time. She waited until the rented Lexus rounded the bend and disappeared. Only then did she realize Sarah Jane had left without her purse or a suitcase.

## Chapter Twenty-One

"So your mate's ex-boyfriend—"

"No. A guy she dated."

"A guy your mate dated shows up here in town and attacks Dylan. Then some Fae guy with a talent for mind whammy shows up to spring Dylan and the other guy out of jail, and it turns out he stalked Ally and Becca and Dylan in town, and his description matches the guy who killed your dad. And then you find out Dec's your uncle, and he knows about the Fae guy, and Sarah Jane does too, and they both know Sindri. Have I got it?"

"Yeah."

Michael was silent for a moment. "Well, that's fucked up."

"Yeah."

"Kinda puts the Stapkis situation into perspective."

"I guess." He thought about it for a minute. "Thanks for not letting me kill my uncle."

Michael shrugged. "If I'd thought you really wanted to kill him, I wouldn't have tried to stop you. But I figured you shouldn't do it in front of Ally." He paused. "Dec's your uncle. That's just weird."

The adrenaline rush of fury Cade had ridden while beating the shit out of MacSorley—or, rather, attempting to beat the shit out of MacSorley, which he hadn't even meant to do—had disappeared the instant he walked out of the house. All the stress and confusion and pain and anger of the night had hit him at once, leaving him exhausted yet still restless.

The glass of the passenger side window was cool against his temple. It would be easy to go to sleep like this.

"So where do we start looking for the guy—what was his

name?"

"Lind."

"Yeah. How do we find out where he is?"

"We talk to the cops. Maybe he told them where he was staying when they booked him. If not, we just call all the hotels in the phone book."

"And how do we find the Fae guy?"

"Hell, I don't know. But we've got what, a dozen wolves in town now?"

"Thirteen."

"Okay. Thirteen guys to track one Fae with long silver hair and a scar on his face. How hard is that?"

"What about his talent? If he can make them believe something, or do something? What then?"

"I don't know."

Michael took a deep breath and shifted in his seat, stretching and flexing. Cade could hear him thinking.

"You say he acted like he knew Dylan?"

"No, I don't think so." He paused, trying to remember exactly what Dylan had said. The events at the police station seemed like days, not hours, ago. "More like he knew who Dylan was. He asked who Dylan's mother was and when Dylan told him, he acted like he didn't believe it. And he kept saying warg olf—'you are warg olf'—or something like that. You ever hear a term like that?"

"No."

"Me neither."

Michael drummed absently on the steering wheel, mouth quirked in concentration. He shrugged. "Warg means wolf, you know. Like my last name—Warg-man."

Cade turned to look at him. "Wow. I'm not sure I ever knew that. So your last name is literally 'wolf man'?"

Michael grinned. "Yep. One of my ancestors had a dangerous sense of humor."

"I knew you had Norwegian ancestry," Cade mused, "but I never thought about the name."

Werewolves evolved in the far north of the Eurasian continent. Asian and Slavic werewolves had never migrated to the extent their western cousins did. Most werewolves who lived outside of northern Europe traced their ancestry back to

Scandinavia and the northern reaches of Scotland.

"Warg is Old Norse," Michael continued. "And your mom was of Norse ancestry too."

"Yeah, so?"

"So...I don't know. But the high Fae come from the same neighborhood."

"Well, obviously. I mean, we know he knew her. But I still don't get what 'warg olf' is supposed to mean. So warg means wolf. What's olf?"

"Beats me. 'Alf' is another Old Norse word, though. Means fairy, or Fae. I've seen it written 'ulf' too. It's where we get the word elf."

Cade stared at his second in amazement. "Since when are you an Old Norse scholar?"

"I've got hidden depths." He laughed. "Actually, I dated this German goth girl when I was stationed at Ramstein. She was obsessed with Nordic mythology, Odinism and all that Lord of the Rings type crap. There are werewolves in the Norse myths, so she was all excited to meet a Norwegian-descended werewolf."

"Did she listen to death metal?"

"Oh yeah, big time. Had a friend who was a druid, went to Stonehenge, got naked in the woods, the whole thing." He and Cade laughed. "Claimed she was possessed by the spirit of a Valkyrie once," he continued.

Cade stopped laughing. "Old Ones aren't supposed to be able to do that anymore."

Michael shrugged. "I'm not saying I believed her. Chick smoked a lot of dope. I'm just saying I've seen some strange stuff. Very strange." He frowned and fell silent for a few seconds, then sighed. "But anyway. So alf means elf, or Fae. And the high Fae were called elves in human folklore. So now we've got the high Fae dude who killed your father calling Dylan a wolf Fae?"

"That's not the only weirdness."

"What? You mean there's more?"

"Yeah. For one thing, MacSorley."

Michael shook his head. "You've never liked the wolf, I know that, but I don't see anything strange about the guy, Cade. I just don't get it."

Cade put his arm across the back of the seat, leaning in to look at Michael more closely. "You didn't notice MacSorley defending himself back there? Since when does a fucking beta *fight back*?"

"But, I thought—" Michael looked at him quizzically. "You were just teaching him a lesson, right? You weren't *loco* or anything."

"First of all, even if I had been disciplining, he didn't submit. But the fact is, I lost it there. He put his hand on my mate and told me how to talk to her. Betas don't do that. And when I turned around to rain down hell on him, he didn't back down. He felt like a fucking alpha, Michael. A strong one. Watch the road, wolf."

Michael had jerked in surprise, the truck swerving toward the center lane. He got the wheel under control, but Cade could see he was rattled.

"What the fuck?"

"Yeah, I know. I've never seen anything like it."

They rode in uneasy silence for a few more minutes.

"Damn," Michael finally said. "And I thought Ally was weird." He gave Cade a sideways glance. "No offense, Alpha."

Cade waved him off. "'s okay. I know she's weird. I might even tell you about it some time." He shifted uncomfortably. "And then there's something else."

Michael groaned. "Don't tell me. Becca's really a cat?"

Cade laughed. "No, not that weird, but still... I don't think I've told you, but when I was fighting Courtlandt... For a minute there, I could read his mind. Like, actually see what he was thinking. I knew Rufus sent him, and I knew he was threatening Aaron to make him spy on me."

"And you're just telling me this *now*? Holy shit, boss." He rubbed his hand across his face, shaking his head once more. "That's kind of...significant. Isn't it?"

"Yeah, it is. But what all of this means, I have no fucking idea." Cade lit a cigarillo and rolled down his window, closing his eyes against the cool breeze blowing into the cab. "Something's going on here. Something huge is happening to my life, something's *changing* it, and I don't know what it is. If I don't know what it is, I can't prepare for it. I just have to wait." He took a long drag. "I don't know how to just wait."

"Hey, Cade..." Michael stopped, cleared his throat, looked

at him sideways.

Cade raised an eyebrow. "What?"

"It's just...Dec kept saying he needed to talk to you. So maybe you should listen."

Cade didn't answer. But he thought about it for the rest of the way into town.

The police station was the first stop.

Hank Cash and Mrs. Holmes retained little of their earlier cheerfulness. They were subdued, uncertain, like people who'd lost track of what was going on but were embarrassed to admit it.

Mrs. Holmes said Lind mentioned staying at the Florence Rose. Even though, according to Dylan, the Fae had told Lind to leave town, they decided to check at the bed-and-breakfast.

Lind was still registered. Michael, who had a very effective sardonic charm on women when he bothered to activate it, chatted up the cute blond on duty at the front desk. He slouched against the counter, his blue eyes fixed on the girl, dazzling her with a smile that melted females and would've shocked most of the wolves who knew him. He asked her name, if she was in college, if she had a boyfriend—oh, she didn't? Did she have plans next week?

She didn't. So he made some for them.

Then he told her they were old friends of Lind and wanted to surprise him. Cade was only a little surprised himself when she gave Michael the room number—and her phone number—and waved them on their way.

Michael was still grinning when they got to the room at the end of the hall.

"You really gonna call her?"

"Sure, why not? She's cute as hell."

Cade snorted. "She's also young as hell. Can't be much over twenty-one."

Michael just shrugged and grinned wider.

They knocked, but they could already hear that no one was in the room.

Michael tried the door. It was unlocked.

They looked at each other.

"So," said Michael.

"Yeah," said Cade. "What the hell, let's take a look around."

Clothes hung in the closet. An open suitcase with more clothes spilling out lay open on one of the two double beds. A razor, toothbrush and various other personal items attested to the fact that Jakob Lind was still staying in the room.

But ten minutes of vigorous snooping yielded nothing of interest.

"Why would he take off without locking the door?" Michael frowned.

"I don't care. I want to know why he's in town to begin with. And what's his deal with the Fae?" He stopped in the middle of the room, crossed his arms and scowled as he surveyed.

"What are you looking at? Or for?" asked Michael.

"Hiding places. Places the maids don't clean." He pulled out the dresser drawers, one at a time, and held them aloft to look at the bottom. On the third one, he got a hit and grunted with satisfaction.

"Here we go." A large manila envelope was taped to the bottom of the drawer. He ripped it off and opened it, spreading the contents on the bed. They stared down at a dozen or so snapshots of Dylan at various places around town, including several close-ups.

"So he's in town looking for Dylan, not Ally," Cade mused as they gazed at the pictures. "Ally said Lind seemed interested in the pup from the first time she met him. It gave her the creeps. Lind told Dylan it took him six months to find them. Maybe he meant it took him six months to find them in Houston? What if he was already interested in Dylan before he ever met Ally?"

"You said he took it bad when Ally quit seeing him?"

"Yeah. He showed up at the stable a while after she dumped him. He attacked her."

"He tried to attack a female who can break a wolf's neck? Fucker's lucky to be alive."

"Yep," Cade said absently. "So. He tracked Dylan down in Houston, then followed them when they came up here, and he's been taking pictures of the pup around town. And when he gets arrested, the Fae gets him out. So was he following Dylan for the Fae, and if so, why?"

Michael looked pensive. "Can't be anything good. If this is the guy who killed your dad, and he's following your nephew around—your nephew who looks a hell of a lot like you did at that age—and he's asking questions about Dylan's mom—"

"And Becca's, remember. He wanted to know about Becca's mother."

"All right. We have to assume the worst about his reasons."

"Agreed. I just can't figure out why now. Why's he come looking for Dylan—or me, or Becca—now? Thirty-three years later?"

They poked around in the bedside tables and under the counter in the bathroom but didn't find any more pictures.

"I don't think we're gonna find anything else, Cade. And you're wasted. You need sleep. Let's get home and think about this in the morning, yeah?"

"Yeah, okay." He sighed, taking one last look around the room. He was missing something, there was something he should remember...but he was so damned tired. "You're right. Let's go."

It hit him halfway down the hall.

"Hey, wait. Wait a minute." They stopped. "Scotland. Scarista Beach."

"Huh?"

"Scarista Beach, in Scotland. It's where we stayed, and where the Fae attacked my dad."

"So?"

"Dylan visited Scarista Beach when he studied in Scotland last year."

Michael looked blank for a minute, then comprehension dawned. "You think the guy would still be hanging out there what, thirty-three years later? I mean, how likely is that?"

"How the hell should I know? I've never known any high Fae. I assume most of them are crazy. So maybe he's been hanging out at the scene of the crime ever since. All I know is Dylan was at Scarista Beach, he looks like me, the Fae guy shows up here after Dylan gets here, Lind is taking pictures of the pup... You know," he murmured more to himself than Michael, "Stapkis doesn't bother me so much. I mean, yeah, he's crazy, but I understand him. I can protect my family from him. But this Fae guy—and Lind, and hell, maybe MacSorley—I have no idea what that's all about, how it relates to me. That's what's got me paranoid and acting like an asshole."

"You're not paranoid, bro. Someone really is after you." Michael shrugged. "The asshole part, that's being a Pack Alpha."

Cade flashed a grin at his best friend. "Thanks, wolf."

"Any time."

They weren't out of town before he started to nod off, his head once more pressed against the cool glass of the passenger window. His cell phone rang. He started in surprise, then pulled it out and stared at it.

Michael looked over. "You going to answer that?"

"Yeah, I—yeah. I just don't know what to—" He sighed and hit the call button. "Hey. Look, baby, I know I was an asshole back there—" he felt Michael smirking at him "—and as soon as we—"

"I don't care about that right now, Cade," Ally cut in. He sat up, adrenaline instantly triggered by the fear in her voice. "You need to get back here *now*."

Michael kept his eyes on the road but attended every word.

"Ally, what happened? Are you okay? Is Becca, or Dylan, or—"

"No one's hurt, but it's creepy as hell, Cade." She sounded breathless, unsteady, but she wasn't crying. "It's Lind."

"Lind showed up there?" He could feel the change coming on again. His self-control was near tatters.

"His body did."

"His—what? He's dead? Who killed him?"

"How the hell should I know?" she shrieked. Both wolves winced. "I'm sorry, Cade, I didn't mean to do that, but I'm really freaked out. I have no idea what happened. I walked outside five minutes ago. He was there on the porch, all trussed up. No one saw a damn thing! We didn't hear anyone, smell anyone, nothing."

"What do you mean trussed up, baby?"

"I mean trussed up! Okay, not technically trussed—his feet are bound together and his hands are tied behind his back. And that's not the really fucking disturbing part!"

By now he knew her well enough to know that "fuck" meant she was on edge. He tried to keep the tension out of his own voice. "What else is there?"

"His neck is broken and his eyes were plucked out."

"Whoa. Shit," muttered Michael.

"Whoa shit is right," Ally snapped.

"What, she can hear like a wolf too?" Michael asked. When Cade waved his hand irritably, he sighed. "Never mind, not important right now."

"Ally, you say the body just turned up? Ally? Baby, answer me!"

After another few seconds of silence, she exhaled loudly. "Okay. I've got it under control now. I didn't mean to go all girly on you but—damn, that scared the hell out of me. Yes, out of nowhere! I walked out on the porch to go for a run and I nearly fell over him. The porch light's on, the guys are all up and around, and none of us heard or smelled *anything!* Who could get all the way to the house, dump a corpse and then disappear without me or a bunch of werewolves noticing?"

Michael and Cade's eyes met. He knew both of them were thinking *a Fae.*

"If Becca had seen this I don't know what I would've done. Thank God I'd put her back to bed."

Shame, love and a sweet, fierce pride washed over him as he heard the concern for Becca in her voice. He'd lost control tonight, let his anger and fear and confusion overrule him. He had a feeling he might even have accidentally struck her while he was going after MacSorley. The thought was too disgusting to contemplate right now.

An alpha of his strength was expected to use violence deliberately, judiciously, with control and purpose. He wasn't supposed to strike out like a wounded animal when his emotions got the better of him. He wasn't an animal, and he wasn't a human. He was a werewolf, and he was supposed to be the last one in his pack to lose control.

And in spite of his behavior tonight, she was worried about his child.

"Cade? Cade, say something! When will you be home?"

He smiled at the irritated tone of voice, so much more welcome to him than her fear. "We'll be there in another twenty minutes. I'm going to figure this out, I swear."

"There's one more thing. Whoever dumped Jakob on the porch left a note with the body. Which would be helpful, except that it's in a language I don't recognize. Looks almost like runes."

Seth and some others had done something with the body—she didn't know and she didn't want to know. They were freaking a little at the way she had freaked. She would have to get a firmer handle on her emotions if she was going to live with a bunch of werewolves. But even an alpha chick got disconcerted at finding her erstwhile ex-boyfriend dead, bound, neck broken and eyes missing on her front porch in the middle of the night.

After conferring with Dylan about the note, and then Googling matters of high Fae etiquette on her laptop, sleep was out of the question, so she took a hot shower. She got into bed with a book, gave up trying to read after five minutes, and ended up sitting cross-legged in the middle of the bed, staring at the door and waiting for Cade to walk in.

She heard him enter the house, climb the stairs to check on Becca, then come back down. When he walked into the bedroom he started in surprise, like he hadn't expected to find her sitting there on high alert.

Finally he said, "Hi."

"Hi yourself," she replied softly. "Are you okay?"

"Yeah. Maybe. I don't know. Fuck." He sighed and ran both hands through his hair. "No. Probably not."

A painful silence settled as she wondered what to say next. Maybe he was as uncomfortable as she was, but if so, it wouldn't show. He watched her in the big dresser mirror as he emptied his pockets and took off his watch.

She cleared her throat. "Something really weird happened tonight."

Their eyes met in the mirror. He raised an eyebrow.

She smiled and shrugged. "Okay, yeah. I mean besides jail, and the Fae, and Dec, and Jakob's corpse on the front porch." She fidgeted for a minute and cleared her throat again. "Tonight Dylan found out he could speak whatever language Dec and Sindri were speaking. And he could read the note left on Jakob's body."

He spun to face her. "What the hell?"

"Swear to God. How can something like that happen? I mean, when we moved to Texas, he seemed to pick up Spanish in like a day, but he was five years old. He's always made straight A's in French. But he hasn't been studying whatever this language is!"

"Where's the note?"

"Here."

She picked it up from the bedside table and held it out. He crossed the room to take it from her. Staring at the paper, he nodded.

"I don't think it's Icelandic, but it's similar."

He looked up at her but didn't come any nearer. "Where's Dylan now?"

"In bed. He was exhausted. It upset him when he realized what he was doing."

"What do you mean?"

"He didn't even know they were speaking another language. He said he heard it as English."

Cade didn't seem as shocked as she'd expected, or had been herself. "This happened tonight? While I was here?"

"Yes. He did it one other time I know of, the day we took Baby Girl to get her hair cut."

He finally smiled at her, a warm, tender grin that erased all the worry in his face and the tension in his body.

"What are you smiling at?"

"Nothing." He stared at her another minute, then sat down on the bed. She scooted out of his way, sitting back against the headboard with her knees drawn up. He didn't seem angry with her, just distant.

"So?"

"So what?"

He sighed and ran a hand through his hair. "So what did the note say, Ally?"

"Oh!" she exclaimed, reddening. "It's an apology. To your mother. He regretted what the human—Jakob—did to her son. He thinks your mom's alive, and he thinks Dylan is you."

"He ran off before—before Mama went into the sea. She cut him with the knife and he ran." He was silent for a minute. "Still doesn't explain why he thinks I'm a teenager thirty-three years later."

It seemed like he was going to say something else. When he didn't, she continued, "Well, he'd told Jakob—he says *the human*, he never uses Jakob's name—not to have any contact with the boy again, and the human's disobedience shames him. Shames Adnar, I mean. He presents the human's body as atonement for the offense."

"Shit."

"I know. I'm not an expert on the Fae, so I got on Google. Sure enough, there's a huge Wikipedia entry on high Fae rituals. It's a shame and honor culture. Giving unintended offense is a big deal. They don't think much of humans—or werewolves, or the non-high Fae, really. When a high Fae's inferior, like an employee or someone under their command, commits some kind of grievous offense, killing the offender and offering the body to the offended party—the way he left Jakob with the eyes and the bonds and everything—that's an ancient way of apologizing."

"That doesn't surprise me. I'm surprised he apologized to my mother, but the whole killing thing—they're a barbaric bunch. And Dylan had no trouble reading this? He was sure he understood it?"

"Yes."

"Well," he grunted as he pulled off his boots, "it's weird, but no weirder than everything else that's been happening around here."

He told her that when he'd fought Courtlandt, he'd had a sudden flash of genuine, honest-to-God telepathy.

"You've never experienced that before?"

"No. And it only lasted a few minutes."

She started to ask him why the hell he hadn't mentioned that before but realized she'd sound like a hypocritical bitch.

"Shit," he groaned, flopping back on the bed and throwing an arm across his eyes. "I'm tired. I'm just so fucking tired."

Working up her nerve, she crawled down the bed to run her fingers through his hair. "Hey," she said against his ear.

"What?" He lifted his arm and turned his head to her. The wariness in his eyes made her heart hurt.

"Take off your shirt and stretch out on your stomach."

He gazed at her as if trying to figure out what she was up

to. Then he stood, stripped off his T-shirt and lay down in his normal spot. When she straddled his back and began to knead his neck and shoulders, he groaned again.

"God, that feels good."

She leaned down to plant a quick kiss on his neck and resumed the massage.

"You're gonna put me to sleep."

"You need it."

"But I should go talk to Sindri." His voice was muffled, his head buried in his folded arms. "I got so angry at him. I need to make sure he's okay, and ask him...damn. Everything."

His warm skin felt good beneath her hands, smooth and solid and safe. In her head she pictured all her love and remorse flowing out of her fingers and into him.

Stupid. Silly, romantic and stupid.

"Sindri's been in his nook since Dec and Sarah Jane left. I'm pretty sure he's hiding."

"Did he say anything?"

"Only to Dec, but it was in Icelandic."

"That's the worst part of all this."

Something in his words made her pause. His voice sounded normal, his usual mellow baritone, if a little raspy from stress and exhaustion. It was something behind the words—something a little wistful, a little sad.

"What's the worst part, baby?"

He turned his head to lay his cheek on his arm. "Sindri. All of a sudden, I don't know him. He's the only person left who's known me all my life, and he's kept secrets from me. Like the way he was with MacSorley."

"The way he ran to Dec and not to you?"

"Yeah. And another time, something I'd forgotten about. When I was recovering, I was asleep most of the time, but once in a while I'd come to for just a few minutes..."

"And? Cade, what happened?"

He gestured with his chin to the green suede sofa. "One time when I woke up, they were over there, on Mama's couch. Sindri was asleep with his head in MacSorley's lap, and MacSorley was petting him, like I would do to Becca. When he saw me looking at him, he told me I was dreaming. I knew I wasn't, but I couldn't answer."

She didn't pause in her work as she thought about that. Her nerves needed the feel of his skin as much as his cramped muscles needed the massage. "You know, tonight he was hugging Sindri like you would a child. Right before he left, I swear Dec called Sindri *barn*. Doesn't that mean child?"

"Yeah. But Sindri's four hundred years old."

"Maybe Dec's protective of him? It would make sense for them to be close, if Sindri was with your mom for so many years, right?"

"Okay, wait."

"What?"

"Stop. Get off." He sat up, sending her sprawling onto the mattress beside him. She started to sit up, but he pressed her back down with one hand and stared, hard, into her eyes. "Tell me everything you know about MacSorley. Now."

"But..." She paused, confused until she realized he thought she was still holding out on him. With the strength she normally kept in reserve, she pushed him off.

"I'm sorry." She brushed his face with her fingertips. "Okay? I'm sorry. I kept hoping he'd tell you himself and— The longer it went on, the harder it got. I know he cares about you, Cade, I know he's a good guy because I've lived with him for four years. But I swear, I don't know any more about him now than you do."

"How do you know he's a good guy if you don't know anything about him? His past, his family—my family, if he's even telling the truth about that?"

"Because, I just—" She sighed in frustration and sat up all the way, turning to face him as she leaned across his long, outstretched legs. "You're right—I don't really know anything about him. I didn't know anything about him when I let him move in with us, and that sounds stupid. It *is* stupid. But in four years he's been a good friend. I know he's telling the truth about who he is because one, he looks so much like you and Dylan—I don't know why I didn't notice it before—and two, he talked a little about your mom and Carson, and, I mean...it just *sounded* like the truth, okay?"

"What did he say about them?"

"He said your mom was kind and loving, but reckless. Heedless, he said. And that Carson was like her, but you were like your dad, and that's why Carson fell apart and you didn't."

He didn't close his eyes to hide the haunted misery in them. "There's nothing else you know about MacSorley that you haven't told me?"

"No. Nothing. I swear. I can't lie to you, can I?"

"No. It's just— I thought everything was finally working out." She heard anguish in his voice, and it made her ache for him. "I lost my brother but found my nephew. My pack's growing, we're getting recognized. I found out I had a mate, and I liked her. I was even okay with having Sarah Jane around. Then this happens—MacSorley, the Fae, Sindri and Sarah Jane. Ally, I don't know who my own family is, who my enemies are. And now I don't know if I can trust my mate. I can't read you like I can read most people."

Almost roughly, he took her chin in his hand and tilted her head back, staring at her eyes. It sure as hell felt like he could read her, like he could see straight through her. When they were like this, skin to skin but without the distraction of passion or tenderness—that was when the force of him nearly overwhelmed her, that was when she realized just what she'd gotten herself into. Yes, she'd lived with wolves for years, but not grown alphas, and not as a mate.

This would be nothing like living with a human male, either, nothing like the short, tentative relationships she'd had before. Those affairs seemed so bland and superficial to her now—but safe, and predictable, and within her control. This would be none of those things.

Yet she didn't feel—much—fear. Mostly she felt love and remorse and something a little too close to pity for this powerful wolf who'd struggled so hard, for so long, to build a pack and a family.

You couldn't tell a Pack Alpha you felt sorry for him. He wouldn't understand.

"I won't keep secrets from you again, I promise. I should've had the balls to tell you." She was absurdly thrilled to see a tiny grin at that. "You've had a horrible day. I'm sorry I made it worse."

In a low voice she couldn't decide was angry or not, he asked, "Are you feeling sorry for me?"

She couldn't laugh, because his gaze was hard and impersonal. He was sizing her up with some kind of finality. If she didn't pass, she wouldn't get another chance. Turning her head to rub her cheek against his palm, she said quietly, "Maybe. A little. Because I love you, and I know you're hurting, and I don't like knowing I caused some of it. I don't want you to doubt me. I want you to lean on me."

"Alphas don't lean. Alphas protect."

"I don't need protection. And Alphas lean on their mates, don't they?"

"If they're lucky. I was starting to think I was lucky." He stared at her some more. "You love me?"

"Yes," she whispered, afraid that if she tried to say anything more she'd start crying.

"Me too. It's not automatic, you know. There have been wolves who got stuck with mates they didn't love, women they didn't want to need. I always thought that sounded like a kind of hell."

She pulled his hand away from her face. "So, you love me and I love you. Right?"

He nodded curtly.

"Then maybe we could kiss? You could let me hug you? Or something?"

Nodding again, and with a frown, he hooked an arm around her waist and dragged her onto his lap. He brushed a quick, hard kiss across her mouth before he buried his face in her neck, hugging her so tight she let out a little squeak. His hold relaxed a bit. She wrapped her arms around his shoulders and cradled his head.

They rocked together like that until she said softly, "Hey. Cade?"

"Mmm?"

"I said I wouldn't keep secrets from you anymore, and I won't. I know you're exhausted, but..."

"But what?"

She pushed his hair back from his eyes and kissed his forehead. "But, baby, you really, really need a shower."

A slow, tired grin spread across his face. "I'm pretty wiped. Can you help me?"

"Happy to."

## Chapter Twenty-Two

The next day he declared the ranch on lockdown—no one to enter or leave without his approval. Pack members living in town were still looking for Stapkis and the Fae. His wolves understood without being told that the lockdown instructions were primarily for the protection of Ally and Rebecca. He'd expected Ally to raise holy hell at being told she couldn't leave the ranch without his permission and an escort. His mate still pretended to be unclear on the overall concept of submission to the Pack Alpha.

To his surprise, though, she agreed to the restrictions after only token protest. Then he figured out why. She was obsessed with the MacSorley situation.

Both Ally and Michael spent the day hounding him to call the Irishwolf. He'd been glad his best friend and his mate got along so well, but now he wished they didn't. They'd spent all morning speculating about MacSorley's role in Cade's past. Neither paid any attention to Cade's repeated order to drop the subject.

After a dinner of cold sandwiches and chips—and still no sign of Sindri—Cade lost his temper, roaring for both of them to shut the fuck up and leave him alone, which they finally did—at least for a while.

It wasn't just the nagging, though. That pissed him off, but Sindri's behavior disturbed him more. The old man was the rock and the rudder of Cade's life. If he was too distraught to speak to them or come out of his den—not even Becca, kneeling by the door and pleading, could get a response—Cade would do whatever necessary to get some answers. Even if that meant talking to the wolf he still couldn't think of as his uncle.

He locked himself in his office before dialing MacSorley's cell phone because he didn't want Michael or Ally to know they'd finally worn him down. And after all that, he got the bastard's voicemail. He left a two word message: "Call me."

It figured, Cade thought sourly two days later, that his uncle would finally call back just as a new crisis erupted.

"Cade? I apologize for not calling you sooner, pup, but I've been out of pocket." His tone held none of its usual cockiness. Only the *pup* kept him from sounding downright submissive.

"Are you still in town, MacSorley?"

"Yes."

"Sarah Jane back yet?"

"She should—wait, did Ally tell you where she went?"

"Ally's not keeping secrets from me anymore. I want to know why Sarah Jane went to Iceland and how she's involved in all this. I want to know a lot of things, but at the moment I've got something else to worry about."

"What's that?"

"Becca's sick."

"What's wrong?"

"She's got a fever. It's up to a hundred and two. I've had the ranch on lockdown, but Ally wants to take her to the doctor."

"Could you ask the doctor to come to you?"

"Ally swears it's strep, and that means they'll need a culture. I won't send them into town alone."

"No, of course not. Until we know where Stapkis is, I don't think she should go anywhere without a couple of wolves with her."

Two days ago, Cade would've demanded to know who the hell the insolent son of a bitch thought *we* might be. Now, with a superlupine effort he wished Ally were there to witness, he said instead, "Michael and I are going."

"Why don't I meet you there? Maybe we can grab some lunch, talk a bit?" When Cade didn't answer immediately, Dec added, somewhat hesitantly, "If that's okay with you. If you want me to wait, I under—"

"No, no. I was just thinking. Yeah, why don't you meet us at the doctor's. I'll take another wolf as well, just in case we run into the Fae. Fremont Pediatric Associates, on McCoy, two blocks off Field. We'll be there in about an hour."

"Good. I'll see you then. And Cade—thank you."

He'd planned on taking Roman and Michael, but Dylan asked to come along. It pleased him that the pup wanted an active role in the pack.

Michael slid behind the wheel of the Rover, starting the engine while everyone else piled in. "Look, Cade, I've been thinking. Maybe we need to take a few more guys with us."

"Why?"

"Well, it's just—" He frowned at the steering wheel. Cade got the distinct impression his second was embarrassed. "I'm just thinking—if Rufus is in town and decides to do something crazy, the more muscle we've got, the better."

"You were just saying yesterday how you thought Stapkis had probably killed himself already."

"Yeah, but what if he didn't? What if he's just been lying low, waiting for us to give up?"

"He's got a point," Ally said from the backseat.

"Thirteen guys would've found one broken-down, crazy old wolf by now." When Michael turned his head to look at him, Cade was shocked at his expression. "Michael. What's got you so worried all of a sudden?"

His lieutenant shrugged miserably. "It's just—just a feeling, that's all. Like something bad is gonna happen."

"There are three of us right now, four when we meet up with MacSorley."

"Five, you mean," Dylan piped up from the backseat. "We've got Ally too."

Michael rolled his eyes while Cade and Dylan grinned at each other. Cade had no idea how he'd explain Ally's nature to Michael. He wasn't even sure he wanted to try. If Michael thought he'd seen strange stuff... "Five against one, bro. Stapkis shows up, we'll handle it."

Michael gazed at him another minute and then sighed. "Yeah. You're right. We'll handle it. I'm acting like a chick."

Cade laughed, then glanced back to see Ally leaning over with her cheek against Baby Girl's forehead.

"I gave her Tylenol before we left, and she's still hot, and it's hurting her to swallow." She looked up at him. "Definitely strep."

"She didn't tell me about the swallowing."

"Me neither. I could just tell by watching her eat."

"So where'd she pick it up?" It wouldn't have been from the wolves.

Ally shrugged. "Some other kid she's been around."

"Shit," he muttered, turning back around in his seat. "It's the kids in town. Town kids have germs."

She seemed to find that funny. "All kids have germs, baby, even Becca. She just hasn't had a chance to build her immunity."

"She didn't need immunity before y'all started taking her into town all the time."

"So what do you want to do, keep her on the ranch?"

"For a few more years, yes."

"Well, we're not doing that."

He turned to look at her. "What do you mean, *we*?"

The car got quiet. Michael kept his eyes locked on the road. Dylan stared out his window.

Cade and Ally stared at each other.

Her jaw trembled—just the tiniest bit, but enough that he noticed. "We—you and me. I just assumed— I mean, I'm your mate." Her voice began to quiver as she dropped her gaze. "She needs a mother, Cade."

"No." He cleared his throat to cover the catch in his own voice. "She needs you."

Her eyes snapped back up to his. He took a deep breath. "And I guess if you're going to adopt her, we need to get married first."

Ally smiled.

The air in the car felt lighter. So did his heart. When he tried to speak, his voice caught again. Just as well—he didn't have words for what he felt. He reached back to touch her face. She took his hand, pressing her cheek to his palm. Her damp lashes tickled his skin.

"What, Tough Girl's crying now? What a pansy," cracked Michael.

"Watch it, dude," Dylan said softly. "Don't fuck with her

when she's crying."

"Don't say fuck," Ally hiccupped. She brushed a kiss against Cade's palm and pushed his hand away, rolling her eyes. Barely sniffling, she said, "Michael's just jealous 'cause he doesn't have a female."

Michael snorted. "Michael's got plenty of females. Don't worry about old Michael."

"Yeah, well, you don't have a mate."

"Yeah, well, why would I want a mate? Only sleeping with one female, having her telling you what to do all the time, not being able to break up with her even if she's a bitch—shit! Watch it, I'm driving here!"

She'd thumped him on the back of the head. Dylan started laughing.

Michael was on a roll. "Women can't stand to see males running around loose. Reminds all the collared guys of their free range life, everything they had before they got tied down. See, like poor Cade over here—"

"*Poor Cade?*" squealed Ally.

"Hush, you'll wake up Stinky Butt. Now, poor Cade probably looks at me and thinks, damn, three months ago I would've gone into town and picked up a hot college girl just like Michael's doing, but now I have to stay here and—"

"Cade? Did you spend a lot of time chasing hot college girls?"

"I can't remember anything before you, baby."

She didn't hear him. She was too busy explaining to Michael that he only fucked lots of different women because he was afraid to fall in love, while Michael was trying not to laugh long enough to explain that he fucked lots of different women because he *could*. Dylan was laughing at both of them, Baby Girl slept right through it, and Cade put his head back, closed his eyes, and basked in the sound of his family.

The doctor deemed Becca's strep a mild case and said she'd be better in twenty-four hours with the antibiotic he prescribed. Ally didn't say I told you so, which made Cade love her a little bit more.

As they walked out of the doctor's office, MacSorley waved

to them from across the street, where he stood chatting with Michael and Dylan next to Sarah Jane's rental car. Cade pressed the remote to pop the lock on the Rover. "I'm hungry," Becca whined. She was grumpy too. He walked around the car to join them.

"Hi Daddy," Becca slurred, sleepy once more.

"Hey, baby."

Ally turned to smile at him as she finished buckling the car seat. A honey blond hank of ponytail had worked its way loose. He tucked it behind her ear, skimming his thumb across the soft curve of her cheek.

"We could send the guys home with Becca and go get some lunch."

"Sounds great, but aren't you supposed to sit down with Dec?"

He pressed a kiss to her forehead.

"I'd rather lay down with you. Let him wait. We can grab a few hours alone, maybe talk about a wedding. I'll look at rings if you want to."

A car pulled into an empty spot a few feet away.

Michael yelled his name.

Ally smiled more easily this time, one hand still on Becca's knee. He bent his head for a kiss, blocking out everything but the beloved scent of saltwater and lavender.

Her eyes flew open. She gave a little start. Some corner of his brain registered the scent of a strange wolf.

Michael called to him again.

As he raised his head, a vaguely familiar voice said, "Got yourself a mate now? Think you're gonna have a wife and family like I did, you son of a bitch?"

Before he turned his head to look at the interloper, he noted two things simultaneously.

The voice belonged to Rufus Stapkis.

And there was a red dot on Ally's chest, just below the hollow of her throat.

# Chapter Twenty-Three

Michael, who'd been paying attention the way Cade should've been, yelled again.

Transfixed by the red dot of the laser sight, Cade didn't turn his head to Stapkis or look up at Michael across the street.

For the first time in over twenty years, he'd ignored his surroundings, too busy mooning over his mate to protect her. As a result, his worst enemy stood a foot away with a gun pointed at Ally and his daughter. Their daughter.

A funny taste burned the back of his mouth. He felt dizzy and sick to his stomach. This was worse than the sudden, powerful urge to shift, which he could control.

This was fear—abject, borderline hysterical fear. He'd never felt this before, not even in combat.

He raised his eyes to Michael, whose face mirrored his own queasy fright. Michael, Dec and Dylan stood paralyzed. No wolf could move faster than a bullet fired at so short a distance. If it were only Cade, they'd take their chances, but not with Becca and Ally there.

Thirty, maybe forty-five seconds had passed. Now, when it was too late, he could smell nothing but the Seattle Alpha's madness and rage.

And Ally. He could still smell Ally.

God bless his magical mate, he caught barely a whiff of fear. Mostly he smelled anger. She was still, as still as a wolf, and she was staring at him, waiting for him to show her what to do, because she trusted him.

It calmed him and helped him resist the urge to change. He needed to be on two feet to handle this.

So when he spoke, holding her gaze and drawing a strength

from her he'd never imagined he would need, his voice was as steady and dry as when he discussed ranch business.

"Rufus. Why aren't you off somewhere killing yourself like an honorable wolf?"

"What honor? You took my honor, MacDougall. Like you took my pup."

"I didn't take Aaron. He left you. He tried to kill himself because of you. Whatever Courtlandt told him, it must've been bad if he thought suicide—"

"Shut up!" Cade recognized murderous fury in Stapkis' snarl. He shut up.

"In the car, female."

Ally's eyes went to Stapkis. "Excuse me?"

"Get in the truck. MacDougall, give me your keys."

Now he turned to face his enemy. This wolf barely resembled the barrel-chested giant Cade had seen in photos. Stapkis' salt-and-pepper hair, a matted, tangled mess, trailed below the collar of his sweat-stained white shirt. His stringy gray beard straggled halfway to his chest. The Alpha hadn't slept or shaved in some time. A quick glance at his pale brown eyes revealed empty madness. This wolf probably couldn't even shift right now.

"Leave them out of this, Rufus. You want me, you got me."

Stapkis' harsh laughter serrated Cade's nerves.

"I'll get to you. Give me the keys and back off or one of your females dies."

"I'll go with you, but leave Becca here." There was no trace of fear in Ally's voice. "She's only four, and she's sick."

"Shut up and get in the truck. Don't make me tell you again."

"You'd never get out of here alive, Rufus."

Stapkis smiled. "Think I care about that anymore?"

And there it was. Cade had no options. Stapkis didn't care about his own life, and Cade didn't care about anything but Becca and Ally's lives, and the two Alphas knew it. He handed the keys to Stapkis and stepped away, keeping his hands out to either side. He could feel his wolves' frustration. He trusted them not to do anything stupid.

His heart lodged in his throat when Ally tried to climb into the backseat with Becca. Stapkis shoved her toward the front seat.

With a morbid despair, Cade realized he might never see either of his girls again. It took all the strength he had, and more self-control than he'd known he possessed, not to ask Stapkis to let him kiss Becca.

But another thought occurred to him then, a thought that immediately banished the despair.

Stapkis believed he held a human hostage. He didn't know he had a female with strength, speed and senses to rival his own.

To his amazement, Cade found he had to suppress a smile as a new, more familiar sense of control and resolve flooded through him.

"How'd you track me, Rufus?"

Stapkis' lip curled in a sneer. "Easy. I spotted you in town the other night. While you were in the police station, I slapped a GPS locator on the Rover. A real Pack Alpha's not so careless about security, MacDougall."

This time Cade let the smile break out across his face. He shrugged. "It's embarrassing, I gotta admit."

"I'll call you with instructions. Don't even think about following me."

Stapkis slammed the driver's door and took off with Cade's whole world.


"Think you're a tough little thing, don't you?"

"You have no idea."

Staring out the window on her side as if she didn't care they'd been kidnapped by a sociopath, she kept an eye on the rearview mirror. She saw several cars behind them, but couldn't tell which one was Sarah Jane's rented Lexus. She had no doubt Cade and the others had followed immediately—she just worried they wouldn't be able to keep up without Stapkis spotting them.

So far she'd succeeded in stuffing the fear deep, deep down inside. She was almost certain he couldn't smell any on her, and she hoped it was freaking him out.

"How old are you, anyway? MacDougall land himself a teenager?"

She didn't answer.

"That's fine. You just sit there and keep quiet. You and the kid will be fine as long as your wolf does what I tell him."

She was trying to make a plan, be prepared for what she'd do when they got to wherever they were going. If she attacked Stapkis the minute he parked the car, just went fists and nails and teeth on him before he had a chance to unbuckle his seat belt...

Behind her, Becca stirred. "Ally?" The sleepy little voice set her pulse racing. For a second, she was afraid her control would slip.

"Shh, baby. Go back to sleep."

But could she catch him by surprise, even with her speed? A Pack Alpha would be faster. Maybe his age would slow him down, though...

"Where's Daddy?"

"We'll see Daddy in just a little bit, Becca."

No matter how many scenarios she envisioned, they all ran into the same problem—Becca. Alone, there would've been a half dozen things she could try, up to and including throwing herself out of the moving car, or jumping Stapkis as he drove. Alone, she'd have taken her chances. But she couldn't do anything that would endanger Becca.

As much as she hated it, she had to bide her time and see what Stapkis would—

"Ally, I want to go home! Take me home!"

"Shh, honey, we'll be home soon."

She turned her head toward the backseat but wouldn't look straight at Becca for fear she'd start crying and upset the girl even more. It made no difference—with that sixth sense small children seemed to have for knowing when an adult was frightened, Baby Girl started crying.

"I told you to keep the kid quiet!"

"Shut up! She's sick and scared!"

He didn't slow down as he made a sudden right turn off the highway onto a two-lane blacktop. She'd never ventured this far out of town. The ranch lay sixty miles behind them on the other side of Fremont. They were alone, no traffic or any other sign of life. Apparently someone had paved a road through the trees without bothering to add buildings, cars or people.

There was no time to wonder about it because she suddenly smelled something terrifying.

"Are you *changing?*" She didn't want to imagine what would happen if Stapkis changed while he was driving. Would they be ripped to pieces even as they spun out of control?

"What the hell are you talking about?" he snarled.

"I can smell the change on you! You can't tell you're doing it?"

His eyes were normal, though—red-rimmed and filled with madness, yes, but the sclera weren't yellow and the pupils weren't elongated. And it wasn't the typical change scent, either. It was lighter, more floral...

"Ally!"

This time, the panic in Becca's cry made Ally spin around. "Baby? What's wrong?"

Becca thrashed against the car seat straps, eyes clenched shut, mouth wide open in a silent scream. Ally ripped off her seat belt so she could turn all the way around.

"What the fuck do you think you're doing?" Stapkis shouted.

"Leave me alone! Something's wrong with her!"

He grabbed her right arm. She jerked it free. The Rover careened across the deserted road, but she ignored Stapkis' yells and curses as he fought the steering wheel to stop the tires sliding off the blacktop. One arm wrapped around her headrest to keep herself upright, she leaned across the backseat and brushed the hair out of Becca's face.

"Becca? Breathe! Right now, baby! *Breathe!*" The child's face was hot, far hotter than a fever could make it, as hot as...

...as hot as a werewolf's skin.

Unconsciously, instinctively, she snatched her hand back as she realized the strange, almost-change scent was coming from her little girl. Now it filled the car.

"Ally..." Becca whimpered. Her voice was mutating, stretching. Ally stared in silent shock as the small body began to flex and undulate. She didn't hear bones popping as when a wolf shifted—these bones were softer, more malleable. The shift was almost silent.

To Ally's horror and shame, a part of her recoiled. She'd never been entirely comfortable watching her own wolves shift.

The sensation of rippling flesh, the sight of sprouting hair, morphing limbs and emerging claws—it was all so alien, so *physical.*

As she witnessed the unthinkable transformation, the past three months flashed through her mind. How many times Becca had chattered about changing into a kitten, how she wished she could do it on purpose, but she couldn't, how it only happened sometimes, and not for very long, and it wasn't scary but sometimes it hurt a little, and...

And then it was over, in far less than the minutes it took the strongest alpha wolf to shift. A tiny black kitten huddled, shivering, in the midst of Becca's white Winnie the Pooh T-shirt and pink shorts.

The kitten, jet-black like her father—and cousin, and uncle—blinked her bright green eyes and mewled softly.

"Oh, baby," Ally whispered in awe. For the space of one caught breath, she forgot their mortal danger, wonderstruck at the sight of Becca, a *female shifter.*

Was she the first? The only? If there were others, why did no one know about them, and why—

"Hey! What do you think you're doing?"

Stapkis grabbed her arm again, much harder this time. It felt like it would snap under the pressure of his huge hand.

Ally yelped in pain.

Becca screeched in fright.

Stapkis whipped his head around, saw a cat in the backseat, and hollered, "What the fuck?" He shoved Ally against the passenger window, then reached back to grab Becca.

The kitten yowled again and leapt straight for Stapkis' head, her claws digging into his scalp and face. He pulled her off and flung her away. Becca went sailing over the backseat. The Rover swerved off the road and bumped down to the gravel shoulder, fishtailing until Stapkis got his hands back on the wheel.

When Ally heard the tiny body hit the rear window, a white hot rage engulfed her. Bracing herself against the passenger door, she gave the werewolf a mighty kick across the jaw. Before he had a chance to recover, she planted another one in his ribs. Once she started kicking, she just couldn't stop.

Which was unfortunate, because this time when Stapkis let go of the steering wheel and the Rover veered onto the gravel shoulder, it kept going. He was too busy blocking her kicks to regain control of the truck. As he struggled, his foot jammed the accelerator to the floor.

The Rover plunged into the dense brush, spinning and skidding a few feet before the rear end crashed sideways into a pine tree and the back window shattered.

"Run, Becca! Go!" Ally screamed.

Giving Stapkis one last kick to the face, she launched herself across the backseat.

# Chapter Twenty-Four

Cade and Michael were in the Lexus before Stapkis reached the end of the street. Michael threw the car into reverse and was about to take off when Cade realized Dec and Dylan weren't in the backseat.

MacSorley stood motionless on the sidewalk, one arm outstretched toward Dylan. But Dylan wasn't looking at his uncle.

He was staring at Adnar, who'd appeared from—where? Nowhere. Thin air. The Fae hadn't been on the sidewalk thirty seconds ago when Cade had leapt across the street and into the car.

Cade jumped out of the car. "Dylan! What are you doing?"

The teenager walked right up to the Fae and said something in a foreign language. Adnar listened for a moment. Then he said something. Dylan's reply had a strange effect on the Fae. While his stoic expression didn't alter, at least as far as Cade could tell, something in his posture, his demeanor, changed. If Cade had to guess, he'd have said the Fae appeared surprised.

The Fae raised his head. His eyes met Cade's, and then Cade was certain. Something Dylan said had shocked him.

Cade reckoned he'd spent hundreds of hours in the past thirty-three years imagining what he'd do if he ever came face-to-face with his father's killer. In some fantasies he was on two feet, in others, four. No matter what form he was in, every scenario ended with him ripping the bastard's throat out.

Now, in the glow of the fading afternoon sunshine, with his mate and his daughter in the hands of one enemy and his nephew inches from another, Cade did...nothing.

Adnar turned and disappeared.

Just like that. There one minute, gone the next.

Dylan elbowed MacSorley out of the way and slid into the backseat. MacSorley climbed in beside him, and Cade got back in the car.

"We're not gonna wait for him to call, are we?" Michael asked.

"Fuck no. After him."

They took off. The sedan was a little crowded with four large werewolves.

"What the bloody hell were you thinking?" MacSorley barked at Dylan.

"There he is," Michael said. "I see the Rover."

"Yeah, me too," Cade replied. "Hang back. Keep him in sight, but I don't want him—"

"I know how to tail someone, Cade."

Michael was as scared as he was, and Cade loved him for it, so he ignored the insubordination. He dialed the ranch and told Seth to forward all calls straight to his Blackberry. He didn't say anything about what had just happened.

"All right," he said as he ended the call. "Just what the fuck was that about, Dylan?"

"I told Adnar that Stapkis kidnapped my little sister, and that we're Eirny's grandchildren, and that Eirny's dead and it's his fault."

Silence greeted this announcement.

"What did you do that for?" Cade asked quietly.

"I figured we could use his help, and he owes us. Fae can move faster than wolves, you know. So I thought he could keep up with them until we got there." He paused for a moment before continuing thoughtfully, "I don't know if he could fight Stapkis, though."

"No, he couldn't," MacSorley snarled. "They can move faster than wolves, and they have their talents, but high Fae are no stronger than humans. The really old purebreds like Adnar are usually weaklings. He'd be able to make Stapkis believe what he wanted him to. That's it."

"Well, I wouldn't know that, would I? Since you've never told me about any of this, *Uncle* Dec."

"If he tells Rufus to let the girls go, like he told the cops to release Dylan, Rufus would do it?" Cade asked.

"If the wolf didn't eat him first, yeah."

"So, what, this Adnar guy followed us from the ranch?" Michael interjected. "You think he could've been there for two days without us knowing it?"

"Shite, I don't know. I've been looking for the wanker for two fucking days and for all I know, he's been tracking *me*. Christ. When did I become so fucking useless?"

No one said anything to that. They rode in silence, maintaining a steady distance between themselves and the Rover.

In the rearview, MacSorley put his head back and closed his eyes.

"Dylan, d'you really think Adnar will feel guilty, pup? You don't think he'll try to attack one of us, one of the girls?"

"What's he gonna do? Tell us to waste ourselves or something?"

MacSorley sighed. "No, he couldn't do that. Only Michael would be susceptible to his talent. And I'm not sure about Michael."

"What the fuck does that mean?" Michael asked.

"He came here to see Eirny, didn't he?" Dylan interrupted. "He killed Jakob for her. Why would he try to hurt us?"

MacSorley made a startled sound and opened his eyes. "What? When did he kill Jakob?"

Dylan quickly—and, Cade noted, curtly—told his great-uncle about Jakob Lind's body and the note accompanying it. The teenager had grown both quieter and more assertive, more confident, in his months on the ranch. Cade liked watching the wolf his nephew was becoming.

"The mad bastard," said MacSorley, shaking his head. "God, I hate him."

"He loved my grandmother, though, didn't he?"

"If you want to call it that. He loved her so much he killed her children's father."

"Dec," Dylan asked calmly, "what's the deal with our family?"

Cade turned to the backseat again, surprised at the question. MacSorley appeared to take it in stride.

"It's a long story, pup."

"I mean the way I can understand languages and Cade can—"

"Yes, I know. I said, it's a long story. Let's get the girls back, then we can talk about it."

"Hey!" Michael interrupted. "He just turned off the highway onto, onto—shit! He turned onto Fourmile!" He banged a hand on the steering wheel.

"Huh?" Cade turned back around. "Why would—God damn it! The son of bitch is squatting at the—"

"—Fourmile Inn," Michael finished for him.

"Why the fuck didn't anyone—?"

"I don't know, Cade!" Michael shouted. "I don't fucking know!"

"What's so exciting about the Fourmile Inn, pups?" asked Dec.

"Nothing," Cade said in disgust. "Just a bed-and-breakfast that closed about ten years ago because no one wanted to stay so far outside town."

"It's the only building on Fourmile Road," Michael added. "If I wanted to hide out and plan an attack on someone I was stalking, that would be a real good place to do it." He banged the steering wheel again, still cursing and muttering to himself. "I can't *believe* we missed that. If we'd looked for the Fae out here, we could've—"

"Never mind, it doesn't matter," Cade said tightly. "I didn't think of it either. Just speed up. I don't care if he knows we're behind him now."

Fourmile Road was a literally descriptive name. While a werewolf could see much better than a human, he couldn't see for a mile. By the time they turned onto the two lane blacktop, there was no other vehicle in sight.

"Faster," he muttered, and Michael obeyed. Harrowing minutes passed as they flew down the empty road. Hoping to catch a whiff or a sound of the Rover, Cade rolled the window down.

What he heard, and what he didn't smell, kicked the primitive wolf part of his brain into panic mode. When the change began, he knew he wouldn't be able to stop it.

He heard Ally screaming for Becca. He heard Stapkis roaring wordless bellows of rage.

He could smell Ally. He could smell Stapkis.

He couldn't smell Becca.

"Over there!" Michael shouted, pointing to the other side of the road.

The Rover was half on its side, the rear side crunched up against a pine tree, back window shattered, tailgate hanging.

*Oh, Christ. Oh, Baby Girl.*

The pheromones flooding his body—fear, alarm, aggression—had an immediate effect on the other wolves, who ripped off their seat belts. Dylan and MacSorley slammed against the front seat as Michael threw the Lexus into park. Cade pressed an elbow against his door and fell to the ground, gasping in agony as he struggled out of his clothes. He hadn't changed involuntarily since his baptism by fire in the Rangers. The change was only painful if you fought it, and he couldn't help fighting it, even though he knew it was useless.

"Michael," he panted, "can you keep—? You need to stop, don't—"

He couldn't believe how fast he was changing. Less than a minute had passed but speech was almost impossible, the fur was pushing through his skin, his neck was stretching, his shoulder blades popping...

"I can do it, Cade," Michael, panting heavily, replied from the other side of the car, "but I have to— I need—" Cade heard the effort in his second's voice, knew how hard Michael was fighting the change.

"Go!" Cade screamed. "Go!"

Not even an alpha as strong as Michael could keep from changing if he was in close proximity to a Pack Alpha involuntarily shifting. Dylan would be changing right now. A beta like MacSorley wouldn't have a chance...

MacSorley stood staring down at him, still two-footed and impossibly, unbelievably calm. He knelt beside Cade.

"Stop fighting it, pup. You're almost done. Michael and I will do the thinking. You go find Stapkis."

For the first time, Cade was grateful for his uncle's presence.

Change completed, the wolf raced after his enemy.

Stapkis' fingers were iron bands around her ankle. She tried to kick, but she couldn't get any leverage, stretched as she was across the backseat of the Rover, scrabbling furiously at the seat to steady herself.

"Becca! *Go!*"

The kitten arched her back, hissing and yowling, crouched amid the glass shards covering the floor of the cargo space.

Why wouldn't she jump?

Stapkis yanked on Ally's leg to drag her back. She dug her fingernails into the carpet but couldn't grab hold of anything.

He growled as he pulled her back. She wiggled and kicked and fought as hard as she could, but a second later she was back in the front seat where she'd started.

He let go of her ankle and grabbed her by the hair, yanking her head so she was forced to look up at his mottled face and his crazy, crazy eyes. His breath stank.

"What happened to the kid? What did you do with her?"

Becca was still mewling in the cargo space. Ally had the most insane urge to giggle.

She tugged at his hand, but she couldn't dislodge it. He was pulling her hair so tight her eyes watered. Hoping to buy some time, she went limp. He relaxed his hold and she headbutted him straight in the nose.

It hurt like hell.

It hurt him worse. As the blood gushed, he dropped her head to put a hand to his face.

"You fucking bitch!" he roared.

*This time, Becca. Please listen to me this time.*

As she shouted for Becca to run, she kicked the passenger door. It went flying, and she with it. Her skull still ringing from the headbutt, she staggered for the first few steps, then ran around to the back of the Rover.

"Becca!"

The kitten sprang out of the cargo hold, sailing over Ally's shoulder. Becca hit the ground and rolled. Then a streak of black fur disappeared into the trees.

Ally took off in the same direction, running for all she was worth, Stapkis right behind her.

She couldn't outrun a Pack Alpha. She just couldn't.

Every breath burned her lungs. Her legs ached as they

pumped. She'd never run this fast in her life.

Becca. Where the hell was—?

Sound exploded behind her. Something went whizzing past her ear.

*Great. He remembered to grab the gun.*

Where was Becca? Ally couldn't hear her, couldn't smell her. She prayed the kitten had run up a tree, out of reach of natural wolves and other predators. At least she was safe from Stapkis for the moment.

A few feet behind her, he bellowed and took another shot. This one hit a tree, bark exploding everywhere. Thank God werewolves couldn't change while in motion or she'd have been long dead.

Though it slowed her down, she started running between the trees, zigzagging to make it harder for him to shoot at her.

Where were Cade and the others? What happened to them?

"Ally!"

"Ally!"

Dec and Michael's voices echoed through the woods.

Stapkis yelled again, right behind her.

Wolves howled, first Dylan and then, thank God, Cade.

Relief washed through her, so profound her legs went weak and she stumbled.

*Keep running, Dead Girl.* Would Eir resurrect her a second time? She didn't want to find out.

Racing into a clearing, she paused a fraction of a millisecond. That was all it took.

Stapkis was right behind her. As she plunged back into the woods, he shot again. A burning pain sliced through her right thigh. Pure adrenaline kept her going a few more yards before her leg buckled.

She heard him right behind her, fancied she could smell his rancid breath. Curled into a tight little ball, her arms covering her head, she tensed and waited for the next shot. Or for Stapkis to start tearing her apart with his bare hands. Or for Stapkis to shift, then eat her. Or…

Cade howled. It sounded like he was on top of them.

Eyes still screwed shut, she heard Stapkis' yell climb several octaves and turn into a scream. She felt a rush of air as something huge flew over her, heard a crash, and felt the ground reverberate.

Cade. It had to be Cade and Stapkis—

Dec and Michael were still calling her name, closer now. Dylan was still howling. But the loudest noise was near her head—teeth ripping through flesh. Stapkis didn't make a sound, and she knew why.

She stuffed her fingers in her ears, but even without her wolf's hearing it wouldn't have blocked the wet, squishy noise of werewolf teeth and werewolf claws slicing through human guts. The smell of the blood made her gag. She swallowed hard against the bile rising in her throat. Knowing what a wolf could do was completely different from having him do it three feet away.

"Ally!"

Dec dropped to his knees beside her, took one look at her leg and started ripping her jeans up to the bullet hole.

"Where's Becca? What happened to Becca?" yelled Michael.

"I don't know!" she sobbed. "She ran, I don't know where, I lost her, I— Dec, she's a cat! Becca's a cat!"

"Shh, love, I know. Lay back and let me look at your leg."

"The hell with my leg! It'll heal!" she shrieked. Both wolves winced. She was screaming so she wouldn't have to listen to Cade. She couldn't look at him. "Would one of you make him stop that?"

"We can't. You can," said Dec.

"How?"

"Yell at him," Michael replied. "Isn't that what you usually do?"

"*Cade! Stop eating Stapkis!*"

The squishy, crunching sounds ceased immediately.

"Okay, he wasn't really eating him, Ally. We're not cannibals..."

"Shut up, Michael! Go find Becca!"

But he stayed where he was, his body fairly vibrating with tension, the odor of distress rolling off him. "She's a cat? You said Becca's a cat?"

"Yes. I know it sounds crazy, but I swear—"

He swallowed and closed his eyes. "I believe you. I do. I dreamed it. Sometimes I dream stuff and then it happens, but I thought— I thought this, this would be too fucked up, you

273

know? I mean, how—?"

"Michael, please, let's look for Becca. Dec will explain all this later because if he doesn't, I'll make Cade eat him. Got that, Dec?"

"Yes, love."

"Help me up."

She held out her hand, he hauled her up, and she stood with all her weight on her left foot.

"You can't walk around like that!" Michael exclaimed. "You're gonna collapse! It'll get infected. You can't—"

"I won't get an infection. It'll heal. Until it does, I'll limp."

"But you're—"

"A freak. Let's get moving."

Dylan howled from somewhere nearby.

"What will we do about Cade?" she fretted, not looking at him or Stapkis' body.

Dec waved a hand impatiently. "I'll stay with him. You two find Rebecca."

Michael nodded and put an arm around Ally's waist. They started off, she leaning on him for support.

"Ally," said Dec.

They stopped.

"She's not dead. I'd feel it if she were. Our girls are almost as tough to kill as we are."

"But, Dec, she must be scared to death! And these woods are enormous, and how—"

He gave her a quick hug. "Shh. Go. We'll find her."

As she limped away into the trees, she heard him say, with rough tenderness, "All right, pup. You need to get two-footed, quick. I'll be right back."

He came out of the change with his uncle standing over him, holding his clothes. MacSorley waited patiently for Cade to return to himself, giving him time to figure out where he was, to grab the memories of what had just happened before they dissolved into distant, hazy impressions.

*Becca.* Stapkis was dead. Ally was alive. Where was Becca?

MacSorley knew what he was thinking. "Easy, pup. I know she's around here. We'll find her."

He leapt to his feet and grabbed his clothes.

When MacSorley handed him the shirt, Cade said, "Why'd you bring this? I ripped it to shreds."

"Not for wearing, for wiping down. Clean Stapkis off yourself. Your mate's never been up close to a wolf while he was ripping someone's throat. She was disturbed."

They both looked down at Stapkis' remains.

"Did she think I was gonna hold him until the cops showed up or something?"

MacSorley shrugged. "Females. Six hundred years and I still don't understand 'em."

"Baby Girl! It's Daddy! I'm here!"

They'd been calling to her, stopping every few feet to listen and smell.

"Do you think Adnar would keep her from me?"

"No. I think Dylan's right. Adnar came here to see Eirny, not to hurt her family. He loved your mother." MacSorley stopped, frowning. "I'd always assumed he'd hate you because you were Louis' son."

"Why would he think she'd ever want to see him again?"

They didn't stop walking, scanning the ground and the branches of trees as they talked.

"Becca! Baby, where are you?"

"Cade, he's a fourteen-hundred-year-old Fae. They don't think like we do. Besides, he's been crazy, even for a Fae, for a very long time. He never accepted the loss of your mother, never stopped thinking of her as his wife. Killing your father, to him, was justified. For all I know, he thought she'd had time to get over it and would be ready to return to him. Even though she never loved him in the first place, which he also never accepted."

His uncle hadn't noticed that while he was babbling, Cade had stopped, frozen in his tracks, staring at him. His mouth was hanging open. He shut it. He opened it again but nothing came out. His mind seemed to have gotten stuck like a record needle, the same words going in circles around and around in his head.

*Females. Six hundred years and I still don't understand 'em.*

*Loss of your mother...her as his wife...she never loved him in the first place...*

MacSorley stopped, put his hands on his hips, and looked around with an exasperated sigh. "But if he did follow Stapkis, I don't know why the hell he hasn't shown up. Surely he can hear us."

Cade found his voice. "One of us is insane. I hope it's you, because I don't have time to lose my mind right now."

MacSorley was still talking to himself. "She's a tiny little thing, and if she's hiding under something...what was that, pup? What did you say?"

"I said, I hope to God you're crazy."

It would explain a lot. Hell, maybe MacSorley wasn't even his uncle.

But Sindri trusted him, so that part, at least, had to be true.

Okay, so the wolf was his mother's brother. And Adnar was definitely his father's murderer. But the rest of it...

"My mother wasn't married to that—that freak. And I don't know what the hell the crack about six hundred years was supposed to be about. Uncle or not, you're out of your mind."

The Irishwolf gave him a look of such sorrow and pity that Cade wanted to kill him.

"No, pup. No, I'm not crazy." MacSorley sighed and ran a hand through his hair. Cade felt like he was looking in a mirror. He had to repress a shudder.

"I'm old, I'm careless, I'm selfish and I've forgotten how to be part of a family," MacSorley continued. "It takes me far too fucking long to do the right thing. I should've sat down and talked to you two months ago. You might have still hated me, but Christ, we could've avoided some of this." He held his hands out in a helpless gesture at the woods surrounding them. "But I'm not crazy."

"Then you're a liar."

MacSorley shook his head. Again with the sorrowful pity. "No. I've not lied. You're a Vargalf, Cade, just like me and your grandfather and great-grandfather and uncles and cousins."

An icy shiver snaked up Cade's back and across his scalp.

*Vargalf.* So that was the word.

If he wanted proof his uncle was crazy, he wasn't getting it.

He didn't want to ask the next question. Something loomed. Something was about to change his life more profoundly, and less positively, than Ally or Dylan had. He sensed a chasm opening in front of him and he didn't want to look down or take one step.

With a deep breath he growled, "So what's a Vargalf, Uncle Dec?"

"A Vargalf is a Fae wolf. A werewolf with Fae talent and Fae longevity."

The chasm loomed wider. He felt himself teetering on the brink.

"Sometimes Vargalfs have shape-shifting daughters," MacSorley continued. "Which is why your daughter is a cat. And your mother was a selkie."

Cade lost his mental footing and went sliding down the side of the abyss, bumping his mind the whole way down. MacSorley just kept talking.

"Many years ago, Adnar stole Eirny's coat, so she had to live with him as his wife. I stole it back from him and freed her. He tried to kill me. That was the first time the Fae put him in prison. He escaped and found your family in Scotland. After he killed your father, they imprisoned him a second time. He escaped again." Dec paused. "I don't know if they're stupid or if they just don't fucking care. I suspect they just don't fucking care." He trailed off and cast a worried glance at Cade. "You okay, pup?"

*Not by a long shot.* He felt lightheaded, like he'd been holding his breath way too long.

It made Ally's tale of death and superhuman revival sound kind of normal.

After what seemed an eternity, all he could think to say was, "And no one ever thought to tell me all this?"

MacSorley smiled sadly. Suddenly Cade could believe the wolf was six hundred years old. "Oh, *barn*. If your mother had lived… But she didn't, and Sindri blamed himself, and Louis' family took the two of you away. And Sindri kept pesterin' me to come and find you, and I kept saying I would, but I never did, and the years passed, and the longer I stayed away, the harder it got to come, and…"

There was a rustle of leaves behind him. MacSorley broke off with a startled exclamation, his eyes widening. Cade spun around.

Adnar stepped forward with a small black cat in his arms.

"Becca! Baby, where are you? Becca!"

The wound was healing. She could feel the bullet lodged in her thigh working its way to the surface.

Michael walked slowly, allowing her to keep pace with him. They scanned the ground and the trees as they called.

"And she just shifted? Right there?"

"Yeah. And Michael, it was *fast*. Less than a minute, I swear."

He quirked his mouth, thinking. "Makes sense, I guess, someone so small. I don't know of any species that starts shifting before puberty, though. Holy shit," he murmured, shaking his head for the thousandth time. "A female. Shifting. It's bizarre."

She remembered what he'd said a few minutes earlier. "What was that about a dream you had?"

He sighed and shook his head again. "It's—it's weird. Not as weird as Becca turning into a cat, but weird. Let's find Stinky Butt first." He started calling for her again as he walked away. Ally followed, only to stop short a few yards later.

"Sarah Jane! How'd you get here? And who are those guys?"

"I'll explain in a minute. Am I too late? Where's Adnar?"

"It's her."

"Yes, pup. It's her."

"It's her," he repeated to himself. "God almighty. It's really her."

The kitten leapt from Adnar's arms to Cade's.

In one swift, fluid motion, Adnar dropped to his knee and, quicker than Cade's eye could register, pulled out an enormous, curved silver knife. It was bigger than any hunting blade Cade had ever encountered. The Fae held it out, handle first, to Cade, his expression betraying nothing as their gazes met. The wickedly beautiful blade glinted in the late afternoon sunshine trickling through the canopy of leaves above them.

Cade's head swam as he stared at the weapon. For a moment—a mercifully short but gut-wrenching moment—he was back on Scarista Beach.

"Oh, fuck me," MacSorley said softly.

Cade opened his eyes. "What? What's he doing?"

Voice heavy with disgust, the Irishwolf replied, "I think he wants you to kill him."

"*What?*" Cade whirled to face his uncle, who crossed his arms and sighed.

MacSorley said something to the Fae. The Irishwolf's voice was suddenly deeper, rougher, carrying an authority Cade had never heard in it before. He realized with a shock that his uncle now smelled like an alpha. Cade had never known of a wolf switching between beta and alpha, turning his dominance on or off. That phenomenon, as far as he knew, existed only in human bedrooms.

He'd never seen the real Declan MacSorley before. Neither, he was certain, had Ally or Dylan or Seth.

The Fae responded without looking at MacSorley, his gaze fixed squarely on Cade. Cade found Adnar's lack of emotion unsettling. He wasn't just stoic—he was cold, alien in a way Sindri and the other lesser Fae Cade had known were not. No flicker of feeling crossed Adnar's face, and he never so much as glanced at MacSorley. Still, Cade suspected he wouldn't have needed his telepathic gifts to recognize the Fae's loathing for the Irishwolf.

When Adnar quit speaking, Cade looked at his uncle expectantly.

"It's like what he did with Lind," the Irishwolf said, "only because the offense is so much greater, he's offering his own life."

"What offense?"

"Eirny's death. Bastard's feeling sorry for himself," MacSorley sneered. "Says he doesn't want to live knowing she's dead because of him."

"So he wants me to kill him."

"Yes. He wants you to slit his throat. This is unbelievable, Cade. Suicide is almost unheard of among the high Fae. And I've never heard of one offering the ultimate atonement to the likes of us."

"The likes of us?"

"Vargalf." His uncle smiled grimly. "They like us even less than normal werewolves. We're beneath them."

"Huh. Well, fuck you too," Cade said to Adnar, who remained motionless, arm raised, fingers gripping the blade of the knife. "Is that why he won't speak to me directly?" he asked his uncle.

"Huh? Oh, no. He doesn't speak English."

"Okay. Weird." *Then how'd he tell Cash and Mrs...never mind. Least of my worries right now.*

"So. What are you thinking, pup?"

"What happens if I don't take his life?"

"He goes back to prison." MacSorley lifted his head and gazed about him. "And very soon, I'd say."

"But if he goes back, how do I know he won't just escape again?"

"You don't. Of course, he might not have a reason to. Both times he's escaped, it's been to look for your mother. And to be fair, the first time they locked him up, they managed to keep him for two hundred years. I do rather like the idea of him living another century or two knowing he killed the only woman he ever loved. On the other hand, I dearly love the idea of you slitting his goddamned evil fairy throat." He looked up and scanned the woods again. Something caught Cade's attention as well—not a scent, exactly, and not a sound, but something weirdly between the two.

"Someone else is here, aren't they?" he asked.

MacSorley nodded. "I think the cavalry's arrived and if they know what he's trying to do, they'll stop it." His uncle turned to look at Cade. "Would you like some advice?"

"No." He thought another moment. "Right. Here, take Becca."

The kitten mewled and scrabbled at his shirt. Cade dropped a kiss on the furry black head—his *daughter,* a *cat*—and Becca allowed her great-uncle to take her.

"Come on, my love," Dec said, nuzzling her to his cheek. "Let's go find your mama and grandmother."

Cade took the knife.

"I don't like the idea of her running around out here, either," Sarah Jane said once Ally had explained the situation, "but there's nothing telling me she's in danger any longer. Stapkis is dead and Adnar wouldn't harm a child. And in cat form she's very fast. She'll be fine. You need to get off that leg, honey."

Ally waved her away. "My stupid leg is already healing. I noticed you're not shocked by the whole Becca-is-a-cat thing."

"Well, no, I'm not. I already knew she was a dyrkona." At Ally's blank look, she added, "That's the Old Norse word for a female shapeshifter."

"You knew—" Ally gaped at Sarah Jane's calm expression for a second.

Then she lost it. "No. You know what, Sarah Jane? No. I'm sick of this. I'm sick of the way you and Dec have been keeping secrets and dropping hints and acting like you're so anxious to tell us what's going on, but you never seem to actually get around to telling us what's going on, and you pop up out of fucking nowhere in the middle of the fucking woods acting like everything is just hunky dory—where the hell did you just come from, anyway?—and I swear *to God* if I find out *any* of this could've been avoided by one of you just talking to us, I'll kick both your asses off the ranch and it'll be a very, very long time before you see that little girl again, you hear me? Grandmother or not, you can't just swan around here like— Are you crying? Oh hell, Sarah Jane, stop crying." She put her arms around the older woman and hugged her.

*Nice going, Dead Girl. Make the grandmother cry.*

"You're right," Sarah Jane sobbed. "I'm sorry. I should've told Cade everything years ago, and so should Declan, but none of that had anything to with Stapkis, I promise. And—and I promise we'll tell you everything as soon as we find Becca." She cried a little more, then broke away with a small shake, wiping her eyes. "But your leg, honey, really, you need to sit down. We're not far from that old hotel. Have Michael—"

"What old hotel?"

"She's talking about the Fourmile Inn. It's that way." Michael pointed in a vaguely western direction. "We think that's where Stapkis has been holed up."

"Wait," said Ally. "Why didn't the guys check—?"

"I DON'T FUCKING KNOW!" he roared. The surrounding

trees and underbrush exploded as startled birds took flight and small mammals dove for cover.

Michael closed his eyes, shook his head, and took a deep, exasperated breath. "Sarah Jane," he said wearily, "who are those guys?" He jerked his head toward three silent men standing beneath the trees lining the clearing.

Ally knew at a glance they were high Fae. They were very tall and slender, all pale blond and beautiful in a way that made her skin crawl.

"They're here to take Adnar back to Keflavík."

"They might just be takin' his body back, old girl," said Dec, appearing with a black kitten in his arms.

"Becca!" Ally shouted as she sprang to them. Or tried to spring to them. If Michael hadn't caught her at the last minute, she would've collapsed. Her leg was healing, but it still wasn't interested in doing its part to hold her up. Dec handed her the kitten.

"What are you talking about?" Sarah Jane asked.

Declan looked over at the three Fae. "You are the most useless fuckers I've ever seen in me life, and I'm deeply, deeply ashamed to be related to you, no matter how distantly. Every goddamn species on this earth evolves except you lot."

One Fae looked at Dec as if he smelled bad. The other two stared pointedly elsewhere.

"Just checking if they speak English or not." He winked at Ally.

"And a good thing for you they don't," said Sarah Jane. "One of them has a talent for pain infliction and one can throw fire."

"What's the third one's talent?"

She rolled her eyes. "Location, of course."

"If he has a talent for locating, why aren't they with Adnar already?" asked Ally.

"His talent can't pinpoint it so precisely. It doesn't work that way."

Dec grinned. "See? Fucking useless."

"Take us to them, Declan. Right now," said Sarah Jane, tears vanished and air of elegant authority restored. She stroked Becca's head and patted Ally on the arm. "We'll see you in a minute, dear."

"Wait!" Ally said as they walked away. "Dec, where's Cade? What's he doing with Adnar? Dec? *Shit*! I'm sick of the way they ignore me like that!"

Michael and Ally looked at each other.

"She played you with that crying bit."

"Yeah. I know."

"All right. Let's get going." He scooped her up in his arms.

"*What the hell are you doing?*" she shrieked, nearly dropping Becca.

"It's either this or I sling you over my shoulder. You really shouldn't walk anymore, Freaky Girl."

"It's Dead Girl. And I can feel my leg healing."

"Whatever."

# Chapter Twenty-Five

He forced himself to toss the beautiful blade in the air a few times, catching it by the embossed leather and gilt bronze haft, pretending to admire the weight and feel of it.

He was ashamed, but not surprised, at the fear and revulsion coursing through him. It wasn't the knife that had butchered his father, and he wasn't the child who had witnessed it—but he found he had to keep reminding himself of that as he stared at Adnar.

In spite of all the countless scenarios he'd devised for slaying his own personal monster, he'd never imagined it would be so easy and still so terrifying.

Ally and Michael were talking somewhere nearby. For a moment he thought he heard Sarah Jane's voice as well. He let it all fade into the background as he stared at the Fae who'd killed his father, driven his mother to suicide and his brother to an early grave, and haunted his childhood dreams off and on for over thirty years.

"Nothing, *nothing*, has frightened me since I was eleven years old, because you were the scariest goddamned thing I'd ever seen in my life," he surprised himself by saying out loud.

If Adnar shared his surprise, he didn't show it. It wasn't like the Fae could understand him. Cade supposed he could call Dec back, or go find Dylan to translate. But he doubted Adnar would have much to say, and he didn't really care if he was talking to himself.

"I always thought killing you would...I don't know. Help, somehow. Ally would say I was looking for closure." He shrugged. "Maybe I don't need closure. Maybe I've always had what I needed—my family and my pack. Whatever Dec has to tell me won't change that. I don't even think I'm gonna have The Dream anymore."

Adnar remained on his knees, motionless, but his eyes followed the knife as Cade talked, tracking its path up into the air and back down, again and again.

Suddenly Cade caught it, wrapping his hand around the haft with the blade pointing up. Their gazes locked.

He fought the shudder that threatened to rack him as he met Adnar's cold and alien stare. He wouldn't swallow, or take a deep breath, or do anything which might betray even a hint of what he was feeling.

If you couldn't make everyone else believe that *you* believed you were the most fearless son of a bitch on the planet, you had no business being a Pack Alpha.

"I think you're the one who needs closure. You spent thirty years waiting for another chance to go after my mother, and now you find out she's been dead the whole time and it's all your fault. I mean, Jesus. Killing you would be a mercy."

He finally took a deep breath and adjusted his grip on the knife. "But I'm gonna do it anyway."

One clean motion, right to left, ear to ear. He sidestepped the geyser of blood, as dark and red as any human's or werewolf's. The body pitched forward. With the toe of his boot, he turned it over and stared, waiting until the last, faintest flicker of life was gone.

Then he exhaled.


At three stories, with gabled windows and a big front porch, the Queen Anne-style bed-and-breakfast looked like it must have been charming at one time. Now it looked like something out of a bad horror movie, the kind of place where unsuspecting teenagers seek shelter after their car breaks down, only to be picked off one by one by the freaky caretaker or the family of cannibals who live in the attic.

"Ick," she said as Michael helped her up the sagging front steps.

Once inside, they found themselves in a small, dusty parlor. Something had chewed away part of the reception desk. A tattered couch and nasty-looking armchair were the only furniture. Leaves and trash were strewn about the floor, as well as something that looked like animals bones, which Ally resolved to ignore.

Near the couch were some coolers, along with some blankets and cardboard boxes. She couldn't sit on that couch. Clutching Michael's hand, she lowered herself down to the dirty hardwood floor and put Becca down next to her. The kitten crawled under the armchair, curled up and fell asleep.

Michael opened one of the coolers, took out a couple of bottles of water, and passed one to her.

"I smell booze," she said.

"You shouldn't be able to do that. But yeah. Scotch. Maybe later."

They drank in comfortable silence for a few minutes.

"So. You break one wolf's neck, you outrun another one, your leg's healing, you can hear and smell as well as we can. What's your deal?"

"I don't like to talk about it." She took another swig of water. "So. You have dreams that come true. What's your deal?"

"Don't wanna talk about it."

"Okay." A few more minutes of silence passed. "What do you think Sarah Jane's deal is?"

"I'll bet you money she's Fae."

Ally sighed. "Shit."


"You all right there?" murmured a voice at his shoulder.

"I didn't know Fae were so easy to kill."

"They're not, but you nearly took his fecking head off," his uncle replied. "Most anything will die if you cut off its head."

Cade wasn't surprised at MacSorley's reappearance; he'd figured he would be sticking close by. Rather more disconcerting was the person with his uncle.

"Where the hell did you come from?" Cade asked Sarah Jane. "And don't tell me it's a long story."

After a pause, she said, "Keflavík."

"It's in Iceland," MacSorley explained. "That's where Adnar was imprisoned. She's the one who brought the cavalry."

"You just happened to catch a flight all the way from Iceland and showed up out here in the middle of nowhere, right when all this goes down?"

Sarah Jane pursed her mouth and stared at him for a few seconds before replying, very evenly, "I didn't have to catch a plane because I'm half high Fae and can transpose myself wherever I need to go. My talent is precognition, and I had a vision of you killing Adnar. I brought a few of his jailers back with me. They wanted to capture him before you had a chance to do it."

"For Christ's sake, woman," groaned Dec. "Give him some time to adjust!"

"Well, he's the one who didn't want to hear it's a long story." She frowned down at the corpse. "But now they'll be taking his body back instead, and I think I have to go with them to explain everything." She looked back up at him with a wry smile. "I'm sorry, Cade. Revenge is never as satisfying as you expect it to be."

"Actually, Sarah Jane, it was satisfying as hell. And now I don't have to worry about him showing up in a few years thinking Rebecca is my mother." He took a second to savor her shock as she thought about that one. Then he turned to his uncle. "Where is she? And where's Ally?"

"Michael was taking them to that Fourmile Inn place."

"Good. Let's go. Have fun in Iceland, Sarah Jane. Don't hurry back on our account."

She looked like she was going to say something more, but he turned his back on her and took off west through the woods. His uncle was right behind him.

"Are you all right, Cade?"

"You already asked me that."

"Aye, and you didn't answer."

"Don't put your arm around me, MacSorley."

"Could you at least start calling me by my first name?"

"I'll think about it."

They walked the rest of the way in silence.


"Cade!" She flew to him when he walked through the door, wrapping her arms around his waist and hugging him with all her strength.

All her strength was exactly what he needed that that moment.

"Oh, thank Christ," MacSorley said. "I smell scotch." He made straight for a cardboard box and pulled out a bottle of Glenfiddich. "Who'd like to join me?" He settled down on a doubtful-looking sofa, ignoring the cloud of dust that rose around him.

"Where's Dylan?" Ally asked with her face pressed into Cade's chest.

"I imagine he's still running around out there," said Dec. "He needs to hear what I've got to say."

"I'll go find him," said Michael.

"Would you stop by the Rover while you're out there and grab Becca's clothes?" asked Ally. "They're in the backseat. I won't have her running around naked when she shifts."

His mate—practical even in the midst of the weirdest shit.

"You're such a mom," Cade murmured into her hair as he pulled her back in and locked her in his arms.

He reeked of blood and guts. MacSorley had said she was disturbed by his attack on Stapkis. He could understand that, but he couldn't let go of her right now. He needed her warmth, her steely soft strength.

She propped her chin on his chest to gaze up at him. "Are you okay, baby?"

"I'm filthy and bloody, but fine. What's wrong with your leg? Where's Becca?"

"I got shot, but it's healing. Becca's sound asleep under the chair."

"Under the—oh." Baby Girl was still furry. "I guess she'll shift after she's had time to rest. I wonder if she can control it."

"She can't," MacSorley said. "Not for a few more years."

"But if she can't control the shift, then it could happen in public, or..." He trailed off as the implications sank in.

"Yep," MacSorley said. "You'll have to be aware of it at all times, and you'll have to teach her to be aware of it too. Fortunately, at this age she doesn't shift often. It's usually under stress. If you ask her what happened the afternoon the nanny ran off, you'll probably find she was upset about something. Now. Glasses. Where are the glasses?"

"Never mind the glasses. Where's Sarah Jane?" Ally asked.

"I'll tell you about it later," Cade replied. "I promise. I don't want to talk about Sarah Jane right now. MacS— Dec, what about that transport shit?"

Declan was busy rifling through one of the cardboard boxes. "Huh? Oh. Not transport—trans*pose*. The ability to move from place to place just by thinking about it. Fae shit. Aha!" A delighted grin broke out across his face. "Styrofoam cups! Now, who wants drinks?"

"Pay attention!" Cade growled. "Transposing. Can Becca do it?" The implications were horrifying.

"No."

"Are you sure?"

"I'm positive. Relax, pup. She doesn't have near enough Fae ancestry. Neither do you. Even humans who have enough Fae blood to have working talents can't transpose. Sarah Jane's father was pure high Fae, and her mother was a half or a quarter or something like that."

"So how old is she?" asked Ally.

"She was born in Ireland in the 1700s, but I'm not sure exactly when."

"Holy shit," Ally breathed.

"That's nothing," Cade said. "My uncle claims to be six hundred."

She broke away with a gasp, spinning around to stare at Declan. Cade got his arms around her again and pulled her back against his chest.

Dec just smiled at them. "Would you care for a drink now, Ally girl?"

She nodded mutely. Cade sank to the floor and stretched out his legs. Ally settled down next to him, and Dec passed them each a cup.

Michael and Dylan walked in, Dylan in his blue jeans but shirtless and shoeless. Michael dropped Becca's clothes on the floor next to Ally and went to pour himself some scotch.

"Okay. Another one," Cade said after a couple sips. "If Adnar didn't speak English, how'd he convince the cops to let Dylan and Lind go?"

Dec shrugged. "Eh. More Fae shit. When he exerts his talent, it works even if the target can't understand the words. It's been a couple of lifetimes since I gave a rat's arse how such stuff works."

"Um, excuse me!" Ally said loudly. "Who cares? Let's get

back to the part about you being six hundred years old."

"What the fuck?" Michael said, thunderstruck.

"Dude!" Dylan looked at his great uncle with awe. "You're *six hundred years old?*"

Declan grinned. "Thereabouts. I'd have to look it up. I was born a year after the Black Plague wiped out half the Faroes."

Cade looked over at Michael. "What we talked about the other night. Vargalf. Fae wolves. Fae longevity, Fae talents. He's one. And I guess I am too, and Dylan." He glanced at his nephew, who'd pulled his iPhone out of his pocket.

"He's six hundred and sixty," Dylan announced as they stared at him. "According to Wikipedia, the black plague wiped out half the Faroe Islands around thirteen forty-nine."

"Do you go anywhere without that thing, pup?" asked Dec.

Dylan grinned. "No."

"But I thought you were Irish," Michael protested weakly.

"Not originally. I was born in the Faroe Islands, as was Cade's mother. We all went to Iceland later. I didn't get to Ireland 'til I was a couple hundred years old." The ancient werewolf shrugged. "For that matter, Declan MacSorley's not my original name. I was born Dougall Mac Sumarliddison."

"Your first name is Dougall?" asked Dylan. "Like MacDougall?"

"Aye. It's a family name. One of Somerled's sons founded the clan MacDougall."

Now Cade was thoroughly confused. "But—you're my maternal uncle."

"And I'm also a direct descendant of Somerled, like your da. Your mother and father were related. Eirny found it kind of funny. She couldn't tell your dad, of course."

"Wait a minute. Sumarliddison was the name of one of Somerled's sons. But it's not in use anymore. Hasn't been for centuries."

"Very good, pup. You do know your family history. Yes, it's an old, old name. And I'm an old, old wolf."

Cade drained his cup and held it out for more. His throat had gone dry. His heart was pounding, his hands clammy. Even after the hints Dec had dropped in the woods, to hear it out loud—a six-hundred-year-old uncle, a shapeshifting daughter, a selkie mother—his mind couldn't stretch much further. At this point, if Dec told him they were aliens from outer space, he'd have no choice but to believe it.

"My mother?" His voice came out in a croak. He took another sip and tried again. "My mother. She was a selkie?"

Dec nodded, no longer smiling.

"How old was she?"

"Fifty years younger than me, pup."

Cade's eyes went to the open window on the other side of the room. He stared at the woods beyond, not really seeing them. "Did my father know?"

"No," said Dec.

"You're older than Sindri," he murmured, awestruck.

"I'm his godfather. His mother raised us, like he raised you and Carson. She died giving birth to him." His voice got quiet. "I pulled the wee fella from her body right before she left us."

"Why didn't he ever mention you?"

Dec ran a hand through his hair and blew out a hard breath. "Ah. Well. That's part of the whole story. I always thought I'd meet you and Carson. Your mother meant for me to. She kept waiting for a way to explain things to your father, but she never found it. You know how she was, Cade." Cade's gaze returned to Dec, drawn by the morose tone in his uncle's voice. "Your mother never took the hard way if an easier one was available."

Cade sighed.

"Then she insisted on going back to Scotland, and your father took you all, and Sindri blamed himself for that. And Louis' family took the two of you away to Savannah, and then... The years rolled on, y'see, and I kept finding excuses to stay away. Shame. Fear, pain, guilt. Take your pick. I wasn't wolf enough to do my duty by you." He shook his head, downed his drink in one gulp and poured some more.

"But you stayed in touch with Sindri even after my parents died?"

"Aye. Always. He pointed me to Dylan."

"How did he know?"

"Eir told him. In a dream or a vision or however she communicates with him. I've never understood it and he doesn't talk about it. But she told him Carson had a son. Didn't tell him how to find either of them, of course. She's never that

291

helpful. She gets involved just enough to feck with your life, but not enough to actually help. Took me five years to track down Carson, two more to find Dylan. I'm wasted as a bartender. I'd make one hell of a good P.I."

"Dec," said Ally, "what did Sindri blame himself for?"

"It's a long story, love."

"I think it's time you told it, then, don't you?"

Dec grinned sadly. "Your mate is bossy, Cade, you know that?"

"Yeah. I like it. Now talk."

For the first time since Cade had known him, Declan MacSorley—or Dougall Mac Sumarliddison, or whoever the fuck he was—looked ill at ease and lost for words.

"Well, now...I'm not sure where to start."

Cade snorted. "How about with the fact that my mother was a selkie?"

"That's a seal who turns into a person, right?" asked Michael.

"Or a person who turns into a seal," said Dec. "Like with any shifter, it depends on how you look at it."

"So Stinky Butt isn't the first and only female shifter running around?"

"No. There've never been many of them. Right now there are only six or seven. Maybe eight or nine, with the *barn* here."

Becca snoozed on beneath the chair. He couldn't believe Ally was letting her sleep on the dirty floor, cat form or not.

"They're all related to us. Cousins, and in my case nieces too, I guess. Most of them are cousins *and* nieces at the same time, on account of how thoroughly bollocksed our family tree is."

"Okay, good. The family tree," said Cade. "Start there. But first give me another shot."

Dec poured. "Somerled. It starts with Somerled."

"Wait," said Ally. "That was the Scottish king?"

"Lord of the Isles, yes. Eleven hundred AD or thereabouts." Dec took another swig. "My great-great-grandfather."

"Fuck," Michael said again. "That's just bizarre."

"Somerled was a Vargalf?" asked Dylan.

"No, just a wolf, but he started the whole thing." Dec stretched his legs out and settled back on the couch, keeping a tight grip on the rapidly dwindling Glenfiddich. "You know how his three sons founded the oldest clans." Cade nodded. "Well, Somerled had another son you don't hear much about—Alan Sumarliddison. He didn't found any clans, and he never became a king.

"Alan Sumarliddison was a shame and a horror to his family because he was a Fae wolf—a werewolf with a Fae talent. Telekinesis, specifically. He could move objects with his mind. Needless to say, this disturbed the fuck out of everyone who knew him. Somerled came from old Norse and Gaelic bloodlines, important families. Finding one of his pups with a Fae talent left the old bastard right gobsmacked."

"How'd it happen?" Cade asked, enthralled despite his growing sense of vertigo, the feeling he'd fallen so far down the rabbit hole he'd never climb out.

"Somerled married the King of Man's daughter. The King had a bloodline full of Fae, which he managed to hide. He was determined to marry his homely little girl off to the Lord of the Isles."

"But Fae and wolves can't have kids together."

"According to family legend, Man thought they'd fake a pregnancy and slip a baby in when no one was looking. All he cared about was his daughter becoming Queen of the Isles. Imagine the old schemer's surprise when Ragnild—that was my great-great-grandmother's name—turns up pregnant by her werewolf husband. There weren't a lot of geneticists in twelfth century Scotland, so we're still working this out, but there must've been a mutation, because Ragnild ended up having six or seven kids with Somerled.

"All the sons were wolves, but Alan was a Fae wolf. When they figured out his abnormality, they married him off to a spinster cousin, gave him a pot of gold and a bunch of land in the Faroes, and told him to keep his head down or lose it."

Dec paused for another long swig. "In wealthy families back then, marriage between cousins was the norm. And if your family's carrying weird genes... Sure enough, Alan's three sons were all Vargalf, and so were *their* sons. Alan's youngest grandson was my dad. His sister, my aunt Ingeborg, was a fox. Not fox as in pretty girl. She was as plain as Ragnild. No, Ingeborg turned into a small red canid that you hunt from horseback. She was the first female shifter we know of."

293

"So a Vargalf's daughter is a shifter?" asked Ally. "Wait a second. Sarah Jane called Becca something. I don't remember the word, but she said it was Norse for a female shapeshifter."

"The word's dyrkona," Dec replied. "Actually, it means changing woman. But not every Vargalf's daughter is one. It requires Vargalf lineage from both parents—remember, there was a lot of consanguineous shagging back then. In time, we think, the gene became recessive. I think that's how Eirny managed to have you two—Louis must've carried the recessive gene. One of my cousins is a doctor in Norway. He's obsessed with all this. He'd love to meet you and Dylan, by the way."

Dec fell silent as Cade's brain began to race.

"So...Dad showed up in Scotland researching his ancestry, and..."

"And saw Eirny on Scarista Beach. Which, by the way, is the same beach where Adnar had seen her three hundred years earlier, or thereabouts. God knows how much I loved your mother, Cade, but her judgment was for shite. Anyway. Your da was smitten immediately, and so was she. When Louis told her he was a descendant of Somerled, it tickled her. It made them—what? Distant cousins? Or maybe it made her his great-aunt five hundred years removed?"

"And she didn't tell Louis about being a selkie, or about Vargalfs or anything?" Dylan asked.

"Oh, no. No. We keep our heads down, always have done. There's not as many of us as there used to be. Fae can't stand us. Werewolves, back when they knew about us, didn't like us much either. Wolves have long forgotten about us, but not the high Fae. No, see, when Eirny first met your da, she didn't realize she'd end up marrying him, so she was economical with details about her family.

"But then he claimed her. Well, she didn't know how to tell him at that point that she wasn't at all what she appeared to be. I told her to go ahead and just lay it all out on the table. She was his mate, he wouldn't walk away. But...hard road, easy road. She packed up Sindri, went to Georgia, married Louis. At that point, she was thinking she'd live with Louis until he died and then she'd go back to Iceland. Or Scotland. Point is, she never thought she'd get pregnant. Because at that point we didn't realize Louis had the recessive Vargalf gene. Then she turned up pregnant, and who the fuck expected that?"

His face lit up in an expression of pure delight. "I'm telling ya, pup, when word made its way among the Vargalf that your mama was pregnant by a wolf..." He laughed softly. "Gobsmacked doesn't begin to describe the reaction. You two were the first ones born in about two hundred years, and the first ones ever in the New World. Far as we knew, anyway."

He stared at Michael for a long moment, then said, "Ah, shite. The Glenfiddich is gone." He looked around. "Anybody drunk yet?"

No one was. Ally's metabolism was just like a werewolf's. It would take a few dozen bottles to get all five of them drunk.

"There's a bottle of MacAllen in here," Michael said, pulling it from another of the cardboard boxes. "He didn't drink anything but scotch? I could do with a beer."

"At least he had good taste in whisky." Dec stood and stretched. "I need to step outside for a moment. 'Scuse me, children."

Once he'd left, Ally turned to Cade, laying a hand to his cheek. "You okay? Still with me here?"

"Yeah, it's just...goddamn. Are you believing all this?" He lay back down with a sigh. "Why didn't Sindri ever say anything to me? He's had plenty of time."

"Dec said something about Sindri blaming himself," Ally murmured.

She ran her fingers through his hair, gazing down at him with a worried expression. Did she sense his fear? He hoped to God she didn't. He didn't want anyone, not even his mate, to know how this was messing with his head.

Michael cleared his throat. "Look, wolf, if you'd rather I cleared out and gave y'all some privacy...this is family stuff, and I don't want to intr—"

"No," he answered immediately. "You're family, Michael. You know everything else about me, why not this?" Michael had to know he was freaked out. It wouldn't matter, which was why he trusted Michael more than anyone else on earth. More, even, than Ally. "I don't think anyone outside this house should know about it, though."

"Cade, does this mean we're gonna live hundreds of years?" Dylan asked softly.

Cade and Ally's gazes met.

"Yeah. I think it does."

The room got very quiet.

"Kind of makes me wanna puke," said Dylan.

"Me too, son. Me too."

At least Dylan and Becca would live as long as him. *Oh Christ. What about Ally?* Would he live for centuries after she died?

The room began to spin. He really did think he might puke.

"I have to go outside." He climbed to his feet, growling when he realized how unsteady he was.

"Cade, wait." Michael rose to his feet. Cade pushed him back down.

"No. You stay here. Call the ranch, have someone pick us up. I'll be back in a minute."

Dec, who'd been staring at the ground outside, looked up when he walked onto the porch. "You all right, pup?"

"What the fuck do you think?"

Michael pulled out his phone to call the ranch.

"Talents," he said after hanging up. "Cade's talent is telepathy, and—"

"Oh!" Ally exclaimed. "Yeah! And Dylan's is languages. But...Cade's talent is kind of weak, isn't it? And why didn't we ever realize about Dylan?"

"How the fuck would I know?" Michael asked.

"And what about Dec?" asked Dylan. "What's his talent?"

The three of them sat in silence for a minute.

"Oh, for fuck's sake," Dylan said suddenly.

"Don't say f—"

"I know what it is, and it's *stupid*," the teenager scoffed, ignoring Ally. "Everyone likes him. That's his talent."

"Charm. Huh. I guess if you're going to wander the globe for hundreds of years, it's useful," Ally mused.

"Cade sure as hell didn't like him," said Michael.

"Well, neither did I, when we first met him. But Fae talent doesn't always work on other Fae."

"That doesn't explain why *you* didn't like him," Michael pointed out. "Unless you're Fae yourself. Which would explain all your weirdness, right?" He looked at her expectantly. Dylan raised an eyebrow and smirked, looking exactly like Cade.

Ally quickly changed the subject.

"Now I have a question for you," Dec announced.

"What is it?"

"Did Ally die? Did Eir resurrect her?"

He'd thought nothing could ever surprise him again, but this did. "Yeah. Dylan's stepfather killed her. How'd you know that?"

"The wee fella guessed it. Or perhaps Eir told him. I think she visits him just for company sometimes. Bitch is probably lonely."

Cade sat down on the bottom porch step and patted his chest, where his front pocket should've been. Then he remembered he wasn't wearing a shirt. A cigarillo would've been very welcome.

"I always knew there was a—how should I put it?—an unnatural explanation for the Wendy's oddities." Dec looked down at Cade. "You've had a hell of a couple of months, pup. And now I've loaded all this on you at once. I am truly sorry, if that helps any."

"It doesn't."

His uncle smiled sadly. "All right then. Well, I'm in need of another drop."

He started up the steps. Cade put a hand out to stop him.

"No. We're not done. I don't want to talk about this in there, with them."

"Don't want to talk about what?"

"What Sindri feels so goddamned guilty about. If you're going to tell me something that changes the way I feel about the old man, I need to hear it alone."

"Ah, hell, pup. I don't think it'll do that." He sat down next to Cade. "You have to promise me something, though."

"No. I don't."

Dec fixed him with a penetrating, appraising stare. Cade didn't like the proximity, the two of them sitting shoulder to shoulder.

"Cade. You and Becca are Sindri's whole life. You have to find a way to let him know you don't blame him for what happened. And you can't blame him for never telling you about this, either. You just—you can't. The wee fella's done the best he could. He's suffered like you can't understand, and I'll not see him suffer anymore, you hear me?"

"You tell me what fucking happened and then I'll decide how to feel about it."

They stared at each other for a moment, nearly nose to nose. Dec made an exasperated noise and turned away to look out at the woods again.

"All right. Here comes the bad part."

Dec dropped his head with a sigh and started plucking at some blades of grass.

"I wasn't thrilled when Eirny decided to run off to America with Louis MacDougall five days after meetin' him. It was that kind of impetuousness that lost her coat to Adnar, see? Always rushin' about on a whim and a giggle, never thinking things through. And I was worried, because Louis had no idea what she was and I didn't see how she could spend thirty or forty years with him and him not notice she wasn't aging at all. Remember, we assumed they wouldn't have children.

"But Eirny was in love, and the wee fella was glad they were gettin' away from Europe. He was always afraid Adnar would escape, y'see. He didn't trust the eejits in Keflavik to keep the bastard locked up, even though Adnar had been there almost two hundred years by then. Well. Louis takes Eirny—and Sindri—off to Georgia. And Savannah's on the sea, so that was all right, y'know? Then his uncle leaves him the land, so they moved here, and Louis took over the pack. And then you pups came. Even though we were shocked to learn Louis carried the gene, and we were worried about Eirny bein' landlocked, we were still excited about possible Vargalfs bein' born for the first time in centuries. And Eirny was in heaven."

He paused, turning to look at Cade again. "She loved you pups more than her own life."

Cade nodded once, abruptly.

"Well, and that's what worried her. A selkie, thousands of miles from the ocean... As old as she was, she didn't *have* to shift, but she was afraid she'd grow to miss the sea, afraid that eventually she'd miss it so much she'd leave the three of you in spite of herself, and she didn't want to do that. She had your da build her the swimming pool, and Sindri said it helped, but still she feared the sea's pull would be too strong. So she decided to burn her coat."

"Goddamn," replied Cade, stunned. "What happens to a—" it was still weird to say it out loud "—a selkie when that happens?"

"According to the lore, she'd go crazy. I don't know if anyone alive had ever known a selkie who did it. She'd be stuck in her human form forever, at the cost of half her nature. Sindri was terrified when he found out she was thinkin' about it. So he hid the coat."

He stopped talking and stared at the grass. Cade let him be.

"And everything was okay for a while, until the day Carson found the coat, and took it to his mother, and asked her what it was."

"Carson never said anything," Cade said hollowly. "Why wouldn't he mention something like that?"

"I don't know, pup. I hope he never knew what it was, or what it led to." Dec swallowed hard. Cade heard the almost silent, surely involuntary, whimper of misery.

"And then she did burn it, before Sindri could stop her. And a few months after that, he got word to me that she was growin' melancholy, unstable, withdrawn. She was pesterin' Louis to take them all to feckin' Scotland."

Cade tensed.

"And Louis did it, no doubt thinkin' it would make her happy, bring her back to you all, but it didn't, of course, it couldn't, and..."

His no-longer-quite-Irish accent had grown thicker. His restless fingers still pulled at the grass between his boots, a small bare patch of dirt growing steadily bigger under his hand. "And the goddamn useless pricks in Iceland had already turned their backs on Adnar, and who knows how long he'd been looking for Eirny. He was haunting Scarista Beach, and she went there too, and I wasn't there, and Sindri wasn't there..."

He turned to look up at Cade. His eyes were dry, his voice filled with unshed tears. "It was just you and your brother and father, pup, and Christ, there was nothing Louis could've done, he had no way of knowin'... If I'd come out here sooner, if I'd met them in Scotland, if I'd just done *something*..."

Dec shook his head, blinked and looked away. Cade had a sudden urge to throw an arm around his uncle's neck and comfort him, cry with him.

He resisted it.

Both wolves stood at the approach of an SUV. A second later, Becca began to cry.

"Oh thank God, she shifted."

"Of course she did. It's completely natural. You'll get used to it."

They stepped apart, each suddenly self-conscious, uncomfortable, avoiding the other's eyes.

Ally dashed out. "I thought I heard the Expedition."

"You did," replied Cade.

"Good. Becca just shifted."

"Why's she crying?"

"She sat up under the chair and bumped her head." She looked up at him. "What's wrong?"

"Nothing."

"Bullshit. You tell me—"

"Shh, baby, please." He grabbed her, held her close, inhaling the scent of her, and she didn't ask again, and he loved her for that.

The Expedition screeched to a halt a few feet from the porch. Roman jumped out.

"Hey. Seth and Jesse brought a tow. Y'all okay?" He eyed the rest of the group filing out onto the porch. "So, anybody gonna tell me what happened?"

"No." Michael cupped a hand. "Keys."

Roman tossed them.

"Go help the guys. When y'all get the cars hooked up, take care of Stapkis' body."

"That's Stapkis I smell? Cool."

"Move," Michael growled over his shoulder.

"I'm going, I'm going. Damn. Three bodies in two months. Maybe we should open a morgue next to the woodshop."


It was long past sunset when everyone fell out of the SUV, dirty, cranky and relieved. Becca, incoherent with exhaustion, had fallen asleep halfway home.

"I can't believe I'm putting her to bed like this."

"It's just dirt, baby. Bathe her in the morning when she's conscious."

"Fine. But I'm burning the sheets."

He almost smiled at that.

"You should run around shirtless more often," she murmured, running a hand across his stomach.

"Yeah? You too."

They helped each other kind of stagger down the stairs.

"Hey, you know...I could carry you. Wanna see?"

He gave her a squeeze and kissed the top of her head.

"Sure. Right after I cut off my balls, since I wouldn't need 'em anymore."

"God. The macho shit."

He pulled up short as they passed the kitchen.

"Ooh, great idea. I'm starving."

"Huh? Oh yeah, me too, but—no, I need to do something."

She shrugged. "All right. How about a sandwich?"

"Good. Make me two. No, three. And see what else is in there."

"Got it. What are you up to?"

They hadn't bothered to turn on the light. He walked over to the corner by the back door, stopping next to the hatch in the floor that led to Sindri's nook beneath the house.

"Cade. It's late, maybe you should just—"

"He's awake. He would've heard us come home." He tapped his bootheel firmly on the hatch once, then crouched on his haunches and rapped with his knuckles a couple more times.

"Vacation's over, old man," he said to the floor in a loud voice. "The house is dirty, we're exhausted and Ally can't cook."

"Hey! That's just mean!"

But it was worth it to see the grin he flashed her.

301

# Chapter Twenty-Six

"*Tomorrow?*"

"That's what he said. Day after, at the latest."

"And he just told you this morning."

"Yep. I said 'thanks for the fucking notice, Declan', and he gave me that cocky grin and said 'But I'm givin' you notice now'."

Michael smirked. "I can't say I'm surprised."

"Me neither. From now on, nothing he does can surprise me." She rested her chin on her hands and sighed. "I guess when you're six hundred years old, saying goodbye to someone you've known for four years isn't such a big deal."

He gave her a brotherly shoulder bump and leaned back on his hands. "He loves you. It's just...he feels like you've all got new lives and now he can move on."

"I guess so."

What Dec had actually said was, *"The three of you belong here now, Ally girl. You'll take care of Cade and Becca, he'll take care of you and Dylan, Seth's happier than he's ever been. And I've got things I need to do."*

They were sitting on the front porch, watching Becca wander about as she chattered to a furry Aaron, following close on her heels.

He'd awakened from his coma a few days after their adventure in the woods. Doctors hadn't yet determined if he'd suffered any permanent brain damage, but he wasn't the same wolf. Since coming home, he'd gone four-footed more often than not. Cade was determined to give him whatever he needed to heal. Becca seemed to help.

"Hey, Michael?"

"Hmm?"

"Is it true that if a wolf stays furry long enough, he'll forget how to change back?"

"Eh. It's one of those things that only seems to happen to someone's cousin's best friend's boyfriend. Nothing's on the record, far as I know."

They watched Aaron and Becca for a few more minutes.

"When do you think y'all will tell him about his father?"

He shrugged. "We'll keep an eye on him, see where his head's at. He hasn't mentioned Rufus since he woke up, though, so I think he might be relieved."

"Michael! Even if their relationship was already ruined, losing his father like that was devastating. Aaron's never going to have any closure."

"Fuck closure. Sometimes a dead father's the best thing that can happen to a wolf."

Matching his deadpan attitude, she replied, "Is there something you'd like to talk about, Michael?"

He twisted his mouth like he was trying not to smile. "No. No, there's not."

"Okay, then. Just checking."

He didn't answer, and she didn't press. She'd grown comfortable with the silences that were a part of any conversation with Michael.

"I'm just disappointed," she said after a few minutes.

"He's a good friend of yours. You'll miss him for a while."

"That's part of it, but I was just hoping...you know. That he'd stick around for a while and Cade would get to like having a father figure."

He wasn't trying not to smile anymore.

"And Sarah Jane would come back, and Dec could rekindle his romance with her, and we'd have this big extended—hey! Stop it!" She punched him in the upper arm.

He didn't say anything because he was rocking back and forth in silent laughter.

"All right," she grumbled with a blush. "Maybe it's a fantasy."

"*Maybe?*" he hooted.

"Why couldn't something like that happen?"

"Because this is life, not Lifetime!"

"I don't want a Lifetime movie," she shot back. Gazing at Becca and Aaron, she tucked her hair behind an ear. "I want a Hallmark Channel movie. Something warm and uplifting and happily ever after." *We're almost there.*

"Well, your ever after's gonna last a really long time, so it could still end happily, I suppose."

Her heart clenched when she remembered her question to Dec last night.

*"Have you had any kids?"*
*"Several."*
*"Where are they?"*
*"They're dead, love. I outlived 'em all."*

With an exaggerated carelessness that proved he'd noted her discomfort, Michael said, "Besides, there's nothing to rekindle with Sarah Jane. Dec says they've been friends for a hundred years, and he decided a long time ago to stay away from Fae chicks, even the sane ones like Sarah Jane."

"Ooh! That's it!" she exclaimed, slapping him on the knee with enthusiasm at the change of subject. "Crazy Fae chicks. Tell me about Mary Ann."

"Oh hell no. You talk to Cade about that."

"I can't!" she whined. "He'll think I'm being nosy."

"Ya think?"

"She's my fiancé's baby's mama, Michael. That's not being nosy."

He muttered something nasty and turned away with a grin, pretending to watch the guys working on one of the cabins.

"Fine," she chirped to his back. "We can talk about you instead. So. You have dreams that portend the future—"

"Portend? Who the fuck says *portend*?"

"—*and* rumors about your dad have been floating around Houston for years. Now, I'm starting to think—"

"Fine!" he shouted. The guys by the cabins stopped what they were doing and stared across the yard at him.

"Fine," he growled again, more quietly, and then he sighed in resignation. "Mary Ann."

"*Yes,*" she hissed triumphantly. She crossed her legs Indian style and spun to face him, hugging her arms in anticipation of the whole juicy story.

"So," he began. "Mary Ann was crazy. The kind of female who'd burn your stuff after a fight and then say it just proved how much she loved you. You know the kind I mean?"

"Oh yeah."

"Right. I mean, she was hot as hell, but it's like I told Cade, no amount of hot is worth that much crazy. But he wouldn't listen. He was into the chaos and I couldn't talk him out of anything..."


"Goddamn, Dec. I've never seen anything like this."

His uncle finished stowing his gear away and looked up with a grin. "You like my bike?"

"I like your bike. Saddlebags look like they'll hold suitcases."

"Well, I'd intended to get a car. Something practical. Then I thought—right. Fuck practical. I haven't had a bike in sixty years."

Cade had had a couple of touring cycles, but nothing like Dec's fully tricked out Harley. He walked around the breathtakingly beautiful machine, running a hand over the spacious leather seat and gleaming chrome console. "I need one of these. I really do."

"They make a sidecar, but I don't think Ally would want to ride in it. I think your mate would look rather fierce on the back of this thing."

Cade agreed. He doubted she'd ever had sex on a bike. Something to file away for later...

"So," he said.

"So," his uncle agreed.

His pose was identical to Dec's—rocked back on his heels, arms crossed over his chest, hands tucked under his arms.

Dec noticed at the same time.

Both wolves immediately shifted, shuffling their feet and trying to do something else with their hands. Cade cleared his throat.

"You've said goodbye to everyone?"

"I have. Becca gave me a stuffed animal for company. I promised to photograph him everywhere I stop."

"She'll love that."

"I do appreciate your seeing me off."

"I couldn't let you leave without saying goodbye."

"Wee fella make you do it, did he?"

Cade laughed, a little embarrassed. "I would've done it anyway. Listen. Is there anything you need before you go?"

"Oh no. No, I've got everything."

"You need money?"

"No. But if you ever do, just let me know."

Cade blinked, taken aback.

Dec smiled. "Seriously, if you ever need anything at all, everyone here's got my number."

The kind-of-Irishwolf fixed him with one of those frank and piercing gazes that made him itch. Cade cleared his throat again.

"Well. If you don't need anything, then— Oh, wait, one more thing. Ally says you're expected back here for the holidays."

"Is that okay with you?" Dec asked with a raised eyebrow. Cade wasn't going to miss the frequently creepy sensation of looking in a mirror while talking to another person.

"I wouldn't really have a choice, with Ally and Sindri and Becca, but yes, of course. You'll always have a place here. We're your family. And your pack."

They shook hands. Cade was glad of the bike between them—Dec looked like he might've tried to hug him. Instead, he swung a leg over the Harley. He started to put his helmet on, still watching Cade with that disconcerting stare.

Cade grabbed a handlebar. "What? What is it?"

Dec cut the engine and set the helmet on his lap. He stared at the ground for a minute, then back up at Cade.

"There's a reason she saved her, you know."

They hadn't discussed Ally since that day in the woods. Now he wished they had.

"You think so?" He crossed his arms again, kicking at the grass with the toe of his boot. "I've tried to talk to Sindri about it, but he won't discuss it."

"No, he wouldn't."

"I want to know why she saved Ally when she didn't save Mama or Carson. Do you think—" It sounded too stupid to say out loud, but what the hell. "Do you think she did it because she knew Ally would get Dylan to me? Did she know Ally was my mate?"

"No." The ferocity of Dec's tone surprised him. "Fuck no. She's not God. None of them are. They're immortal, not omniscient. Eir saved Ally because Ally saved Dylan, and our line is precious to her. That's it.

"But you know what, pup? That's not what worries me. I understand why she saved Ally and not Eirny or Carson. What bothers me—what fucking terrifies me—is that Eir could save her at all. It's the twenty-first century. Old Ones haven't messed with our world in a thousand years. I thought evolution had taken care of that."

"I know. That's what I thought about when Ally first told me what happened to her."

"Don't get me wrong—I'm thrilled Ally came back. Thrilled for her sake, and Dylan's, and yours and Becca's. But if Eir can reach out and touch someone, that means others can do it as well. Our world doesn't need that."

"That's why you're leaving now? Is it something to do with Eir?"

Dec nodded.

"What will you do?"

"I'll talk to folks I've not seen in a while. I spent the twentieth century around humans and normal werewolves because I was tired of people as old and tired as me. I need to get back in touch with my folk."

"Where?"

"New York City, to begin with. I have a cousin there who always has an ear to the ground. If there've been any supernatural rumblings, he'll know about it." He put his helmet on.

Cade nodded. "That makes sense. Will you keep in touch? Let me know what you find out, what you hear?"

"Absolutely."

They shook hands again. Dec restarted the engine and roared off down the gravel road.

Cade thought he might actually miss him.


"Seth," he called a few minutes later.

The beta paused on his way to the gym.

"Hey, Cade."

"Do you know where Ally is?"

"No, but I got a late start this morning."

"Okay. Thanks."

He needed to talk to her about what Dec had said.

Despite Sindri's devotion, Cade never gave the Old Ones much thought—not the Aesir of his mother's people, not the Tuatha Dé Danann or the Orishas or any others in the pantheon of pre-historic immortals. They'd withdrawn from the world, or been taken out of it. No one knew which or why. Cade had never cared.

Ally, on the other hand, had spent years learning about Eir and other Old Ones, researching credible stories of physical interaction between mortals and the Immortal Entities Formerly Known As Gods With a Little G.

*Jesus.*

Whom he'd much rather run into, actually.

He checked in the house—no Ally.

They hadn't discussed the subjects each knew was weighing on the other. Ally's lifespan. The lifespan of any children they might have. Where they'd go when they got so old people began to talk. If Becca would be doomed to outlive a string of husbands and all her children.

He saw Michael heading for the Rover.

"You seen Ally?"

"Not since breakfast." Michael buckled up and started the car, clearly not in the mood to chat.

"Where you off to in such a hurry?"

He leered. "Town. Tara."

Cade had tried to discuss the whole Vargalf thing with Michael a couple times. On both occasions, Michael changed the subject. Michael was going to have to think about it at some point but for now, Cade wouldn't push him.

If she wasn't with Becca, and she wasn't working out, maybe she'd gone for a ride.

As he approached the barns, a groom jogged out to meet him, a big, goofy grin on his face.

"What is it, Felipe?"

"Ally's looking for you, Boss. She's in B."

"Oh, good. Is she saddling up?"

Felipe shrugged. "I dunno. She kicked me out, told me to find you and to tell everyone else to stay away."

Cade mustered his best Pack Alpha scowl-and-growl. "You're about to bust a gut there, son. You got a joke you need to tell me?"

Properly abashed, Felipe reddened and dropped his gaze. "No, Alpha. Um, sorry."

He wouldn't laugh. "Fine. Go see if Doyle can use you in A-Barn."

"Yes, sir."

Cade strolled into B. "Ally?"

She sighed loudly. "Took you long enough." She didn't sound annoyed, though—she sounded relaxed. Happy.

"I've been looking for you."

"Well, I've been waiting for you."

"Where are you, baby?" But he knew.

Something floated down from above, landing on his shoulder. Lavender-scented fabric.

A bra.

He looked up to see her peeking over the railing of the hayloft.

"You coming up or not?"

"Yes, ma'am."

Springing up the wooden ladder three steps at a time, he hauled himself into the loft to find her lying naked in the hay like a centerfold. He forced himself to undress slowly, so he could just stare at her a few minutes. It excited him all the more because he knew that stripping down in an open barn in the middle of the afternoon wasn't an easy thing for her.

He wondered how long it would take before the sight of her like this no longer summoned a wave of desire that left his head spinning. How long it would be before he could look at her with something less than amazement, before he could think without wonderment of the way she'd slipped into his life, his child's life, and made herself necessary without even trying.

No mate bond could account for that on its own.

She looked a little cross as she stretched and wiggled. "Since when does it take you so long to get naked?"

"Sorry. Here. I'm done."

He covered her body with his, and she wrapped her arms around him.

"We need to discuss some very serious subjects," he murmured into her ear, loving the way she shivered beneath him.

"Can it wait 'til later?" she whispered.

"Yeah. Yeah, it can wait. We've got time."

# About the Author

Kinsey Holley lives in Houston, Texas, where a lot of people know about her Secret Romance Writer Identity. Hopefully those people don't include her mother or the folks she goes to church with. She's married to the Hub, mommy to the Diva, and works part time as a law librarian.

She enjoys reading SF, UF, history and romance and is addicted to pop culture and several television series. She dreams of moving to the mountains of Colorado, which she'd never really do because all her friends and family are in Houston and she loves them and besides, she can't imagine being more than an hour's drive from a beach. Besides her *Werewolves in Love* series, she's working on a Regency and a big, glitzy contemporary that she hopes will evoke comparisons to the sexy melodramas of the 80s (Models! Rock stars! Monaco! Alexis Morrell Carrington Colby Dexter Dexter Rowan! No, not her...)

Kinsey takes her mail at kinseywholley@live.com, lives at www.kinseyholley.com and ninenaughtynovelists.blogspot.com, and hangs out way too much at Twitter (@kinseyholley).

Pop round and say hi.

*It's all about the story...*

# Romance

# HORROR

www.samhainpublishing.com

CPSIA information can be obtained at www.ICGtesting.com
Printed in the USA
BVOW071207220112

281106BV00003B/5/P